LOST TRUTH

LOST LAKE LOCATORS BOOK TWO

SUSAN SLEEMAN

1

Hayden Kraus had never killed anyone.

Please don't let that change now.

He drew his sidearm and eased through the cottage's murky shadows, advancing on the intruder. A sliver of moonlight pierced through a gap in the blinds, illuminating a narrow path, but it did nothing to help him identify the intruder, not even their gender. Burglary statistics said he was likely facing a male so he would go with that.

The person dug through a storage box located on ceiling-high bookshelves consuming the far wall of a compact living room. With his back to Hayden, he seemed oblivious to Hayden's presence as he tread softly over the wooden floor.

Please, please, don't creak.

Hayden eased closer. Closer.

Sharp summer ocean winds buffeted the meager cliffside cottage, rocking the structure. Aged wood creaked and protested like the bones of a hundred-year-old man set into motion.

Hayden felt like an intruder himself, but he had every right to be there. His Lost Lake Locators team had been hired just hours ago to find Kai Nakoa, the cottage owner. He'd been missing for several days, and it was Hayden's turn to take charge of an investigation. Before the team met to create a plan, he wanted surveillance cameras placed on the property but arrived to discover someone sneaking through a window.

The intruder stilled.

Hayden halted. Held his breath. Waited for the guy to turn. To see him. Perhaps attack.

His heart pounded in his head like a conga drum sending out a warning message.

The intruder shrugged and moved on to another box.

Good. The building's groans must have covered the sound of his favorite tactical boots as they'd hit the floor.

Still, he waited a moment longer—let the intruder settle down. He studied the man's shadowy figure. Small, slight in build. Dressed all in black.

Hayden scanned for a weapon. Squinted. Spotted nothing. Not necessarily because the intruder wasn't armed, but the dim lighting prevented Hayden from making out a weapon. Didn't matter. If Hayden wanted to live to tell about this event, he had to assume an armed foe awaited him.

His heart thundered harder. As a former Customs and Border Protection agent he'd handled far more dangerous situations, but it'd been a while.

Breathe. Calm down.

He steadied his weapon. Sucked in air. Moved through the small dining room. Ten feet between him and the intruder. He reached up to a higher shelf.

Slowly, Hayden advanced. Inch by inch. Closer and closer. The person showed no sign of knowing he was moving in.

Five feet away now. He would soon be within arm's

length. Nothing for it but to call out and hope the shock didn't produce a weapon.

He took a deep breath and dredged up the commanding tone he'd used while serving as a CBP agent. "I have a gun at your back. Stop what you're doing."

The person spun. Gasped. "I—"

"Hands!" Hayden held his sidearm steady. "Your hands up where I can see them."

The intruder raised trembling hands.

Good. No weapon. No assault. Hayden flicked on his flashlight and aimed the beam at his face.

Stunned, he blinked. Once. Twice. Cadence Vaughn. Even with her curly hair pulled up behind her, he would recognize that unique red color anywhere. But that couldn't be her, could it?

No. No. Impossible. Or was it?

"What're you doing here, Cadence?"

"Is that you, Hayden?" Her shocked voice rose into the rush of raging winds.

"In the flesh." He exhaled, sucked in more air, and holstered his weapon.

She lowered her hands and propped them on her hips, jutting one out in the familiar way she had of standing. "Never mind why I'm here. What're you doing here?"

Say what? She thought she could demand his reason for being at the cottage when she was the intruder. "I have a right to be here. You don't. This is private property. I could charge you with breaking and entering."

"Um, Hayden." She cocked her head. "You're not a law enforcement officer anymore, and you can't charge me with anything."

Good point. "Maybe not, but I can hold you here and call the sheriff. Mina wouldn't be happy to arrest you, but she would do it."

For several months, Sheriff Mina Parks had been dating the LLL team founder, Nolan Orr. Hayden and the rest of the team had gotten to know her in that time, and Hayden was certain she wouldn't want to arrest Cadence.

Cadence sighed. "Why don't we sit down and talk about what's going on instead of trading barbs like this?"

No thanks. The last thing he wanted was to turn on the lights. See her face. Look into her chocolatey warm brown eyes. Swirly, crazy emotions that hit him every time he saw her would leave him feeling out of control, pushing his hot buttons, and he would have to struggle to remain in charge. Not how he wanted to spend his night. Not at all. But she didn't deserve for him to be rude and not explain what was going on.

He backed away and pointed at the dining room table. "Have a seat. I'll get the lights."

She crossed the room, her steps pointed and urgent as she rushed to pull out a chair. Heading in the other direction, he flipped on the overhead light, flooding the room in brightness.

His eyes were blinded by the sudden glare. Fine by him. Stopped him from looking into her eyes and sinking hopelessly under her control again.

He remained in place until his vision cleared enough to cross the room without face-planting. At the table, he turned a chair around to straddle it, but avoided looking at her full on. "So start talking, Cadence."

She waved a hand. "I thought we'd resolved that by now. Cadence is my byline for the paper, but everyone calls me Cady."

"Okay, *Cady*," he said. "What's going on?"

"Sounds like you're here on official business," she said not answering his question.

Fine. He would answer her and hope she would reciprocate. "Our team has been hired to find the cottage owner."

"Find the owner?" Her voice rose sharply. "Kai Nakoa is missing?"

He looked directly at her then. "He's been gone for a few days. I would think if you knew him that you would've heard that."

"I've never met the man." Her firm tone was almost a challenge.

Was she telling the truth? No reason to ask. He hadn't known her for long, but he *knew* her and had no doubt she was speaking the truth. "Are you doing a story on him for the newspaper?"

"Story?" She shook her head. "No. No. No story."

"Then why are you here?"

"My dad. A few weeks ago. He... he... even now it's almost impossible to say." She looked up at the ceiling and shook her head. "He passed away."

"Oh man, Cady." Hayden wanted to put his hand over hers to offer comfort, but they didn't have that kind of relationship, and even with the strong attraction between them, he would never act on it.

He finally met her gaze head-on. The light caught the shimmer of tears in her eyes. He shouldn't have looked. It was like watching someone tear a chapter from his own book of sorrow. Her tears didn't just move him—they struck with the force of a punch.

He paused just long enough to steady himself, careful not to reveal how deeply her grief shook him. "What happened?"

She drew in an agonizing breath. "He was poisoned."

"Poisoned? No way." Hayden shook his head as he tried to come to grips with more shocking news. "Who would want to poison your father?"

"That's what I'm here trying to find out."

Okay. This was getting weirder and weirder. "You think your father's death has something to do with Kai?"

"I'm not certain. I'm just following up on things in Dad's journals, and Kai was frequently mentioned in them."

"But what about the police? Aren't they investigating?"

"Sort of, but they don't have any leads and have back-burnered his case to move on to other pressing investigations. They didn't say that, but I could read between the lines. So you see, it's up to me to find his killer."

"This is crazy." He hesitated, searching for the right words to say. "I mean, I don't know you all that well, but it seems like your dad was an ordinary guy. Nothing outstanding or outrageous going on with him, other than his dementia. Why would someone want to poison him?"

"I don't get it either." She kept wringing her hands, as if the motion alone could keep her from falling apart. "At first, the medical examiner ruled his death natural causes. Blaming the dementia. She said she found his organs filled with blood and there was foamy blood in his lungs, too, which she said could occur in heart failure deaths."

"Then how did you find out about the poison?"

Cady pressed her lips into a flat line. "I argued with her. Made sure she understood his dementia hadn't reached the point where it affected his autonomic nervous system. I asked her what else could account for these symptoms, and she said an overdose."

Interesting, but not fitting for Percy. "Overdose of what? It's not like your dad was a drug addict."

"Exactly. And I told her he didn't have access to any of the medications he *did* take. When he moved in with me, I locked them all up and gave them to him when they were due, so I begged her to run a drug test. It came back positive for fentanyl, and then she went back to his body and found a needle mark. He could never have gotten his hands on these drugs. Even if he had, he was terrified of needles. Someone would've had to administer it to him."

"Wow." He rested his arms on the back of the chair. "That's surreal."

"Agreed, and like I said, I don't actually think it's real yet. I mean, I'll never forget finding him in his bed that morning. His body cold. His skin dark. But..." She shuddered.

Hayden couldn't ignore the anguish causing her to nearly fall apart. He took her trembling hands in his and held them still. They were arctic cold, and he rubbed her silky skin to try to warm it.

Their joined hands looked like they belonged together. He was in a quandary and couldn't let his emotions color his decisions. Did he still report her to the sheriff for breaking and entering? What kind of man would he be if he turned her in or even left her alone in such distress? Not the kind of man he wanted to be, that was for sure.

Helping her find her dad's killer was the only option. "If you think Kai's disappearance could have something to do with your father's death, then we should meet with the team and discuss working together on finding the killer while we look for Kai."

Her eyes widened, a hint of relief breaking through. "That would be amazing."

Fighting the urge to press her for answers about how her father's death connected to Kai, he gave her hands a gentle squeeze before letting go. Time was of the essence when looking for a missing person, and Hayden needed more information—but he would wait. She'd have to share the full story with the team soon enough. Holding back now would give her a chance to pull herself together—and spare her the pain of reliving it twice.

But first... "Before I even suggest our partnership to the

others, I'll need to confirm you aren't planning on writing a story about it."

Her posture stiffened. "I would never turn my father's death into a story for the paper. It's private." She stabbed her thumb at her chest. "*My* wound. *My* grief. No one else's and certainly not the public's."

Seeing her like that tore him up inside. He was witnessing her pain raw and unfiltered, and no matter how seasoned she was as one of Portland's top crime reporters, he knew this story would never be just another headline—it would live close to her heart.

He dug out his phone. "Let me give Nolan a call. The team's meeting at the inn to plan our investigation into Kai's disappearance, and it would be really helpful if you could be there—if you're okay with that."

"It's more than okay. I'll be forever grateful." She looked up at him with those luminous eyes, and he was once again lost, not only in the surprising way she'd affected him when he'd first met her, but in the grief and pain he would carry with him as if it were his own.

Oh, man. She really got to him, and he would do anything to take her pain away. From this moment on, she could count on him—not just to stand by her in her grief, but to find her father's killer.

No matter what it took. No matter the personal cost.

Cady had assumed she and Hayden would head straight to the old inn where the team lived and worked. Instead, they'd stopped outside Kai's cottage in the warmth of the summer evening, while a sharp wind swept across the cliffside.

She huddled out of the flow of air near the house, but

8

Mr. Adventure didn't care about the forceful winds. He climbed a swaying tree to install security cameras, moving from limb to limb like a monkey at ease off the ground.

"There." He jumped down from the lowest tree branch, sticking his landing. "Not as fun as scaling a mountain or skiing down one, but climbing a tree still has its rewards." He grinned in the moonlight.

Her heart did a crazy somersault. From their first meeting, something about him drew her in a way she'd never experienced. Physical, yes. He was the proverbial tall, dark, and handsome. Piercing charcoal eyes able to cut right through a person but were often tempered by a gentle side she hadn't witnessed in a man in a long time.

Several times while her father's dementia held him captive and terror had him flailing about, Hayden had tenderly approached him and coaxed him into a relaxed state. If she had any question about Hayden's character, his compassionate behavior told her he was a stand-up guy.

Compassion and keeper material. Too bad she wouldn't follow her interest in him. She had way too many things to do and accomplish before settling down. If she ever said *I do*—an unlikely event—she would be all in. Everything, including starting a family. But she had big goals for her job as a reporter and couldn't be traveling around the world and be the kind of mother she wanted to be.

The kind she never had.

The familiar ache that thoughts of her mother always brought to the surface over the years gnawed a hole in her heart.

Remember that when he flashes that sweet smile at you. And remember that your mom and dad proved serious relationships didn't work.

Hayden shoved a pair of pliers into a low cargo pocket of

his khaki pants. "Would you like to ride with me or take your own car?"

"I'll follow you in my car." She didn't wait for his response, but hiked across the property to her old Honda Accord. The engine grumbled and complained, coughing a few times and then catching. She needed to buy a new car. Chalk it up to another thing that wouldn't happen in her life. Not after depleting her savings to pay for her father's caregivers. She wasn't complaining. Making his last days on this earth the best they could be had been the most important thing to her.

Hayden, on the other hand, drove a newer model blue metallic Ford Bronco Raptor that purred like a grown cat. He eased out of the driveway onto the main road cutting through Lost Lake. She followed close behind as he navigated through the quaint coastal town, steering toward the large inn perched on the ocean cliff ahead.

In the inn's front lot, he smoothly backed into a spot among other vehicles—all parked the same way by the front door. As former law enforcement officers, they all backed in to be ready to move at a moment's notice. Backing up wasn't her forte. She bumped over a few potholes before coming to a stop nearby.

Laptop tucked under his arm, Hayden strode to her car in that eager, confident way he had of walking and stood waiting near the hood. "Welcome to Lost Lake Locators headquarters."

She shoved hard on her groaning door and had to use her hip to fully slam it closed. "Interesting location for your type of business."

He arched an eyebrow. "Yeah, this probably does push the envelope for a team who finds missing people, but Nolan got the place for a great price, and it suits our needs."

She cast a look over the horizon, where the moon glistened off rolling waves crashing into the shoreline below. "With these views, it's probably a great place to live and work."

"You got that right." He jerked a thumb over his shoulder. "Let's go in and meet the whole team."

He led her over a crumbling walkway. "Careful. We need to get the disintegrating concrete fixed, among a million other things."

She wore her favorite red Chuck Taylor All-Stars and didn't want to ruin them, so she watched the ground until the sidewalk improved. He tugged open the bright orange front door and held it for her.

A small sign near the door, displaying the team's name and logo, was the only hint of their business. Worn furnishings in faded oranges and mustards—styles she guessed dated back to the fifties or sixties—filled the spacious but dark and gloomy lobby. Without hesitation, Hayden walked past the wood-paneled check-in desk and continued down the hallway.

He stopped near the first door and glanced over his shoulder. "This used to be the dining room, but we turned it into our conference room."

The door stood open, and the savory scent of fresh popcorn drifted out. She'd opted to skip dinner to save money on buying takeout food, and her stomach grumbled.

He raised an eyebrow but didn't mention the noise as he gestured at the doorway. "After you."

Inside the large room, she found the outdated dining tables pushed together to form a long conference table and worn wooden chairs pressed up to its side. At the wall, two long folding tables held refreshments. His teammates stood in small groups, talking and laughing.

"Popcorn, stat," Hayden announced and set his

computer on the conference table. "We have a hungry one here."

A slender woman locked startling blue eyes on Cady and held out her hand. "I'm Reece Waters."

"Cady Vaughn." She took her hand—her grip surprisingly strong despite her slight frame. Cady couldn't help but want Reece's luscious blond hair, wishing her own wild tangle of red curls were as sleek and smooth.

"I'm glad to get you some popcorn, but have you had dinner?" Reece angled her head in question.

"Not yet." Cady was embarrassed to admit she hadn't eaten because she couldn't bring herself to go into her dad's house yet, and she couldn't afford takeout food.

Reece rested her hands on slender hips. "Then let me rustle something up. Any allergies?"

"No, but don't go to any bother." Now she was really embarrassed that Reece was making a special effort for her. "Popcorn would be wonderful."

"No bother." She spun and wound her way toward the swinging double doors that must lead to their kitchen.

"If you're making a sandwich, you might as well up your number to a dozen or so," a guy with ebony hair and a matching beard perfectly trimmed close to his jaw called after her.

She glanced back at him. "Are you serious or is this another one of your jokes?"

"Serious." He straightened his shoulders, but a hint of humor clung to his expression. "I mean, take a vote. I'm sure most everyone would take one of your famous sandwiches."

"Well?" She scanned the group. "Do I have any other takers?"

Two guys, also with dark hair and close-cut beards, nodded their affirmatives. The closest one of the pair she recognized as Nolan Orr, the team leader and once a Secret

Service agent. She'd met him when her father had gone to the local sheriff with a lead related to the murder of Lost Lake's mayor.

"None for me." A petite woman with short brunette hair shook her head. "No way I can eat like the rest of these guys and not gain weight."

"Be right back." Reece pushed through the swinging doors.

"Come on, let's go meet the others." Hayden took off across the room. "Everyone, this is Cady Vaughn. She's Percy's daughter." He clapped a hand on the shoulder of the guy who'd requested a sandwich. "This would be Jude French. He's our resident joker and a former FBI agent."

"Perfect timing on the sandwich. My stomach thanks you." He grinned, his smile playfully devious.

It did nothing to help Cady relax, and she released her nerves by unzipping her lightweight jacket. "I didn't mean to cause anyone extra work."

Hayden lifted his hands in an easy-going gesture. "Don't worry about it. Reece is the team mom, and she loves spoiling us all."

"But I'm not part of the team," she said, even though she had to admit they were welcoming—and no one made her feel like an outsider.

"I mean, if you want to feel special you can, but seriously, Reece will mother anyone who allows it." Jude laughed.

The other guy she hadn't met stared at his teammate. "Doesn't mean we should take advantage of her. Unless of course she's grilling burgers. Then we must always, always agree to them." He chuckled, his deep amusement rumbling through the room.

Hayden shot the guy a sideways look dripping with sarcasm. "This is Gabe Irving. He served as an Oregon

State Trooper and can rate every burger joint in the entire state."

"Hey, don't limit me to Oregon." Gabe gave a sly smile. "I can rate a ton of them in Washington too."

Hayden looked away as if biting back a comment and shrugged out of his jacket. "You remember Nolan, right?"

"I do." Cady smiled at the team founder. "Glad to see you again."

Nolan nodded. "Sounds like we might be working together."

Oh, how she prayed his statement was true. "I would very much appreciate your help if it's possible."

His unyielding attention remained locked on her as if assessing her. "As soon as Reece comes back, we'll sit down and iron it all out."

Hayden had called Nolan from Kai's place, and Nolan made it clear that she'd have to sign a nondisclosure agreement with LLL before they'd even consider working with her.

The other woman stuck out her hand. "I'm Abby Day. A sheriff, once upon a time in a land far, far away. I hope we can help you." She ended with a very pleasant smile Cady wouldn't necessarily associate with a tough sheriff.

But Cady liked her humor and smiled as she shook hands. "Nice to meet you."

Holding a large tray laden with thick sandwiches and a big bowl of fresh fruit, Reece pushed back through the swinging doors, which flapped closed behind her. "Back off, all of you, and let Cady have first choice."

"That's not necessary." Cady's embarrassment surged as Reece fussed over her, especially since she'd already interrupted their evening.

"I assure you it's very necessary." Reece set the tray on one of the long tables pushed against the wall and stood in front of it. "You've never seen these guys when food is put in front of them."

"She's not wrong." Gabe grinned. "Reece has schooled us on proper manners more times than I can count, but we don't always follow them."

"Try seldom follow them." Abby reached into a cabinet and withdrew plates to set next to the sandwiches, then she glanced at Cady. "Quick. We can only hold them off for so long." She laughed and stepped out of the way.

"The sandwiches are turkey with sharp cheddar cheese," Reece said. "Sandwiches on the right half of the tray are loaded with jalapeños, the left half have sweet pickles."

"Which are you?" Hayden looked at her, flirtatious humor lighting his eyes. "Spicy or sweet?"

She caught his gaze and held it, though getting lost in their mutual attraction was the last thing she should be doing in front of this team. But that pull—that instant connection with him—was too hard to resist, and she let his playful mood override her common sense.

Someone coughed, and she broke free, but she couldn't let the moment end. She offered a Cheshire cat grin and took half of each kind of sandwich before dishing up a generous portion of mixed fruit.

"Yes," she said in answer to his spicy or sweet question.

He blinked a few times. Good, she'd caught him by surprise as she'd hoped, but he recovered quickly. "Take any clear spot at the table if you can find one. Our team won't win any awards for neatness."

"Hah." Jude pushed up to the food table. "Our team might not, but you would."

"And proud of it." Hayden glanced at Cady.

He seemed to be searching for her response to his need for order. She wished she could say she shared that trait, but honestly, she was a bit of a mess. Maybe neatness and orga-

15

nization weren't important to him in a life partner—or maybe he couldn't be with someone who didn't value those traits.

Grr. Stop thinking about being with him.

She found an open slot in the middle of the table, dropped her jacket over the back of the chair, and sat. Her stomach rumbled again, and she stabbed her fork into a plump red strawberry.

Before she could bite into it, Nolan joined her and held out a piece of paper. "Here's the nondisclosure we spoke about. I need to make sure everything we discuss tonight and in the future isn't shared with anyone else and especially not published in any public format. If you'd look it over and sign it while we eat, then we'll talk about working together."

She took the document with her free hand and gave him a tight smile when she really wanted to grit her teeth. She'd told him and Hayden both in no uncertain terms she wasn't here in a reporter's capacity and wouldn't be writing about this situation, but they couldn't seem to let it go.

She understood their caution, though. They needed to protect their business and their clients. She would do the same thing in their shoes.

Stuffing the strawberry in her mouth, she laid the page down and chewed as the fresh sweetness saturated her tastebuds. She glanced through the legalese, bored after the first sentence. Too bad. She needed to continue to read. At least she had the tasty sandwich with the sweet pickles—something she'd never had on a turkey sandwich before—to chomp into as she tried to decipher the lawyer speak. It took her exactly half a sandwich to skim the agreement. Before starting the jalapeño one, she grabbed the pen and scribbled her signature.

Holding it in the air, she caught Nolan's attention. "Here you go. Signed."

He stepped over to her and collected it. "I hope you're not offended by this. It's routine business for us."

"I understand," she said, and tried her hardest not to be offended.

As a reporter, she'd developed a thick skin and was rarely put out by anything. Somehow, this seemed more personal. Maybe she believed because she was interested in Hayden, he and his team should trust her. But they knew nothing about her feelings, and her belief didn't make sense.

She might be attracted to him. She might want to get to know him. She might even want a potential relationship with him. But the fact of the matter was, she *didn't* know him, and he didn't know her.

They would spend time together searching for her father's killer, and she was sure she'd learn more about who he really was. Maybe, just maybe, they'd find they weren't compatible at all. She didn't expect that, though—just like she never imagined he'd hold her at gunpoint in a stranger's house.

She had no idea what lay ahead—and maybe that was for the best. Hunting a killer was dangerous enough, but Hayden had shown her tonight just how quickly the search could turn into a life-or-death situation.

2

Hayden would like to believe Cady was at home in his group. Not just his group, but his family—the people who meant the most to him in the world. Not so. The moment Nolan plopped the nondisclosure agreement in front of her, an unease took over, and her wary expression as she finished her sandwich left his stomach in a knot.

Standing at the end of the table, Nolan cleared his throat. "Go ahead, Cady. Tell us what brought you to Kai's house."

She pushed away her plate, holding a partial sandwich, and sat up straighter. "First, let me say thank you to Reece again for the sandwich. It was very tasty and much appreciated. I'll be adding pickles to my sandwiches in the future."

Reece gave a camera-worthy smile perfected in her college modeling days. "I'm always glad to keep the group fed so they can work at peak performance."

"More like so we're not grumpy." Gabe chuckled.

Cady waited for the laughter to die down, then started her story. "So, I was at Kai Nakoa's house because I was following up on... Well, I... My father was murdered and I..."

Her voice broke, and she clapped a hand over her mouth. "Sorry. Sorry. I don't mean to be so emotional. I-I'm just getting used to the fact that he's gone."

Abby got up from the other end of the table and came to sit next to Cady. "Oh, sweetheart. I'm so sorry about your father. I wish I'd known him better, but from everything I've heard, he was a wonderful man. And don't you worry about being emotional. If you need to cry, we want you to cry. Let it all out. This is a safe space."

Hayden couldn't agree more, but he wished he could be the one comforting her. She was clearly in the beginning stages of grieving her father's loss, and he was thankful Abby stepped in. If he couldn't provide the needed comfort, Abby would be his second choice.

On the outside, she was all tough law enforcement officer, but she'd suffered hardship and loss herself and knew how to empathize. She was gutsy and true, loyal to the end, and if she came alongside someone, that person's life was enriched in a special way. Maybe she and Cady could form a real bond.

Tears flowed from Cady's eyes. "Th-thank you. I'm..." She shrugged. "Just thank you."

Abby slipped an arm around Cady's shoulders and gave her a hug. "We'll sit here until you're ready to talk. No pressure. Take your time."

Cady's lips parted in a wobbly smile, and she took a few measured breaths. "It was just such a shock. Not only to lose him so suddenly, but having someone take his life. The medical examiner says someone administered a lethal dose of fentanyl. We don't know how or who gave him the injection or why. This happened a few weeks ago. The police have investigated, but they don't have any leads and have basically given up."

"I'll ask Mina if she can get us a copy of the police investigation files for your father's death," Nolan said.

"Thank you," Cady said.

Hayden didn't want to say anything, but she probably shouldn't be thanking Nolan when he was likely wanting the files to confirm her story. "Once in law enforcement always in law enforcement" meant a healthy measure of distrust without proof. Or maybe unhealthy for some people.

"So you're investigating," Nolan clarified.

"I had to." Cady's forceful tone confirmed her dedication to this task. "Figured I'd start with Dad's journals. He wrote in one every day when he still had clarity of mind. I've been reading through the books to see if he noted anything to help me find his killer."

"What about the secret he said Mayor Sutton was keeping?" Reece cupped a coffee mug in delicate hands. "We never did find out what that was."

Hayden, like the rest of the team and Mina, wanted details of that secret. They thought it was related to the mayor's murder a few months ago. The team helped to find his killer, and there was absolutely no question they'd found the guilty party. But the killer didn't seem to have anything to do with this secret Percy said the mayor had been keeping.

Cady frowned. "I haven't found out what it is either. I asked Dad several times, but he couldn't recall anything other than it had to do with people. His journals didn't reference the secret either."

Reece leaned forward. A strand of hair fell over her forehead, and she swatted it away. "But there was something in the journal about Kai?"

Cady nodded. "You may not believe this based on the man you met, but until the dementia set in, my dad was very active. When he moved here, he hired Kai to teach him how to surf. Dad noted in his journal that he stopped by Kai's surf shop to talk to him every day. I hoped Kai might have information that could help."

"But you didn't see him?" Hayden asked.

"No. I went to his shop, but the employee working said he was taking time off. So I asked people in the area if they knew where he was, and no one did. They *did* say it was unlike him to take more than a day off." She exhaled. "I was disappointed, but I couldn't just turn around and go back home. I had to do something, so I kept talking to people until finally someone gave me his home address."

"And you went to his house where I found you." Where he thought she was an intruder who might turn on him with a gun, and he could've fired on her in the dark.

"I didn't intend to go inside without permission." She bit her lower lip. "I only wanted to talk to him, but he didn't answer. So I sat outside for the rest of the day to wait for him. When it got late and he didn't show, I decided to take a look around. I found a window open and—"

"You went inside," Hayden finished for her.

"I know I shouldn't have been digging around in his house, but I didn't mean any harm. I'm just so desperate to figure out who killed my father." Her voice collapsed again, and her shoulders curled in. "Losing Dad. Not knowing who killed him. This is so much harder than I thought it would be."

Abby patted her hand. "It'll take time, sweetheart. Just let the emotions flow, and you'll heal faster."

Cady fixed her attention on Abby. "Sounds like you speak from experience."

"Something like that." She'd lost her mother less than a year ago, and all the teammates knew her wounds were still too fresh to open up, even with someone on the team.

"I don't mean to pry." Abby's steady, lower-pitched voice signaled to everyone who knew her that a change of subject was coming. "Are you a woman of faith?"

Hayden watched Cady with interest to see how she handled Abby's direct approach.

She angled her head. "I am. Why do you ask?"

"Would you mind if we prayed with you?" Abby asked, but it sounded as if it were a foregone conclusion.

"Mind?" Cady blinked a few times. "No. Of course not. I'd appreciate it."

Abby reached out to clasp hands with Cady and each team member joined hands with their neighbor until they were all connected.

Abby offered a poignant prayer. Not only did she listen the most intently of anyone in the group and clarify vague things, but her clear understanding of what was going on around them allowed her to pray in a way that always seemed most effective.

When the prayer ended, Cady lifted her head. "Thank you. Your compassion and knowing that God heard your prayers help more than you can know."

"Not to seem insensitive, because I agree prayer is important." Nolan glanced around the group. "But Kai is out there waiting for us. Maybe depending on us to bring him home, and we need to move ahead on figuring out if he's in trouble. As in any missing person's investigation, time is of the essence."

"Of course, I'm sorry for taking up so much time," Cady said. "I'm in complete agreement with you. I know Kai isn't married, so who reported him missing?"

"He was once married, but his wife passed away fifteen years ago," Nolan said. "Their son, Rocco, is certain his dad's in trouble. Kai didn't tell Rocco he was taking time off, and according to Rocco, his dad hasn't been gone for three days since his wife died. So the son's freaked out."

"Did he go to the sheriff?" Cady asked.

Nolan nodded. "But there's not much Mina can do with it. Kai told his staff he wouldn't be in and scheduled them accordingly, so no missing persons investigation can be filed at this point. It'll be a different story if Kai doesn't return to work as scheduled. Still, she did look into it as much as she could without an official investigation but concluded nothing untoward had happened to Kai. Rocco doesn't agree."

Cady pressed her hands flat out on the table. "I don't suppose Sheriff Park was willing to share what she'd learned."

"Hah!" Gabe shot Nolan a sideways look. "Nolan and Mina are dating, and he's got an inside track."

Nolan's eyes flicked upward. "Not in this case, as there really wasn't anything to tell. She did bring me up to speed on the steps she took, but she couldn't determine any possible reason for his going missing and didn't find anything out of the ordinary."

"Did she rule out health issues or a mental health crisis?" Reece asked.

Nolan nodded. "No dementia or other issues, but as much as I trust Mina's and her team's investigative abilities, you know I'll want us to follow up. And before one of you suggests it, I've already told her we'll revisit everything she's ruled out."

"Good thinking." Reece gave him her complete attention. "You wouldn't want to throw a monkey wrench in your relationship this early in the game."

"Something to consider for sure." Nolan's lips pressed together in a slight grimace, then he firmed his shoulders. "Mina's involvement or not, I'll do whatever I need to do to find Kai until I'm positive nothing bad has happened to him. You can be certain of that."

No doubt Nolan believed his statement, but if push came to shove, Hayden couldn't see his buddy risking his forever kind of relationship with Mina. It was up to the rest of the team to do their best to keep an eye out for any potential landmines he might step in with her and make sure it didn't come to that.

"I'd be glad to get ahold of his doctor to see if Kai has any of these issues," Abby offered, probably thinking along the same lines as Hayden.

"You got it." Hayden went over to one of their large whiteboards near the head of the table and noted her assignment.

Cady cleared her throat. "What exactly do you know about Kai?"

"Not much." Jude rubbed the back of his neck. "We've been in town less than a year, and most of that time we've had our noses to the grindstone. No time for fun and games or getting to know the locals."

Abby nodded. "Basically the only information we have on him is he's a former champion surfer. As you're aware, he owns Ride the Tide Surf Shop, where he sells and rents surfing gear plus beach things like umbrellas and chairs. He also gives surfing lessons, as you mentioned. And everyone loves him and speaks highly of him."

Gabe's pinched expression fell on Cady. "Nothing on the surface would make you think someone abducted him, but a superficial look like Mina's team did can often be wrong."

"Which is why we need to do a deep dive on him." Hayden noted the item on the board. "I'll get some algorithms running, and I should have basic background information soon." He looked at Cady. "I'm kind of the computer geek of the team. Need anything done related to computers, and I'm your guy."

She tilted her head like a confused little puppy. "Not something I would've guessed."

"He hides his geekiness quite well." Jude grinned.

Hayden rolled his eyes at his teammate's joke and kept his gaze on Cady. "I'm sorry, but I also have to do a background check on you and your father. We did a cursory look at you both during the mayor's murder investigation, but I'll go much deeper this time. If there's anything you think we should be aware of, now would be the time to tell us."

He didn't know if she quite understood her life was about to become an open book within the LLL team. *Dear God, don't let me find anything in the search to put her on our suspect list.*

Her breath was long, controlled—forced calm. "I've got nothing to hide, but you'll discover my finances are a disaster at the moment. I wiped out my savings to pay for Dad's caregivers. I exist on Ramen noodles and pray my Model T of a car doesn't bite the dust."

Hayden had heard many times over the years how medical expenses had destroyed families, leaving them vulnerable and in need. He hated this for her. "Since there's been no ransom demand for Kai, I don't think your lack of money will play into his disappearance."

"Wait..." Her gaze lifted skyward for a moment, then she blinked long eyelashes as she glanced at the team, stopping to linger on each person's face. "You all aren't considering me a suspect in Kai's disappearance, are you?"

"Not really," Nolan said. "But we can't ignore your unauthorized entry into his home to search his personal possessions. It appears as if you have a solid reason for being there, but we wouldn't be doing our jobs if we didn't perform our due diligence."

"Oh, right." She sagged as if deflating in her chair. "That makes sense, and I guess it's why you're so good at finding people."

"Not good." Gabe puffed up his chest. "Great."

"I wouldn't have put it that way, but we are good at our jobs." Nolan caught Hayden's attention. "Will you be able to obtain Kai's phone records and financial information?"

Hayden shrugged. "I can't answer that until I look into it. What would help most is if there's action on his credit or debit card since he's been gone. I wish I could obtain up-to-date phone records and financial transactions, but it's tricky without a warrant."

"There's no way at all you can do it?" Jude aimed a pointed look in Hayden's direction. "I mean, you're the IT wonder boy of the team."

He resisted sighing or pointing out that he didn't have an official background in IT, it was just an area he spent a lot of time dabbling in. "I won't hack a bank or phone company, but it's possible we can locate the financial information in his home or business. And if we're lucky, we might find online banking passwords, giving us access to his accounts and his real-time data."

"When Rocco gave me keys to Kai's cottage and the surf shop, he also gave us full permission to search both of them," Nolan said. "We should do a detailed search first thing in the morning. In addition to the financial records, it could turn something up to change our priorities."

"Count me in on that." Hayden added the item to the board.

"Me too?" A gleam shone in Abby's eyes. "I've done my share of property searches in my sheriff days and got to know where people hide things."

"Thanks." Hayden made a note on the board.

"We need to talk to Kai's staff and fellow store owners.

Neighbors too." Jude leaned forward to peer at Hayden. "I suppose you'll want to do that so you can also ask about Percy."

"You know it." He made sure his tone brooked no argument. "In addition to questioning them, we could ask for any video footage of Kai's movements. We should also talk to the mayor's former assistant to see if she learned anything new about Percy's secret. Or even if she's heard anything about Percy at all."

Cady scratched her cheek. "Not that I'm questioning your logic, but why would she have heard anything about my dad?"

"Daisy was Mayor Sutton's assistant for years, and she's basically the local 411." Jude chuckled. "She stayed on with the new mayor and is still the numero uno source for everything going on in Lost Lake."

"We need to talk to Mayor Sutton's daughter, Becca, too," Nolan said. "She might've learned more about the secret. Plus, we never figured out what her dad did with the big cash withdrawals from his account after selling off his sports memorabilia. Maybe the secret is related to that."

Cady perked up. "Then for sure I'd like to talk to her *and* Daisy. And I want to talk to my dad's birdwatching group. It's questionable if they can give us any info to locate Kai, but I think it could help find my dad's killer."

"Do you have a list of the group members?" Gabe asked.

Cady nodded. "In one of his journals. Unfortunately, that particular journal is a few years old. I figured I'd start with the first name on the list to see if that person could give me the names of current group members."

Nolan cleared his throat and looked at her. "I hope we've made it clear that we want to help you figure out who killed your father."

"But?" she asked.

His eyes narrowed. "But Kai's disappearance is top priority. If he wasn't involved in birdwatching, I don't want any of our resources allocated to investigating that group."

Hayden fired a testy look at his partner. "This is really important to her, so I'll do it off hours then."

Nolan gave an offhand shrug. "I'm not saying we shouldn't do it. I'm just saying it takes a back burner."

Hayden didn't like his buddy's answer. So what? It was the right answer. A missing person could be in danger here, and Percy's life was no longer in the balance.

Nolan turned to Cady. "What about searching your father's house? Have you done that?"

She shook her head and clamped her hands together on the table. "I've only looked at his journals. He insisted on bringing them to my apartment when he came to stay with me. After reading them, I came here to talk to Kai. I'm not sure if I can bring myself to search through Dad's other things."

Reece gave her a sad smile. "Do you think you'd be up to it if you have one of us along for the ride?"

"I hope so," she said, her answer tentative.

"I can go with you." Hayden watched her expression to see what she thought of him accompanying her.

She offered him a hint of a soft smile. "We'll see how I feel at the time."

His heart rolled in that funny somersault it did when she looked at him in such a sweet, innocent way.

"Oh-h-h. Oh." Abby's eyes widened with sudden clarity. "So it's like that for sure, huh?"

She was talking about Hayden's feelings for Cady, but now wasn't the time to discuss it. Not like there was ever a time to have such a talk in this group. Any group for that matter.

He fired a look at Abby, warning her to leave it alone.

28

"We'll make time for you to visit your father's house in between our other duties tomorrow." He pulled the cap from the marker and added the visit to the board. "Mina's team called the hospital and homeless shelter in town, but I think we should expand the calls to the surrounding area."

"I'll be glad to make those calls," Reece offered.

"Thank you." Hayden jotted the information on the board with Reece's name.

"Do we have any information on Kai's vehicle?" Gabe asked.

"There isn't one parked in his driveway or garage," Cady said.

Nolan shifted in his chair. "Mina didn't mention anything about it."

"Let me see if I can get the vehicle details through one of my trooper buddies." Gabe's Oregon state trooper connections had come in handy more than once.

Hayden scribbled down the additional information and toyed with the marker in his fingers. He looked at Jude. "You good with keeping us organized and manning the phone?"

A crooked smile formed on his face. "Never met a person I couldn't charm so you know I'll handle the phones just fine."

"Are you sure about this assignment?" Gabe looked between Nolan and Jude. "I mean, you've known him for years. Organization isn't really his thing."

"Hey, I resemble that." Jude laughed. "I know where each and every thing is and can put my finger on it in a flash."

"You couldn't have been an FBI agent if you couldn't organize case files." Hayden tossed the closed marker to the whiteboard tray. "You might not like it, but you can do it."

"You're right." Jude grimaced. "It's time for me to take one for the team."

"Good," Hayden said.

"This is a solid start," Nolan said." I'll check in with Mina in the morning. See if she has any other leads or if she might have phone or financial information she'll share."

"We all have our assignments," Hayden said. "Just remember as you go about your tasks, we might not have any proof at this point of Kai's abduction, but we need to move forward believing he's in danger and needs our immediate attention."

He believed what he'd just said, though he preferred his number one priority to be helping Cady find her father's killer. But he'd have to resist his feelings. Kai's life could be on the line, and the hunt for her father's killer had to be put on the back burner so they could focus on Kai and bring him home before he came to grievous harm.

3

Cady charged down the hallway, Hayden tailing her. He'd insisted on walking her to the door, but she hurried ahead to collect herself. She plunged into the cool night filled with sparkling stars overhead as a sharp wind coming from the ocean beat against her body. If only it could blow away the thoughts whirling through her mind. A plethora of thoughts. Conflicting thoughts.

She resisted, groaning over her unease, and tugged her jacket closed, then zipped it to her chin as if she could zip out her anxiety. The meeting had done nothing to settle her thoughts. Was partnering with the LLL team in her best interest? Sure, they'd offered to help, but their goal differed from hers. In the long run, would working with them distract her from her mission?

Maybe she should search her father's home and talk with his fellow birdwatchers on her own. Or not. She just didn't know. This team had far more experience in questioning people and searching properties, and they might find something she would miss. Plus, she had to admit it would be far easier to look through her dad's things if she had someone with her, as Reece had suggested.

Oh, man. What was in her best interest anyway? Was she letting her chemistry with Hayden cloud everything?

The words her father shared whenever she wanted to quit echoed in her brain.

Come on, Cady girl. You can do anything you set your mind to. Just be true to yourself and your faith, and you'll succeed.

Right. Do as her father said. Do her best to take her emotions out of the equation. Approach this situation dispassionately like she would as a reporter hot on a story. Make a plan. Stick to it until other information presented itself. Then revise and move on. Rinse and repeat until she reached her goal.

"Feels like we might get frost tonight, though it's really not the time of year for it," Hayden said from behind.

She jumped and spun.

He tipped his head and studied her. "Sorry. Didn't mean to scare you."

"Lost in my thoughts, I guess." She forced out a smile. "Mind if I leave my car here for the night? I'd like to walk to clear my head."

"No problem." His eyes narrowed much the same way as when he'd first laid eyes on her at Kai's house, but she had no idea what had prompted such a reaction. "I'll walk with you."

No. No! That was not in her best interest or his. "Thank you, but I'd rather be alone to think about everything that's happened tonight."

He widened his stance and didn't look away. "There's no way I'll let you walk alone at this time of night."

Was he concerned for her safety? Was that all this was about? Her safety here in little Lost Lake. "Um, Hayden. I walk alone in big cities all the time. I think Lost Lake is safe."

He remained resolute and didn't budge. "You never know where crime will strike."

"I'll take the chance."

"But I won't." His expression solidified into a hardened rock, and he gestured for her to go first.

Clearly, this meant a lot to him, and she wouldn't keep arguing, so she started down the hill.

He caught up and stepped into place beside her. "I'm sorry. I kind of have this protective thing. I might overdo it, but I don't ever want someone I care about to be hurt."

She looked up at him to discover worry had replaced his rigid expression. "Sounds like something happened in your past, and you don't want it to happen again."

"Yeah," he said, but his voice trailed off in the wind.

Now he'd really piqued her curiosity. "Want to tell me about it?"

He glanced at her, but quickly looked away. "Want to? Not really."

"But will you so I can understand?" she asked, but did she really want to understand what was behind his actions when she had no intentions of getting involved with him? What was the point?

He clenched his fists, and his footsteps faltered.

She'd caused his negative reaction, and she didn't much like being the source of his pain. "You don't have to tell me. It's up to you."

"My parents died when I was fourteen, and I was put in foster care," he blurted, the words racing like a train barreling out of control down the tracks.

"Oh, Hayden." She clutched his arm. "I'm so sorry. I didn't mean to bring up old wounds. Especially now that I know what it's like to lose a parent. And I can't imagine losing both of them and to have it happen at fourteen."

"It was hard, there's no denying that. I'd like to say I

handled it well, but I didn't. I was angry and confused and conflicted." He started walking again.

She released her grip on his arm and kept up with him. "Of course you were. The unthinkable happened to you."

He waved a hand. "I have nothing to complain about. Not really. I was one of the lucky ones. I had excellent foster parents—patient, loving Christians. They didn't push me beyond what I could handle, and they were always there for me when I screwed up."

"I'm glad of that. You see horror stories in the news about terrible foster parents. I know there are more good ones than bad, but those stories aren't sensational enough to make the news."

"Yeah." He grimaced in opposition to his response. "I wish I could say I was worthy of them. I wasn't. Not at all. They tried their best to connect with me, but I put up a wall between us. I was too angry to see reason, and I wouldn't let it go. So when I aged out of the system, I walked away and never looked back. They didn't deserve such a callous response from me. They deserved so much more."

She hated hearing how he suffered and about his sincere guilt for how he treated his foster parents, but he was just a teen and should cut himself some slack. "I'm sure they understood."

"Maybe. Probably, anyway." He shrugged. "They'd been foster parents for a long time before I came to stay with them and had likely seen a lot of different reactions in kids they took in. Especially since they only fostered teenagers."

She gave him what she hoped was an empathetic smile. "Losing your parents would be a good reason for wanting to be protective tonight."

"Nah, that's not it. There's more. There was this foster girl in the same house as me. Lexi." He stared over Cady's shoulders. "I was supposed to walk her home from school,

34

but one of my teachers kept me after class to talk about a project. It only took five minutes, and I figured Lexi would wait for me, but when I got out front, she was gone."

Cady could only imagine where this story was going. She was already sympathetic to his past trouble and the effect it still had on him.

He swiped a hand over his face. "By the time I caught up with her, three guys were dragging her toward an alley. I charged them in the alley. One guy held onto her. The other two beat the crud out of me, and I lost consciousness. When I came to, I found one of the guys on top of her. She was sobbing hard. I mean crazy hard. I somehow got up and ripped the guy off her, then started pummeling him. He ran."

He stopped talking and blinked a few times. "By the time I turned back to Lexi, she'd gotten her clothes back on and was trying to stand. I helped her up and told her we were going to the police. She refused and begged me to take her home." He looked at Cady then, his mouth pinched. "She was my responsibility, and I failed her. I won't let something like that happen again. Ever!"

He took her hand and started walking, this time at a fast clip as if this difficult memory made him more eager to get her off the street. She enjoyed holding his hand but wished it were under a different circumstance, like when he really wanted to be holding her hand, not dragging her to her dad's house.

They reached his small bungalow overlooking the ocean, and she stopped at the walkway to stare at the cute home she'd helped him purchase. Seemed like just yesterday when they'd laughingly walked up the brick sidewalk arm in arm for him to open the door to his new home. Such wonderful possibilities had been written all over his face. Possibilities that could only occur to him before his dementia struck.

But now? Now all possibilities had come abruptly to an end earlier than she'd imagined. Sure, his dementia had quickly ended life as they had known it together—robbing him of his identity and his ability to recognize her—but at least he'd been alive and lucid at times. Times she'd learned to cherish more than any other memories of their lives.

Now he was gone. Her rock. Her mentor.

Pain gutted her, and she blinked back mounting tears. She'd been inside only once since he died. Just for a moment when she arrived in town and put her suitcase in the entryway. She'd wanted to go in and unpack, but she hadn't been able to step any deeper.

Could she now?

She took a long breath and swallowed hard to get the words out. "What time should we meet in the morning and where?"

He watched her carefully like a circling hawk, alert to every flicker of emotion on her face. "I'll pick you up at eight. We'll head straight to Kai's cottage, then we'll search the surf shop."

"Then good night, and thanks for all your help." She dredged up a smile and hoped it looked sincere because she really was thankful for his help. "And thank you for walking me home."

"Of course." He didn't make any moves to leave.

"You can go now."

"You don't want me to come with you in case it's harder than you thought?"

"I'll wait for daylight before searching through his things and let you know if I need your help then."

"Okay." He widened his stance. "But I'll wait to leave until you get inside with the door locked behind you."

She dug out her keys and sifted through them one by one to locate the right one. She was stalling. No question about that. Not because she didn't want Hayden to leave, but because she couldn't bring herself to move even a fraction of an inch toward the house.

C'mon, Cady. Move. You have to go inside at some point.

She turned. Tried to force her foot one brick forward. Froze.

Hayden was right behind her in a flash, his hand on her elbow. "What's wrong?"

"I-I don't think I can go in."

"Do you want me to come with you?"

"I don't know. Maybe. I'm not sure I'm ready." The gentle concern on his face was nearly her undoing, and her tears threatened to break free again.

"You don't have to do this right now. You've already had a tough day." He squeezed her elbow. "You can stay with us at the inn. We've left a couple of the rooms as is for visitors."

She would be thankful to be anywhere but where she was right now, but was spending the night under the same roof with him a good idea? Probably not, but spending the night here didn't seem like a good one either. "I don't want to impose or be any trouble for you."

"You won't be imposing. Everyone will understand."

"If you're sure, I'll stay tonight, and maybe I'll be braver in the daylight."

He released her elbow. "It's not about being brave. Trust me. I understand. It's about acceptance and finding the ability to move forward."

"You probably didn't have the luxury of time when your parents died but were forced to deal with the harsh reality of leaving your home right away."

"Yeah. Yeah." He dragged a hand through his hair. "Like

I said. It was rough, but hey, maybe I can use my experience to help you through this pain."

"You know what I could use right now?" she asked, even though she knew she shouldn't. "A hug. A simple friend-to-friend hug."

His brows drew together as he looked at her. "I haven't done a good job of hiding the fact that I'm interested in you, but I'll do my best to offer the friendly hug you need."

She stepped toward him and made the mistake of looking into his eyes. That interest he talked about burned brightly, and she had to be transmitting the same signals. She quickly looked away as his powerful arms encapsulated her and drew her close. His body hid the house from her view, and the warmth emanating from him helped ease out a fraction of her grief.

Enough that she didn't want to move and face the full realities again. He seemed okay with holding her, so they stood in the shadow of the moon, feeling as one to her. She wanted to wrap her arms around his waist and cling to him for as long as possible, but she wasn't a child like he'd been when he lost his family. She was a grown-up and had to face the loss of her father head on.

The sooner she internalized his death and could move forward, the better she would do in finding the person who killed him. She needed to keep the reason she was in town a greater priority than her comfort.

All the time.

Even if Hayden offered her solace, the hunt for her dad's killer had to take top priority.

~

Hayden opened the guest room door for Cady, just three doors down from his own suite. When he'd told her the team had left a few rooms untouched, he wasn't misleading her. They cleaned and disinfected the spaces but had left them decorated exactly as the prior owners had intended.

A nautical theme dominated this room, and not in a good way. Colored buoys with ropes were strung on the wall above the queen-sized bed, and cut-out anchors hung on the other wall. Faded linen drapes boasting colorful sailboats on a bright blue background to match a worn bedspread blocked the view over the ocean through French doors.

He stood back to let her enter. "It doesn't look like much, but we replaced the mattress and keep the room as clean as possible. And, of course, the bedding is all freshly washed too."

She turned, her expression blank as she took it in. "The inn must've been an interesting place before you all bought it."

"Actually, it sat vacant for two years. Thankfully no one vandalized it or tried to squat on the property."

"You wouldn't have wanted to lose these priceless buoys or anchors." She laughed.

He appreciated her humor, but her sweet giggle, like pretty much everything else about her, made him want to get to know her better.

What in the world had possessed him to ask her to stay at the inn? Sure, her pain impacted him in a way many people couldn't comprehend. Her anguish brought back so many memories, making them as fresh as if they'd happened the other day instead of twenty years ago. Memories he never wanted to call up again. Could be why he was so quick to offer her an out. Not only so she didn't have to live with the pain tonight, but so he could keep an eye on her and make sure she remained safe.

"Sorry," she said. "I didn't mean to diss your property."

"Don't be sorry. You're right. Someday we'll work on these rooms, but we currently devote our free time and money to upgrading the suites we live in."

"I'd be very interested in seeing your suite sometime."

"Of course," he said, but he doubted that would be a good idea. He set her small suitcase he'd retrieved from her father's house on a luggage rack at the end of the bed, then grabbed the ice bucket. "Glasses for water are by the sink, but I'll get you some ice. Do you want a snack too?"

"I'd appreciate the ice. Otherwise I'm good, but thank you for asking."

"Then I'll be right back with this." He held up the bucket. "And if you change your mind about a snack, you know where the kitchen is. Reece always has some wonderful home-baked stuff, so help yourself to anything you find."

He nearly fled from the room and jogged down the hall to the kitchen. Reece was unloading the dishwasher, and Nolan sat at the table with Mina, cups of hot cocoa in front of them. It looked and smelled chocolatey good. Maybe Hayden should take a cup back to Cady.

Nolan cast him a quizzical look. "The freezer go out in your suite or something?"

"Cady had a hard time going into her dad's place, so she'll be staying in a guest room. For tonight at least."

"Of course she had a hard time going there." Reece brought a container of mini marshmallows to the table. "I don't suppose you offered to go in with her."

"I do have *some* empathy, you know," Hayden said.

"Oh, I know you do, but you guys aren't always the first to pick up on such things."

"Well, I did, and she still didn't think she could stay there."

"I'm proud of you for thinking to ask." Reece opened the

container and handed it to Mina. "I should've thought to offer one of our guest rooms to begin with."

"None of us did," Nolan said. "We're too focused on the investigation."

Reece plopped down on a hard wooden chair. "Well, I for one hope we watch out for that. The day we start prioritizing an investigation over the mental health of our team or the people we help is the day we need to get out of this business."

Nolan held up a hand. "Hey, now. I hear you, but let's not be too quick to shut the business down when we've only gotten started."

"She does have a good point, though." Mina set down her cocoa. "You both do, actually. Like everything in life, there has to be a compromise, and I have confidence you'll find it."

Reece looked from Mina to Nolan. "Seriously, dude. How did you manage to sweep this woman off her feet?"

"I get it." Nolan smiled at Mina. "She's way out of my league, but for some reason she let me into the game."

Mina took his hand in hers, and an impish smile crossed her face. "It's exactly analogies like that one that hooked me."

Reece mocked gagging, but Hayden saw through the joking to Nolan and Mina's solid relationship. What he wanted in his own life. They hadn't been together for very long, but everyone on the team knew they had a forever kind of relationship. When all the team members were old and in their rockers, Mina and Nolan would be side by side, still holding hands.

He didn't like the way his thoughts were moving, so he held up the ice bucket. "I'll just grab the ice."

He marched across the room to the ice maker, taking

giant steps as if he could flee his thoughts, but they came with him.

"Make sure Cady has my suite number and knows I'm available if she needs anything," Reece called after him.

He plunged the bucket into the frozen cubes, the chilly temperature doing nothing to cool his thoughts. What was he going to tell Cady when he got back to the room? Would he tell her how to find Reece in case she needed something? Or would he give her his suite number and ask her to find him instead?

Argh. He lifted the bucket and closed the lid on the ice maker.

He didn't like it, but his answer would be decided by what she seemed to need. The part of him who was interested in her but shouldn't pursue those feelings hoped she would go see Reece if she needed help. Not so with the part of him who needed to protect Cady. If she was in any trouble, he would insist on her searching him out, no matter the consequences.

4

The morning came way before Cady was ready to face the day and all of the pain losing her father brought, but she couldn't hide out in her room. She strolled toward the kitchen, the comforting smell of bread toasting drawing her closer.

Voices drifted down the hall to greet her, and she tried to find a smile for the kind men and women on the team. She'd cried herself to sleep the night before, and the mirror reflected her red and puffy eyes, but she couldn't fault her accommodations. The bed was comfy, the shower hot, and the room held zero negative memories as her dad's place would've raised.

She reached the door and paused to take in the situation. Abby sat at a small table, and Reece's back was to Cady as she cooked at the stove.

Abby looked up and pointed at the chair across from her. "Join me. Reece is scrambling some eggs and making toast."

Cady pulled out a chair and sat.

Reece spun, frying pan in hand. "Would you like coffee with your breakfast?"

"Yes, please." Cady gave her a sincere smile. "That's the best question I've been asked in eons."

Carrying a coffee carafe, Reece crossed the room. "Rough night?"

"The room was wonderful, thank you, but I had a hard time sleeping. Spent way too much time thinking about my dad."

Abby rested a reassuring hand on Cady's. "If there's anything I can do to help, please let me know. And I mean that sincerely."

"Ditto for me." Reece flipped over a cup and poured in rich black coffee. "Cream and sugar are on the table. The guys have already destroyed the breakfast I made them and are outside doing who knows what. Now I'm scrambling eggs for Abby and me. I can make them any way you want or make you something else."

"Scrambled eggs would be lovely." She smiled up at Reece. "Thank you so much. Is there anything I can do to help?"

"Now you've done it." Abby grinned. "We're about to hear how too many cooks in the kitchen spoil the meal."

Reece wrinkled her nose at Abby. "Actually, I was about to say, 'No thank you, I have everything under control.'"

"Translated, too many cooks in the kitchen spoil the meal." Abby laughed.

Their good-natured banter brightened Cady's mood, probably the considerate duo's plan. She could easily see herself becoming friends with these women. Not that it mattered in any way. She wasn't about to move to Lost Lake anytime soon. Sure, she could see living in this charming town in retirement like her dad had done or if she ever lost all sense and decided to settle down and have children. It was probably a great place to raise kids, but as a reporter who wanted to make her mark on the world? No, Lost Lake wasn't her choice for her career goals.

Besides, there was still the lesson her mother taught her. Still the pain she'd inflicted. The doubt she'd created. After having a late-term miscarriage, she couldn't handle seeing Cady without thinking of the lost baby. The pain was so intense she couldn't deal and walked out on Cady and her dad, never to return again. Cady had no idea where she was or even if she was still alive. Heartbreaking in itself, but it also proved marriage didn't last. Didn't withstand the trials and hardships.

Why would Cady's marriage be any different?

"Be right back with the eggs." Reece hurried back to the stove.

Cady turned her attention to the coffee, sipping from her mug and nearly groaning at the piping-hot liquid with a hint of hazelnut.

Abby set down her mug. "I really do know what you're going through. My mom recently passed away."

"Oh, Abby, I'm so sorry. Here I am wrapped up in my own grief when you must be suffering too."

"There's a difference though," Abby said. "My mom and I didn't get along. In fact, I'm pretty much the black sheep of my family."

Cady worked hard to keep her mouth from falling open. "I would never peg you for a black sheep."

"I didn't see myself that way either, but both my parents, along with my siblings and their spouses, are defense attorneys. It was pretty much expected I'd become one too. When I decided to go into law enforcement instead, everyone was horrified over my career choice. They didn't give me an ultimatum that said to change or I'd be ostracized. They just grew away from me."

"That has to hurt."

A pensive look on her face, she ran a finger along the rim of her mug, emitting a humming sound. "You'd think I'd be used to it by now, but it's still painful in a way I really didn't expect. Their disapproval was hard to take, and I pretty much stopped visiting or communicating with them. Now that my mom is gone, I have so many regrets over not trying to iron this out between us and spend more time with her. One of the hardest parts about losing a parent, is knowing you'll never be able to reconcile with them."

Cady took Abby's hand and held it tightly. "You'll be in my prayers for sure, but is there anything else I can do for you?"

She smiled, barely—like she couldn't manage a full smile. "I can't think of anything, but you've already helped. Until now I haven't been able to tell anyone how I felt. I guess seeing you work through your loss helped me be willing to say it."

Cady squeezed Abby's hand and let go. "I'm here for you for as long as I'm in town, and we can stay in touch even after I go back to Portland."

"Order coming up," Reece called out, ending the moment. She brought over two plates with fluffy eggs and slices of thick whole wheat bread toasted to a crisp brown. "I hope you like the toast. It's a new bread recipe I've been working on. I'm trying to get the perfect balance of wheat flour to white flour to make a hearty yet light wheat bread."

Cady blinked at her new friend. "Are you actually telling me you bake your own bread?"

"I do. Like I said, I hope you like it." Reece headed back to the stove.

Cady glanced at Abby. "I don't think I've ever met anyone who bakes her own bread."

"I hadn't either until we met Reece, but trust me, you'll never taste anything better."

Cady leaned closer and tapped a jar of strawberry jam on the table. "Will she be offended if I put some jam on it?"

"First off, remember who all she cooks for and know that nothing could offend her or she would've stopped cooking for all of us a long time ago." Abby chuckled. "But then, you should know she made the jam too, so I'm sure she'll be more than happy for you to enjoy it."

Cady shook her head over Reece's abilities and dipped into the thick jar of strawberries wrapped in a sweet syrup and slathered it on her toast. She took a bite and moaned. "Oh. Oh. Man, is this good. Thank you so much for making me breakfast."

"Glad you like it. It's nice to be so appreciated." Reece joined them with her own plate of eggs and toast.

Cady shouldn't have wolfed down half of her breakfast instead of waiting for her.

Abby frowned and looked at Reece. "I guess we've started taking you for granted, haven't we?"

She waved a hand. "You know I don't do it for praise and thanks. Feeding you all is my love language. Seeing you enjoy it is all I need."

"But..." Abby took a bite of her eggs.

"Yeah, but." Reece chuckled.

The front door closed and footfalls tromped down the hallway.

"The guys have returned," Abby said. "It's been at least thirty minutes since they've eaten, so protect your plate, especially the toast, or you might lose some of your food."

Cady laughed, but her heart warmed at seeing how much this team cared about each other. Sure, their comments were mostly joking, but behind it all, their love for each other rang out as loudly as if they shouted, "I love you."

Gabe barreled into the room, followed by Hayden, who

entered with a more cautious approach. He never seemed to rush into things but wanted to consider his options and perhaps control his surroundings.

"Yo. Second breakfast. Wait, where's ours?" Gabe reached toward Reece's plate, and she playfully slapped his hand. He chuckled and crossed the room to lift the coffee pot. "Is it okay if I have more coffee?"

Hayden gave a look like he'd been in the place many times before. "I think the right question is do any of you want more coffee before I take some?"

"Well, yeah. What he said." Gabe laughed again. "But seriously, if I have to sit behind a desk this morning and track down Kai's vehicle, I need something to keep my eyes open."

"Go ahead," Reece said. "I can always make more."

Hayden turned his attention to Cady, and her heart tripped into high speed, as usual.

"Sorry I wasn't here when you got up," he said. "We had some rain overnight, and we sprung a roof leak. One that should've been repaired years ago, and it took all of us to patch it. Hopefully we fixed it for the time being."

"Thankfully, now that the rainy season has ended," Abby said, "we can do a proper job of fixing or replacing it."

"If we have enough money." Gabe leaned against the counter and took a sip of his coffee.

Looked like the business might be suffering from startup costs, which didn't surprise Cady. It didn't sit right with her for taking up their time to find her father's killer. She'd like to say it bothered her enough to tell them to forget it, but she needed to know what had become of her dad. Needed to know as badly as she needed to breathe.

Hayden looked at Cady again. "Whenever you and Abby are done, we'll head over to Kai's house to do a thorough search."

Having eaten every bite of her delicious breakfast, Cady pushed her plate away. "I'm ready to go whenever you are. Unless, of course, I can help do the dishes first."

Reece waved a hand. "No worries. I'm sure Gabe will be glad to help me load the dishwasher." She gave him a pointed look.

"Right," he said, but looked like he wanted to groan. "What she said."

"I'm good to go, too." Abby slid back. "I'll help with dinner dishes tonight."

"As long as you don't help me cook." Reece laughed.

"No chance of that happening." Abby winked.

Cady scooted off her chair. "Thank you again for breakfast, Reece. If you're ever in the Portland area, I'll be glad to repay you."

"No need to repay me, but I'd be glad to go out for a meal the next time I'm there."

"We can take my vehicle." Hayden held his hand toward the door and directed them to his Raptor, then soon had them pulling up to Kai's cottage.

Cady followed him to the door of the quaint place, tucking the front of her jacket closed to the sharp wind curling off the ocean. The sun might be shining bright, but with temps in the low fifties and the breeze a cooler temperature still, the chill seeped through her jacket.

Hayden pushed open the door and stepped back to let her and Abby enter first.

Abby marched straight inside and looked around the room, her hand on her sidearm. "I'll clear the place as a precaution before we get started."

She disappeared in the hallway.

Hayden's gaze tracked her. "You can take the person out of law enforcement, but you can't take the law enforcement out of the person."

"I heard that," Abby called back. "The same could be said of you, and if you'd entered before me, you'd be doing the same thing."

"She's got me there." He gave Cady a lopsided smile.

Her heartstrings reverberated in her chest, but before she could fall prey to her emotions, Abby zoomed back into the room.

She handed disposable gloves to Cady, and then to Hayden. "Cady will search the kitchen and you have the living area. I've got the bedroom and bathroom."

"I'll get right on that, boss." Hayden saluted her.

If she was bothered by his playful response when she seemed quite serious, she didn't show it.

Cady glanced into the small kitchen. "I assume you gave me this space because nobody ever hides things there."

"Actually, criminals stash stuff in their kitchens all the time." Abby slipped into her gloves. "They figure we won't think they would do such a thing and it's safer."

"Be particularly mindful of the freezer and refrigerator and any openable containers holding food in the pantry," Hayden added.

Cady nodded and took a few steps to the kitchen, struggling to put on the gloves, unlike Abby's practiced movements with hers. Cady decided to start with the refrigerator-freezer and then work her way through the pantry, since those were the areas Hayden mentioned.

His and Abby's footsteps on the wooden floor signaled their departure, but she soon lost herself in the search. It was a tedious job to look through containers of rice and beans for small items, but she didn't want to dump them on the floor and leave a mess for Kai when he returned. She'd just eaten breakfast, but the pungent spice smells stimulated her appetite, especially the exotic curry powder.

Either she wasn't very good at searching, or there was

nothing to be found, but she struck out in the prime locations. She climbed up on the counter to begin a search of the upper cabinets. If she wanted to hide something in a kitchen, she would use these harder to reach cupboards.

"I'm not finding any bank or phone records," Hayden called out.

She glanced around the refrigerator to look at him as he closed a desk drawer. "That would seem odd, right? Many people his age still get paper bills in the mail."

"I was thinking the same thing too." Hayden leaned against the bookshelf behind him. "But lots of people don't get them at all, and others shred their bills after they pay them."

"Not me. I'm a keeper." Albeit a messy one.

"Me too. At least until the end of the year. Then I get rid of everything I don't need for my taxes." He peered around the space. "But I don't see a shredder."

"Maybe he has one at his business, and he shreds them there."

He pushed off the bookshelf. "We'll have to ask when we go to the shop."

She went back to the cupboards and pulled dishes in and out. Kai's neat cabinets continued to show his organizational skills. Thirty minutes later, she reached the final cabinet, holding coffee mugs from various surfing locations across the United States. Based on the mugs being stored high up, she doubted he ever used them but had collected them on his travels.

She took out a vintage mug from Hawaii where a plastic surfer moved in gel on one side and shook it like she'd done with the mugs on lower shelves. Something clinked. Her excitement built. She looked inside. A small blue metal device lay in the bottom. Her heart soared.

"I found something!" she yelled loud enough for Abby

to hear in the bedroom. "Looks like a flash drive, but it's kind of big."

She hopped down with mug in hand. Hayden met her between the two rooms, and she handed him the mug. Abby rushed into the room.

He picked up the drive and turned it round and round, but instead of excitement over the lead, he frowned. "It's a flash drive, all right."

A confusing response, for sure. "I thought you'd be happy I found it."

"I would be if it wasn't one of these." He pulled the ring on the end to release a case and reveal the end of the USB drive that plugged into a computer. Nothing unusual there, but when he flipped it over, the backside of the device held a tiny black keypad.

Something she'd never seen before. "Are those keys used to access the device?"

"Yeah," he said. "You need to know the PIN and enter it here before you have any hope of getting to the data. It could be any random string of up to fifteen characters. Drives like these often use military-grade encryption that's oblivious to any kind of hacking. Almost impossible to figure out the password."

Cady's excitement was dashed to the curb. She held back a sigh of frustration.

"So unless we get the PIN, you won't likely be able to open this," Abby said. "Even then, it'll be iffy."

"Exactly." Hayden shoved the drive back into the sleeve. "Only one hope that I know of to get it open. We need to contact Nick Thorne at the Veritas Center."

"Veritas Center?" Cady asked.

"World-class forensics experts in Portland," Hayden said. "Nick is their cyber specialist, and I've never seen anything he can't do. Problem is, he's highly sought after, and he or his team might not have time to handle this drive."

"Then together we'll convince them to do it." Abby bounced on her toes. "We have to. It must hold something big. Your average surf shop owner in a small town like Lost Lake doesn't need to own a drive with this level of security."

"Yeah." Hayden's gaze grew uncertain. "It's seeming more likely Kai is indeed missing, and there's something on this drive that will help us find him."

Cady had to agree with him and prayed the drive didn't reveal something terribly wrong. Wrong enough to have cost Kai his life.

5

Clouds rolled over the sun as Hayden stood outside Kai's cottage and ended his call with Nick. With the way things were going, he wondered if the sun going away was a warning of upcoming difficulties. Thankfully, he'd piqued Nick's interest with the drive. Nothing negative about that.

Hayden texted Nolan to tell him about their discovery and asked him to inform Mina and get her buy-in before he turned the drive over to Nick. She also needed to know they were following chain of custody protocol with the evidence. Whenever she arrested a suspect and brought him to trial, proper procedures like this would increase their chances of successfully introducing the evidence. The last thing they wanted was for a sharp defense attorney to get the drive thrown out on a technicality.

Nolan texted his acknowledgment, and Hayden joined Abby and Cady on the small porch.

"Did Nick agree, or do I need to work my charms on him?" Abby chuckled, but her expression was deadly serious.

"He agreed," Hayden said. "Once I told him about the type of drive and the encryption, I think he might've actually driven down here to get it just for the challenge of cracking it."

Abby let out a quick whoop and high-fived him. "I knew you could do it."

"Thank goodness." Cady's breath came out in a wave of relief.

Hayden couldn't agree more. "He suggested overnighting the drive to him, but I don't want to wait that long or risk the carrier losing it. I'll drive it to him tonight or ask someone on the team to do it. Nick will start working on it the minute it arrives."

"Someone else can drive. You're needed here." Abby maintained direct eye contact, her confidence in her decision typical for her.

"Yoo-hoo," Kai's silvery-haired neighbor called out as she bustled down her walkway, her cane thumping. "I don't believe I know you folks."

"Great, a nosy neighbor," Abby said. "I'll handle it. I'm used to dealing with situations like this."

The three of them met the elderly woman at the sidewalk. She wore a flowery dress and pink cushioned slippers and looked to be in her eighties. She poked out a wrinkly hand. "I'm Dorothy Green."

Abby pushed forward, a smile on her face. "Abby Day, and these are my associates. We work with the Lost Lake Locators. Have you heard of our business?"

"Who in this town hasn't?" Dorothy looked each of them over with a critical eye. "You made quite a splash by buying the inn, but then the big news was your involvement with the mayor's death. That was something, wasn't it? I was so impressed when you figured out who killed him." She clutched the buttons on her dress. "And what a shocking conclusion!"

Abby nodded, and Hayden hoped she would change the

subject before they went down a rabbit hole into their investigation of Mayor Sutton's murder.

She smiled at the woman as if humoring a child. "Do you know Kai?"

"Well, of course I do." She sniffed as if offended. "I've lived in this neighborhood since I met and married my dear Walter, may he rest in peace. Then Kai bought his house about twenty years ago. I think you could say I know him better than anyone in town."

"So he told you he was going on vacation then," Abby pressed her gently.

"Yes, and it's about time." Her expression softened. "The poor man rarely takes time off, and I was so glad to see he decided to get away for a week."

"Did he mention where he was going?" Abby asked.

Dorothy turned her head just a bit. Did she want to avoid this question?

"He didn't say what his destination was, and I didn't ask. I figured he would tell me if he wanted me to know, and he wanted his privacy. Also, he didn't want anyone bothering him this week."

How odd that this woman, who appeared to be quite nosy, hadn't questioned Kai about his destination. But she seemed to really care for him, so maybe she was respecting his wishes.

Abby stared more intensely at Dorothy. "Can you think of anyone he might have shared his vacation plans with?"

Dorothy tipped her head in the direction of the tall two-story house on the other side of Kai's cottage. "Maybe Jake."

"Jake?"

"Jake—Jacob Hill. He lives on the other side of Kai, and they're surfing buddies."

Hayden made a mental note of the name, but Cady scribbled it down in her notepad. If the man was home, they still had time to question him before heading to the surf shop.

"So everything seemed okay with Kai, then?" Abby circled back as all good detectives would do in an interview to be sure the person replied with the same answer.

Dorothy shifted her cane to the other hand, her expression turning suspicious. "Don't tell me you're here on business? That you think he's missing or something? He's just on vacation."

"His son is concerned," Abby said. "He said it's very unlike his dad to take time off, but to do so in peak surfing season and at the spur of the moment, even more unlikely. So Rocco wants to err on the side of caution and make sure Kai's all right."

Dorothy gave a sage nod. "That's just like Rocco. He's such a good son. Ever since his mother passed away, he's stepped in to make sure everything is going okay with his dad. But with this? No. I think he's just overreacting."

"You could very well be right." Hayden smiled, trying to deflect any concern Dorothy might have. "Other than the surprising vacation, has everything seemed normal with Kai?"

"Hmm." She tapped her chin. "He's been a little busier at work, and I haven't seen a lot of him, so I'm not sure how to answer that. The few times I *have* seen him, he seemed a bit preoccupied, but again, it's the beginning of his busy season, so that's not unusual."

"Do you know if Kai has a personal computer?" Abby asked. "There wasn't one in his cottage."

"A computer? Kai?" She snorted. "That's like mixing oil and water. He's never had one, and he claims he never will. He doesn't have one of those smartphones or been on the internet." She tsked. "For goodness' sake, I do that, and I'm about as ancient as they come." She chuckled, and a sudden gust of wind buffeted against the cliff, carrying the sound away.

Abby brushed hair, also caught by the blast, from her face. "Do you have any security cameras on the property that could've recorded his movements?"

"No. No way. No how." Dorothy stomped her cane on the sidewalk with a reverberating thump. "The day I have to install those at my place is the day you might as well put me six feet under."

The raised-brow look Abby gave Hayden said she wanted to know if he had additional questions. He shook his head.

"Thank you for your time, Mrs. Green." Abby sent the woman a warm, reassuring smile. "We very much appreciate it."

"I really think everything is fine, but I pray for Kai every day, and I'll make sure to add his safety to my petitions." Dorothy raised her cane and tapped it on the sidewalk in front of each person one at a time. "If you discover anything is wrong, you will promise to tell me, won't you?"

"Yes, ma'am." He wasn't about to argue with this sweet, yet fiery older woman. He gave her his business card. "If you think of anything that might help us find Kai, I'd appreciate it if you would give me a call."

"Don't you worry. I can see his surf shop from my back deck, and of course, his house is right next door. So I'll watch for anything out of the ordinary." She turned carefully and strode to her house, the thud of her cane getting lost in the wind.

Abby's gaze lifted to Hayden's face. "She seems like she keeps an eagle eye on things around her, and if there's anything fishy going on, she would know."

He nodded, but he wasn't ready to concede that Kai

wasn't in danger. "Let's go see if Jake Hill is home. He might have a different story to tell."

He waved the women ahead of him, then followed behind.

Cady slowed and fell into step beside him. "Despite Dorothy's lack of concern, I'm starting to get a bad feeling about this."

"I'd like to say I'm not, but I'm with you." He dredged up what he hoped was a comforting look to ease her concerns. "But we don't need to overreact. Especially not this soon in the investigation. Each little piece put together will hopefully reveal the true picture."

"You're right. Jake could tell us something that changes everything." She frowned. "Let's hope whatever he says is good."

They climbed the walkway at a determined pace toward the two-story house. It appeared as if it was once a single story cottage similar to other houses on the street and had been renovated to add a story.

Abby reached the door first and stabbed her finger into the doorbell. She tapped her foot and stared straight ahead. She might've been gentle with Dorothy, but she'd moved into her former sheriff mode. She'd developed the ability to be what she needed to be for the person she was interviewing. Such skills had made her a good sheriff.

Hayden searched the front of the building for security cameras but didn't see any. Not a surprise. In small, low-crime-rate towns like Lost Lake, residents felt safe enough not to have protective devices on their homes, which made finding missing persons more difficult.

The sound of footsteps clipping toward the door brought Hayden's attention back to the entrance. A guy Hayden put in his late thirties, pulled the door open. His cheeks were covered with freckles, and his fiery red hair was messed up like he'd just crawled out of bed. Baggy, unhemmed khaki pants hung from his hips.

He planted bare feet with a slap on the tile floor and rested a hand on a hip. "Help you with something?"

"Are you Jacob Hill?" Abby asked.

"Yeah. What's this about?"

Abby gave him her business card and introduced herself and the others. "We've been hired by Kai's son to make sure he's all right, and Dorothy thought you might know something about his vacation."

"Wait, what?" A crease formed between his brows. "Did something happen to him on vacation?"

Hayden held up a hand. "Sorry, Mr. Hill. We didn't mean to worry you."

"Please call me Jake."

"We don't have any information to suggest something bad has happened to Kai." Hayden explained Rocco's concerns.

Jake hissed air through his teeth. "Man, I'd hate to have something bad happen to that dude. He's like my amigo, you know?"

Abby continued to peer at him. "Since you're close to him, did he tell you where he was going?"

"Nah, he said if no one knew where he was, no one could bother him." He took a few exaggerated blinks. "I didn't think anything of it at the time, but now that you mention it, it *is* kind of odd for him. He's really an open book. A what-you-see-is-what-you-get kind of person. He doesn't hold back." A grin spread across his face. "I can't tell you how many times he's blurted something out that's gotten him into trouble. Never a dull moment with him."

"We've been told he doesn't much like computers." Hayden let his statement rest in the air.

"Hah!" Jake shook his head. "*Doesn't much like* is an

understatement. He hates them, and he hates what they're doing to our society. He gets that we need technology and understands it can make things better. But it irks him when people come here for vacation or to take surfing lessons with him and every second he's not talking to them or they're not in the water, their noses are buried in their phones. They're missing God's creation and all of the beauty around us."

Even though Hayden was a geek and probably spent too much time on his phone, he had to agree with Jake's comment. "So it's fair to say he didn't own a computer."

"Not only no computer, but no tablet, and his phone is a basic device for making calls only." Jake shook his head. "He didn't even want that phone, but since he spends so much time away from his business and out on the beach, Rocco insisted so he could check in on his dad at any time."

"Sounds like Rocco might be a little overprotective," Abby said.

"Yeah, he got that way after his mom suddenly died of a heart attack. She was alone and unable to call for help. He didn't want the same thing to happen to his dad."

"Understandable." Cady's grief over losing her father lingered in her tone, but she raised her pen over her notepad. "Other than Kai going off on a vacation when he doesn't take vacations, have you noticed anything off or unusual with him?"

Jake shifted, his bare feet smacking the tile. "Not really. I mean, maybe he was more intense and less relaxed or easy-going. He hasn't had time to surf with me like he usually does. He said the business was taking up more of his time. I'm self-employed, so I get that and didn't think anything of it."

"Do you think Rocco is overreacting?" Hayden asked.

Jake shrugged. "I mean, who am I to say someone is

overreacting? I guess something could be up with Kai, and I think you should probably keep looking into it just to make sure he's okay."

"I don't see any security cameras on the property," Hayden said. "Do you have any that might've caught Kai's movements?"

"Nope. No need for them in this town. At least not in most of the neighborhoods."

"Is there anything else you think we need to know that might help us locate him?" Cady tapped her pen against her notepad with growing intensity. "Like maybe places he's ever said he would like to go on vacation?"

"Hmm, a vacation for Kai would have to involve surfing, but honestly, he's surfed every one of the best areas in the world. He talks about the positives of each one, so I couldn't begin to pick which one he might go back to." Jake scrunched up his face. "But then, if this really is a vacation to get away from everything, he probably wouldn't go anywhere that had anything to do with surfing."

"Does he have a favorite surfboard he would take along on a surfing vacation?" Abby asked. "If it's not where he stores it, it might tell us he's gone surfing."

"Oh, yeah." Jake grinned. "We all have favorites."

"Can you tell us what his looks like and where he stores it?" Cady asked.

"At his shop, he has a storage area in the back. You can access it from outside." He got out his phone. "I'm sure I have a picture of the board."

Jake thumbed through his phone, then held out a photo of a well-used surfboard.

"Text it to me." Hayden held out his own phone. "Here's my number."

"Sure." Jake tapped his screen. "Done."

Hayden's phone dinged, and he confirmed the receipt of the picture. "Thank you for your help, Jake."

"Yes, thanks," Abby said, sounding sincere. "If you think of anything else we need to know, you can reach us at the phone number on my card."

"Hey, yeah, man." Jake frowned. "I'll keep thinking, and maybe something will come to mind, but hey, can you let me know once you find out he's okay?"

Abby offered Jake a comforting smile. "Of course we will."

They turned down the walkway, but Hayden didn't hear the door close. Hayden glanced back and Jake stood intently watching them. He'd seemed sincere, and Hayden really had no reason to believe he was lying to them, but why was he watching them this way?

Maybe he was just shocked by the fact that an investigator was asking about his best friend. Or maybe he was in contact with Kai and Jake was making sure they left the area so he could call Kai and tell him people were asking for him. Kai might not have gone on vacation and could be hiding out at Jake's house for all Hayden knew.

But if Hayden were to follow on that thought, then his next question would be—what was going on in Kai's life that he felt a need to hide from everyone around him?

6

Hayden motioned for Cady and Abby to follow him up the boardwalk to Ride the Tide Surf Shop, his conversation with Nick Thorn still on his mind. The thumb drive might be the key to their entire investigation. But Kai might need them now, and Nick had no idea how long it might take to get to the data.

Time. Their investigations always came down to time. The last thing his team had when they were hunting for a missing person, and the pressure to find Kai was already starting to weigh on Hayden.

He took a moment to compose himself, then pushed open the door. Brightly colored surf and boogie boards, along with wetsuits, beachwear, and diving paraphernalia, stuffed the small shop.

Behind a long counter located close to the door, a blond-haired twenty-something guy stood pricing T-shirts. He looked up and shoved a wayward strand of hair behind his ear. "Yo. Welcome."

Hayden passed a stand of Ride the Tide logo T-shirts and stopped at the counter. The guy's surfboard-shaped name tag pinned to his tie-dyed T-shirt read "Ziggy."

"Hayden Kraus." Hayden smiled. "I work with the Lost Lake Locators."

"Oh, right, dude. You bought the inn." He pointed in the direction of their building up the cliff. "Super cool what you do." He looked over Hayden's shoulder. "You two locators too?"

"I am." Abby gave a little wave. "Abby Day."

"Cool. Cool. I love that chicks do something like this too."

"Abby is a former sheriff," Hayden said, hoping to make this guy think twice about lying to them.

"Dude, I hope we never crossed paths." He grinned, looking about twelve years old, then glanced at Cady and sobered. "I know you somehow."

Cady offered a faint, unsteady smile. "I'm Cadence Vaughn."

"Oh, yeah. Yeah. Percy's daughter." Ziggy shook his head slowly. "I heard he passed. Sorry, man. He was a great guy. A good surfer for an old dude. He was big-time buds with Kai."

Cady's smile gained confidence. "He always spoke highly of Kai and his surfing skills."

"Man, Kai's the best. Taught me so much. He shoulda gone pro, you know?" He stared ahead as if lost in memories. "But then I wouldn't have this awesome job. If you're here to see him, he's on vacay."

"We heard he'd be gone for a week," Hayden said.

Ziggy's gaze drifted back to Hayden, a flicker of hesitation in his eyes. "Yeah, man. Kinda weird. It's hard to get him to take a day off, and then he ups and goes for a week. And at the start of the summer season." Ziggy scratched his head. "Strangest thing is, he didn't even take his board with him, and he never goes out of town without it."

Perfect. Information they needed without asking.

Hayden held out the picture Jake had given him of Kai's favorite board. "So this board is still here?"

"Yep, so I doubt he's surfing. I dunno. He didn't even say where he was going and doesn't want us to call him unless the place is on fire. His words not mine."

"Have you tried calling him?" Hayden asked, though Rocco had called and hadn't gotten an answer.

"As you can see, the place isn't on fire, so..." Ziggy laughed.

"You said *us* call him." Cady looked up from her notepad with a pen poised over it. "Who all works here?"

"Full-time, just me and Bodhi. I do days. He does nights. Guy likes to party and can't get up before ten to save his life." Ziggy gave a long-suffering look. "Then we have a couple of college kids for the summer too. Kind of hopeless cause they don't really surf, but I've done my best to train them on the lingo and gear. When they put down their phones, that is. Bodhi and I have keys. I open. He closes."

"Kai's son is worried about his dad," Abby said. "He thinks something bad has happened to him."

"Rocco? Weird. He didn't call to say anything about it to me. Don't know about Kai being in trouble, but like I said, leaving like this is odd. Especially this time of year." He frowned. "And another thing. He said if anyone came looking for him not to tell them anything. I don't think he meant you guys, but he whispered it like it was some deep secret."

Cady took a step closer. "Do you have any idea what that might be about?"

He shrugged. "Maybe something to do with money."

Hayden's interest perked up. "You have a reason to think Kai had money issues?"

Ziggy waved a hand. "Nothing like that. I get my paycheck on time, and the shop is doing well. So nah. He seemed good, but it was the way he mentioned someone might come looking for him."

"Can you think of any other reason for his statement?" Hayden asked.

"Nope. He's like honest and doesn't break or even bend the law, so I doubt he was in any trouble."

"So it couldn't be drugs or something else illegal?" Abby asked.

"Drugs and Kai?" Ziggy gave a low grunt. "No way. Not even legal MaryJane. Or even alcohol. Guy's into fitness for strong surfing."

Cady finished scribbling on her notepad and looked up. "What about friends? Is he close to anyone besides my dad?"

"Everyone in town loves the dude. He's got like celebrity status for all of his surfing awards you see on the wall." Ziggy pointed at framed photographs and trophies on the far wall. "But close friends? I mean he was good friends with the mayor and your dad when he lived here, but otherwise I've never seen him with anyone in particular."

Cady jotted down another note.

Hayden was beginning to wonder with all the notes she was taking, if she was indeed going to do a story, or if the reporter in her just had to record everything. He'd ask about it later, but for now he dug a set of keys from his pocket. "Rocco gave us keys so we could have a look around." He splayed out the six keys on the ring. "This bronze one is for his house, but can you tell me what the others are for?"

Ziggy tapped the two largest silver ones. "Front and back door." He poked a smaller one. "Office, and the littlest one is for the outside board and equipment storage area. Never seen the other one before."

"I guess we'll have to figure that one out." Hayden took a breath and slowly let it out, so he didn't sound eager to gain an answer to his next question. "I assume your cash register is computerized. Does that mean Kai has an office computer it connects to?"

"Hah! Kai and computers don't mix. He doesn't have a machine here and fights any suggestion of adding one. This register doesn't even print receipts." He tapped a rectangular metal box holding two-part paper receipts sitting on the countertop. "We do it all by hand. Write it out and give it to the customer."

Abby studied the cash register. "Then what does this thing actually do then?"

"We enter the product information into it, and it records everything. At the end of the day, Kai's bookkeeper is able to electronically poll the machine somehow to get the sales data for her records. I think she's tried to give Kai reports, but he doesn't even look at them."

Not the way Hayden would run a business at all. "So he must do all the inventory by hand."

"Yep, he just walks around and looks at what we're running out of. I keep telling him automation would save him so much time and effort, and nothing would ever be out of stock, but he totally doesn't trust computers. I don't think that'll ever change."

With Kai's hatred of computers, having a high-tech drive like the one they'd found at his house could mean he'd stolen it from someone. Maybe that someone had abducted him to get it back.

Could Hayden be putting Kai in more danger by taking the drive? What if Kai was being tortured, and he finally cracked and gave up the location of the drive? The abductors wouldn't find it. Then what would they do to Kai?

"Okay, thanks for the information," he said. "We'll take a look at his office. Maybe while we do, you can think about anything I've forgotten to ask you, but might help us."

"Yeah, sure. Sure thing." He bobbed his head up and down like a puppet. "You've got me worried now too."

Hayden didn't want to worry this employee, but he also didn't want to downplay the situation Kai might be in, so he left the comment alone and turned to Abby and Cady. "Follow me."

"I wouldn't recommend the three of you going in there," Ziggy said. "The space is really small. I mean ti-nee! It'll be a challenge for two people to move around in there. No way three could, unless you like to be up in each other's business."

Cady closed her notepad and looked at Hayden. "I want to go with you, but you guys are more experienced than me, so I'll stay here and talk to Ziggy."

Hayden hated to leave her behind, but he nodded and headed for the door labeled private. The key turned without a hitch, and he entered a room he put at about six feet wide and ten feet long. A desk was built into one side wall with file cabinets and a small safe beneath. A bookshelf filled with binders and stacked with papers stood against the back wall.

"Ziggy wasn't exaggerating." Abby went straight to the desk. "As small as this space is, it shouldn't take us long at all."

"You go ahead and start there, and I'll do the bookshelf." Hayden turned his back to Abby and riffled through binders filled with records, pausing to take stock of the financial condition of the business. "Kai might not be looking at the reports he gets, but he's filing them. It's everything we need and we shouldn't need to interview the bookkeeper unless any red flags are raised. His income has steadily gone up. I'd say strong performance and solid stability."

"Doesn't seem like this is about money then," Abby said.

Hayden turned to see what she was searching and

leaned against the bookshelf. It moved under his hand. "What in the world?"

He spun to find it had pulled away from the wall. "There's something behind here."

He grabbed the back of the case and dragged it forward, revealing a door. He turned the knob. Didn't budge. "Locked."

"Maybe the key Ziggy couldn't identify opens it." Abby stood by him, her eyes ablaze with the same excitement burning through his gut.

He dug the key from his pocket and inserted it. The lock came free. "Jackpot."

Pushing open the door, he took a step into the dark room. His foot dropped into space. He lurched back, his heart rate kicking up at his near miss. "Floor disappears, and I almost took a nosedive. Stairway, I think."

"Stairs?" Abby's confused voice rose and echoed back at them from the space ahead. "Surely this place doesn't have a basement."

Hayden ran his fingers over the wall until he connected with a light switch. A quick flip and a single bulb hanging from the ceiling illuminated the area. A stone ceiling and walls with steps carved out of the rock stood in front of him. "Not a basement. A cave."

Abby bumped him aside and peered ahead. "This is creepy."

"You can say that again." He tried to keep the hesitation out of his tone. "You stay here while I check it out."

Frowning, she slowly backed off. "Don't take any risks. If anything seems off, hightail it back here."

He nodded and pushed past her, illuminating his feet with the flashlight on his phone to start down the steps. No handrail, so he ran his hands along the cold stone wall. Six steps led him down to a stone floor. He flicked his flashlight to the right, revealing a short tunnel. It seemed to open into a large room.

He listened for any noise. Any sound at all. A slow drip plunking into a pool of water reached his ears. Nothing for it but to follow the tunnel.

Using his light to mark his way, he bent forward to safely move under the low ceiling. A stale, musty odor permeated the stone cavern surrounding him as he approached the room.

What in the world would he find? He had no idea. Couldn't be good if Kai had to hide it like this, could it? His heart beat faster, and he rested his hand on his sidearm for quick access if needed.

The ceiling gently slanted up at the end of the tunnel. The urge to rush ahead hit him, but he flashed his light around the space before taking another step. His light revealed a large room with smooth walls. Not walls built by man, but a natural cave.

He ran his light down the length. Reached the end and jerked to a stop.

Man, oh man!

His mouth fell open as he studied three women of Asian descent huddling together on the floor. Near them sat three cots and shelves lined with food and various other toiletry items. A composting toilet had been placed on the opposite wall, and a foul odor emitted from the area.

He stepped a few feet into the space. The women cringed.

"No hurt." The oldest one with large terrified eyes shielded the other two behind her.

Hayden held up a hand to give him time to process the scene before him. Was Kai into human smuggling or trafficking? Did his disappearance have something to do with these three women?

He didn't know Kai well at all, but the man was well loved in town, and Hayden found it hard to believe he would be involved in such a horrific thing.

"Please, no hurt." The woman's panicked voice rose. "You ask. We do."

"Don't worry. I won't hurt you." He took a step closer.

She jerked back farther. The fear was alive on their faces and in their eyes, their arms gripped tightly around their waists. As a former border patrol agent, he'd seen the same expressions more times than he would like to count from people trying to illegally cross the border or those who made it across only to be discovered by authorities. When he'd left CBP, he'd hoped he would never have to face such human fear again.

But here it was. Fresh. Intense. And not more than ten feet away from him in quaint Lost Lake.

Sadly, the women's reaction to him said they'd been abused. No question in his mind. Likely by men. Likely in the worst way possible.

A wave of nausea rolled through him, and the urge to flee the room and not look back hit hard. They needed him to rescue them, and he didn't want to fail.

Please let us help them.

Us. He should probably call Abby down here. As a former sheriff, she would know how to handle this situation, and the woman would probably trust a female more. He should call her, but he didn't want to bring her into this ugly experience if he didn't have to, and he definitely wouldn't allow Cady down here.

So what, then?

"Hayden?" Abby's voice came from the end of the tunnel.

Of course she didn't listen and stay in the office. She'd sensed a problem, and as his backup, she came to check on him. If he didn't stop her from entering the room, she would see more than she bargained for.

He turned, but he was too late. Her light beam preceded her into the room. A short cry escaped her mouth, and she flashed a look at Hayden. "Oh my. Is this what I think it is?"

"Probably," Hayden said, trying to downplay it.

Abby twisted to appraise the women. "We need to call Mina. Get some deputies out here and the women to the hospital for treatment."

"No!" the woman all but shrieked. "No police. Bad people. Very bad people. No police."

Her distrust of law enforcement wasn't unexpected, and she needed reassurance. "Our sheriff is a wonderful woman. She'll help you."

The woman's gaze remained skeptical, but she seemed to calm down a bit. Perhaps knowing a female sheriff would rescue them offered comfort.

Abby had gotten out her phone. "No signal. I'll step out to make the call and be right back."

Hayden nodded. He'd come in here, hoping for a lead telling them how to find Kai. Instead, he'd discovered helpless women in captivity, something Kai had to know about and was potentially involved in.

Hayden's stomach rolled like the waves crashing against the rocky beach outside.

Was this merely the tip of a horrific iceberg their search for Kai would reveal? As they continued their search, what other horrors might they find?

≈

Cady spun as Abby, phone to her ear, raced past her and Ziggy and out the front door. Her face had lost color, and her eyes narrowed as she requested backup and ambulances.

Ziggy stared out the door. "Something's really wrong."

Had Hayden been hurt? If so, why more than one ambulance? "Something's definitely wrong. Wait here, and I'll check with Hayden." Cady took off before Ziggy insisted on going in her place. She was too worried about Hayden not to check on him.

In the office, when an open door on the back wall came into view, her footsteps faltered. What in the world? Had it been hidden by the bookshelf? Eager to find out where the opening went, she raced to it and screeched to a halt when she almost tumbled down steps. They led to a stone cave-like structure.

Should she go down the steps? No question. Hayden had to be down there, so of course she would go. She got out her phone to light the way and traversed slick stone steps to a tunnel where she had to duck to follow it.

What could be ahead of her? Something horrific, if Abby's request for ambulances and law enforcement officers told her anything. Cady's heart ramped up with each step, and her palms started sweating.

She eased through the opening. Not looking injured, Hayden stood tall, his back to her. She peered around him. Three terrified women gazed up at her.

"Oh. Oh. Oh, no." The realization of what was happening in front of her hit hard, and she clapped her free hand over her mouth, resisting the urge to gag.

Hayden spun. "No. You don't want to be here. Turn around and go back."

"Did Kai do this?" She couldn't seem to control her voice as it turned shrill and bounced off the walls. "Is he trafficking these women? Or smuggling them into our country?"

"I don't know. They aren't talking."

"Do they speak English?"

"A little, but you don't need to see all of this." He took her arm as if he planned to turn her around. "Abby's calling Mina, and she'll soon handle it."

Cady couldn't take her eyes off the three trembling women. "But they're terrified. Maybe I can talk to them. They might respond to a woman."

He released her arm as if conceding her point.

She didn't wait for his approval, but stepped past him and squatted in front of the women. "I'm Cady." She pointed at herself, then at them. "Your names?"

The women blinked at her. Did they not understand her, or were they hiding their names? Cady continued to transmit her concern through her expression, mentally willing them to share their names, but they remained silent.

"Did Kai do this to you?" Cady asked quietly.

"Kai. Kai." The older woman's eyes lit up. "He gone."

Not the reaction Cady expected. "Do you know where he went?"

"He gone. Help."

Wait, what? Was she asking for help because of what Kai had done to them or was she saying Kai had gone to get help? "Did Kai go for help?"

She blinked again, saying nothing more.

Cady had to pursue another line of questioning and hope they understood her. "Where are you from?"

"From Beijing."

"China?" Cady clarified.

She nodded, her eyes widening. "Yes. Yes. Home Beijing."

"Do you want to be here?"

She blinked again, clearly not understanding. Seems as if all Cady could do at this point was to offer comfort and wait for an interpreter to fully understand their predicament.

Cady reached out to pat the terrified woman's leg, but she jerked back.

"It's okay." Cady withdrew her hand, holding it up as she slowly stood. "I'm here to help you, not hurt you, but I'll step away so you're more comfortable."

She backed up, easing her way to Hayden, and leaned close to him. "Man, this is awful. I can't imagine many things more heartbreaking. How can someone do this to another person?"

He clutched his fingers into a fist. "It's beyond imaginable."

She took a long look into his eyes. "I know we're not supposed to question God, but how can He let something like this happen?"

"Yeah." Hayden released his fist and scrubbed his hand over his face. "I struggle with that too. The only thing I can do when faced with something like this is try to remember that even in moments of hardship, God is arranging events for a greater good. For something we can't see or know."

A somber stillness took hold of her body, and she felt frozen in place, but she managed to rip her focus free from the women to look at Hayden. "It's hard to see how this could turn out positive. We'll just have to watch it play out." Could Kai be involved in such a terrible thing? She just couldn't see it. "One thing I know for sure, my dad was tops in his ability to judge someone's character. If Kai was capable of such an atrocity, Dad wouldn't have spent so much time with him."

"Let's hope you're right." Hayden's gaze locked on hers, unflinching. "But it's not looking very good in his favor right now."

No, it wasn't.

The women huddled tight against the wall like a trio of trembling kittens abandoned by their mother to fend for themselves.

A lump rose in Cady's throat as their suffering and the consequences of what they would face in the future sank into her heart.

Oh, please. Just please. Hear my prayers for these women. Help them. Help them now.

Cady wanted to believe her frantic prayer—to believe God could really work this out for good. She was guessing these women weren't thinking that could ever happen, but she believed in God's almighty power and prayed He would indeed find good in this terrible, terrible tragedy unfolding in front of them.

7

Hayden leaned against a signpost outside the surf shop with Cady and Abby, while Mina and her team were in the cave. He stared at crime scene tape fluttering in the wind, but not even the warm summer breeze and glaring sunshine could thaw his frozen emotions.

How had something this horrific happened in the small beach town of Lost Lake? He couldn't fathom it. Not at all. What would the locals think when they found out about it?

The news would travel like wildfire, starting with sparks from the large contingency of beachgoers and locals who'd seen the flashing lights and heard the sirens. They'd assembled outside the fluttering tape, watching the action, calling out questions, demanding answers.

Near them sat three patrol vehicles, along with Mina's SUV. All were parked haphazardly, almost looking like someone had dropped them from above, letting them sit wherever they landed. Medics positioned three ambulances in a precision row with open rear doors facing the front of the surf shop.

Mina's detective, El—Elaina—Lyons, had accompanied her inside, where they'd remained since their arrival thirty minutes ago. Hayden had expected Mina would move the women right away, but she said she would hold off until an interpreter arrived to explain to the women what they could expect next. Thankfully, a deputy from a nearby county spoke Mandarin and had joined them in the cave.

Abby pointed at a deputy erecting a portable canopy by the building entrance. "The canopy is a nice touch. Respects their privacy."

The portable structure looked more like a tunnel, the fabric going all the way to the ground and one open end abutted the building. Mina didn't want to parade the women in front of the onlookers, so she'd made provisions to back one ambulance at a time close to the canopy and take them out through the shelter for privacy.

"Mina seems like a very compassionate sheriff," Cady said. "I suspect a lot of people in her position wouldn't care about how the crowd might affect these women."

"Agreed." Abby's vehement tone carried a lot of respect. "She can really empathize with people when needed, but she also has a tough side when it's called for. The perfect combination, and I have a lot of admiration for her."

She might admire Mina, but Abby was a similar kind of sheriff back in her day.

The crowd stirred, and Hayden returned his attention to the front of the building now hidden by the canopy. Dressed in her county uniform, Mina stepped around the structure and spoke to Sergeant Abell. The six-foot-tall, beefy man with buzzed blond hair raised a hand above his eyes and glanced around. Mina had made him the officer of record and put him in charge of logging names of anyone entering the crime scene. He also followed protocol to take photos of the crowd in case someone involved in putting these women in the cave had shown up to watch the drama unfold.

"Something's about to happen." Abby leaned around

Hayden, trying to get a better view of the action. "Mina's body language gives it away."

Mina glanced over her shoulder at them and clamped her hands on her hips. Abby was right. Mina's words and posture seemed urgent. Abell gave a sharp nod, and she spun to return to the building.

He moved to the tape holding back the crowd from the crime scene. "Okay folks, there's nothing to see here. Go on about your business. Enjoy this beautiful day at the beach."

He strode down the line of people shooing them away. They reluctantly moved back about twenty feet, but still remained glued to the scene. Abell marched toward Hayden, Cady, and Abby.

Hayden braced himself for whatever Abell was about to tell him.

The sergeant stopped in front of them, the sand swishing out from under his booted feet into little mounds. "Sheriff Park wants the area clear and that means *everyone*. So I'll ask you to please step outside the crime scene tape, and she'll contact you for your formal statements."

The beeping sound from one of the ambulances backing to the canopy distracted Hayden before he looked back at the sergeant. "Is she bringing the women out now?"

Abell's eyes narrowed. "As I said, I need you to move along. Now!"

Hayden had never liked this guy. He'd run for sheriff against Mina and lost, at times making her life difficult. She handled it well, but the guy had an attitude at times. Still, he was a capable officer and did an excellent job.

Hayden looked at Abby and Cady. "After you."

The three of them strode to the tape and stepped under the flapping plastic.

An SUV pulled into the beach parking area, and Nolan climbed from behind the wheel and charged down the hill, the breeze whisking away sand his boots kicked up. He approached Hayden. "What's happening?"

Hayden brought him up to speed. "Seems like Mina's moving the women out of the cave now. Ziggy's still inside providing information they might need, but she's probably done with him by this point. Hopefully, now will be a good time for you to talk to her. See what you might learn."

He frowned. "Don't expect too much. She'll see right through my reason for being here and won't release any information she doesn't want us to have."

"Someone's coming out of the building now," Cady announced.

They all turned to look at the shop and could see feet move in a slit of space where the tarp met the sand. Moments later, the ambulance drove away, and the next one backed into place. The process was repeated twice more. It didn't take long before Ziggy, head down, trudged out of the building and toward the fluttering tape. Sergeant Abell lifted it for him, and he scooted under as if fleeing from arrest.

Dragging his feet as he approached, he made eye contact with Hayden. "I'm glad you're still here. You don't think Kai did this, do you? I mean, he's not the kind of dude to mistreat women. To treat anyone badly. I think he's being set up."

Hayden had considered that Kai actually went on a legit vacation, and while he was gone, someone broke into the building and placed the women in the cave. But who other than Kai even knew about the cave? Doubtful many people did. Plus, there wasn't any sign of a break-in, so if someone did place these women here, they would need keys. And the women obviously recognized Kai's name.

"Did you know there was a cave under the building?" Hayden asked.

Ziggy shook his head, his long hair flapping against his face. "News to me."

"Is there anything you can think of that might help us understand all of this?" Abby asked him.

"Nah, I've been thinking about it the whole time they made me wait. Couldn't come up with anything to explain it. Nothing at all." The desolate bent to his tone said all that needed to be said. He'd made it clear that he'd hero-worshiped Kai, and if Kai was guilty of trafficking women, he'd fallen off the pedestal.

"I know this isn't exactly a fire, but did you call Kai?" Hayden asked.

"Yeah, man, more times than I can count while I was waiting inside. He didn't answer. Left him a few messages."

"You'll let us know right away if he calls you back." Hayden made sure his words didn't sound optional.

"Right after I let the sheriff know." He glanced over his shoulder. Mina was stepping out from the building. Ziggy swallowed hard. "She told me not to talk to you or anybody about this. I gotta go before she decides to arrest me."

"I don't think that's likely, but go ahead." Hayden gave the terrified guy a comforting smile.

Ziggy nodded, and after one more glance over his shoulder, he jogged up the hill and out of sight.

Mina, a stern look on her face, slipped under the crime scene tape and joined them. "I see Ziggy didn't listen to me."

"You can't blame him for wanting to talk to us," Hayden said. "We built a rapport before we found the women, so he's more comfortable with us."

"I get it, and I honestly don't care if he talks to you all about it. What I don't want is for him to confirm the discovery of these women to people all over town, so I made sure he knew I wouldn't be happy if he went around blabbing about it." She shifted her focus to Nolan, and a soft smile crossed her face. "Before you say anything, I know why you're here, so let me save you the trouble of questioning me and striking out."

"Way to let a guy down gently." He grinned.

"Actually, I have information I'm prepared to give to you." She ran her gaze from person to person. "Thought that would surprise you."

"What is it?" Cady asked as she grabbed her notepad and pen again.

Mina arched an eyebrow and stared at Cady's pen.

Cady raised her shoulders. "I don't want to forget anything that might be important."

Mina shrugged as if it wasn't worth battling over. "I interviewed the women and recorded the session. After I have a chance to review the video, I'll send you a copy. I wouldn't normally do this, and it's not proper police procedure, but I believe it could help in finding Kai."

"Definitely not proper police procedure," Abby said, prompting a frown from Mina.

Hayden wanted to sock his teammate's arm. The last thing they needed right now was to convince Mina not to share the information.

She eyed Abby. "Sometimes you have to make a judgment call, right?"

"Right," Abby said. "And we all trust your calls."

"No need to butter me up." Mina's lips tightened into a flat line. "As a quick overview, you'll find out Kai is indeed involved in this. Odds are, it's the reason for him taking off or being abducted. Even if I asked you to, I know you all won't stop looking for him, so we need to work together. In fact, I'm glad to have you looking for him as long as we aren't at odds. Means we'll have to coordinate. Detective Lyons will take lead on the investigation, I'll serve as liaison with you all."

Nolan couldn't seem to take his eyes off her. "Which means I'll get to spend more time with you."

"You never know what'll happen." She smiled at him in that quiet, intimate way Hayden had only seen her direct at Nolan.

Nolan's face flushed red, and he took a step back. Hayden had been observing the relationship develop between the couple and had to admit to jealousy he knew was wrong. He wanted his friend to be happy. Of course he did, but he also wanted the same thing in his own life. Not a likely possibility. Not if he couldn't relax his need to control pretty much every aspect of his life.

He glanced at Cady. Could she be the one to help him get over being a control freak? A potential future with her sure seemed to be worth the attempt to change.

"I'm headed back to my office to review the video, and then I'll email it to you," Mina said. "After you watch the interview, I'd like to get together to discuss it."

Nolan glanced at his watch. "With everything going on, you probably won't stop to eat. We could have an early dinner meeting and kill two birds with one stone."

"Sounds like a plan." Mina glanced over her shoulder as the third ambulance departed. "That's my signal to go. Let's say around six o'clock at your place."

"I'll walk you to the perimeter," Nolan said.

Mina gave a sharp nod and pivoted. He came alongside her, barely a hair's width between them as they strolled toward the crime scene.

The relentless jealousy hammered at Hayden, teasing him with something just out of reach. Focus on the work— *that* he could control. Shoving aside the unwelcome emotions, he turned to face the others. "I'd like to talk to Dorothy and Jake again. See if they've ever seen Kai with a woman. I'd also like to interview Becca and Daisy before we watch the video."

"Makes sense to talk to Dorothy and Jake first since they're just up the hill," Cady said.

"Then let's go." Abby didn't wait for agreement but started for the many steps leading up to Kai's neighborhood. At the top, she looked at them. "Which house first?"

Hayden gave it some thought. "Let's try Jake. He might be a less emotional and a more reliable witness."

Abby headed straight for Jake's house, marching up to the door. She stabbed her finger into the doorbell before Cady and Hayden could even put a foot on Jake's walkway.

"She's a real spitfire." Cady's words carried quiet admiration. "She'd make a good reporter for sure."

"As much as I respect what you do, I don't think that's a job Abby would ever want. She's faced too many antagonistic reporters during her time as a sheriff."

"I get that. My profession often gets a bad rap when reporters come off as aggressive in the pursuit of a story they can't crack." She glanced at Hayden and then back at the sidewalk.

He had no clue what her look meant, and he didn't want to get sidetracked by asking—not when they needed to stay focused on the investigation—so he fixed his attention on the walkway as well.

By the time they reached the door, Jake was jerking it open and rubbing his chin. "I hoped I'd see you after the commotion at Kai's shop. Is he all right?"

"Kai wasn't present." Abby's response was blunt and to the point.

"Phew." Jake let out a breath and ran a hand over his already messy hair. "I'm glad he wasn't in one of those ambulances. So what's happening down there?"

"We're unable to share any details," Hayden said. "But we do have some questions for you."

Jake frowned. "Can't say I'm happy about that, but go ahead. Ask away."

"Does Kai have a woman in his life?" Abby's tone was open, as was her expression.

"Woman? Nah." Jake rolled his shoulders. "He's been a hermit since his wife died. The only woman I've seen him with is Dorothy, and I'm certain they're not dating." He chuckled, but grew fidgety.

Such a nervous reaction could mean he knew something about the women, and he was keeping it from them.

Hayden needed to probe for more details. "What about anything unusual going on at his shop after it was closed for the night?"

"At night? No. I mean, I don't think so. It's not like I've looked. Only one spot on the corner of my deck gives me a view of his place. Even then, I have to lean out for a clear view, and I don't have reason to do it. Well, except for today when I heard all the sirens." He grimaced. "You sure you can't tell me what's going on?"

"Sorry, no." Abby gave him a look meant to pacify. "But there's nothing for you or the general public to worry about."

Jake snorted and eyed her. "Sounds like some nonanswer law enforcement might give in a news conference."

"I can see how it could come across that way," Abby said, not at all sounding upset by his comment. "But I simply wanted to assure you there isn't a threat to your safety."

"Okay," he responded, but his skeptical look said he didn't buy her answer. "I'll just have to trust you on that. Anything else you want to know?"

"Just the same question we asked earlier," Hayden said. "Have you seen anything unusual or suspicious?"

"I've been thinking about it since you left." He wrapped his arms around his body. "But nothing, and I mean nothing at all has been out of the ordinary. Just the same old same old until Kai went on vacation."

"Then thank you for your time," Hayden said before Jake could continue to nag them for information they wouldn't provide. "You have our card. Call if you think of anything."

Jake's lips twisted in a dissatisfied grimace. "I guess I'll have to watch the news to find out what's going on down there."

Unfortunately, he spoke the truth, but thankfully, zero reporters had been on scene. Well, no one, except Cady, and Hayden was pretty sure she wouldn't report on this situation.

They made their way to Dorothy's house. Hayden knocked, and they waited a good three minutes before they heard her coming toward them.

She pulled the door open. "Oh my, I'm so glad it's you. I've been watching things unfold at the surf shop, and I can't imagine what could've happened. Please tell me Kai is okay."

"Kai wasn't present," Hayden said before Abby had to handle the same situation again. "Unfortunately, we don't know anything more about his whereabouts than we did when we talked to you earlier. We were wondering if you'd ever seen him with a woman."

"Woman? Now that's an interesting question. I can't say as I have." Dorothy lowered her gaze and rubbed her chin thoughtfully. "Oh. Oh." Her eyes opened wide. "Yes. Yes, I did. Not too long ago. It was three in the morning on the beach by his shop. He went into his shop with her."

Abby was too much of a professional to show any excitement she might feel, but she took a step closer to Dorothy. "Where were you when you saw this?"

"It's easier to show you than tell you. Follow me." She pushed past them and hurried around the side of her house.

Hayden trailed the women through the side yard leading to a wide-open backyard, and a large wooden deck protruded over the hillside. Dorothy hustled up the steps, her slippers whispering on the wood, and pointed out over the ocean. "See? See? You can see his shop clear as day from here. That's what I was doing when you arrived. Watching to see what was going on down there."

Hayden joined her on the deck and looked over the edge. She had a perfect view of the beach and of Ride the Tide. "And you were out here at three in the morning?"

Dorothy frowned. "I have insomnia, and I often come out at night when the weather's nice." She rested a hand on a glider with a plush cushion. "I rock myself to sleep in this all the time. That night was no exception. I saw Kai with his arm on this woman's back escorting her to his surf shop. I tried to stay awake to see what else happened, but I fell asleep."

"Can you describe this woman?" Cady asked, her pen poised over her notebook.

Dorothy shook her head. "It was too dark, and my vision isn't the best anymore."

"If so, are you even sure it was a woman?"

Dorothy sniffed as if she was offended by Cady's continued questioning. "This person was very petite and moved in a feminine way. I guess I can't really describe it well, but I think you can often tell when you're looking at a man or a woman based on how they move. Wouldn't you agree?"

"Yes," Abby said. "Sometimes we're fooled when we get up close, but I think your assessment is on target."

Cady looked up from jotting on her notepad. "Did you ask Kai about it?"

"Of course I did." Dorothy dropped down in her chair, the cushion hissing a release of air. "He said I must've been dreaming. He wasn't on the beach. He was home sleeping at that time. I trust him completely and figured he was right and I must've seen someone else. Until you asked. Now I feel certain I was right, and he didn't want me to know about this woman."

"Could be," Hayden said.

Her gaze stayed anchored on Hayden. "What's going on down there, anyway? Since you asked about a woman, it seems like it must have to do with women. Maybe with the woman I saw."

"As I said, we're not at liberty to discuss that." Hayden planted his feet wide so she didn't think this topic was open for debate. "Did you notice anything else that night on the beach? Anything at all?"

She leaned her head back against the cushion and closed her eyes. Her fingers drummed rapidly on the armrests, sounding like a woodpecker. She bolted forward and her eyes flashed open. "A ship. There was a ship anchored offshore. Not a fishing boat or personal boat. One of those big ones. Like a commercial shipping one. I'm not sure, but I think it might've had those big containers on it."

Hayden took a moment to force himself to calm down before he let his excitement over these leads creep into his tone. "Where was it anchored in relationship to the surf shop?"

She heaved herself out of the chair and went to the deck railing. She pointed to the left of the shop near Outlook Rock. The over two-hundred-foot-high rock formation just offshore was a tourist destination and people climbed it to get a better view of the ocean.

"I'm not good with distances," she said. "But it was near Outlook Rock. I suppose it was as close as it could get for a big ship without grounding itself. And it was straight out from the Rock."

Cady's hand holding her notepad trembled. "Did you catch the name of the ship?"

Dorothy shook her head. "I was too far away for that. From the way you sound, I should've gone in to get my binoculars, but there've been ships out there other times, so I didn't think it was important."

"Was it still there when you woke up?" Cady asked.

Dorothy shook her head. "No. No. That I'm sure of. No ship when I woke up."

Abby lifted her foot to the upper step. "When you saw Kai and the woman, what direction were they coming from?"

"From the left, but I didn't see where their path originated. It's like they suddenly appeared from nowhere."

"Were there any other boats?" Cady didn't bother hiding her enthusiasm over this lead. "Like a small craft that could've brought them to shore from the big ship?"

Dorothy blinked a few times. "I don't think so. At least I don't remember seeing one."

"You've been most helpful." Hayden looked at the others. "Does anyone have any further questions for Dorothy?"

"None for me," Abby said.

Cady shook her head and pocketed her notebook and pen.

He glanced back at Dorothy. "Can you think of anything else we need to know about that night?"

"I don't remember anything else." She gripped the arms of her chair. "But I promise to sit here and think about it. If I come up with something, I'll give you a call."

"Thank you so much, Dorothy." Hayden smiled at her. "We'll see ourselves out."

Hayden waited for Abby and Cady to step down to the gravel path, and they crunched over the rocks to the front of the house.

Abby looked at him. "You're thinking the trafficked women came from a ship."

"It's possible. I don't think this is a route commonly used for trafficking though. At least I don't remember seeing a mention of it when I was a border patrol agent. But I can make a few calls and have the answer right away."

"Then I'd get on the phone if I were you." Abby gave him a penetrating look, her eyes narrowing. "If Kai is involved in trafficking women, and he did something to anger the people in charge, he's most likely in danger of the worst kind."

Hayden agreed, and the sense of urgency put a bead of sweat across his lip. "I'll see what I can find out."

As the women walked ahead, he stood back to take a few beats and gain control of his mounting anxiety.

Because Abby was right. Very right. He'd seen traffickers and human smugglers over his years working for CBP. These felons were some of the most ruthless people he'd ever encountered. If Kai was in their hands, and the team didn't find him soon, he likely didn't stand a chance.

8

At Percy's cottage, Hayden told himself to keep his hands off Cady, but at her trembling, he ignored his warning and circled his arm around her as they walked to the door. She didn't object to his touch. In fact, she moved closer to him, firing off all of his senses. There really was something about this woman that got to him, and he couldn't put a finger on it. It wasn't tangible. It was, well, mysterious and fantastic.

Problem was, he didn't know what to do with it. Since his parents died, he'd been unable to trust loving someone again, and he'd controlled everything within his power. It took him a good year after he met his teammates before he began to trust the affection he'd developed for them and to believe he wasn't going to lose them too. Not like the fear ever totally went away. It was there. Mostly dormant, but it surfaced at times to remind him to be careful. Like now with Cady.

Could he set aside his fear as he'd done with his teammates for a woman who might share every day of his life with him? A woman he would undoubtedly be closer to than to his best friends? His family?

Crazy thinking. Maybe he shouldn't be alone with her

and should've asked Abby to stay with them instead of going back to the inn. Too late now.

Cady broke away from him to insert the key in the lock. Her hand shook as she pushed the door open. A musty scent wafted out, a testament to the challenge of owning a home located near the ocean that wasn't aired out on a regular basis.

Cady shook her head. "The place has lost my dad's unique scent. It smells like he's gone and feels so final."

Did that make things easier for her or more difficult? Her expression became unreadable, and her body language warned him not to comment.

She stepped inside and hesitated in the entryway, where an open layout unfolded before them. The dining area anchored the front of the space, while the living room stretched across the back of the cottage. Spanning nearly the entire width of the living room, large glass sliding doors offered a sweeping view of the ocean. Tucked to the left was a simple yet functional kitchen.

Cady's eyes lifted to his, searching for something—comfort, understanding, anything. "I know Dad didn't live here long, but he brought as many of the furnishings from my childhood home as would fit here, and the memories of time with him are so vivid."

Helpless to ease her pain, he stayed close, silently offering his presence, ready to move if she so much as reached for him. "I can only imagine what you're going through."

She hesitantly met his gaze. "I'm sorry, that was insensitive of me. What happened to your family's belongings?"

"I don't actually know." He didn't like how his voice was so low, thick with feeling, indicating he was about to lose control, so he paused and breathed before telling his story. "They immediately assigned a social worker, and she brought me back to the house to collect my things. My parents didn't have a will, but the worker let me choose a few items to take with me."

At the memory of the day, he curled his fingers into fists and let the nails bite into his palms. "Problem was, I wasn't allowed to take as much as I would've liked. I asked if we could put some things in a storage unit, but they rejected that request. It cost money to pay for the unit, and I wouldn't have any until the estate went through probate, if then. And as it turns out, they had barely enough money to pay off their debts and outstanding bills, leaving nothing for me."

She loosened his grip with a tender touch, then enclosed his hands in her own, grounding him. "I'm so sorry, Hayden. That must've been hard."

A hard swallow caught in his throat, and he hesitated, gathering the strength to speak again. "It was, and it's something that stuck with me."

She studied his face for a long time, and opened her mouth as if she wanted to say something, but closed it and turned to the room. "Dad kept his journals in his nightstand, but we cleared out those drawers when he came to live with me. If we start in the office, we could find something in his desk or filing cabinet. Or even on the bookshelves."

With a reassuring nod, Hayden conveyed his full confidence in her strategy. "Lead the way."

Closed window blinds cast the room in shadows portraying a heavy, almost suffocating atmosphere. A masculine energy radiated from two dark leather chairs positioned before an imposing desk that dominated the center of the room. Beside it, a sturdy wooden filing cabinet stood as if guarding the space, while two overflowing bookshelves flanked the window like silent sentinels.

She opened the blinds and flooded the room with warm

rays of sunshine. "If it's okay with you, I'll start with the desk, and you can do the bookshelves."

"Sounds good."

She pulled out a vintage wooden chair from behind the desk. He stepped to the bookcases and started combing through stacks of paper, looking for any possible lead. The grating sound of desk drawers scraping open and then slamming closed broke the silence in the room as they each continued their search.

"Oh. Oh!" The pain in Cady's voice had him spinning to look at her. She clasped a hand over her mouth.

He rushed to her, not just to offer his support, but to learn what she had discovered. "What is it? What did you find?"

She held up a butterscotch candy. "When I was a little girl, I would always get pencils from the middle drawer and sit on the floor next to Dad and draw while he did paperwork. He always tucked my favorite butterscotch candy in the drawer as a surprise for me.

"Sorry." She glanced up, heat rising up her neck as she didn't like being caught in such a moment of vulnerability. "You probably think I'm crazy reacting over something as simple as a piece of candy."

"Not at all." He flashed her a comforting smile while he perched on the corner of the desk. "My experience with grief says it's the little things that are sometimes the hardest to overcome. But I also know, as time passes and memories fade, you become afraid you'll forget so much about your loved one, and you'll welcome the little memories."

She tilted her head. "I can really see that happening. I want to think I won't forget anything about my dad, but I know it's natural for memories to fade."

Maybe he wasn't supposed to try to help her. It continued to stir up the painful memories of losing his parents, leaving his emotions so raw that saying anything felt like it might lead to that lack of control he so desperately craved. And yet, she was the first person he'd ever wanted to talk with about his parents. But before he said something he might not come back from, he swallowed the words, and simply nodded.

His lack of reply seemed to trouble her, and she inhaled a deep breath. "We should get back to work."

He returned to the bookshelves. The crinkling of a butterscotch candy wrapper had him glancing back to see her reaction. The taste would either soothe her soul or break her heart.

He tried to get a read on her, but she shot back from the desk, a drawer handle clutched in her hand. "This drawer won't open, but there's no lock. I've seen Dad open it so it's not a false drawer."

She tugged harder, planting her feet, and putting her whole body into it, to no avail. "It won't release."

"Let me look at it." He squatted and ran his fingers around the outside of the drawer, but couldn't find any reason why it wasn't opening. He sat back for a minute to think. "What if it's one of those drawers where you have to open two drawers at the same time to release a mechanism."

"I'll try it." She yanked the top drawer open part way, then tugged on the second one. "Not the top one."

After shoving that drawer closed, she jerked on the bottom one. Her hand flew back to the second one. Pulled. It moved.

"Yes! Yes!" Eyes alight with victory, she bounced in the chair. "You're right."

He caught her excitement, but when he looked inside the emotion evaporated. "Nothing in there. Not a single thing."

She let out a defeated whoosh of air and sat back.

Hayden felt her defeat, but he wasn't done with the drawer yet. "What's the point of having a locked drawer with nothing inside?"

"Good question," she said, but didn't move.

Hayden eased closer and traced the wood inside with his fingers. He revealed a gap between the bottom and the sides.

False drawer? Maybe.

"Do you have a letter opener or something else thin I can pry with?" he asked.

"Letter opener. Here." She jerked out the middle drawer, her hands frantically searching until she waved a shiny opener at him.

He took it and inserted it in the tiny gap, then lifted the bottom panel. "Just like I thought. The drawer has a false bottom."

He raised the bottom higher and revealed a stack of papers, an old bank deposit book, and a journal embossed with colorful birds.

"A journal." The words came out on a whisper as she reached for the book and quickly pressed it open on the desktop. "Dated November of last year. He didn't bring a journal for this time period to my house, so I thought he'd stopped journaling. I questioned him, but he couldn't remember if he'd stopped or not, and if so, where he'd kept the book."

"It's got to be very frightening to lose your memory that way. I can't even imagine."

She nodded, though her distant gaze made it clear her mind was elsewhere. She suddenly locked gazes with him. "Why would he have put this one in a secret place? He was still lucid most of the time then. He didn't really go downhill until February, so he must not have wanted anyone to find it."

Hayden didn't know the answer, but he could share his

best guess. "Makes sense that the journal contains some-thing he didn't want anyone else to read."

She planted her hands on the desk and pulled herself closer. "I got pencils from his desk so many times as a child. How did I not know this false drawer was here?"

"If he wanted to keep it a secret, he would've been very careful to make sure you didn't know about it."

She could chalk this up as one of those things she would desperately want to ask her father and then realize she could never ask him about things no one else could answer for her, and the depth of pain at his passing would hit her all over again.

"The journal might provide some answers," he said, trying to sound upbeat. "Do you want to read it now, or would you rather do it when you're alone?"

Her finger tapped nervously on the journal, her gaze fixed downward. After a long pause, she straightened her posture as if bracing herself. "I'll skim through it now to see if there's anything to help us and read it in more detail later."

"Then I'll go back to the bookshelves, and you can let me know if you find something."

She smiled up at him, her expression warm, and he caught the hint of a smile that seemed to promise some-thing more. "Thank you for coming here with me. Being with you makes this much easier."

"Anytime you need me, I'm here for you." He gently squeezed her shoulder on the way back to the bookshelves.

Offering her comfort in that way was the right thing to do, but he had to stop touching her. Yes, he only meant to show his support, but a simple touch could grow into so much more.

Something he didn't want, and it wasn't fair to lead her on. To let her believe she could ever have a relationship with him. A future with him. As much as the possibility of being with her intrigued him, he wasn't sure a future with any woman was possible.

~

With each journal page Cady touched, the fear of what she might discover left her emotions raw, and her senses on high alert. The paper felt hot under her fingers, like it might burst into flame at any time.

But so far, the days were filled with her father's routine. He'd journaled every day for as long as she could remember, noting ordinary things that wouldn't seem important to most people. Things like every bird he'd seen in a day. Not only notes about the birds, but pictures drawn in colored pencil.

The happy and contented tone of the book warmed her heart as did the days he'd recorded her visits and phone calls. Guilt often ate at her for living away from him, but his journal writings cleared that up as he thought she'd made him a priority in her life, and he knew how much she loved him.

She took a moment to let the good news settle in. She couldn't ask for anything more. But still, this journal was much like his other ones, and she saw no reason why he would hide it.

She flipped to March, and mid-month his writing changed to sharp, crisp characters instead of his usual flowing script. The urgency in his words raised her concern.

He'd added a message in his familiar handwriting two months before he'd come to live with her. A message directly for her.

Dearest daughter,

If you're reading this journal, I've either passed on or the

dementia has taken me and you're looking through my posses-
sions. I'm sorry about the locked drawer, but I had to be certain
no one but you would find this information. You'll find a memory
stick taped to the back of the same drawer. Please listen to it
immediately. Hopefully you'll write about it in an article for your
paper.

Love, Dad

Tears blinded her as she reached into the drawer and pushed items around to locate the drive he'd left behind. She swiveled in her chair, the same comforting squeak it'd made for many years drawing Hayden's attention.

"You'll want to look at this," she said.

He laid down an open binder and took urgent steps in her direction. She sat back, giving him access to the journal. "Dad left me a personal message."

Hayden leaned over the desk, his fingers running along the lines of writing. "Mid-March. That wasn't long before Mayor Sutton's murder, but it seems like your dad's thoughts were more organized than when we met him."

"His disease wasn't as advanced." She swallowed down the memories threatening to swamp her. "He didn't have basic dementia or even Alzheimer's. A specialist in Portland diagnosed him with Creutzfeldt–Jakob disease. This is a rapidly progressing dementia that can advance very quickly. Sometimes in months or even weeks."

"I've never heard of it. What a horrible disease."

She swallowed down tears for her dad *and* herself. She had to change the subject or she would lose it. She held out her hand. "I found the drive."

Hayden studied it intently. "Same question again. Do you want to listen to it here or in the privacy of your room at the inn?"

"Here," she said quickly. She had no doubt about her answer. "With you by my side this time, if you're willing."

"Of course I am." He took the memory stick from her hand. "You never have to ask if I'm willing to support you."

She fought the urge to sigh. "I've been so needy since I met you, and that's not who I am. Believe it or not I'm a pretty strong, independent woman."

He leaned close, his gaze filled with empathy and understanding. "Give yourself a break. You just lost your father. You're grieving, and everyone needs extra support at a time like that."

His continued care radiated through her, and she found herself captivated and unable to tear her gaze free. "You're a good man, Hayden Kraus, and I'm glad God brought you into my life."

"I'm glad He did too." He squeezed her hand, and apprehension settled into his gaze. "I think I'm falling for you. Big time."

Oh! So was she. Falling for him, but his uneasy look disturbed her. "It doesn't seem like you're glad of that."

"Yes and no." He released her hand as if he suddenly realized he'd been holding it. "I've told you my past left me with commitment issues. You've probably noticed I like to be in control."

She grinned. "That would be hard to miss."

No smiles from Hayden. "It's more than liking to take charge. I *need* to do it. Falling in love takes everything out of my control, every last piece of it. I feel like I could easily fall in love with you, but I don't think I can live with that kind of uncertainty."

"You don't want to go through the pain again. I understand that," she said, her voice soft but firm. And she truly did understand—she didn't like it, but she got it. "Don't worry, I'm not looking for anything serious either."

He jerked back. "I didn't realize that."

"Sorry. I should probably have told you. I don't do things

halfway, and I have too many goals I want to accomplish in my job before I settle down and raise a family." She opted not to tell him about her parents' failed marriage. Her mother's abandonment. In all these years, she'd never brought that out in the open. Too much pain.

His brow furrowed. "You don't think you can work and have a family too?"

Good. He continued in the area she *could* talk about. "No, that's not it. I believe you need to give your full commitment to your spouse and children. That doesn't mean you can't work, it just means your work/life balance must be in line with each other. Right now, my life balance is seriously out of whack with my work time. Well, at least normally. Once I find out who killed my dad, work will once again consume my life."

"Got it." He sounded as if he understood her conflict, but didn't seem too pleased about it. He reached for her father's laptop, then squatted next to her to insert the drive. "Ready for me to start playing this?"

Glad he'd moved on and didn't seem upset with her, she nodded.

He clicked on the video. The screen came to life, revealing her father sitting in the same chair she now sat in.

"Hi, my Cady girl." Her dad smiled.

She gasped, and her heart clutched. "Oh, Dad. I miss—" The words slipped out, but a sob swallowed them.

Hayden paused the video and took her hand again. "Are you okay to go on? Maybe you'll want to take this to your room after all."

She shook her head hard and gripped his hand. "I need you here. To hold your hand. Start it again."

Without a word, he clicked the mouse, and her dad appeared on screen.

"First I want you to know how special you are to me."

Her father beamed at her. "I know as my dementia gets worse, you won't believe me, so I want to tell you before it's too late. I couldn't have been prouder of the woman you've become. You have so many wonderful qualities that will take you far in your job. Sadly, I set the example of letting work be all-consuming. But my move to Lost Lake taught me to slow down and appreciate everything life has to offer. I found such a richness here I wish I'd embraced in my younger years. Don't make the same mistake as I did, Cady girl. Live life to the fullest, the life God wants you to have, and you'll have no regrets."

"It's almost as if he heard our conversation," she said and waited for him to continue.

"Now, about the information you need to pass along." The gentleness disappeared from his tone, and his expression turned to stone. "I'm sorry to have to share it this way, but Ernie swore me to secrecy and gave me no choice."

Cady flashed a look at Hayden. "It's about Mayor Sutton."

He released her hand and leaned forward.

"Since I promised never to tell anyone for the rest of my life," her dad said. "I figured this was the only way to make sure the secret didn't die with me. Ernie stumbled on a human trafficking ring in our area and tried to stop it."

"Human trafficking!" She flashed a horrified look at Hayden. "This could be related to the women in the cave."

"Let me explain," her dad said. "He's partners in a charter fishing boat with his brother-in-law Wade Collins. Their fishing business has been losing money for some time, and Ernie planned to sell the boat. He had a potential buyer who wanted to compare the boat engine hours to the maintenance records."

Cady paused the video. "Any idea what boat engine hours are?"

Hayden nodded. "It's the equivalent to an odometer on an automobile. You can't record the miles driven in a boat, but you can record how many hours the engine has run. Gives the buyer an idea of the longevity of the engine going forward."

"Makes sense." She clicked to start the video again.

"But when Ernie recorded the information at his office, it didn't match the records Wade had turned in. And the gallons per hour the boat should've been getting for the fuel used was way off from what Wade had been charging to the business."

Hayden paused the video this time. "We interviewed Collins when the mayor was murdered, and he seemed like kind of a shady guy. He could've been cheating the mayor for sure."

"Hopefully my dad will tell us what he was up to."

Hayden restarted the video.

"Ernie wondered if Wade was using the boat for something else and faking the reports, so he downloaded the boat's GPS data. It showed Wade taking the boat out every Thursday night at three a.m. to coordinates in the Pacific where there was nothing but water."

Surprised, Cady glanced at Hayden. "Did you discover anything about this when you investigated the mayor's death?"

"No," he said, his focus still fixed on the screen.

She looked back at her dad.

"So Ernie called to ask if I would go with him to trail Wade the next Thursday." Her dad grinned in a way she hadn't seen for months before he died, and it filled her heart with such joy she almost broke down. "You know I said yes. The excitement and adventure was too much to say no to."

She paused and looked at Hayden. "That was my dad

before the dementia took hold. An adventurer, for sure. You probably would've had a lot in common with him."

"Seems like it." Hayden smiled, a boyish glint in his expression that tugged at something deep inside her—reminding her of her father when he was in one of his playful or adventurous moods.

A calming peace settled over her as if God Himself had sent Hayden to fill the void left behind from her father's passing. God's gentle reminder that she was never truly alone. He was always with her. Always.

Before she got sidetracked again, she clicked play on the video.

"Kai Nakoa, who owns the surf shop, is a good friend with Ernie," her dad said, "and he offered to take us in his boat. We waited in the shadows until Wade departed on the boat, then we hopped into Kai's boat and trailed him to a location just offshore from Lost Lake where a ship called the *Red Dragon Voyager* had anchored." He shook his head. "What happened next blew us away."

His smile evaporated, and he chewed on his lower lip. "Ten people got off the ship and boarded Wade's boat. Men, women, and children. He traveled toward land and loaded them in a dinghy. They disembarked on the beach about a mile down from my place. Three men with semi-automatic rifles waited for them. They had the people sit on the beach until everyone was on shore, then they separated the women from the men and children—some of them force-fully—and took them to a cargo van. The others marched to another van. Ernie suspected these men planned to traffic the women."

Cady couldn't speak. Couldn't move. At the thought of her father having to discover this, her stomach churned, and she had to keep swallowing to prevent upchucking on the desk.

"I urged Ernie to report this incident to Sheriff Park," he continued, but his voice was broken as he seemed to choke back tears. "He said she wouldn't have the authority to deal with it, but he had contacts at ICE who handled this kind of situation. He'd give them a call and let them take charge. They never arrested Wade. I saw him make the same Thursday trips. What changed was three vans showed up and several women were split off and taken to the third vehicle. I snuck down to the beach one night, and it turned out Ernie was driving."

Cady gaped at the screen. "The mayor was involved in trafficking women?"

"Sounds like it." Hayden gritted his teeth.

Her dad grimaced. "I confronted him the next day. That's when he shared the information he made me promise never to tell. He told Wade he was selling the boat and confronted him about his illegal activities. Wade lost it. Said he got into something far more sinister than he expected. If he didn't have the boat, he would no longer be of use to the men he was dealing with, and they would kill him."

Her dad took a long pause as if he barely had control of his emotions.

"I can't believe Collins's attitude." Hayden shook his head. "What did he expect from men who trafficked innocent women?"

"I know. Disgusting."

The video continued. "Ernie couldn't let Wade come to any harm, so he didn't sell the boat, but he also couldn't let these men continue to traffic women. He called his buddies at ICE, and they opened an investigation. He didn't tell Wade. He might not have wanted him dead, but thought he deserved to pay for his crimes. Turns out Wade turned on the traffickers and agreed to work undercover for ICE in exchange for them cutting him a deal."

Cady pounded a fist on the desk. "He doesn't deserve a deal. Not with what he's done."

"Agreed." Hayden might've spoken only one word, but the gravity of his tone told her how deep his anger ran.

"But Ernie couldn't leave it at that," her dad said. "By then he knew he was dying from cancer and had nothing to lose, so until ICE took care of the situation, he had Wade take him to the beach on a Thursday night. He met with the traffickers, and the guy in charge agreed to sell a woman each week to him for cash. Ernie started selling off his memorabilia and anything else he could to raise money. He paid anywhere between ten and twenty thousand dollars for each woman. Then he had Becca process her through the charity where she works."

Cady paused the video. "This has to be the people my dad was talking about when he said Ernie had a secret."

"And it explains what Ernie did with his large cash withdrawals from his checking account. Also explains why he continued to share the fishing business with Collins." Hayden gripped the edge of the desk. "What it doesn't explain is when your dad said, 'they killed Ernie because he couldn't get the money fast enough. They wanted it right then. All of it.' We found Ernie's killer, and these men weren't responsible."

"I'm not sure everything he had to say when he met with Mina was totally reliable. But this video was filmed before he really slipped. If there's a conflict in what he's told us then and now, this is what I would go by." She pondered everything they'd learned. "I wonder if ICE has shut down the smuggling or if the women Kai held in his cave came from this trafficking ring."

Hayden didn't answer right away—just stared ahead, clearly weighing her words. "Ernie left the boat to Collins, but only because he died before he could file a change in his will. If what Collins said about the trafficker wanting to kill him if he was no longer useful was true, he's probably still involved. Or ICE still has an ongoing investigation, and he's part of it. Either way, we can stake out his boat on Thursday night or somehow check the GPS history on his boat."

"Shouldn't we just talk to him and get his side of the story?"

Hayden shook his head. "Not if he has Kai. If he finds out we're onto him, he could go to ground, and we might not ever find out what happened to Kai. Far better to keep a covert watch on him until we know more."

"I see." She had to trust his reason for not confronting Collins was sound. "But what if ICE has an open investigation, and we interfere with it?"

His eyes narrowed. "That could be problematic. I'll call a contact at ICE and find out if they have anything going on before we step on their toes." He stood. "But first, we finish this video, then go see Becca to find out what she knows about the women her dad was bringing to her charity."

"Even if she knows anything, her dad probably swore her to secrecy too."

"It would make sense she wouldn't say anything to keep her uncle's name clean."

"But maybe now that we've heard the story from my dad, she could be persuaded to tell everything." Cady hoped a woman who ran a charity to help people would want to keep innocent women safe and would tell the truth.

If not, they might have to actually stake out the boat as Hayden suggested. She really didn't want to do that. She'd never shied away from difficult challenges in her job, and some of the things she'd had to do to get a story were outrageous, but this was different.

This situation could turn deadly.

9

_____

Hayden made the last turn to *Begin Again* to interview Becca while Cady huddled in the passenger seat, her arms wrapped around her body as if needing to defend herself. If it was possible to increase her distress from losing her dad, seeing him on video appeared to have overwhelmed her in grief.

If his parents had left a video where they talked to him after they'd died, he would've lost it. Odds were good he wouldn't have been able to watch them. Sure, he was much younger and didn't have Cady's maturity, but grief didn't know age. Grief was non-discriminating. All-inclusive for everyone, even the littlest of children who felt the loss but couldn't express their pain with words.

He parked in front of BAG, located in a storefront on the corner of Main Street and Ocean Drive, and faced Cady. "Would you like to join me in interviewing Becca or take some time alone?"

She released her seatbelt, and it slid into the holder with a whoosh. "I definitely want to go with you. After seeing that video, I need answers more than ever."

He nodded and opened his door. She followed suit. He

took a long look around to see if anyone was watching them. Satisfied they were alone, he escorted Cady to the building painted a pale yellow with black trim. Matching colors had been used for the sign, reminding him of a bumblebee. If it was symbolic, he didn't know how.

He opened the door for Cady, and a bell jingled from above. The small room held several round tables with chairs painted similar colors to the outside. Becca sat at one of the tables near the back of the room. She resembled her late father with a prominent chin and large green eyes, but unlike her dad, she had a full head of brown hair that fell to her shoulders.

She looked up and tilted her head. "Hayden. What brings you here?"

"You remember me?"

"How can I forget one of the people who helped free me from my abductor?" Her smile melted away, leaving only a shadow of unease etched across her face.

Obviously her traumatic kidnapping still impacted her. How could it not? "I'm sorry you had to go through that."

She waved a hand. "Thank you, but I know you didn't come to talk about that."

She seemed as if she still needed to talk about the pain, but he would leave it alone for today. He would continue to pray for her. "We have a couple of questions about your father as related to our current investigation, if you don't mind answering them."

She didn't speak right away, her expression thick with emotion. "I heard you were looking for Kai. He was a good buddy of my dad, but what could that have to do with Kai going missing?"

Cady stepped forward. "I'm Cady Vaughn. My dad, Percy, was a friend of your father's too."

"Oh, Cady, honey. I'm so sorry for your loss." Becca came

around the table, pulled Cady into a hug, then let go—though her hands stayed on Cady's upper arms. "I know what you're going through. Such a sudden and unexpected loss."

Cady gave a small nod, her lips parting as if she wanted to say something, but no words came.

"Sure, my dad had cancer and yours had dementia," Becca continued, "and we would've lost them soon anyway, but we would've had a chance to prepare and say goodbye. But this way?" She shrugged, and tears shimmered in her eyes.

"We have so much in common." Cady returned the hug then leaned back. "We should get together and talk. Not now, but after I find out who's behind my dad's death."

"Talking could really be helpful for both of us." Becca sniffled, her attention returning to Hayden. "Now, how can I help you?"

"Percy left a video where he said your father had learned about trafficking of women in the area."

Becca gasped and clutched her chest.

Hayden forged on before she started asking questions. "He supposedly contacted ICE to resolve it, but until they could, he used his own money to buy women from the trafficker."

Becca's mouth fell open, and she blinked.

"Looks like you knew nothing about it." Hayden wished that weren't the case because he didn't want this to be a dead end.

She shook her head, then stilled. "Oh. O-o-oh! Now I get it. I didn't know anything about the trafficking, but before Dad died, he brought several women to our refugee program."

"Did he say where they came from?" Cady asked.

"He said he learned about them through law enforcement, but he was never specific. I figured if he could share more details he would, so I didn't push him on it." Her hands tangled together, shifting and twitching.

She sounded and acted so earnest that Hayden believed her, but that didn't mean he wouldn't dig deeper. "Is it possible for us to talk to these women?"

Becca chewed on her lip. "Are they somehow related to Kai's investigation?"

"We believe so," Hayden said. "And also we believe his disappearance could have to do with that."

She released her hands and stared at him. "Don't tell me he was trafficking women?"

What could he say to such a loaded question? "I don't have an answer for you."

She grimaced. "And you really think talking to the women my dad saved could help you find him?"

Hayden nodded.

Becca picked up a paperclip from the table and fidgeted with it. "If what you say about having been trafficked is true, I'm not sure it's good for them to bring up their past."

"My understanding is your dad rescued them just after they arrived in our country. They might've been afraid— maybe terrified—for a short time, but at least they didn't experience the worst things possible."

Becca looked down at the paperclip. "I don't suppose I'd have time to think about it."

"Time is of the essence when you're looking for a missing person." Hayden made sure his words held the intensity he felt for locating missing people.

"I understand that more than most." She frowned and looked down again. "Let me get a hold of them to see if they'll talk to you. I'll call you as soon as I know something."

"Thank you." Hayden got out his business card. "Is there

anything else you can think of to help us find whoever is trafficking these women?"

"I doubt it, but I'll think about it. I probably won't think about anything else until Kai is home safe and sound." A long sigh escaped from her lips. "This explains what my dad was doing with all the cash he had withdrawn though, right?"

"Percy did mention it in the video," he said. "At least you now have closure on that."

She bit on the inside of her cheek. "And it's great to hear he used the money for something good. You can't put a price on giving a person a new lease on life."

"No you can't." Hayden laid his business card on the table next to her. "My cell number is on here. Call me anytime if you have any questions or think of anything we should know. And the sooner you can find out if the women will talk to us, the better."

She nodded and grabbed her own business card from a holder on the table. She handed it to Cady. "When this is all over, give me a call."

Cady flung her arms around her, and the pair hugged for a long moment before Becca released her and stepped back. "I'm sorry for your loss, too, but I'm grateful you're willing to talk with me about it."

"I'm sure you'll help me deal with this as much as I help you." Becca's words cracked at the end, fading into a breathless silence.

Cady swiped at tears on her cheeks and rushed toward the exit.

"Thanks again." Hayden hurried after Cady.

A tight knot formed in his gut. The weight of her grief left him feeling useless. He was a doer. A fixer. A take-action guy. And as much as he wanted to fix this for Cady, he couldn't. Not in any way.

~

Despite the waves of feelings Cady was riding, she followed Hayden into the courthouse. After watching the video, her emotional state was fragile, and she really didn't want to melt down in front of the mayor's assistant. But more than that, she wanted answers to questions.

Or did she?

What if she learned something else about her father she didn't want to hear? True, he'd fulfilled his promise and had taken the mayor's secret to the grave with him, but he did make provision for the story to come out in the end. And, it didn't seem as if keeping the secret harmed anyone, but she couldn't be certain until Hayden talked to his buddy at ICE.

That's what she should be focusing on. Not her emotions. Not the way she'd wanted to throw herself at Hayden outside the BAG office and let him hold her until the fresh rush of grief from talking to Becca disappeared. He'd looked concerned for her, but he didn't seem inclined to provide any additional support. Made sense, she supposed. After all, she'd put up a wall. Told him to back off on any interest he might have in her. How else should she expect him to act?

He pulled the door open to the mayor's office, revealing a waiting area where an older woman sat behind the desk. Her dyed-blond hair was pulled back in a sleek bun, and she wore a green paisley dress with a fitted waist. The name plaque perched on the desk read *Daisy Ellington*.

"Why Hayden Kraus." Her smooth Southern voice drifted over Cady like a warm summer breeze. "To what do we owe the pleasure of your company?"

"I wasn't sure if you'd remember me."

"It's my business to remember the people of our town." She gave a pointed look at Cady. "Not so with you, young lady. I know I've seen you before, but I'm certain we've never met."

Cady stepped to the desk. "I'm Cadence Vaughn. My dad is—"

"Of course." Daisy stood and held out her hand. "You're Percy's daughter. I was so sorry to hear about his passing. He was such a good friend to Mayor Sutton."

"Thank you," Cady said and left it at that as she didn't yet know how to react when someone offered their sympathy. Maybe it was something she would learn as time went on, but right now these interactions were uncomfortable. She did shake Daisy's hand, though, as it would be awkward not to.

Daisy gave a sincere shake, then held out a manicured hand toward the chairs in front of her desk. "Please have a seat, and tell me how I can help you."

Hayden pulled out a chair for Cady, then took the seat next to her. She didn't often encounter men today who had such old-fashioned manners. Most guys she interacted with thought it was outdated. Probably because a lot of modern women didn't like things like door opening and chair holding and wanted to demonstrate their own independence. She respected their choice, but she loved the considerate attention, and the more she got to know him, the more she liked him.

"We've come about the incident at the surf shop," he said. "I'm sure being the mayor's assistant you've heard about it."

"Sickening." Daisy clasped her hands together on the desk. "I sure hope our sweet Kai wasn't involved in such a horrible thing, but it doesn't look good for him. Not when the women were found in the cave beneath his property with the only exit being through his shop."

Hayden nodded.

Daisy stared at him. "I'm not sure how I can help, though. Unless of course you want to schedule an appointment with the mayor to discuss it. That I can help you with."

"No," Hayden said. "This is about Mayor Sutton."

"Ernie." Daisy looked off into the distance. "But Ernie's been gone for months. How could he have any part in trafficking these women?"

Hayden shared the information they'd learned, leaving Cady's father out of it.

Daisy fell back into her chair and gripped the arms, her fingers turning white. "I had no idea. If I had, I would've let you know that's how he spent the cash he'd withdrawn or that it was the reason for selling his prized collection."

"What do you think about the mayor's brother-in-law being involved in this?" Cady asked.

Daisy scoffed. "No big surprise there. He's been taking advantage of Ernie for years, sponging off of him. Taking money Ernie really didn't have to give. But to honor his wife, Ernie helped her brother." She tapped her fingers on the end of the chair, then shot back up. "This is probably why Ernie continued to support Collins for so long after she passed, isn't it?"

Hayden nodded. "Other than Collins, do you know of anyone who could be involved in the trafficking ring?"

"Me?" Daisy's hand flew to her chest. "No. No way."

Hayden held up his hands. "I'm not suggesting you knew anything about this. I'm just asking if there were any men or women who Mayor Sutton dealt with that you didn't know or know why they'd come to this office to talk to him."

"You can be sure I find out what anyone needs before I allow them to schedule an appointment with our mayor." Daisy tapped a calendar on the desk. "And before you ask me if they were potentially lying to me, I followed up on every appointment with Ernie. If I'm at all in question about the person's credentials, I follow up with them as they exit the office too."

Cady didn't doubt what she said was true. If Mayor Sutton had any contact with the traffickers, it would've had to be outside the office.

"Is there anything else you can think of that we should know?" Hayden asked.

"How can there be?" Daisy blinked. "I told you everything I knew about Ernie's life when you were looking for Becca and trying to find his killer."

"I figured as much," Hayden said. "But I thought maybe this would jog your memory regarding something else."

She shook her head. "But I'll think about it and call you if I do come up with anything." She shifted to lock eyes on Cady. "Was your father involved in this?"

Cady explained his role. "I have to say the video made me thankful the dementia kept him from remembering something so troubling to him."

"Like I said." Daisy paused to smile. "He was a good friend to Ernie, and after hearing how he kept Ernie's secret, it sounds like an even better friend than I knew."

"Do you know if Mayor Sutton ever contacted ICE?" Hayden asked.

"He never met with an ICE official in the office, so if he did call them, it was outside of here." She planted her hands on the desk. "But if you'd like, I can review his phone records to see if I can find anything."

"Thank you. That could be helpful." He smiled and stood.

"I'll get to it right away and also keep my eyes and ears open for any information I can find about trafficking."

"Don't go digging for information," Hayden said. "These men are dangerous."

Cady stood too. If people were talking about trafficking

and information slipped, this go-getter of a woman wouldn't let them down. Problem was, Cady didn't believe the information could easily be found. No, it would take some super investigating to get to the men in charge.

But more importantly, there would be extreme danger to anyone who dared look into a ring of men who were willing to sell women to the highest bidder. That meant she and all of the fine members of the Lost Lake Locators team needed to watch their backs.

10

Closing her eyes, Cady sat back in the conference room at the inn while the LLL team settled into chairs at the long table. They'd gathered for an update and to watch the video from Mina's interview.

The more Cady was learning, the more she wondered if her father's murder was related to the trafficking. She had to accept the fact that his death really could be part of this investigation, and though she'd rather do anything other than watch this video, she would stay at Hayden's side while it played.

She glanced at him. He sat rigid and tense, his hands curled on the table. He'd made a call to his ICE contact, hoping to discover if Mayor Sutton had requested an investigation and if smuggling routes were prevalent in this area. He'd had to leave a message, his disappointment obvious to anyone who looked at him. She was frustrated with the delay, too, but she was consumed by the upcoming video and the search they'd made of her dad's place.

She'd totally freaked out after the search and completely forgot the faith principle she'd tried to employ after her dad's passing. She'd been trying her hardest to believe no matter what she planned, no matter what happened, God's behind-the-scenes purpose prevailed. Always and forever.

But now? What possible purpose could He have behind these difficult situations? She shouldn't question. She'd just discussed this with Hayden, and yet here she was, wanting to know how her dad was involved and why, when she should accept and make the best of any situation God allowed her to be in.

No. No! That wasn't it. She not only had to make the best, but *thrive* in every circumstance to serve as a role model for others and bring glory to God.

She closed her eyes and bowed her head. *I'm sorry I'm constantly failing. Help me to do better.*

Hayden leaned close to her. "Are you okay?"

She flashed her eyes open. If only she could alleviate the concern she found on his face, but she couldn't. "I won't lie and say I am. I don't want to watch this video, but I will."

"You don't have to do it. I can update you on anything new."

She smiled at him. "I appreciate your willingness to take this problem from me, but God put me in this situation for a reason, and I can't run from it."

"I'm proud of you for thinking that way." He reached under the table and took her hand.

His touch was warm and comforting, and despite her brain saying *Don't let this thing develop even more*, she didn't pull away.

"If it helps," he said. "Our team has a motto that's gotten us through a lot in the past. Maybe it can help you. 'The best is yet to come.'"

"Something to hold on to for sure," she said, but did she really believe it? Not now. Not when her grief was so fresh, but maybe later.

"I'll be here the whole time the video is playing," he said, looking deeply into her eyes. "If it gets to be too much, tell me, and we'll stop."

Her heart rate kicked up and not from the danger—from the anxiety. The genuine caring and compassion she saw in his eyes had fired it off. He was the real deal. A guy who could be strong and in control, and yet had a softer side he was willing to expose to her. Even here in front of his whole team.

He smiled softly, then squeezed her hand and let go. She instantly missed his touch and almost reached for him again, but clasped her hands together instead.

He leaned forward to peer down the table. "Before we watch the video, I wanted to let you know the information in my deep dive into Kai has come back, but hasn't returned anything unusual. He seems to be exactly who he presented himself to be."

"As much as I'm glad he's what we think he is," Cady said, "it would be better for the investigation if he wasn't, right? Because it could give us something to go on."

"Exactly," Hayden said. "Okay on to the video. Someone kill the lights so we can see the screen better."

"Got it." Gabe bolted to his feet and charged at the light switch as if it were some treat and not a chore. He never seemed to let anything interfere with his passion for life.

He flicked off the light, putting the room in darkness. Cady squeezed her eyes closed, then blinked a few times to adjust to the dim light.

The screen came alive, showing Mina in her uniform. She announced her name and title, plus the date, time, and location. She panned the camera, naming Detective Elaina Lyons and Olive Simpson, the interpreter.

After a long pause, the camera swung to the imprisoned women who huddled together on one of the small cots.

Olive knelt next to them and took the hand of the woman who'd been speaking for the trio.

Mina stepped into place next to her detective in full view of the camera. "I have Li Zhang with me, and the other women have asked her to serve as their spokesperson for this initial interview."

Olive shifted to look at Mina. "Go ahead, Sheriff. How do you want to proceed?"

Mina rested her hand on her hip. "Ask Li to tell us how she came to be in this cave."

Olive translated the request for Li.

Li's chin trembled, but she rubbed a hand over her face, then started speaking, distress spilling from her words. She stopped.

Cady waited for Olive to translate the words that impacted Li so deeply, scooting to the edge of her seat as if it would move Olive along.

Olive shifted to the side, allowing her to look between Mina and Li at the same time. "The women left China with their families because of religious persecution and hoped to make a new home in the United States. They boarded a ship with twenty other people wanting new lives too. Men, women, and children. They were put in a smelly cargo area for the ocean voyage. As they neared our coastline, the men who'd arranged their illegal passage came to them and separated the women from their families."

Olive stopped to listen again, then she cringed before speaking. "They didn't dock in the Port of Portland as they were told would happen, but the ship anchored off the coast near this shop. The women were hustled into a charter fishing boat that made its way to shore, where three men with guns waited for them."

"Can they identify the ship or the fishing boat?" Mina asked.

"Or the men with guns?" Detective Lyons added.

Olive asked the question. Li gave a quick answer.

"The ship was called the *Red Dragon Voyager*," Olive said. "But they have no idea who owns it. The charter fishing boat was named *Off The Hook*. They'd never seen the men before."

Nolan paused the video.

Hayden shot a look at the team. "The *Red Dragon Voyager* is the ship Percy said was involved in trafficking."

"Not only that," Nolan said, "but *Off The Hook* is the name of Wade Collins's boat."

"I need to do a deep dive into the *Red Dragon Voyager* to see who owns it," Hayden said.

Nolan started the video again where Mina was facing Olive. "How many women were there?"

Olive asked the question of Li, then said, "Fifteen."

"Were all fifteen of the women brought to shore?" Detective Lyons asked.

Olive translated, and Li nodded.

"What happened to the other women?" Mina asked.

Olive relayed the question and Li's expression tightened.

Olive cringed. "After they were unloaded from the boat, they were marched across the beach toward the cliffs and an idling, run-down van. She knew what was waiting for them and was terrified. She was at the back of the line with her two friends here and wanted to run, but they were surrounded by gunmen. One man walked in front, one to the side, and the last one behind them, leaving no avenue of escape."

Cady studied Li. Fear emanated from her as if it were a stench permeating the room. Imagine the terror she must've felt knowing the terrible future awaiting her. Tears flooded Cady's eyes, and she had to swallow a sob to keep from drawing attention to herself.

Li continued her story, and Olive sat unwavering until she clutched her arms around her waist and faced Mina. "She said everything changed then. The van had a flat tire, so the man in the middle and the one in the back went to change it while the women were forced to sit in a line. Li still brought up the rear, and she saw movement off to the side. It was a man trying his best to conceal himself. She later learned it was Kai. He waved for her to come join him. She wouldn't leave her friends behind so gave a slight shake of her head and pointed at her two friends. Kai continued to wave frantically. Li touched her friend's legs and let them know without speaking that they should slip away when the guard was distracted."

Oh, my goodness! Cady couldn't even imagine having to make such a life-threatening decision. Escape with a gun-brandishing man standing over you and risk being shot, or go into slavery. Would Cady be brave enough to risk escaping as Li did? She wasn't sure what she would do.

Li lifted her shoulders, and her words spilled out in an uncertain cadence.

"One by one, they slipped into the darkness unnoticed," Olive translated. "Kai raced through the landscape and brought them into a tunnel hidden in large rocks below the cliff. It opened into a tiny cave, the space so small they could barely fit. Barely breathe. He spoke to them in broken Mandarin, telling them they had to wait until the men left, and then he would make sure they were properly taken care of."

Olive listened again, then glanced back. "They could hear the men outside. Searching, looking hard. Cursing. Demanding. Threatening. They clung together, trying not to make a sound as Kai stood guard at the mouth of their cave. They heard the men say they were leaving, and then the van's engine rumbled as it took off. Still, Kai kept them in the cave for what seemed like eternity, but was probably more like an hour before he slipped out to check for the men."

Li sighed and released her tightly clutched hands, and her tone cheered up for the next part of her story.

Olive's shoulders sagged. "At first, Li didn't believe they'd been rescued. She doubted Kai all the way to his shop and into this cave. Actually, even beyond that because she feared he'd taken them for his own enjoyment. But he continued to care for them until he could make arrangements for sanctuary. And then he promised he would locate the men who did this and make sure they paid."

Detective Lyons swiped her fingers under her eye. A tear in the woman who had seemed detached? "Was Kai the only man in this cave?"

Olive asked the questions. "Kai only. They haven't seen the gunmen since the beach."

"How long have the women been here?" Mina asked.

Li leaned back and pointed to Roman numerals scratched into the wall, marking seven days.

A week! These poor women had been living in the tiny cave for a week. They must've been frightened. At least they could start to believe Kai was trying to help them, but honestly, if Cady had been in their situation, she might not have trusted him.

Li started talking again, her words coming out fast.

Olive held up a hand, stopping her. "Then Kai came to them and said he had a lead on the men, and he had to leave. He left them with enough food, water, and other supplies for a week and told them to be quiet until he returned. She begged him not to go, but he said if he didn't, he might miss the opportunity to prove who'd abducted them and bring the men to justice. He couldn't risk them going free and trying to hunt them down. And hopefully he could find out where the women's families had been taken."

Their families! Cady hadn't even thought about what had happened to them. They'd been separated on the ship. That's all they knew. Were their families placed into forced labor somewhere, and if so, would anyone be able to locate them?

"Did Kai give any detail about where he was going?" Mina asked.

Olive repeated the question, then shook her head.

Mina closed her eyes and stopped speaking for a moment, then she looked at her detective. "I don't have any other questions. Do you?"

The detective solemnly shook her head.

Mina turned to Olive. "Please tell them we have ambulances here to take them to the hospital for a checkup. Then we'll escort them to a house where they'll stay until we're certain it's safe for them to relocate."

"What if they ask what happens after that?" Olive asked.

Mina frowned. "Tell them I don't know. I'll do my best to find and reunite them with their families, but that'll be a challenge. I can't guarantee anything."

"I'll tell them." Olive gritted her teeth. "Some days I really hate this job."

"Same," Detective Lyons said, her voice cracking.

Olive gave the women the bad news. They took it stoically and gripped hands. Cady couldn't imagine being in their position to then find out they might or might never be reunited with their families. How horrible. No one deserved such treatment. *No one.*

The video went black, and Hayden stood, his face a mask of anger. "So Kai *is* involved, but not in the way we first suspected."

"I'm really glad to see that." Abby might have been

trying to be positive, but her eyes were damp. "From everything other people told us, him being involved in human trafficking didn't fit who he was."

"I agree." Cady tried to sound in control of her emotions as she would as a reporter, but it was difficult when her heart was shattered for these women. "I know my dad could never have been friends with someone who could do something so appalling."

"But his journals tell us he found out about it and didn't report it to the sheriff," Gabe said, a challenge in his tone. "So maybe he didn't tell you everything."

"Don't take any offense, Cady," Hayden was quick to say. "Gabe loves to call our theories and facts into question."

She nodded, but she couldn't say Gabe's comment didn't sting. "Maybe my dad would've reported it in time if his memory hadn't been taken from him."

"Maybe," Gabe said, now sounding disbelieving. "But we need to keep watching for anything to suggest his involvement."

He had a good point, and if they weren't talking about her father, she would agree with him. She needed to set aside her personal feelings and look at the situation objectively. "I can understand that."

Hayden met her gaze, and she didn't like the thread of worry in his expression. "Equally, if not more important, we need to question if we're the only ones who know he had this secret. Because it doesn't sound like these are the kind of people you keep a secret from."

Abby's expression tightened, her eyes narrowing in concern. "In my experience, people who engage in such heinous crimes are quite capable of committing murder. They wouldn't hesitate to act if they fear being reported to the authorities."

Cady almost gasped at the blunt statement, but Abby

was right. The traffickers could have been afraid her father would talk, and they'd thought their only option was to end his life.

She already knew everyone had to watch their backs, but how much more so if the traffickers learned not only Cady knew the secret her dad had been hiding, but this entire room of professionals knew the secret too?

11

The pizza was delivered a few minutes before Mina and El had arrived for dinner and the meeting, but Hayden wasn't hungry after watching Mina's video. The others seemed to share his feelings. In fact, the tangy scent of pepperoni filling the air turned his stomach. Or maybe it was seeing Cady broken again. He'd watched like a spectator with a quick touch here and there as she'd ridden a roller coaster of emotions since he'd found her breaking into Kai's house. But figuring out these traffickers could seriously be the men who killed her father might be too much for her.

Could he remain hands off?

He bolted to his feet before he discovered the answer to his question was an emphatic no. "I'm gonna grab some pizza. Would you like some?"

She shook her head. "I don't know how you can eat after seeing such a horrible interview."

"I don't know that I can, but maybe it'll keep my mind occupied, and I won't be thinking about the women. Besides, we'll be working late tonight, and we should eat something if we want to be effective."

"I suppose you're right." She sighed. "Go ahead and bring a slice of sausage, and I'll try to eat it."

He charged across the room before he acted on the impulse to comfort her.

The table by the wall had been loaded with utensils, plates, and napkins, and bottled water rested in a tub of ice. Reece was doing something in the kitchen, and Abby was brewing coffee. The nutty scent took over the strong pepperoni smell. On the far end of the table, Reece's famous two-layer chocolate cake waited on a glass serving plate. Usually, his mouth watered when he laid eyes on the fluffy chocolate frosting he knew would melt in his mouth and fire off all of his sweet taste buds, but not tonight.

"It'll be hard to eat after that video, but I'm..." Abby looked up from the coffee maker. "Whoa, what's up with you?"

"What do you mean?" He reached for a slice of sausage pizza dripping with cheese and managed to plate it without strands of gooeyness dangling behind.

"I get that you're concerned for Kai, but your infamous intensity is even more intimidating than usual."

He knew the look she meant, but he didn't want to admit his feelings for Cady to anyone, so he didn't answer. He took a plate to load three slices of pepperoni pizza for himself.

Abby clutched his arm. "You've fallen for her, haven't you?"

He glanced at his friend, striving to keep his tone even as he responded before she raised her voice, repeating the question loud enough for everyone else to hear. "You could be right."

She tightened her grip. "Hah! Could be? Nah. You're in. Hook, line, and sinker."

Yeah, he was drowning, but what could he do about it?

She arched an eyebrow. "So you finally met someone who's threatening the tight hold you have on life."

He grabbed two bottles of water, relishing the coldness in his hands. "How do you always know what's going on with us?"

"In this case, just looking at you is a dead giveaway. If that isn't enough, we all know you're Mr. Control Freak. Just add the fact that falling in love means you're putting all your control in the other person's hands, and I can figure it out."

"Yeah, you nailed it, but I don't know what I'm going to do about it."

"Wish I could help. I really do." She squeezed his arm. "Along with some serious talking to God, only you can figure that out."

The *talking to God* part was the component he'd missed when it should've been the first thing he did, but as usual, he was trying to work his problem out himself. He'd had to fend for himself since his parents died. Or at least he thought depending on himself was the only option. So now, he believed he didn't need anyone's help. That sometimes meant God's help either. To be honest, he often forgot to ask until he came to the end of his abilities. By then he'd exhausted himself in worry and struggling when he could've made his life easier simply by going to God on a more regular basis, and especially when a problem first arose.

He picked up Cady's plate and carefully balanced everything. "Thanks. You've given me something to think about."

"Hopefully more than think. Do." She wrinkled her nose. "There might never be another woman who can break through your rigid control, so whatever you do, don't let Cady get away."

Abby was probably right. At least he'd never met a

woman who tempted him to get involved in a long-term relationship. To that end, Cady was a miracle worker.

Back at the table, he placed the pizza and bottled water in front of her and took the next chair again. He didn't speak, but attacked the first piece of pizza, which despite its oozing cheese and crispy pepperoni, still tasted like sawdust.

"Everyone have a seat, and let's get started," Nolan said from where he sat next to Mina at the far end of the table.

She wiped her mouth with a napkin and got up. "Does anyone have questions about the video?"

"No questions about that, but I do have questions about the crime scene," Hayden said. "Who'll be processing the forensics for the surf shop and cave?"

"County forensics techs will be here in the morning."

"Have you considered using Sierra at the Veritas Center?" Abby asked as she joined them at the table.

Hayden leaned close to Cady. "The forensics team in Portland I told you about where Nick works. Their skills are exemplary, and if anyone can recover forensics, it's them. They've supported us on a past investigation."

Mina took a sip of water and eyed Abby. "You know the expense would prohibit that."

"Sure, I get that." Abby uncapped her water bottle. "You have a budget to keep, but they could do the work pro bono."

"Right." Mina let the word hang in the air. "But it's a big job, and I can't imagine them offering to handle it."

"I'd be happy to talk to Sierra after the meeting to see if she's free and willing to do the work pro bono," Nolan said.

"I'd appreciate that." Mina smiled at him. "But until I hear back from you, we'll move ahead with County techs."

Hayden's phone rang from the table. Aha! His friend Adam was calling back. He pushed to his feet and grabbed the phone. "I need to take this. It's my source at ICE."

He didn't wait for anyone to agree with him, but strode out of the room and closed the door behind him. "Thanks for calling me back, bro."

"Like I could even consider ignoring you after you left such a cryptic message." Adam laughed.

"I didn't think it was safe to leave details on your voicemail."

"Oka-a-y." His drawn-out word was followed by silence. "Now you *really* have my attention."

Adam responded best to plain talking, so Hayden came right out with it. "We've encountered a human smuggling and trafficking ring here on the coast in Lost Lake, Oregon."

"No way, dude!" His deep voice rumbled over the phone, sounding like one of the guys who recorded movie trailers. "That's odd, for sure. Definitely not a route commonly used by traffickers."

"That's what I thought, too, but we rescued three women who shared their story of travel from China on a ship to a charter fishing boat on our coast, where they were offloaded and put into vans."

"Interesting." Adam fell silent. "Sounds like an investigation we'd pursue. I'll run it up the flagpole. I—"

"No, wait," Hayden jumped in. "Your agency should already have an active investigation. Ernie Sutton, the former mayor here, reported the situation a few months back."

"Odd. I haven't heard anything about it. Hang on, and I'll check our records." The rapid click of fingers racing over a keyboard came through the phone. "Nothing here, man. Nothing comes up. Could be a classified investigation, but I doubt it."

Hayden could've been hit over the head with a baseball bat and not have been more shocked. "Is there any chance the mayor reported it, and the case has already been closed?"

"No chance." The forcefulness in his friend's tone took Hayden by surprise. "I looked at active, inactive, and closed investigations. Nothing under any classification."

Weird. But Hayden wouldn't give up. "Is there any way you can ask about it being classified?"

"Will do when I check with my supervisor. You can be sure now that I know about this, we'll open an investigation."

"Excellent," Hayden said. "We need this smuggling to end."

"Amen to that, bro." The strength behind his words spoke volumes as to his feelings on trafficking. "Let me ask some questions, and I'll call you back. Since you brought this to me, I'll do my best to take lead if a new investigation is warranted."

"Sounds good." Hayden could count on Adam to do a thorough job. "Also, I need to let you know how we happened upon the trafficking ring." He explained about Kai's disappearance.

A rustling noise came through the phone. "Making a note of his name now. I'll be sure to keep it on top of my mind if we start an investigation."

"Get back to me as soon as you can."

The call ended, and Hayden shoved his phone in his pocket to go back to the meeting. Everyone raised expectant gazes to him. He remained standing at the head of the table and explained the situation. "So it's possible Mayor Sutton didn't report the trafficking."

"How can that be?" Cady cried out. "What in the world could he have to gain by not reporting such a horrible thing and then turn around to use his own money to save some of the women?"

"Wade Collins is his brother-in-law," Abby said. "Was Ernie trying to protect him?"

"Maybe from getting killed by the traffickers," Cady said. "At least that's what my dad said in the video."

"Most everyone knows about the mayor only tolerating his brother-in-law because of his wife," Mina said. "After she died there was no love lost between them, but he continued to support Collins with the boat long after that."

"Maybe the mayor was in on the trafficking," Hayden said.

"No!" Mina lifted her chin. "No way. There has to be a legitimate explanation for why he didn't report this, and it's our job to find out what it is while we bring in the traffickers."

Hayden moved over to the whiteboard. "Then let's review our assignments to see if we've gotten any closer to resolving this mystery."

He tapped the first item for the algorithms that he was assigned to run for gathering background information about Cady and Kai. "I got alerts that the reports are done running. When the meeting breaks up, I'll review the results and email reports."

"I'd be glad to analyze the results for Cady." Abby gave Hayden a pointed look.

Ah, she didn't trust him to be impartial, but he would probably do the same thing in her shoes.

"Thanks. Two of us will make quicker work than one." He gave her a look loaded with meaning, a silent plea to keep his involvement to herself. "I'll also add Percy to my algorithms. Seems like he's involved in some capacity, and we don't want to miss anything."

"Just ask if you need his financial or phone records. Or mine, for that matter," Cady said. "I can give you access to our accounts too."

He gave a simple nod, tempted to praise her for being so cooperative—but with Abby already sensing his feelings for Cady, he held back. If anyone else hadn't noticed yet, he wasn't about to give them a reason to.

He moved on to the second item. "Abby, were you able to check with Kai's doctor for any mental or physical issues that could've explained him simply wandering off?"

"Yeah, nothing out of the ordinary," she replied.

Hayden crossed the item off the board and looked back at the group. "You all know we searched Kai's house and business today. He doesn't use computers, and we didn't locate any personal financial or phone records. I'll need someone to contact his bank and phone company for that information."

El shifted uncomfortably and leaned at an awkward angle to make eye contact with him. Her unnatural position was probably to keep Gabe out of her sightline. The pair had been fighting the same emotions Hayden and Cady were losing the battle against. Everyone on the team knew it, and they were all rooting for them to get together.

Big problem was El was a by-the-book, stickler kind of woman, while Gabe was an easy-going, whatever will be will be kind of guy. Opposites attract, or so they say, but the big question was, could the pair get beyond the initial attraction?

Maybe a bigger question was, could Hayden and Cady get beyond it too? He stole a glance at her, and the strength behind his resolve began to fade.

El cleared her throat. Hayden snapped his attention back to her.

"I already have warrant requests in the works," she said. "I should be able to serve them tomorrow morning."

Nolan aimed a challenging look at the detective. "But are you planning to share the information with us?"

El glanced at Mina for direction.

Mina sighed. "I wish we could, but that's not information we can share."

El beamed a smile at her boss. Yeah, she was a stickler for protocol, too, and would likely have argued if Mina had agreed.

"Then I'll take care of it," Abby stated plainly, sounding not in the least bit put out. "Wouldn't be the first time I've tried to get those kinds of records without a warrant."

"Speaking of getting records." Hayden looked at Mina. "Any chance you were able to get copies of the police investigation into Percy Vaughn's death?"

She shook her head. "I've put in a request with the lieutenant in charge, but even if I'm able to get the file, I can't share it with you."

Nolan looked at his girlfriend. "But you can review it, and reaffirm Cady's take on things."

"What?" Cady asked, her eyes wide. "You doubt me?"

Hayden held up a placating hand. "He's merely trying to confirm every aspect of the investigation so nothing gets missed."

She crossed her arms and slumped in her chair, but Hayden couldn't offer a better explanation. He tapped the whiteboard.

"Before you ask." Reece's gaze zeroed in on him. "I've called hospitals and shelters in a tri-county area. No one matching Kai's description has been seen at any of the locations. In case he did show up, I urged them to be on the lookout for him."

Hayden slashed a red mark through the item.

"You can cross off my thing too." Gabe was sitting up straight, his usual, relaxed posture missing. "Kai's Jeep Wrangler isn't at his home or business, and that's about all we can do. I'll text everyone the details so you can be on the lookout for it as you're working the investigation."

Gabe glanced at El, a flash of emotion crossing his face, then he quickly looked away to Mina. "I assume you'll be putting out an alert for the vehicle."

"Already done," Mina replied.

Hayden crossed the item off, then backed up to a skipped step. "We interviewed Becca, Daisy, and both of Kai's immediate neighbors." He explained the information they'd learned. "Becca will let us know if we can interview any of the women Mayor Sutton brought to her, and Daisy is reviewing the mayor's phone logs to see if any record exists of a phone call to ICE."

"They'll both get back to us if they can be of more help," Cady added.

Hayden gave a nod. "It's possible they could remember something to help move us forward too. We also checked the houses in Kai's neighborhood for security cameras. Nada."

"Dorothy kept an eagle eye on the area and seemed almost as good as a camera." Abby chuckled.

"Problem is, she doesn't have video playback." Hayden laughed.

Cady laughed, but it seemed halfhearted. "I plan to interview my dad's birdwatching friends tomorrow. See if they spotted a ship or boat or anything out of the ordinary on our coast."

"Like I said," Hayden continued. "I'll look into registration records for the *Red Dragon Voyager*. But if my ICE buddy is right about his agency not having an open investigation, then the trafficking is likely still going on. Percy said Collins went out every Thursday night, and Collins could still be actively involved."

"That's tomorrow night." Cady's excitement echoed in her voice as it carried easily through the room.

"Which means we could put him under surveillance and perhaps get a registration number for the ship, which will help ID the owners," Jude said, weighing in for the first time, which was surprising to Hayden when his teammate was often very vocal.

Gabe rubbed his hands together. "You can count me in on that."

"Hold up." Mina scanned both sides of the table, her gaze meeting each person's eyes with quiet intention. "That's a job best left to law enforcement. And I'm not the only one who'll tell you that. I'm sure your ICE contact will ask you to back off and not interfere too."

She was right again, but that didn't matter to Hayden. Not one bit.

"I can't do that." Hayden set his feet firmly apart, grounding himself with a solid stance. "Not when we've been hired to find a missing man, and we committed to help Cady find the person who gave her father the lethal fentanyl dose."

"I understand your commitment, but we'll take care of Collins." Mina's gaze swept toward Nolan, expectant, as though she was silently asking him to break into the tense exchange with Hayden.

Nolan cleared his throat, but didn't shy away from looking at her. "I can't say we won't watch Collins and tail him if he goes to the ship, but we won't get in your way."

Mina cocked her head. "Then we might have to arrest you."

"For what?" Gabe shot forward, seeming to forget his awkwardness around El, and stared at Mina. "Taking a boat ride at night? Hayden's always looking for the next thrill, and you don't have a legal reason to stop him—us from taking a joyride."

Mina's gaze sharpened, her silent plea to Nolan growing more insistent.

"Sorry." He offered a smile, but it was tight with tension. "But we knew at some point we'd get into a situation where we'd be at odds with each other. None of us will break the law, and we won't get in your way. That's all I can promise right now."

Hayden wanted to high-five his teammate but refrained from moving and watched carefully to see how Mina and Nolan handled this disagreement.

"You're right. We did, and I guess this is one of those times." She gave Nolan a gentle, sincere smile. "If we're both on the water tomorrow night, we'll coordinate with you so there's zero chance of interference."

He beamed back at her, but El glared at her boss's back. Obviously El didn't like the decision, but she held her tongue. At least for now. She would probably share her thoughts with Mina when they were alone. Not that it would change anything. One thing Hayden had learned about Mina was, when she'd made up her mind, it was hard to change it.

Thankfully, this decision was in the team's favor. They were now free to tail Collins to the ship, bringing them one step closer to identifying the traffickers.

12

The meeting had ended a few minutes ago and Cady had no idea what would happen next. Mina and El had departed, and Nolan walked out with them to call Sierra as he promised. The rest of the team remained in the room.

Earlier, Hayden said to prepare for a long night ahead, so maybe the team planned to do some research. She had something to do too. During the update, an idea had formed in her head. One she could do something about without any assistance from the team, but she didn't share it yet. No point in discussing an idea that might not pan out.

Hayden approached Abby at the food table. "I'll email the files from Cady's background check to you."

Abby poured a cup of coffee, which she held out to him. "Let me get some caffeine on board, and then I'll get right on it."

Jude joined Hayden at the table and grabbed a mug that said, *I heart Lost Lake*.

Hayden blew on his steaming coffee as he faced his teammate. "If Cady gives you a list of her dad's birdwatcher friends, would you locate their home addresses so we can hit the ground running in the morning?"

"You got it." Jude quickly dumped coffee into his mug, splashing the deep brown liquid on the table.

Abby swiped a cloth over the table behind him. "Dude, you have so got to learn to clean up after yourself."

He raised three fingers. "I'll be more careful. Scout's honor."

"Empty promise." She gave him a patronizing look. "You were never a scout and don't think for one second your little-boy I'm-sorry look will cut it." Her words carried a bite, but a playful grin tugged at her lips as she looked at her friend.

He flashed a winning smile that left her shaking her head.

He sauntered toward Cady as if he had all the time in the world.

"I'll jot down the names for you." Cady grabbed her notebook and wrote quickly, but glanced up as Hayden approached. He set down his mug and dropped heavily behind his computer as if the weight of the investigation was too much for him.

She couldn't even imagine being responsible for finding a missing person. Sure, she did stories where lives were on the line, but it wasn't her responsibility to save a life, or at least she'd never investigated a story that required her to keep someone alive.

She quickly finished the list for Jude. "Thank you for doing this."

"Of course." He swiped the paper from her hand. "But don't be thinking I'm a pushover and I'll accept just any to-do item. I definitely draw the line at cleaning toilets." He laughed and strode to the same seat he'd occupied before.

Cady shook her head but couldn't help grinning as he walked away. Of all of the teammates, he seemed the most fun-loving, or at least he was the team joker, as Hayden had said. Every team had someone like Jude to lighten the mood. She was starting to see how each person's strengths and quirks shaped the dynamic of a team that meshed well together.

"Just a heads up." Hayden opened his laptop. "Jude might be a real charmer and doesn't seem reliable, but you can depend on him to do whatever he's asked and do it to the very best of his ability."

Her thoughts exactly. "Dependability and reliability seem to be one of the hallmarks of this team."

He squared his shoulders, the pride in his expression unmistakable as he relaxed against the back of his chair. "I'd like to think that's true. I know we all would give up everything, even our lives, to rescue someone in danger.

Oh, man. How did she respond to such a statement? She didn't like to think of him in any kind of danger. Anyone on the team facing danger, for that matter. But her concern for Hayden exceeded her worry for the rest of the team. He was finding a place in her heart, and losing him to violence wasn't something she even wanted to contemplate.

Hayden sat forward again. "Give me a minute to get this information emailed to Abby, then we can talk about what I hope to accomplish tonight."

"I actually have an idea. I don't know if it'll pan out, but I'd like to run with it for a bit. I'll grab my computer from my room and be right back." She got up before he asked questions and tried to talk her out of branching out on her own.

A quick trip down the hallway, and she was in the large open foyer. The musty, old-building smell seemed more overpowering tonight, but she quickly made a turn down another hallway to her room. No musty smell here. They'd used sweet-smelling coconut and orange-scented cleaners, reminding her of vacations at the beach.

What would it be like to live here with pristine beaches and an ocean right outside your door? Calming at times, she was sure, but storms could rage and destroy. She didn't much like that part of beach living. Could she get used to it?

She reached for the light switch, then paused—drawn instead to the soft glow of the moon pouring in through the French doors. Why not take a short break, just long enough to feel the ocean's calm before confronting the world's ugliness again?

As she pushed through the doors, a gusty wind pounded her backward. The ocean air between gusts was warm and comforting, so she braved the wind and stepped outside to the sound of waves crashing into the craggy rocks. Clear skies let the moon's glow stretch across the water, and the stars above glittered like tiny fragments of glass tossed across black velvet.

She made her way to the white wooden railing. It wobbled under her hands, and she spotted a warning sign on a tall post, but couldn't make it out in the dim light. Hayden's warning came back to her from her first night here. *Don't trust the railing and go no further than the barrier.* The cliff ahead had experienced erosion before Nolan had bought the inn, and they needed to fix it to make the area safe.

She backed over cracked concrete and looked up at the sky again. The stars, the moon. How could anyone not believe in an all-powerful God when such splendor was revealed in front of them?

Releasing a sigh of contentment, she fell onto the cushioned redwood bench on the patio. She leaned back, and her eyes drifted closed. She rehashed the meeting in her mind.

She never expected the team would stand up against law enforcement to help find her father's killer, but they had. All the way. Nolan even went against the woman he loved to help Cady and to find Kai. What an amazing team. Thank God for putting them in her path. Sure, she had strong investigative skills, but she didn't think getting in a boat and trailing a human trafficker was in her wheelhouse, and she'd always known when to seek help on the job.

Might this end tomorrow night when they located the traffickers' ship? Would the team find proof of their crimes? Proof of their connection to her father and that they'd murdered him? Would they also find Kai so Mina could arrest the murderers?

Such an outcome would be too good to be true, and she couldn't count on it. Which meant she needed to start her research tonight. Soon. Just five more minutes with the soft breeze caressing her skin. With the rhythmic sound of waves rushing in and out from the shore. With the moon and stars above.

"There you are." Hayden's voice sounded from above.

She flashed her eyes open. "I couldn't resist the scene through my French doors. I don't know how you all get anything done living in such a beautiful area."

He settled on the cushion next to her, the bench shifting under his weight. "When someone's life could depend on you finding them, staying motivated is easier."

"Yeah, I can see that. I was just about to come back to the conference room and get to work."

"Doing what?"

"Hear me out before you shoot me down." She sat forward and pivoted to face him. "I got to thinking the trafficking situation could be bigger than we think. Maybe our smugglers are working elsewhere in the state, and there are news reports regarding it. I'd like to search for any stories done on this issue to see if potential names are mentioned or if anyone has been arrested."

He swiveled too. "Why would I shoot you down? Sounds like a great idea."

"Oh," she said, surprised at his easy acquiescence. "I'm glad."

"I can even piggyback off your idea and run some algorithms to automate the search."

"That would be great, but I'm an expert at finding information like this online. I could even do as well as your computer."

"Say it isn't so." He mocked pulling a knife out of his chest and laughed.

Every one of his joyful glances, every vibrant smile, wrapped around her, drawing her in. It was as if God Himself had woven their paths together—and she didn't want to fight it.

He slid to the edge of the cushion and took her hands, his fingers strong and warm. "You feel it, don't you?"

"If by *it*, you mean the unrelenting attraction between us. Yes, I feel it. Question is, what are we going to do about it?"

"Maybe tonight, we stop overthinking. Just let it be—let whatever this is take the lead." His hand rose to gently cradle her cheek. "Maybe we let the moonlight and stars show us the way."

Man, oh, man. The air practically sizzled between them, and she was lost. He was going to kiss her. That was clear. Did she want his kiss? Even if it ended up being one kiss tonight with no possible future?

He slid his fingers into her hair, his touch electrifying as if a star had fallen from the sky and grazed her skin.

"I want to kiss you," he said, his voice breathless. "But I don't want there to be any mistake or lead you on. A kiss is all I can offer right now."

She touched his cheek. "We're both in the same boat. One kiss. One time. Nothing more."

He sighed softly and lowered his head toward her. Unable to resist, she leaned in, and their lips met in a tender, shy kiss.

Oh. Oh!

Everything else faded away—only his touch remained, filling her with a sense of belonging, of warmth, and the promise of a future together.

No. She jerked back.

She'd only wanted one kiss, right? Just one. But that was a lie she'd been telling herself. She wanted more. Much more.

Still, the emotions swimming through her said to be cautious or she would be lost. She couldn't let her feelings for this wonderful man get the best of her. She couldn't risk abandoning her dreams. Not for something fleeting, something her parents had shown her didn't last.

Behind his computer in the conference room, Hayden pretended to review results from the background checks that had recently completed. Tried was the operative word. His brain wouldn't concentrate on the job. Not after that kiss.

What had come over him? Why on earth had he kissed Cady? Not only kissed her, but wished he could go on kissing her. Not for a minute. Not for an hour. Not for a day. For infinity.

Had he completely fallen for her? The kiss sure made it seem like it. His heart had soared. His skin tingled. He felt lightheaded. Not in a dizzy, 'he was going to fall' way, but in a wonderful spinning of joy. These emotions were most definitely going beyond physical attraction.

He glanced at Cady, her attention glued to her computer where it had been since they entered the conference room. Had she found what she was looking for or was she avoiding him?

On the patio, she'd pulled away and fled from him as if he'd done something wrong. Dare he hope she'd taken off because he'd done something right, making her struggle in the same battle he was facing?

But did he *really* hope for such a reaction? They would still go their separate ways when this was all over, and this type of connection would simply cause misery for both of them.

Nolan strode into the room. "Just heard back from Sierra at Veritas. She's glad to do the job, but the partners need to weigh in on the pro bono status. They have a meeting at eight in the morning, and she'll get back to me when she has a definite answer."

"That sounds encouraging, though," Hayden said.

"Yeah, I got the feeling she thought they would do it, but let's keep it between us for now in case it falls apart."

Hayden could read between the lines. Nolan didn't want to give Mina hope, and then disappoint her. Made total sense.

Cady's head popped up, and she made eye contact with Hayden. "I found something. A news story. A Chinese refugee named Emei Gau came to our country illegally with her family on a ship and boat."

"Just like our women," Hayden said.

She nodded. "Emei escaped after she was loaded in a van to be delivered to a man in California. Malnourished and dehydrated, she collapsed on the side of the road. A good Samaritan called an ambulance, and she told her story to the police. She was blindfolded and didn't know the exact location where the boat landed or the route the van had taken."

"Was she able to give them any details to find and arrest these parasites?" Hayden asked.

Cady shook her head. "But the detective found a safe place for her to live and arranged for a reporter to write the story in hopes of locating her family."

"Did they find the family?" Abby asked, an unusual hint of optimism alive in her voice.

Cady shook her head. "The only good outcome noted in the story is that she was able to get free."

"We need to talk to her," Hayden said, his mind firmly back on the investigation.

"I already sent an email to the reporter," Cady said. "If he's like most reporters, he'll check his email often and reply right away. If not, I'll call his newspaper in the morning."

"Sounds like a plan." Hayden smiled at her, doing his best to keep anything personal out of the smile.

She gave a crisp nod and avoided his gaze.

"Maybe when Mina looks for the family of the women we rescued, she can look for Emei's family too." Abby's hopeful tone had turned hesitant.

Hayden knew how important it was for a former law enforcement officer who was used to being disappointed by outcomes and investigations to find a positive outcome in the one they were working. All law enforcement officers hoped for good, but wouldn't put voice to it. Likely in fear of dooming the outcome, because no matter how hard they hoped—prayed—in their field of work, disappointment was the norm.

"On an encouraging note." Jude crossed over to them in his usual lighthearted saunter. "I got a hold of the guy who heads up the birdwatching group. He's agreed to gather as many members as he can to meet with you in the morning at eight."

"Thank you." Cady smiled at Jude.

Hayden gritted his teeth. Just as he suspected. The tension in the room from the investigation hadn't stolen her smile. It was worse. Way worse. It was what happened between them on the patio. The kiss. The amazing, life-changing kiss had turned her off to him.

But even worse, he had no idea how to fix it or even if he wanted to.

13

A minute before eight, the sun caressing her shoulders, Cady knocked on Tom Young's door. Hayden stood behind her. He'd been trying to engage her in conversation this morning, but after having kissed him, she didn't have a clue what to say. It wasn't an ordinary, run-of-the-mill first kiss. Not for her anyway. It was a fireworks bursting in the sky, explosions of emotions, and a sense of permanence and well-being at the same time kind of kiss.

In other words, she'd set her mind to thinking about what it would be like to be in a serious relationship. Not with just anyone, but with him. So how was she to handle such a realization? Behave around him? Do?

She had no idea. None. Until she did, she would do her best to keep him at arm's length. She might come across as being rude, and she might have to tone it down some from last night as they worked in the conference room, but she had to be watchful and not fall even harder for him.

The door opened, and a man with the most interesting hair color smiled at her. A flaming red color topped the upper half of his hair, but a beautiful silvery color that spoke to his age circled around the bottom.

He shot out a hand. "Tom Young."

Cady clasped his calloused hand and introduced herself and Hayden.

"I'm real sorry to hear about your dad, Cady." Tom's joyful expression disappeared. "He was a great guy. One of the best. We all liked having him as part of the club, and we all miss him a lot."

"Thank you," she said sincerely, as it was special to hear such wonderful things about her dad.

Tom stood back. "Come on in. I could only round up a few of the guys on such short notice, but they're here already."

She entered a cottage reminiscent of Kai's place, but larger. Three men in the living area shifted their attention to Cady from where they sat on a sofa and club chairs. She marched straight to them, hoping her quick steps would give her the confidence she needed to potentially hear bad news about her father's past.

She stopped by two wooden chairs placed near the end of the sofa. Tom pressed past her and introduced her and Hayden to the men.

"Have a seat." Tom gestured at the sofa as he settled on one of the wooden chairs.

She sat in the middle, inching close to the baldheaded man named Larry on the end, leaving Hayden plenty of room. Didn't matter. He perched on the arm. Why he didn't want to sit next to her she didn't know, but maybe after last night he didn't feel comfortable with her so close either.

Tom looked at her. "So tell us what we can do to help."

She forced herself to relax. "As you know, my father passed away unexpectedly. Perhaps you thought it was from his quick-moving dementia. But the medical examiner determined Dad had a high level of fentanyl in his blood."

"Fentanyl?" Tom lurched to his feet. "You're kidding,

right? Or am I misunderstanding you to say someone murdered Percy, because we all know he wouldn't be taking fentanyl?"

"No misunderstanding. He wouldn't take that drug." She clutched her hands together in her lap. "He was murdered. I'm in town hoping to find out why and who killed him."

Larry gaped at her. "You don't think we can help with that, do you? We wouldn't have a clue who might possess fentanyl."

She smiled at him. "I didn't think you would. At this point, I'm just gathering facts."

Hayden leaned forward, looking at Larry. "Facts can often be put together to help formulate an investigative strategy or just give us another piece to the puzzle."

"Okay." Tom dropped onto his chair, the shock still lingering in his expression. "What do you want to know?"

"Did my father act any differently in the last few months before he moved?" she asked.

"Well, the dementia had started in by then." Tom's shocked expression morphed into sadness. "So he was forgetting things. Maybe now that I think about it, he did seem a little preoccupied about something, but at the time, I thought he was just trying to deal with the shock of the dementia diagnosis, you know?"

"Same here." Norbert pushed up his thick glasses. "He didn't want to talk about the diagnosis, but we all could see it was taking a toll on him."

They were right. She'd seen the same thing, and it broke her heart to remember it, and she had to fight hard not to start crying. But... "Now that we believe someone murdered him, I'm not sure if it was fear of this person or the dementia bothering him. Did you observe anything else out of the ordinary with him?"

Murmurs of *no* broke out. She looked around the group to see shaking of heads.

"What about anything unusual you might have seen while birdwatching?" Hayden asked.

"I'm assuming you're not talking about birds." Tom gave a wobbly smile. "I don't recall anything unusual." He looked at the other men. "Any of you remember anything odd?"

More head shaking. Her frustration began to build. She had no idea what she expected these men to tell her, but she hoped they could give her a lead of some sort. Maybe it was time to be more specific. "What about any unusual boats or ships in the area?"

"Wait!" Tom sat up in his chair. "I heard the women found in the cave under the surf shop came off of a ship. You don't think this has to do with them, do you?"

Hayden held up a hand. "Once again, we're just fact-finding. What happened at the surf shop was out of the ordinary, and we're looking for things out of the ordinary."

Tom looked at the other men.

"Well, there *is* the boat that ran aground up the coast." Silas's droopy eyelids tightened. "It's a forty-two-foot sport-fishing boat and has been rumored to be linked to smugglers. Smuggling what, I don't know. Could be people like those women, I suppose, but I never heard such a thing mentioned." He looked at his fellow birdwatchers. "Any of you guys hear anything about that?"

"Not me," Tom said.

"Me either," Larry said. "But I thought everyone in town knew about that boat since they have crime scene tape strung all around it and a sign warning people not to board it."

Tom studied Larry. "Don't tell me you ignored the sign and boarded it? 'Cause that sounds exactly like something you would do."

Larry's eyes twinkled with mischief. "I thought about it. I mean, who doesn't want to see inside such an expensive boat? But I didn't do it."

"So your wife was with you, then?" Tom chuckled.

Larry nodded and laughed.

"Is this boat within our city limits or the county's jurisdiction?" Hayden asked, no humor in his tone or appearance.

"County," Silas said. "Not sure who's in charge of getting rid of it, but it hasn't happened. If it involves smuggling, maybe they had to call in the feds, and you know how fast they work." Silas rolled his eyes.

"How long has it been there?" Hayden asked.

"At least a month," Tom said. "If you want a more exact date, you could check old newspapers. They did several stories on it."

Silas crossed his arms. "They should've done a follow-up on why it's still there. It's a magnificent boat for sure, but it still makes our beach look like a dumping ground."

Cady glanced at Hayden to see if he thought this was an interesting lead. But if he did, his expression didn't give it away. If indeed the boat was involved in smuggling, maybe Mina had been called in to search it. She could possess evidence that made no sense at the time but could be relevant to the human trafficking ring.

"What about Kai Nakoa?" Cady asked. "He was good friends with Dad. Was he a bird watcher too?"

"Nope," Tom said. "That guy was happier on water than on land."

"Is there anything else unusual you all can think of?" she asked before they voiced additional questions about Kai.

"Nah." Tom frowned.

Hayden stood and gave Tom a business card. "If you'd

give it some thought and get back to us if anything comes up, I'd appreciate it."

Cady pushed to her feet. "Perhaps, if you would review any pictures you took while birdwatching with Dad in the last few months, you might have captured something to help."

"We'll be glad to check them." Tom got up and saw them out.

After he closed the door, she turned to Hayden. "Do you think we should see Mina in case she has additional information on this beached boat?"

"She'll know something, for sure, but let's head back to the inn and have Nolan call her. If the information is important to an investigation, she might not share it with us. But that could tell us something."

Cady doubted Mina would disclose the info with anyone. Especially if it was related to the cave investigation. All Cady could do was pray and hope Nolan was more persuasive than he'd been in their earlier meetings.

Hayden watched Nolan deep in conversation with Mina as they walked into the conference room. Nolan hadn't been too happy about calling Mina to ask about the boat, but he said he wasn't about to let a potential lead pass them by. Plus, he'd heard back from Sierra. They would take on processing the shop and cave, but they couldn't get anyone on scene until the following morning. Still, it was a big win to have the Veritas team handle forensics.

Cady, along with the rest of the team, were seated around the table where they'd been tossing out their many thoughts on the forty-two-footer that had run aground.

Hayden couldn't believe such a big boat could get

beached until he searched YouTube and saw several even bigger boats plow into the sand. That might answer one of his questions, but he had no idea why the owner would abandon such a pricey boat unless he was engaged in illegal activity.

"We need to get a registration number and find out who owns that thing." Cady took out her notepad and pen, but her gaze shifted to Mina, watching her every move.

Mina, seeming oblivious to Cady's interest, put the large paper evidence bag she carried on the table across from Hayden without any explanation.

He tried to make out the information written on the outside of the bag, but she'd left it at the wrong angle, and he wasn't about to grab official evidence without permission.

He made eye contact with her. "I hope you have answers for us."

She tilted her head and gave him a quizzical look. "Depends on your questions. But if you don't mind, I'd like to grab a cup of coffee before we get started."

"Sorry. I should've offered you one." Hayden gave her a sincere smile. Not that he wanted to wait for answers to his questions. Not with Kai missing and women obviously being trafficked, but that didn't mean he should ignore common courtesy. His mother taught him proper manners before she died. One of the many lessons he carried with him from both of his parents and tried to implement in their honor.

Mina stepped to the long table where Reece had stocked soft drinks in a tray with ice and a big pitcher of iced tea. She'd also brewed two pots of coffee. Mina grabbed a mug and poured the coffee, taking it black. She also picked up a large blueberry muffin fresh from the oven and took an empty chair across from Hayden.

After a long pull on her mug, she glanced around the table. "Before we get started, I wanted to make it clear that I still can't share most investigative details with you. It's not that I don't want to, but my job requires me to follow investigative protocols. I know all of you except Cady can understand my position from your prior law enforcement jobs."

"We do." Nolan searched the team's faces. "And we'll respect that, right?"

Everyone except Cady nodded.

"I'm not sure I understand all the technical rules of what you're allowed to share and not share," she said. "But I'll assume if you don't tell us, you can't."

"Thank you for understanding." Mina smiled at her.

"In that vein," Cady said, "were you able to get my father's police reports?"

Mina nodded. "There's nothing in them to dispute your story."

Cady gave a shaky exhale. "Do they include anything that could help?"

"Maybe. El is reviewing the file in more detail, but like I said, I won't be able to share that information with you."

"Understood," Cady said, but her expression gave away her disappointment.

Mina shifted her attention to Hayden. "Okay. Fire away."

Hayden realized he'd been shaking his leg as he waited. He didn't want to come across as being overeager to get answers so forced himself to plant his foot solidly on the floor. "We heard a rumor that the boat washed up on the beach is associated with smuggling. Is that true?"

Mina rested her hands near the muffin, but didn't touch it. "I suppose it *could* be related. But at this time, we don't have any evidence to suggest that it is."

"But you don't have any evidence to suggest that it isn't either, do you?" Cady asked.

"No. Nothing either way."

"Have you found the boat's owners?" Cady pressed harder.

"No, and it's not for a lack of trying." Mina peeled the paper from her muffin. "We pulled information from the state's boat registration database only to learn it was registered in Delaware to a shell corporation called Marine Investment Associates, LLC."

Cady quickly scribbled in her notepad. "Is Delaware significant?"

"Good question." Mina looked up from her muffin. "Delaware has strong laws that prevent government from revealing the beneficial owner of a given shell corporation. So shell corps aren't required to publicly list the company's owner, which means we couldn't use that route to locate the owner's name. We were able to track down registered company directors, but the names were phony —three guys who agreed to sign their names for a few dollars."

"So it was a wild goose chase." Abby's frustration lingered in her tone. "My experience says shell corps can be legit but also a front for illegal activities. Having bogus directors in play likely indicates someone was trying to skirt the law."

"Exactly." Mina broke off a piece of her muffin, but held it in her hand. "Which is why we had a state forensics team process the boat like we might a crime scene."

"I'm assuming since the boat is still there," Hayden said, "the search and evidence collected were a bust, and you didn't find anything to help locate the owner."

"That's correct." Mina popped the muffin in her mouth, then reached for the evidence bag. She pulled out a plastic bag holding something made of cloth and laid it on the table in front of Hayden. "One thing we did find was a monogrammed handkerchief. It'd fallen behind bench cushions. Note the initials. CAP."

Hayden examined the handkerchief. "Who even carries monogrammed handkerchiefs these days? But that aside, where do you begin to look for someone with those initials? You're probably not looking for your garden variety criminal."

"Precisely our dilemma." She put another bite of the muffin in her mouth.

Hayden passed the bag down the table so each team member could look at the handkerchief.

Mina finished chewing. "Problem is, I need to resolve it soon, as we have to notify the owner he's in violation of the Abandoned and Derelict Vessels Law. The Oregon State Marine Board contracts with us for marine law enforcement services. So this is *my* problem, and I haven't been able to seize the boat without proper notification to the owner."

The handkerchief reached Abby. "Oh, wow!" Her eyes widened in a lightbulb-gone-off moment. "Cody Palmer."

"Palmer?" Hayden closed his eyes for a moment to think. The man owned Tidewater Mansion. A few months ago the team had been accused of stashing Mayor Sutton's body there after they'd supposedly killed him. "How could he be connected to the boat?"

"I don't know that he is." Abby handed the bag to Jude. "But remember I organized all of the records for Mayor Sutton's investigation. That included contracts for Tidewater Mansion, all signed by Palmer. His signature included his middle initial."

"Let me guess." Gabe smirked slightly. "It was A."

Abby nodded. "It could just be a coincidence, but I really don't believe in coincidences."

"Neither do I," Mina said. "Nor do most law enforcement officers."

Nolan shifted his attention to Mina. "Do you think Palmer could be the boat owner? The man behind the shell corp?"

She set her coffee mug on the table, her eyes alight with enthusiasm. "It's possible. When we interviewed him about Tidewater Mansion, he was overly antagonistic and evasive, like he had a thing against law enforcement."

"He's also a lawyer and a pretty sharp dresser who might carry a handkerchief," Nolan said.

Gabe planted his hands on the table. "And he didn't have security cameras at the mansion because he said his guests needed privacy. Could be because his guests are involved in illegal activities with him."

Mina rubbed her thumb around the top of her coffee cup. "The more I think about it, the more it seems possible Palmer could be the owner and was using the boat for no good. I'll get El on it right away and see if she can link him to the company or find any indication that he's a boater."

"This might be a long shot," Cady said, "but whoever the owner is, Palmer or someone else, could be using this boat for ferrying people from a ship to shore as my dad said in his video."

"If we embrace your theory," Mina said, "Palmer could be connected to Wade Collins. I'll have El look into that too."

Hayden started to warm to the idea. "You have Palmer's fingerprints and DNA on file from the mayor's investigation, right?"

She nodded. "We do, but we searched databases at that time, and he doesn't have a criminal record."

Abby leaned forward. "What about prints and DNA from the boat?"

Mina frowned. "We have prints, but we didn't get a data-base match, and we only lifted potential DNA samples.

Unfortunately, our budget doesn't stretch to processing them when we don't have a known suspect for comparison."

"But we could have Veritas run the DNA and prints from the boat against the earlier samples they have from Palmer," Hayden said. "We could also have Nick do a deep dive on Palmer to see if he can find a connection to the shell corp."

"Sure thing." Mina frowned. "Only if you all plan to pay for it. I can't see them doing another pro bono job after agreeing to do the surf shop and cave."

"Nick already agreed to crack the drive from Kai's place at no charge, so I think he'd agree to the additional work."

"It's worth a try." Mina continued to look at Hayden, but lifted an eyebrow. "I expect to be looped in on any information Veritas discovers."

"Of course," Hayden said and glanced at his teammates. "To that end, I need someone to take the drive to Nick."

"Road trip." Jude pumped up a hand and grinned at Reece. "You game?"

Hayden wasn't surprised Jude asked Reece to join him. The two of them had a deep friendship going back to their college days. At one point, the rest of the team thought their connection was romantic, but they both emphatically put an end to the notion.

She offered him one of her easy-going smiles. "If it keeps you out of trouble, then I'm in."

"Sweet!" His smile widened. "If we leave right after we break up here, we can be back by six."

Reece wrinkled her nose. "You'll be pushing it, but with the way you drive, I can believe it might be sooner."

"I did not just hear that." Mina laughed but quickly sobered. "It's always good to have a well-respected group like the Veritas team on our side. Too bad we didn't figure out the initials when the boat ran aground, or we could've used them to process that scene. I'm sure Sierra and her forensic staff would've given us better forensics to go on."

"We could ask them now, right?" Cady asked.

Mina frowned. "We could, but the scene hasn't been secured, and despite our warning signs, people will have boarded it to check things out."

She had a point, but they couldn't have a do-over, and Hayden wouldn't spend any time thinking about it. "Let's stay positive. The important thing is we have a world-class forensic team to help us."

Now, all they had to do was hope any information the Veritas staff provided would give the team a viable suspect and a lead on Kai's whereabouts.

14

Cady grew antsy and looked around the group to judge their moods. She wasn't used to this much discussion and planning. Once a story was assigned to her, she was her own boss for the most part. Sure, her editor reviewed her articles and suggested changes most of the time. Even when she didn't agree with the changes, her editor was very reasonable, and they could talk them out until they reached a compromise.

But this? All the rules law enforcement had to consider? Then waiting on forensics. The sitting. The hoping. She was a doer, and if writing a story, she would've rushed right out and interviewed these people. Or if they were unavailable right away, she would've looked for other sources who might give her the information she needed.

She wasn't one to not speak up when she had an opinion, even if others wouldn't like what she had to say. "This forensic business is great, but it feels like we're wasting time waiting for it and not acting. This is our only lead, so what can we do until we have the forensics results?"

"Agreed." Hayden faced Mina. "Do we have your permission to search the boat on the beach?"

She nodded. "But after my deputies and forensics processed the place, I don't expect you'll find anything. If you do by some off chance locate something, make sure I'm the first person to know about it."

Hayden looked away as if he wouldn't promise.

"The team still has plans to tail Wade Collins tomorrow night," Reece said.

He cast Reece a thankful look, likely for the change in subject, though Mina didn't take her eyes off him.

"But to Cady's point," Reece continued. "None of us wants to sit around and wait on the Veritas Center, so we should be keeping a covert eye not only on Collins but Palmer too."

"To be perfectly technical, that's sitting around too." Jude laughed.

Hayden rolled his eyes. "But it's actively sitting around. I call dibs on the first shift with Palmer, and you know there's no way I'll miss tailing Collins when he makes his boat run."

"I'll go with you on both," Cady said and waited for him to disagree.

"Sure thing." He sounded casual, but his hands clenched on the table.

Didn't he want her with him? Maybe he was simply concerned for her safety, but maybe he didn't want to be alone with her.

"Dude, not a one of us thought you'd miss out on that excitement." Gabe chuckled. "I call second dibs on Collins, but watching these guys? Boring. I'll pass if you don't need my help."

Nolan looked at Gabe. "I can prepare a schedule. See if we need you or not. I'll email the details to everyone."

"Just a reminder." Mina made eye contact with everyone at the table. "We coordinate on everything, and none of you are to take any action. Let my team handle it."

Cady wished she could take a picture of the team members' faces. Mina was doing her job, and apparently doing it well, but their disappointment took center stage. Gabe's expression also held a bit of rebellion as he lifted his chin and pointed it at her. He was the wildcard in the group. No question about it. If anyone went rogue and struck out on his own, it would probably be Gabe.

"Other than calling dibs on stakeout times, how do we start?" Cady asked. "I mean, we have to first find the guys."

The team turned to look at Reece.

"Okay, fine." She grinned. "Good old Betty Lou can handle that for you."

Reece put her fingers to her ear and mouth as if on the phone. "Oh, Mr. Palmer. I'm so glad I reached you. This is Betty Lou from the neighborhood watch. We've had a rash of break-ins in the neighborhood. I'm in charge of calling everyone to find out if they've had a break-in or any evidence of an attempted break-in. Are you at home and can you check your front door for any damage?"

"Good old Betty Lou sure can come in handy." Gabe chuckled. "Now all she needs is Palmer's phone number."

"I've got it in the reports I filed for the mayor's investigation." Abby opened her laptop, and within moments, jotted something on a piece of paper and slid it to Reece. "Here you go, Betty Lou. Palmer's cell phone. Best of luck in tracking him down."

Abby and Reece shared a chuckle. Over time, Cady had seen these fine investigators use humor to cover up the awful situations they were involved in. She wasn't sure she could laugh quite as easily with such dire consequences on the line, but she suspected they'd learned it when they witnessed horrific things in their former law enforcement jobs.

Horrific things like the trafficking of defenseless women they encountered in the cave.

Was there anything worse than taking a human being against her will and selling her to the highest bidder? Or forcing someone to participate in slave labor? Or more horrific, to participate in prostitution? Something Cady didn't want to think about.

But she *had* to think about it. She had to think about these men who could be so cruel and even responsible for her father's death. If they were the men she sought, she would make sure they paid in every way allowed by the law.

Cady fidgeted in the passenger seat of Hayden's vehicle and couldn't seem to settle. She'd been jumpy since Hayden took her to their well-stocked equipment room and armory. He'd said they could use the downtime to search the abandoned boat while Reece tracked Palmer's location, and he wouldn't proceed without the right gear.

Guns galore had greeted her. Handguns. Rifles. More ammunition than she could ever imagine anyone needing. Couple all of that with night vision goggles and binoculars, plus many gadget bags stuffed with camera gear, and she'd only been able to stare.

Hayden had fairly glowed when he talked about each piece of equipment and firearm, but he'd said they would take just a few of the weapons as a precaution in case Palmer turned on them. Which Hayden didn't believe he would do.

So forget about it. Relax.

She watched the road ahead as they arrived at the beach, and Hayden parked as close as he could to the abandoned boat.

She stepped out of his vehicle and was met by a bright afternoon sky scattered with soft, white clouds. The air was mild—typical for the Oregon coast, where even in the peak of summer, the temperature rarely climbed above seventy degrees.

A brisk wind swept across the sand, whipping it into the air and stinging her skin. She ducked her head against the gusts and headed for the boat, not bothering to check if Hayden was behind her.

He soon caught up. "It might be broad daylight, but we need to stay alert. Never know who might be watching the boat."

Concern lifting her head, she cupped her hand around her eyes to keep the sand out. Seeing the boat up close made her take a step back. Boat, hah! It was more like a yacht, if you asked her.

She looked at Hayden. "Do you remember the story about a beach near Florence when a whale beached itself on shore?"

He shook his head.

"It was years ago, but authorities didn't have a clue how to get rid of it. So believe it or not they blew up the rotting carcass with dynamite, hoping it would disintegrate."

"They what?" He blinked at her. "Sounds like all kinds of trouble waiting to happen."

"It was. The big kaboom, and then small, foul-smelling pieces of whale showered everyone who'd come to see the event and tainted the beach. It was a failure of epic proportions."

"And one I doubt they'll ever repeat again." Shaking his head, he led the way to a ladder on the side of the boat and looked back at her. "I'll go first and let you know if it's safe to board. Stay alert."

He started up the ladder and climbed over the side, soon disappearing from view. She forgot all about the whale fiasco as unease had her gnawing on her lip. The ladder he'd climbed led to an open area on the first level of the boat, and another one rose up to a top level located above a closed section. It appeared as if the upper level was for the pilot and the living quarters took up the middle.

Hayden poked his head over the side. "It's clear to board."

She took one last look around, then started up the ladder and landed on the boat's open deck. She'd been on plenty of boats in her life, and it felt odd for this one to be stationary and not rocking with the water.

"Let's start in the cabin." Hayden handed her a pair of disposable gloves. "Don't touch anything without these on."

She nodded, and he pointed at a closed door in the middle.

She slipped on the gloves and stepped ahead of him, pushing through the door. Inside, a cozy living area unfolded before her, its mahogany-paneled walls giving the space a warm, refined feel. To her right, a compact kitchen gleamed with stainless steel appliances, and just beyond that, a doorway revealed a stairwell leading below. Windows lined nearly all of the walls, framing the stunning view from every possible angle.

"Straight ahead are two bedrooms," he said. "Mind searching the one on the right, and I'll take the one on the left?"

"Works for me." Before she stressed over being with him in such tight quarters, she set off, passing a small bathroom called a head in the boating world and entering the berth, where a queen-sized bed consumed most of the space.

The boat owner had likely crammed trafficked people in these rooms. Shoulder to shoulder. Terrified. Maybe alone. Maybe beside their family. Everything they'd known and cherished left behind. Wondering what their future would hold.

Shuddering, she got busy with her search before her thoughts made her cry. She tore off the bedding. Flipped the mattress from the platform to the floor. Felt the pillows. Pulled open drawers at the end of the bed.

Nothing.

Backing out, she headed for the other bedroom. "I didn't find anything."

Hayden looked up. "Nothing here either. If you want to go back to the galley, I'll take the bathroom."

She hurried out of the small space and started in the cabinets, going straight for the mugs since she'd been successful in finding the flash drive in a mug at Kai's cottage. She jiggled and peered inside every one, finding nothing. Finally, she moved on to other cupboards until she'd completely searched each one.

Okay, maybe the appliances held a lead. Microwave first. Empty. Small oven next, where she ran her hand over the top in case they taped something inside. Her fingers met only the smooth finish of the oven. Last was the refrigerator and freezer—both warm now, unused since the boat had been abandoned. The fridge held only a few bottles of water. In the freezer sat oversized ice cube trays filled with water, a small pint of strawberry ice cream, and a handful of frozen entrées.

Law enforcement had obviously left these items alone, but why? If what Abby had said at Kai's house held true, criminals hid things in food packaging. The ice cream had been opened, so she started there. She took the carton to the sink and rattled a spoon around the inside. It connected with something hard and reverberated in her hand.

But what?

Holding her breath in hopes the faucet would work, she

turned it on. *Perfect.* A steady stream poured out, and she placed the container beneath it. Light strawberry colored liquid flowed over her gloved hands. Finally something glistened in the container, and she picked it out.

A key!

"Hayden!" She rinsed the key under the water as she waited for him to join her.

His footsteps charged in her direction.

She faced the doorway and held up the key. "It was in the ice cream container. I'm surprised the forensics team missed this."

He shook his head. "Who would leave a container like that without checking it? Not very good policing if you ask me."

"Maybe someone added it after the search."

His eyebrows puzzled together. "That could've happened, I suppose, but why would anyone hide a potential lead when law enforcement could come back?"

"You're right. It doesn't make sense. We need to get this key to Mina."

"We'll do that, for sure." He glanced around as if thinking. "But let's keep this bit of news to ourselves for now. Especially since you rinsed the ice cream away, and it could be construed as tampering with evidence."

She gaped at him. "You don't think she'll believe that, do you? I mean she gave us permission to search the boat."

"Yes, but she wanted to be notified first if we found anything, and she's a by-the-book kind of sheriff. I can see her being irritated with us, but I can't see her charging you with interfering with an investigation or anything."

Cady could only pray he was right.

"Now if we figure out what it's for and check it out before telling her, that might be another story. But I won't let that stop me. Not when she won't share any information about what she locates."

"You're not planning to do that?"

"I am, but you don't need to be involved."

Would she do something that could make Mina press charges against her? Looked like it. "I'm coming with you."

He held out his hand. "Can I see the key?"

"Do you want me to dry it first?"

He shook his head. "If there're any fingerprints, you could wipe them off."

"Oh, right, I didn't think of that. I hope running it under water didn't wash any off." She placed it on his gloved palm.

"Prints can survive water, but it could depend on how forcefully you rinsed it." He turned the key over a few times. "It's engraved with the number twenty-three. Looks to me like it's for an old locker. If we're talking about public lockers, the only ones I know of in Lost Lake are at the bus station, and they're original to the old building."

"The others might know of different places with lockers."

"I'll text them a picture and ask." He laid the key on the counter and used his phone to snap a picture. Then his thumbs raced over the screen. He looked up. "I didn't find anything in the bathroom. All that's left is the entry area and upper deck. Which would you like to take?"

"I'm not real big on heights, so I'd like to stay on this level."

He put the key in a small zipper bag he'd grabbed from a box on the counter and pocketed it. "We'll finish up here, and hopefully we'll still have time to go to the bus station."

She nodded and went outside, her heart thumping. If the key did indeed fit a bus station locker, they might locate that elusive lead that would take them straight to Kai and her father's killer.

15

Hayden pulled into the bus station parking lot in downtown Lost Lake, with Cady riding shotgun. His teammates didn't know of any other public lockers in town, and Nolan had offered to run it by Mina, but Hayden suspected she'd demand control of the key, so he asked Nolan to hold off—at least until he had a chance to check the bus station.

His phone displayed a text. "It's from Reece."

Cady moved closer to him. "What does it say?"

"Palmer's still at his office, but will be home in a little over an hour." He texted his acknowledgment and put his phone away. "We'll make our way over there to set up before he gets home."

"Do we still have time to check the lockers?" Cady asked.

He met her gaze over the console and nodded. "Someone could've been keeping an eye on the boat and saw us search it. So be alert and aware of your surroundings."

She gnawed on her lower lip. "Or someone could even be here watching the lockers, right?"

"I suppose they could know about the locker but didn't have the key." He took another look around the area for anyone acting suspicious. "Even more reason to keep our eyes open."

She gave a quick nod and stepped out of the vehicle without a word.

He quickly slid out and jogged to catch up to her. Together, they made their way to the old station building that had been in service since the 1920s. Wide, black-rimmed glass doors and windows filled the entire front wall of the two-story structure, which was one of the few buildings in town constructed of brick. Not surprising in the big logging state of Oregon.

He gave the heavy door a firm pull and stepped aside to let Cady enter first. Following her into the grand, two-story lobby, he was immediately struck by the sweeping view of the ocean beyond. On the far wall, a set of glass doors mirrored those at the entrance, framing the rolling waves in the distance. Despite the clusters of bolted-down chairs and the steady flow of rushing passengers, the ocean's rhythm remained visible and steady.

The air carried a mixture of scents—the salty tang of the sea mingled with the buttery aroma of fresh popcorn and the faint mustiness of an aging building. Oddly, it comforted him. Maybe it was the familiarity. His parents had always loved antiques, and he'd learned early on to find beauty in things with a little age and history.

He glanced around, checking for anyone casting a suspicious eye in their direction. Finding no one, he leaned closer to Cady. "The lockers are on the right side in the back. Lead the way."

She started out at a quick clip, her shoes thumping a cadence on the marble tile floors. He matched her pace until they reached the wooden lockers with antique brass hardware. Maintenance on these old locks had to be a challenge, and he respected the people of Lost Lake for keeping the history of this place even when it might not be practical.

He pulled out the key and confirmed they were looking for number twenty-three.

Cady beat him to the correct locker and was tapping the brass number. "This one. Hurry."

He crossed the space and inserted the key. Twisted. The lock clicked. The door popped and swung out an inch. She shot a hand in front of him and jerked the door fully open.

"Papers." She frowned and stared at the open locker. "Just a stack of papers. Nothing more." She started to reach inside.

He blocked her with a hand in front of the locker. "We need gloves again."

He dug a pair from his pocket and put them on. Removing the documents, he quickly scanned them. "Wow! Not what I expected at all. Looks like documents linking Kai to financial transactions with a foreign group."

"Kai!" A rapid flurry of blinks revealed her surprise. "Are you sure?"

Hayden nodded, his mind racing with what to do going forward. "We need to thoroughly review these documents and do extensive research on this group." He glanced around, looking for anyone watching them.

She held out her hand. "Let me see."

"Not here. Not out in the open."

Her eyes lost the spark of excitement, and she pinched the bridge of her nose.

"Hang in there. We can start on it while we stake out Palmer's place." Hayden rolled the papers into a cylinder and tucked them under his arm. He secured the locker and pocketed the key. "Let's move."

She started off, but looked back at him. "Why do you

think that key was left in the ice cream? To hide it so they didn't get caught with it or for someone else to pick it up?"

"I'd rather not speculate until I've read through these papers." He accelerated his speed, eyes scanning their surroundings. The terminal buzzed with the usual activity—travelers watching the monitors, chatting with companions, or lining up at food stands.

No one stood out. No one seemed to notice them. And more importantly, no one looked suspicious.

Outside, he doubled his surveillance and drew Cady close to him, but they arrived at his Raptor without any issue.

He handed the documents to her. "I know you'll want to dig into these right away, but resist the urge. I could use help keeping an eye on the area, until I'm sure no one is watching us."

Her pleasant expression vanished. She turned to stare out the window, her back suddenly stiff with tension. Hayden didn't enjoy scaring her, but his priority was keeping them safe.

He fired up the engine and eased out of his space. A vintage black Ford pickup—with a freshly installed bullbar on the front—rolled toward them. Hayden braked, letting it pass. The truck moved slowly at first. Creeping ahead.

"Come on. Get out of the way." Hayden had half a mind to pull out as he didn't want to be late for Palmer's homecoming,

Before he could react, the driver hit the gas, the engine snarling under the sudden strain. The truck surged forward—aimed directly at Hayden's side of the Raptor. He caught sight of not one, but two men inside the cab.

The truck careened toward him.

"Look out!" Cady shouted.

Instinct taking over, Hayden threw an arm out across her. The truck's heavy-duty bullbar crashed into the front end of the Raptor on his side with a brutal force. The vehicle jolted sideways, slamming it into a parked SUV, and airbags rocketed out to slam him in the face. His body rattled from the collision just as the side airbag exploded against him. The Raptor rocked violently, metal groaning under the crushing force.

"Are you okay?" He punched down the airbags, but didn't take his eyes off the Ford.

"Fine," she said. One word, but her shaky tone gave away her fear. "What's going on?"

"Not sure. They could've seen us take the documents from the locker, and they want them." At least that was the only logical explanation at the moment, but he didn't have time to think about it any further.

If he was right, they'd stop at nothing to recover them. It wasn't something he could say out loud without pushing Cady into further panic. But he couldn't ignore the possibility. He needed to prepare himself and take a more defensive stance.

He had to get out of there, but how? The truck pinned his vehicle on the side.

He couldn't wait for them to move again. He backed up to release his vehicle and clear the Ford.

The truck's bullbar caught. He shifted into drive and floored it. Still trapped.

He reversed again. His vehicle moved forward. Yes! He repeated the pattern. Once. Twice. Finally, he was free.

The truck eased back as if planning to charge again.

Hayden had to take quick action. Now!

He shifted into drive but took one last look at the Ford.

The passenger window lowered.

The flash of a silver handgun caught his eye.

"Gun! Down!" He reached across the seat and pressed his hand against Cady's neck until she was folded in half.

A gunshot sounded.

The bullet pierced the rear window, and the air trembled with its wake.

Hayden clasped the steering wheel. "Stay down until I tell you it's safe to sit up."

He ducked as low as he could go and gunned the engine. Two rapid bullets sliced through his vehicle. He kept going and cleared the truck.

Three speedy shots split the air, sounding like a car backfiring.

He floored the gas pedal. Thankfully his off-road vehicle withstood the collision and instantly reacted, screaming out of the parking lot and onto the main road. He'd purchased the Raptor for its big engine, and it didn't disappoint.

The truck raced after them, their powerful engine disturbing the quiet. Not as much as their continued gunfire.

Pop. Pop. Pop.

Cady cringed as each report sounded and the bullets struck his Raptor.

He'd be in his element at this high speed if he didn't have a gunman bearing down on them. "My phone is in the center console. Stay down and call Nolan."

He sensed her reaching for the phone, but didn't risk taking his eyes off the road other than to glance in the rearview mirror. He caught the license plate number on the pickup and memorized it.

The highway led out of town to the coast, an open road where he could really fire up his vehicle and scream away from their tail. The road paralleled a train track. The sharp call of a train whistle pierced the air, signaling the engine's arrival.

Up ahead, the safety gate at the intersection began to lower. He glanced down the tracks, calculating the distance, the timing. Gauging how long he had if he made a hard right and gunned it across before the train arrived.

He could do it. Just barely, but with bullets flying his way, he would risk it.

"Hold on," he said and punched the gas pedal.

His Raptor shot forward and careened around the sharp turn. His muscles strained under the tension of keeping his vehicle on the road. They flew under the gate with precious moments to lose. The truck tailing them slammed on their brakes, fishtailing wildly while the train barreled across the road.

He didn't let up on the gas. "When you connect with Nolan, put him on speaker."

She relayed the information to Nolan, and Hayden looked in the rearview mirror, glad to see a long train rumble toward the south, a solid barrier between them and the truck on the other side of the tracks. His risk had paid off. They now had plenty of time to lose their tail and make their way to Palmer's place without being seen.

Still bent in half, Cady held out the phone.

"We had a little altercation." Hayden described the documents they located along with the Ford's chase and their current location. "I ditched them, and we're still headed to Palmer's place but might need backup."

"We can't risk losing the documents," Nolan said. "We can keep them safe here and make copies too in case something happens with the originals. I'll meet you at Palmer's place to collect them and bring them back here."

"Roger that." He tapped the screen to end the call, then checked his rearview mirror.

The road stretched out as far as he could see without a

vehicle in sight. Good. They'd lost their tail. He glanced at Cady. "Looks like it's safe for you to sit up."

She raised up and stretched. "Who are these guys?"

"Not sure, but I got their license plate and will have someone run it as soon as possible."

"This is surreal." She shook her head. "I've been threatened on the job, but I've never been followed. And I've certainly never been chased by some gun-wielding maniac." She shuddered. "What if they're the men who killed my dad?"

He slowed and met her gaze. "Then we know they're capable of murder, so we need to be vigilant."

And if they were afraid of being exposed and thrown in prison for what they'd done, Hayden doubted they'd draw any lines. They'd do whatever it took—no limits, not even stopping at committing another murder.

16

Cady barely saw the landscape outside her window as their vehicle raced toward Palmer's house. She could hardly hold her tears back either. They'd survived. They were alive! Uninjured. Too many bullets to count had been fired at them. The outside of the vehicle probably looked like it had been through a war zone—riddled with holes.

She reached up to smooth wayward hair back into place, but her hand shook, making it worse. Her heart rate continued to beat at an urgent rate and adrenaline raced through her body.

She needed a distraction. Needed one badly. She picked up the documents and started to read. The papers shook under her trembling hands, but laying the documents on shaky legs wasn't any better. Still, she read on. By the time she reached the third page, she had to share what she'd discovered. "This report details a recent covert plan to traffic women. It was conceived by the Emerald Scorpion Group."

"Never heard of them." Hayden's hands tightened on the steering wheel. "But if they're behind the trafficking, they're not likely a legit business."

"Agreed, but that's not the worst thing. There's a sinister

twist." She braced herself before revealing the next part. "The money to fund the plan was funneled through Kai's shop."

He flashed her a wide-eyed look. "Kai? Can't be, can it? Not when he helped rescue the women we discovered in the cave."

He had a good point. One she hadn't considered yet. "Maybe he was involved in the beginning, but then had a change of heart and was trying to make up for his part in the operation."

"Or maybe they had something on him, and he was funneling the money against his will. Could be why he's missing." Hayden shook his head. "If I'm right, that doesn't bode well for his safety."

If he's even still alive. Hayden didn't say it, but he had to be thinking it just as she was. She wouldn't say it either.

"Let me see what else I can find out before we get to Palmer's place." She turned her attention back to the documents, but her phone rang. "It's Fletcher Jarvis, the reporter I emailed about Emei Gau."

"Answer. Find out what he knows." The vehicle seemed to come alive with the energy behind Hayden's reply.

She accepted the call and chose speaker so Hayden could listen. "Thanks for getting back to me, Fletcher."

"You wanted information on Emei." His professional, no-nonsense tone gave her a moment's pause. Would he actually share information he had most likely painstakingly gathered?

She had to be careful and watch every word. Starting with flattery. "I read your article on human trafficking. Great job."

He didn't speak at first, but then a breath sounding like the hiss of a snake came through the phone. "I don't respond well to compliments when someone wants something from me."

Oops. "It *was* well written, and I wouldn't say that if it wasn't true. But I can understand you calling my motives into question." She paused to gather her thoughts and to make sure she didn't sound desperate for information. "I wondered if you had additional background information you didn't use in the article. Maybe something you couldn't confirm with a source."

That silence filled the phone again. Had she stepped on his toes for a second time? Could be, but she wouldn't say anything to pressure him. Waiting him out seemed like the best course of action.

"Before I share," his sharp voice cut through the stillness, "I need to know the reason for your question."

Not a surprising response. If someone called her and wanted the research she didn't publish behind an article, she would be hard-pressed to share the information. Her best approach was to be totally honest with him and let him know what they were facing. She explained about the women they'd located in the cave. "So, if Emei is somehow linked to these other women, and you share your resources, we might be able to find the traffickers."

"What's in it for me?"

Ooh, selfish much? Cady gritted her teeth. People's lives were on the line, and his behavior was unacceptable. Still, it wasn't unusual in her profession to find people trying to get to the top of their game, whatever the cost. "If you're hoping for an exclusive on this story, we can allow that to some extent after the perpetrators have been found and jailed."

"What does 'to some extent' mean?" He obviously was suspicious of every little detail and questioning until he had an answer. Perfect qualities and approach for a reporter.

At least that's the way she did the job. "We'll have to get

agreement from all parties to allow you to publish the story."

"I don't know." A heavy sigh passed through the speaker. "Odds are good one of them will say no."

She was starting to lose her patience. "You do know we can turn this over to law enforcement, who can subpoena the information from you."

"Doesn't mean I have to give it to them."

"Are you really willing to take a stand over this story? To go to jail for contempt?" She tried to remain calm but her voice rose, revealing her full-blown irritation.

"Nah, probably not."

She drew in a lungful of air, steadying her nerves, and let it slip out silently. "So, did you discover the identity of the people behind the trafficking but couldn't prove it?"

"I think so, yeah." He cleared his throat, but didn't elaborate.

Okay fine. She'd give him a little information to get a little more from him. "Did you happen to run across a man named Kai Nakoa?"

"Yeah. Yeah, I did." His tone grew more animated. "He seemed to be the money man for the Emerald Scorpion Group. Company's registered in Delaware, but definitely has Chinese backing."

Cady shot Hayden a glance and saw the same shock that swept through her when Fletcher mentioned the name of the group she'd discovered in the documents. "So you think Emei was smuggled into the country by this organization?"

"I do, though she was unable to identify any of the officers of the company or Kai Nakoa. But..." He let his voice drop off in a dramatic pause. "I dug into three other locals in this investigation too."

Three? Only two suspects were on their radar, Palmer and Collins.

Cady worked on calming her nerves. If she seemed overeager, he'd know he had the upper hand. "Care to share their names?"

"Sorry, no can do. I don't have actual names, which is why I couldn't use them in my story. I only had code names from the dark web that I wasn't able to connect to actual people."

Oh man, if he'd only had names... But this was a lead nonetheless. "Can you email me the code names and the websites where you found them?"

"Sure, yeah, but you better hold true to your promise."

The implied threat didn't have any impact on her. Not when she was already planning to follow through on her promise. "I will, and if you can think of anything else that might help, include that in the email too."

"Just like a reporter. Always wanting more and more and more." He huffed and ended the call.

She flashed a look at Hayden. "That's a start, right? With your computer skills, you should be able to do something with the code names."

"Maybe." He kept his attention on the road as he turned the corner. "The dark web is a whole other world. It's tough to navigate and almost impossible to locate information. After all, it only exists to hide illegal activities from authorities."

"Sure, yeah, I've run into that in my investigations, but it's not impossible for computer professionals, right?"

He white-knuckled the steering wheel again. "I'll give it my best shot, but I can't promise anything. I have legit skills, if I do say so myself, but I'm an amateur compared to guys like Nick at Veritas. This might be another job for him."

Please let one of them discover the identity of these local men.

"I know you'll do your best, and if you can't figure it out, you'll call Nick."

"No point in waiting to contact Nick. Not with Kai missing and these very dangerous people in his life."

She didn't need to know Kai personally for her stomach to twist at the thought of him in the hands of killers—imagining what he might be enduring, or worse, what terrible things had already happened to him.

She swallowed away the discomforting feeling and went back to reviewing the documents, only putting them away when they neared Palmer's house. Hayden located a wildlife area with a dense cluster of trees that offered cover from the neighbors while still providing a clear view of the house.

"Nolan's not here yet." Hayden shifted into gear and grabbed his phone. "I'll text Nick so when you get the info from Fletcher, we can send it right to him."

He thumbed his phone, and Cady took a long look at Palmer's expansive house perched on a hill overlooking the ocean. Stone steps led up to the two-story building featuring double-height windows with tall shutters, all fronted by a large, perfectly manicured lawn.

The guy had money. No doubt. Question was, did it come from human trafficking or from his work as a lawyer? If the lawyer, then was there someone else in the area with CAP initials? Actually, the person wouldn't even have to be from the area. Deciding the handkerchief belonged to Palmer was a long shot. One she didn't have a lot of confidence in at the moment.

Were they better off reviewing the documents in further detail, or for Hayden to search for the men behind the code names shared by Fletcher than watching this guy?

Hayden's phone chimed. "Nick's on board."

"I hope I get to meet him and offer my thanks."

"That can probably be arranged." He looked up at the rearview mirror. "Nolan's pulling up behind us now. I'm going to greet him."

He didn't suggest she should stay in the vehicle, so she slid out too, bringing the documents with her. She paused to take in the bullet-riddled vehicle, stifling a gasp that might tell Hayden how afraid she'd been in the shooting. She ran her finger over a sharp hole in the rear door. Then over another one. A shudder ran through her body.

She couldn't let Hayden or Nolan see how the damage upset her, or they might suggest she go back to the inn and not participate in any of the missions. She couldn't have that happen. Not at all.

She willed herself to calm down and walked back to Nolan's vehicle.

His window was open, and he leaned his head out. "You two okay?"

Hayden nodded.

"I'm good," she said, and did her best to downplay her continuing unease.

Hayden planted his hands on his hips. "My Raptor sustained a lot of damage, but thankfully it's still drivable."

Nolan peered at the vehicle. "It'll need a lot of bodywork for sure. Thank goodness we have good insurance."

He pointed at the papers in Cady's arms. "Those the documents?"

She nodded. "As much as I want to review them here, I get that it's not safe. Like you said, it's better for you to take and scan them so we have more than one copy." She passed the documents through the window.

Nolan laid the stack on the passenger seat. "After I scan them, we should turn the originals over to Mina, along with the key."

"Agreed." Hayden dug the key from his pocket and handed it to his teammate as he described Cady's phone call with Fletcher.

Nolan narrowed his eyes. "Sounds like you need time to run this lead down."

"I do," Hayden said. "But we can't leave here with Palmer due home any minute."

"Good point," he replied. "I'd stay, but I have an appointment I can't cancel. As soon as that's over I'll make some calls and arrange for someone to replace you."

"Let me know who's coming and when." Hayden stepped back.

Nolan gave a quick salute and cranked his engine.

Cady stood next to Hayden, and they watched Nolan drive away.

"Time to get eyes on Palmer." Hayden spun and marched toward his vehicle.

She had to jog to keep up with him, but they both slid inside at the same time.

He reached behind his seat to grab a tote bag. "Good. The bag escaped any bullets."

"That's remarkable, considering the outside of the vehicle." She worked hard not to shiver at the thought of the bullets and alert Hayden to her ongoing unease.

From the bag, he handed her a pair of binoculars, then took a pair for himself and aimed them at the house. "No sign of Palmer yet. But we're a little early, so that's not surprising."

She lowered her binoculars and swiveled in her seat. "Do you really think this will be helpful? I mean, Palmer will hardly stand out on the sidewalk and tell us he's guilty of human trafficking."

Hayden continued to watch the house. "You're right. It won't be that easy. The best we can hope for is witnessing something he might carry into or bring out of the house. Maybe he goes somewhere, and we tail him. That provides another lead."

He laid his binoculars on the console and retrieved his gadget bag that also looked free of bullet holes. "No matter what happens, we'll be ready for it."

He took out a digital camera. Even with her limited experience with cameras, she knew he held a top-of-the-line 35mm SLR.

He screwed a long lens on the front and lifted the viewfinder to his eyes. "Hold up. He's just pulling onto his street."

She picked up her binoculars again and zoomed in on the front of the property. A black Mercedes drove at a low speed toward the house. The garage door swung open, but the car stopped in the driveway. A tall man wearing a black suit, white shirt, and striped necktie slid out and started for the front door. She zoomed in on his upper body to see his thick head of dark hair, a wide jaw, and buff body. He looked like the pictures she'd seen of Palmer, and since this was his house, he probably was Palmer.

"Man," she said, keeping her binoculars locked on him. "These binoculars can see everything down to the pin on his lapel."

"The very reason we bought the best high-powered binoculars we could afford. It's the little details that can sometimes give you the big leads."

Palmer strode confidently to the front door and squatted in front of the keyless entry lock. He entered his code, giving her full view of the number. "Did you catch his code?"

"Six-three-seven-nine-three. Simple enough to remember in case we need it."

"Speak for yourself. I'm going to jot it down." She grabbed her notepad and a pen from her purse to record the number before quickly returning her attention to Palmer's actions.

Squatting, he was moving the door and studying it up

close. He took out his cell phone and aimed it at the door. "Looks like he's taking pictures of the lock."

"Or he could be magnifying the lock for a better look at any signs of a break-in."

"Something I wouldn't have thought to do," she said, but then she wasn't a suspicious criminal like he might be. "It still amazes me that an astute attorney and businessman like Palmer actually fell for Betty Lou's story."

"Not really." Hayden glanced at her. "I should've let you listen in on Reece's call. She can be very convincing." A lopsided grin crossed his face.

Captivating. She had to look away before getting swamped in emotions.

She lifted her binoculars. Another car pulled up in front of Palmer's house as he went inside and closed his door. She couldn't make out the driver's face. "Who could that be?"

Hayden flashed up his camera and adjusted his lens.

The guy in the car started to get out.

She held her breath as she waited to see his face, her hands trembling.

Hayden clicked away on the shutter. "Collins! It's Wade Collins."

"Really? They know each other?"

"We'll soon find out."

Collins marched up to the door and rang the bell. She counted to five, and Palmer opened the door. His expectant expression morphed into anger, and he appeared to be spewing expletives at Collins, his hands flying in all directions.

"We need to get closer," she said. "Hear what they're saying."

Hayden kept clicking the shutter release button. "No need."

"But..."

He flashed up a hand. "Hold on. You'll see."

His finger went back to pressing the button, and she watched Collins and Palmer through her binoculars. "Looks like they're arguing."

"They both seem mad about something."

Collins spun and marched to his car, then roared away as Palmer slammed the door.

Hayden lowered his camera and opened his door. "Switch places with me."

Before she could ask why he bailed out and came around the back.

She stared at him. "What's going on?"

"You wanted to know what they were saying, right?"

"Yes."

"Then get behind the wheel, and you'll find out."

Why he needed the mystery behind his actions, she didn't know, but she complied and got out of the vehicle.

Hopefully, whatever he had in mind would finally give them the lead they so desperately needed. With the growing fear that Kai was in danger, every second counted. They had to find him before whoever took him made sure he was never found at all.

Reaching into the backseat, Hayden grabbed his laptop and flipped it open. He sank low in the passenger seat, settling it on his lap and keeping himself out of view. "Take us down the hill by Palmer's house."

"Just by it?" She cranked the engine, a bit uncomfortable with the loud roar of power. "Anything more specific?"

He'd opened the system settings on his screen and kept his gaze fixed on it. "I need to be within range of his Wi-Fi signal. I'll tell you when to stop."

She started the vehicle rolling down the road. "You're going to hack his Wi-Fi?"

"That's the plan."

She took a quick look at him. "To what end?"

"I noticed he has a video doorbell." He continued navigating on his computer to the main Wi-Fi window. "Collins rang the doorbell. That means the camera would've started recording their conversation."

"Ahh. I get it now. That's how you plan to hear what they had to say." She turned the corner and coasted down the hill toward Palmer's house.

"Exactly." He looked down the list of Wi-Fi accounts within range of his computer. "No obvious Wi-Fi name that seems to fit with Palmer, so keep going. When we get closer to his signal, the right account will move to the top."

She glanced at him. "But why bother hiding in your seat??"

"I need time to hack his network, and I need to be close to his house, but I don't want him to see me, much less my computer, so pretending to take a phone call will look natural."

"But what about the condition of your vehicle? If he gets a look at it, don't you think he'll call the cops?"

"If he's who we think he is, the last thing he'll do is bring law enforcement to his house."

"Fair point." She shook her head. "I've had to do some sneaky things in my career, but I wouldn't have thought to do this. Probably because of my limited computer knowledge."

"Unfortunately, in law enforcement, to catch a criminal you learn to get into their head."

The vehicle crept toward Palmer's house, and Hayden watched the account names jog for top position on the Wi-Fi list. Finally the account named DontEvenTryIt rose to the top and stayed there. Cheeky name. If he already hadn't planned to hack Palmer's account, this name would make him try it for sure.

"Okay, hold up," he said to Cady. "Leave the engine running and get out your phone."

She reached into her purse on the console for her phone.

He turned his attention to Palmer's account and set to work on what would be an easy task for him. Only one problem. He couldn't fully concentrate the way he usually did. Not after the shooting. His adrenaline had faded, and only now were the true consequences of the incident hitting him.

Collins could come back. Palmer could come outside. Or even their gun-toting assailants could come after them. He had to see what was going on around them.

As he broke through Palmer's security and found the files to download, he weighed his options. If he sat up, what was the worst thing that could happen? Palmer could see him. Sure, his main job was to find Kai, and Palmer catching sight of him outside his house could put a wrinkle in that.

But at this moment, he had one job that trumped everything else. His priority was to keep Cady safe and not let that gun-wielding shooter anywhere near her.

17

With heavy clouds overhead hinting at the evening's forecasted rain, Hayden drove to a secluded stretch of beach just beyond the Lost Lake Locators' headquarters and cut the engine. Fortunately, the inn sat near a boat launch, making this section of the beach legally accessible by vehicle.

He'd gone off-roading on beaches in Oregon before. Plenty of times. Only in legally designated, drivable areas. Still, it always felt odd not to have a road or rules to follow. Other than to obey a slow speed limit, the only real unwritten rule of driving on the beach was simply not to hit anyone or come close enough to beachgoers to spray them with sand. He'd like to say that rule was easy for him to follow, but his innate sense of adventure had him wishing he could press the gas pedal to the floor.

"Done." Cady set her phone on her lap. "Code names and websites off to Nick. Hopefully he'll figure out who these men are."

"As I've said, he's the best."

"So we're here." She sat forward and looked through her window. "You're sure no one followed us?"

"Positive. And even if they did, they'd never expect us to come to the beach."

"I sure didn't." She shook her head. "I mean, who would think you have some sort of secret tunnel leading out of that rocky wall?"

"I know, right?" He grinned. "It goes back to the days when supplies arrived on a ship, and it was easier to carry them in here than traverse a steep cliff wall."

"Whatever the reason, it's fun and exciting."

"I suppose." Hayden tried to remember his feelings when they'd first discovered the tunnel. He probably had a jolt of surprise, but then began thinking about how it could be useful to them. Today was the first day it had come into play. Nolan suggested using this entrance so if anyone was watching the inn, they wouldn't see Hayden and Cady arrive.

He tapped a text to Nolan. *We're here. Open the door.*

On it, came the reply within seconds.

He glanced at Cady. "You ready?"

She nodded, but her expression held a healthy dose of fear.

"Nothing to worry about. We'll head into the tunnel. Easy peasy." He smiled to help her relax.

She gave him a flat smile and opened her door to get out.

He exited the vehicle and retrieved his rifle from the back, shouldering it while keeping his other hand free in case he needed his sidearm. He might've told her they were fine, but that didn't mean he was foolish enough to believe they couldn't run into danger.

He closed and locked the vehicle and met her at the hood of his poor, injured Raptor. Would it ever be the same again? It had to be. He'd put all of his savings into the business and couldn't afford a new vehicle.

They trudged through the thick sand together toward the craggy outcropping.

"I don't see a door," she said.

"It's hidden. Just keep going." Normally he'd tell her to follow him, and he'd show her the way, but with the potential danger, he would have her back.

She set off, and he stayed close to her, but kept scanning the beach behind them. Nearing eight o'clock, the beach was deserted except for a few couples walking along the shoreline in the setting sun.

"Just ahead," he said as they arrived at the worn wooden door with original antique hardware. It stood open just as he expected.

Nolan waited inside. "Any trouble with being followed?"

Hayden shook his head. "But I'll feel better when we're safely inside and the door secured."

Nolan stood back, and they passed him.

"The equipment bags are still in the truck," Hayden said. "I don't want to leave them out there overnight, but wanted to make sure my hands were free until I got Cady safely inside."

"You stay with Cady. I'll get them." Hayden gave him the key fob and Nolan took off.

Hayden waited by the door, and Cady remained nearby until Nolan returned with the bags. He pulled the door closed and settled a solid wood beam across it. Even if someone stumbled upon the door, they'd need power tools to get it open. And if they did, Hayden had put alarm sensors on it and also had a camera with an alarm positioned outside.

"Just follow the tunnel to the stairway," he told Cady.

She stepped off, keeping to the center of the wide stone tunnel where the ceiling was higher. Still, he had to stoop most of the way. Either the people who made the tunnel were shorter—quite possible—or they had to bend to haul the cargo.

The stone stairway led up one flight to a typical exterior door standing open at the top. They entered into what had once served as a living room for guests. A moving bookshelf hid the door. The team used the room as a quiet space, but the outdated and worn furnishings weren't something they wanted to share with others.

Cady turned in a circle. "This room is a blast from the past."

"I'd say sixties or early seventies." Nolan joined them and secured the door behind him.

"Is it wrong to say I love it?" She smiled. "I mean, it's worn out, but I love the design style."

Hayden shook his head. "I've never had much appreciation for mid-century design."

Nolan peered at him. "I didn't even know what mid-century design was. I'm surprised you do."

"It is kind of odd, isn't it?" Hayden said. "My foster family owned an authentic mid-century ranch designed by some famous architect. The building was all square lines and angles. I liked that part of it. Just not the colors used to decorate. Like orange. They had a whole lot of that in the house, and I'd tell them it only belongs on traffic cones."

Cady laughed. "I guess we don't have like-minded design styles then."

Hayden looked at her. "Is that a problem?"

"Okay, then." Nolan shifted his eyes between Hayden and Cady. "This is getting a little too personal for me and where I make my exit. The team's in the conference room whenever you're ready to update them on today's events."

He left the room as if it were on fire. Hayden clenched his jaw. He didn't want to combine personal with business, and here he was talking about decorating a house and comparing it to what Cady might like.

"We should get going." *Before we get distracted and follow down that personal lane.* "Kai is depending on us not to get sidetracked."

She nodded and hustled out of the room without a word.

Hayden trailed behind her, but at a slower pace. He needed to clear his brain and be ready to update his team on the progress they'd made today. Sure, none of it had led to Kai as of yet, but everything pointed them in the right direction.

By the time he reached the room, Cady had poured a mug of coffee and taken a seat next to Abby. She seemed to avoid looking at the door. Hayden ripped his gaze away from her before his teammate saw the battle he was fighting.

Too late.

Abby cocked her head and gave him a pointed look. He ignored it and went to the refreshment table Reece had stocked. Without a word, he took his cup of coffee to the head of the conference table and grabbed a marker, then set his mug down and went to an empty whiteboard.

He started noting the items from today in the order in which they'd learned them. First, he jotted down, *Detailed review of documents from locker and look up license plate for pickup.* Next line, *Look into Emerald Scorpion Group.* Number three was, *Review Palmer's older Wi-Fi files.* And finally he noted, *Search for names on the dark web matching code names.*

He put the marker down and turned. "We had a productive day, but we have a number of items to follow up on."

"Can I barge in to give an update first?" Gabe tapped his finger on the table. "I wanted to put this out there in case it impacts anything else we talk about."

Gabe didn't wait for Hayden to agree, but got up and went to the board to pick up the marker. He wrote the name Sawyer Ellis.

"Sawyer?" Reece blinked her long, mascara-coated eyelashes. "What's he got to do with this?"

"Now, Reece." Jude patted her arm. "Don't go off on Gabe just because you've got a thing for Sawyer."

She gritted her teeth. "I do not have, as you say, *a thing* for Sawyer. I hardly know the man."

"That's because you do your best impression of Bashful every time he's around." Jude laughed.

Reece grumbled something under her breath and turned her attention back to Gabe. "So, why Sawyer?"

"Simple," Gabe said. "I was tasked with finding a boat to tail Collins on his meetup with the trafficking ship, and Sawyer's in the Coast Guard."

Reece crossed her arms. "Surely he won't let you use an official Coast Guard vessel for our off-the-books undercover op."

"Of course not." Gabe dropped the marker into the tray. "But he loves all things water and owns his own boat. One that will outperform Collins's boat in every way. It'll hold the entire team and more, but has a super-fast motor."

"Who will be piloting this thing?" Reece asked, her arms still tight around her body.

"Sawyer, of course. He's chomping at the bit to go on an adventure like this."

"I'll just bet he is." She looked down at the table.

Hayden wasn't certain about her feelings for Sawyer, but the attraction between the two was obvious to all and could interfere with the op. He should talk to her outside the meeting. Her sharpshooting skills meant she was critical to the mission, and he needed her not only on the boat, but zeroed-in on her job. He had to make sure she could manage her emotions while close to Sawyer.

But that was a private discussion for the two of them. For now, he would move on. "Thanks for securing the boat for us, Gabe. Let's review the items we made progress on today. First is related to an attempt to pin our vehicle in and fire at us with a small caliber handgun. We believe the shooter was after the documents we recovered from a bus station storage locker."

He described finding the key, the gunfire, and how they got away. "My Raptor is toast."

"There's no way you can operate incognito anymore," Nolan said. "You should use the company vehicle going forward."

"Thanks." Hayden had never needed to use the SUV the team had sprung for in case of emergency.

"I can get the plate you need run in like five minutes or less." Gabe dropped onto his chair.

"I'll hold you to that timeline." Hayden gave him a challenging grin.

"No worries. My contacts at OSP never fail me." He blew on his fingernails and rubbed them on his shirt. "I'll do it as soon as the meeting ends, and you can time me."

Rolling his eyes, Hayden picked up the marker and wrote Gabe's name next to the item. "We met up with Nolan at Palmer's house and gave the documents to him. It would be good to have a couple sets of eyes on these papers to pull out anything we can use."

Cady sat forward. "I started reviewing the file in the car and found a company called Emerald Scorpion Group. They're behind trafficking the women, but the really big news is they were funneling the money through Kai's shop."

Reece gasped. "But he helped rescue women. Why would he funnel money for them?"

"That's what I hope we'll figure out by doing a detailed review of the documents," Cady said. "I want to finish my review but need help in case I miss something. And research needs to be done on the Emerald Scorpion Group."

Hayden sipped his coffee. "I'll write algorithms to search for the group, but it would be good to get multiple pairs of eyes on the documents."

"I'll volunteer." Reece planted her palms on the table. "My gut says Kai isn't guilty, and he's being set up."

Jude nodded at her. "If Reece's gut thinks he's not guilty, I do too. I'll be glad to help with the documents."

"Thanks." Hayden added their names, along with Cady's, to the list. "Next is Palmer. While we were watching his house, Wade Collins paid him a visit."

Gabe's head jerked back. "Collins? That seals Palmer's connection to the trafficking."

"I wouldn't say 'seals.'" Abby shot Gabe a sidelong glance. "They could be legitimately working together on something else. Like maybe Collins is offering boat cruises for guests at the mansion."

"Were you close enough to hear their conversation?" Nolan asked.

Hayden shook his head. "But Palmer has a doorbell camera. I hacked his Wi-Fi to download recent recordings and reviewed the one from today right away. Collins didn't like the fact that we've been snooping around and wanted to bow out of tonight's meetup. Palmer told him there was no way we could know about their Thursday night pickups, and the meeting would go on as usual. He told Collins that if he didn't show up, he could count on the Chinese coming after him."

Reece shook her head. "Palmer's as nice of a guy as we thought."

Gabe snorted. "A class act, that one. We'll have to hope the guy doesn't rethink this and get cold feet."

"As far as I'm concerned, we're still on for tonight." Hayden controlled his breathing so the others didn't see his extreme level of stress. "Anyone not with me?"

He waited for someone to disagree, likely Gabe, but no one spoke up. "Good. Then we're a go. Until then, we haven't had a chance to review the older videos and need help."

"I've waded through my share of videos in my career." Abby gave him a focused stare. "So count me in."

Hayden smiled at her. Watching video files could be extremely tedious, and he was thankful she stepped up right away. He added her name to the board, then tapped the last item, *Search for names on the dark web matching code names.*

"This will be a tough one," he said. "As you know, it's hard to find information on the dark web, but I'll work on it. Nick at the Veritas Center also agreed to help."

"I'll get a hold of Mina," Nolan said. "And take the original documents you recovered to her to see if she'll share information on the shooting scene."

"She won't be happy we didn't report it." Hayden dropped the marker in the tray. "Or that we used the key to get the documents."

Nolan grimaced. "I'm sure you're right, but what's done is done. I'll just have to face the consequences."

"She probably isn't happy that we fled the shooting scene either."

"Not likely but I'll run interference for you." Nolan gave a tight smile. "I'm sure she'll be fine once she has the key and the original documents. Just be aware, she's not likely to trust us as easily in the future, and that could mean not sharing any findings from today's shooting."

Ruining their trust with Mina was something Hayden

would never want to do. Next time he saw her, he would explain and try to win her back to their side. They couldn't afford to be without law enforcement backup. Not when it looked like some nefarious organization might be behind Kai's disappearance.

18

Hayden fired up his algorithm for searching the dark web for code names. Job done, but he had no time to sit back and take a break. Kai was counting on all of them to keep working.

Abby leaned over to him and tipped her head at the door to the kitchen. "Join me."

Hayden had too much on his plate for a trip to the kitchen. "Is this really important enough to stop working?"

"It is." She kept her voice low and mysterious. "Just come with me and don't say anything to the others."

Okay. Now she'd piqued his interest. He glanced around to see if anybody had noticed their conversation, but his teammates were all busy working on their assignments, so he stood. She tucked her laptop under her arm and eased toward the kitchen as if she was casually getting something to eat. She pushed through the swinging doors, sending them flapping.

Obviously, she wanted to tell him something she didn't want the others to hear. But what? Must involve her computer, so could it be a lead she'd found in her review of videos from Palmer's camera?

Hayden glanced back at Cady, but she hadn't looked up from her laptop and didn't seem to notice him watching her.

Perfect time to slip away. He stepped through the doors, but gently closed them behind him.

Abby stood at the stainless steel island, her computer open and a paused video on the screen. "This is one of the doorbell videos from Palmer's place from several weeks ago. A man I don't recognize arrives at Palmer's house at 2:45 in the morning to talk to him. More like shout at him, but their conversation leads me to believe this guy's the head of the trafficking organization. Or at least Palmer's boss."

"Wow! Great, but why the secrecy? I'm sure everyone would want to see this."

"It's their topic of conversation I want you to see before Cady does."

What could she want to hide from Cady? Only one possible topic.

"It's about her father." Hayden could barely get the words out over his throat closing. "Play it."

The man standing at Palmer's door was short, maybe five foot six, and stocky, but in a muscular way, and had a full head of wavy blond hair. He wore an expensive-looking pair of jeans and an athletic jacket. Hayden thought he might've seen him somewhere in the past, but he didn't know where.

"Are you nuts?" Palmer asked. "Coming by here. We can't have people see us together."

"I needed to talk to you, and you weren't answering my calls. So you gave me no choice."

"What calls?" Palmer pulled his phone from the pocket of his robe. The light illuminated his face and the roll of his eyes. "I didn't answer, because I was in bed sleeping."

"I pay you good money for twenty-four/seven service, so don't use any excuse for not responding." From that tone alone, Hayden got a pretty clear read on the guy.

"Okay, fine," Palmer said. "You're here now. Say what you have to say and get going before anyone sees you."

"You remember that birdwatcher friend of the mayor, Percy Vaughn?"

"Yeah, the old dude with dementia who went to live in Portland with his daughter."

"His daughter, *the reporter*. A fact you failed to tell me about."

"I don't see how it's relevant."

The man glared at him. "That's why I'm in charge and not you. We were counting on him not remembering any information that Sutton might've given him and not tell someone before he kicks the bucket."

Hayden drew in a sharp breath. It would nearly kill Cady to see the cavalier way this man was talking about her father.

"But it's been bothering me," the unidentified man continued. "What if it comes back to him, and he shares it with his daughter? Then she starts digging for a story. Maybe even report us to the sheriff."

"Okay, yeah." Palmer shifted his stance. "I can see how that could be a problem."

"A problem you're gonna take care of for me."

"But how? It's not like I can make sure he doesn't remember."

"You can't recall anything when you're dead, can you?"

Someone gasped behind Hayden and Abby, and they both spun. Reece stood at the door, staring at the computer.

"Pause it," Hayden instructed Abby, who stopped the video.

"I can't believe he just said that." Reece shook her head. "He... I mean... I'd never expect that from him."

"Palmer?"

She shook her head. "No. The other guy."

Abby took a step back. "You know him?"

"I don't know him personally, but I know who he is. And I can hardly believe it." Reece shook her head. "It's Odin Ivers."

Abby shared a baffled look with Hayden, but he was no more in the know than she was.

"Is that name supposed to ring a bell for us?" he asked.

Reece's eyes were wide. "He's our county commissioner."

Abby clapped a hand over her mouth.

"Yeah," Reece said. "If he's in this with Collins and Palmer, there's some high rollers in the group."

Hayden had to agree. The former mayor's brother-in-law, a respected attorney, and the county commissioner. Could they possibly be human traffickers? As Reece said, it was almost unbelievable.

"If I hadn't seen him tell Palmer to kill Percy on this video," Reece said. "We probably wouldn't have believed he was involved."

Hayden agreed. "Start the video again. Let's see if he says anything else to incriminate himself."

Abby clicked "play," and the screen came to life.

Palmer glared at Ivers. "You want me to kill this Vaughn guy? He's just an old dude with dementia. He's gonna die soon enough anyway."

A shrill shriek came from the doorway. Hayden whipped around to see Cady standing there, her mouth hanging open as she gaped at the computer.

Abby stopped the video, but Hayden stepped in front of the screen so Cady couldn't see it.

"He's talking about my father. Did he kill my father?" Each word took her voice higher and higher until it reached an out-of-control range. She rushed across the room, side-stepped Hayden, and stared at the screen. "It's Palmer. Oh my goodness! Palmer killed my dad? But who is the other man?"

Reece stepped forward, concern etched on her face. "His name is Odin Ivers. He's our county commissioner."

Cady lifted her hands and gawked at Reece. "Why would a county commissioner want my father dead?"

"Earlier in the video he admits to being connected to human trafficking," Reece said.

"Seriously?" Cady blinked. Blinked again. "That's almost unbelievable, but at least we have proof of who killed my father." Her expression tightened, and she glanced around the trio. "Where did this video come from, and how long have you had it without telling me?"

Hayden really didn't want to talk about the video with her, much less give her any details. He hadn't even wanted her to know about it, but now that she did, she deserved an answer. "It's one of Palmer's security files. Abby just discovered it."

"And you all decided what I should and shouldn't see." She gritted her teeth. "For now, I'll skip telling you how upset I am that you would keep this from me." Tears glistening in her eyes, she curled her arms around her waist in a protective hug, and glared at them. "I want to see the whole video."

"You really don't want to watch this." Hayden met her gaze, and it gutted him to see her pain. "That's why we didn't tell you about it. You don't need to see this man's cruelty."

"But I do." She lifted her chin and squinted at Hayden. "Don't interfere in this."

He didn't want her to watch these bottom-feeders discuss killing her father, but her body language and tone of voice served as warnings he didn't want to ignore.

"Rewind it to the beginning," he said to Abby.

She frowned, held his gaze for a long moment, but then did as asked.

The footage started playing again. Cady released her arms and leaned forward. The pain in her eyes deepened, and he stepped closer to take her hand. She didn't fight him, but held on tight.

As the recording advanced, her tears intensified, dropping from her cheeks onto their held hands. The video reached the section where she'd come into the room, and Hayden paused it there to see if she wanted to continue.

"I can hardly believe this." She freed her hand to swipe it across her cheeks. "But at least we have the proof we need that they plotted to kill my father."

Hayden didn't want to tell her that, yes, they now likely knew who killed her father, but they still didn't have adequate proof for a court of law. He would have to explain those details later. "Do you want to continue?"

She nodded, but didn't speak.

Abby clicked play.

"Not *want* you to take him out," Ivers said. "I'm telling you to take care of him."

"Why me? Why not Collins or one of your Chinese goons?"

"I might have the backing of that group, but I'm in charge of this operation." He poked himself in the chest with both thumbs. "Me. Get it, and don't forget it."

"I get it, but again I ask, why me? You were going to take Kai Nakoa out yourself. So why is this any different?"

Abby paused the video. "Finally we have information on Kai. Looks like he could be in big trouble."

Hayden nodded. "Or Ivers already took care of him, but doesn't want Palmer to know."

"Keep playing it so we can find out," Cady said.

As the video started up again, Ivers planted his feet

solidly on the concrete, and his nostrils flared. "Nakoa is a different story. He has information on us that could bring down our operation. We're toast if that information gets out, and I'm the best one to retrieve it."

"Likely the encrypted flash drive," Hayden said, and the others nodded.

"Okay, so you don't want to do this," Palmer said. "But Collins has done some pretty underhanded things over the years, and is perfectly capable of handling this. Knowing him, he would be jonesing to do it."

Ivers watched Palmer. "This is going to take finesse. Something Collins doesn't have. Vaughn's death needs to look like natural causes, so it's not like you can go to his place and shoot or stab him."

Cady grabbed Hayden's arm, her fingernails digging in, but he didn't pry them off.

Palmer's shoulders sagged. "Then what do you want me to do?"

From his pocket, Ivers pulled a black container the size of an eyeglass case and shoved it into Palmer's hands. "Use this syringe of fentanyl. One injection, and he'll be gone."

"That's it! The murder weapon!" Cady cried out, her fingers tightening more. "Additional proof of their involvement."

Palmer held the container as if it were some fragile object that might break. "How do you propose I get into the house to inject him without anyone seeing me?"

The man shrugged. "That's your problem. I want it done by end of day tomorrow."

"But I—"

"You do *not* want to disobey a direct order from me. You already mentioned my Beijing connections, and you don't want to bring their wrath down on you too." Ivers walked away, not stopping for Palmer's objections.

Palmer stared after him, still holding the syringe. He suddenly pivoted and entered his house, and the video went black.

"What date is this video from?" Cady asked.

Abby called out the date.

"That's the day before my father died. Don't you see? It's all there. Their intent to murder him, the murder weapon, and even saying what day it was going to happen." A strained smile crossed Cady's face, but she released Hayden's arm. "We got them. We found the men responsible for killing my father. We need to get this file to Mina so she can arrest them."

"About that," Hayden said, hating to have to share this information with her. "If we show her this video now, she won't be able to use it in a court of law."

"What?" Cady stared at him wide-eyed. "Why not?"

"I didn't have a warrant to take these files."

"So we can't use it?"

"Not right now in the way you would hope." Hayden planted his hands on his waist, hoping to show her he was still in control. "She'll need probable cause to get a warrant to search Palmer's house. She's a terrific sheriff, so she'll know to request doorbell files for review. Until then, we now know who did what, so we can work to prove it in other ways. And hopefully along the way, we'll figure out where Ivers stashed Kai."

19

In the team's conference room nearing midnight, Cady fastened the straps for a Kevlar vest around her body, as did the rest of the team. She stared at the whiteboard holding details of their planned event tonight. Event, hah! She had no idea what she should call it, but one thing was for certain. She could call it scary. She shifted the vest to make sure it covered all the essential areas. She'd never worn any kind of bulletproof protection before, but had always imagined herself wearing Kevlar if she ever went to a war zone.

War. Something horrific, but something many good reporters covered. She'd long dreamt of doing that, but did she still want to? The more time she spent with Hayden, the more she wondered if she really needed that kind of success in her life.

Or had she been trying to prove something to herself that she no longer needed to prove now that her father was gone? Maybe so. She no longer needed to make him proud of her. She'd always been driven to succeed, but had never really stopped to figure out why. But could she have been proving her worth because her mother didn't think her worthy enough to stay around?

Hayden joined her. "You look deep in thought."

"It's nothing." She waved a hand. "I've got my mind in the right place, and I'm ready to participate tonight."

He tilted his head and watched her carefully. "I think the word you're looking for is observe."

"I know that's what you said we'll do, but if we see something actionable, and Mina's team isn't in a position to act, we won't sit by, will we?"

"It all depends on what we see and how our actions might hold up in a court of law. A life and death situation trumps everything." His forehead creased. "Even if something occurs that we need to act on, you'll remain an observer. That's not optional. If you don't think you can do that, you'll have to stay here."

Hah! There was no way she was staying behind. No matter what. "Don't worry. I get it. I'm not trained to do anything but observe and report, so I know my limitations." She smiled up at him. "Besides, I trust the team to do whatever they need to do to catch my father's killer. But I want to —no, I need to be there."

"Then let's go." Hayden nodded at his teammates.

"Hold up." Reece lifted the bus locker documents she'd been reviewing. "I thought you'd like to know. I found Odin Ivers's name in this file you got from the bus station locker."

"Not a surprise," Hayden said. "but good to see, we have written documentation of his involvement."

Reese nodded and dropped the document on the table, then joined the team at the door..

They marched silently down the hallway and outside, striding toward the three vehicles loaded and ready for the operation. A sharp wind whipped off the cliff and blew her hair in her face. She brushed it away and looked up at the sky where thick gray clouds threatened a downpour soon.

They put their heads against the wind and split up

based on an earlier decision to ensure each vehicle had a skilled driver and a marksman in case they came under fire. Hayden drove the company SUV and Gabe rode shotgun, while she took the backseat with no other role than to observe. In the second SUV, Abby drove and Nolan served as their marksman. Jude drove his pickup truck, and as a sharpshooter, Reece sat beside him.

Hayden got the vehicle on the road to Seaside Harbor Marina, where Collins moored his boat. Serving as the county seat, Seaside Harbor was more than double the size of Lost Lake. Cady had only been there once, when she took her father to Mina's office to tell her about the secret he hadn't revealed.

That was the first time she'd met Hayden. The moment he'd gently tried to soothe her father, who was wrapped up in one of his panicked dementia states, was the moment she'd fallen for him. Sure, he was a fine looking man— unbelievably attractive, in fact. At least to her. But more attractive were his compassion and care for an elderly man who was clearly suffering.

She caught sight of his strong profile as he continued to search the area to be sure no one was tailing them. She'd thought tonight she would go alone with Hayden, but having Gabe along was much better. With him in the vehicle, she and Hayden couldn't get into a personal discussion as they waited for Collins to act. Because, honestly, she didn't know what she would say to him at this point. Or do, for that matter.

She sighed. Hayden fired a look at her in the mirror. "You're not worried, are you? Because Gabe and I'll make sure nothing bad happens to you."

Gabe looked back at her. "Yeah, relax. I Googled how to aim a rifle, and I'm basically a certified expert now." He wiggled his eyebrows at her.

She laughed and felt the tension leave her body.

"No time for fun and games." Hayden turned down the road leading to the marina. "Keep your eyes peeled."

"Roger that." Gabe shifted the rifle on the floor next to him but kept his gaze roving from window to window.

The humor evaporated in the vehicle. There was no danger around them at the moment, but as their operation commenced, so did her concern.

Hayden crept his vehicle along the fenced marina, passing the main entrance with a large sign announcing Seaside Harbor Marina. Five wooden docks projected into the water like the spokes of a half wheel, and various-sized boats were tied to the docks.

She picked up a pair of binoculars and ran them over the third spoke, which, in their planning meeting, they identified as Collins's boat location. "Which slip number belongs to Collins?"

"Twenty-five," Gabe said. "If you count from the building, it's the fifth one on the third dock."

Hayden parked in a hidden spot behind a large dumpster, and she zoomed in on a large white boat with two decks and fishing pole holders on the sides. She shifted her view to the rear of the boat and spotted *Off The Hook* painted in loopy letters.

"Got it," she said. "But I don't see anyone on board."

Gabe raised his binoculars too. "Agreed. If he's on board, he's inside with the lights out."

"We're plenty early." Hayden cut the engine. "He might not arrive until near time to rendezvous with the ship."

Without the motor rumbling, the sound of waves lapping against boats became clear, as did the sound of the wind gusts sending choppy waves to shore.

Hayden's phone dinged. "Text is from Daisy. She didn't find anything unusual in the mayor's phone records."

"She sure is working late," Cady said. "But we figured she wouldn't find anything."

Hayden nodded, but then continued to look at his phone, time ticking silently by.

Gabe turned toward him. "Gaming at a time like this?"

"Of course not," he said. "Just checking to be sure the tracker Jude placed on the boat this afternoon is operational."

"And is it?" Cady asked.

"It is indeed. We should be able to follow Collins's every move."

"What if he finds the tracker and destroys it?" she asked. "Then what?"

"Then I hack his navigation system to follow him that way." Hayden's confidence in his abilities came through every word. "It's a little more complex and might take longer, but we won't lose him."

She thought he was being unreasonably positive, but what did she know about hacking navigation? She shifted her binoculars to the open ocean, dark in the inky night. "Too bad we can't get out on the water to see where Mina and her team are waiting. It would be comforting to know they were there for sure."

"Don't worry," Hayden said. "If we run into trouble, they're a radio transmission away for Nolan."

"Speaking of Nolan, I'll check in with the others to see if they're in place." Gabe bent his head forward. "Top Dog, this is Outlaw. Are you in position? Over."

Top Dog? Outlaw? She shouldn't be surprised the team members had nicknames. After all, they had to communicate when they were undercover. It would be fun to figure out who was who. Obviously, Gabe was Outlaw, and since he mentioned checking in with Nolan, Top Dog had to be him.

"Will do, Top Dog. Over." Gabe looked at Hayden.

"Nolan's in place, and he's communicated with Mina. Her team is in place too."

Hayden had his binoculars raised and gave a slight nod, but didn't say anything.

"Riddler, this is Outlaw," Gabe said. "Are you in position? Over."

Hmm, Riddler. Though Gabe seemed to have a sarcastic kind of humor, she'd already identified him as Outlaw, so the real team joker could be no other than Jude.

Gabe soon confirmed her suspicions, and that Jude and Reece were in place.

"So what are the other team nicknames?" she asked, particularly eager to find out what they called Hayden.

Hayden lowered his binoculars to look back at her. "Ace, Maverick, and Sidekick."

"You seem to be a fearless adventurer, so you must be Maverick."

"Touché."

"And I just learned that Reece is a sharpshooter so she must be Ace."

"Right again," Gabe said.

"Then that leaves Abby as Sidekick." Cady pondered that one. "I guess Sidekick means she's there to help whenever needed, which I see in her, but that's not really a good nickname for a leader like a sheriff."

"Our names go way back to college days," Hayden said. "Back then she didn't show any desire to be a leader, but people change. Problem is, she'll always be Sidekick to us, no matter what happens."

Gabe leaned between the seats to look at Cady. "Impressive reasoning. Looks like you've already got us pegged."

"I'm not sure my skills are all that impressive, but you all definitely have defined roles in the group."

"Hmm." Gabe tapped his chin and a snarky grin crossed his face. "Now what should we call you?"

"Me?" She stared at him. "I don't need a nickname."

"Humor me," he said, and turned back to his binoculars. "It'll help pass the time until Collins shows up."

"You don't seem to miss a thing so how about Eagle Eye?" Hayden asked.

"That might work," Gabe said, not sounding all that impressed. "At least it's a starter."

Hayden glanced back at her. "What do you want us to call you?"

"Oh no." Gabe shook his head. "No. No. No. You don't give yourself a nickname. I like Snoop."

"Snoop!" she cried out in her defense. "That sounds negative."

"Sorry, but I like it too." Hayden grinned at her in the rearview mirror. "Not that I think you're a snoop in the rest of your life, but I like the sound of it, and it is kind of what reporters do."

"I suppose," she admitted reluctantly.

"Then Snoop it is." Gabe laughed.

She opened her mouth to argue, but a truck entered the parking lot and all joking stopped. The three of them watched the oversized silver pickup pull into a parking space near the marina entrance.

Cady held her breath and inspected the driver through her binoculars. Thankfully, she'd seen Collins at Palmer's place and could easily recognize him—if he was in the truck, that is, since he hadn't driven a pickup to Palmer's house.

The door groaned open, and a man slid down.

"That's Collins," Hayden said, then leaned forward. "This is Maverick. We have eyes on suspect in west parking lot. Repeat, we have eyes on suspect. Hold positions until further notified. Over."

Collins's boots hit the ground with a thump. He remained stationary, casting cautious glances around. It gave Cady time to give him a good once-over. He had a thickset body, bordering on overweight, and was average height. He didn't have much of a chin, and his face was pudgy and soft. Definitely not the strong masculine type she would expect in such a devious position.

She was looking at Wade Collins. Not her father's killer, but someone who worked for the man who'd arranged and carried out his murder. For all she knew, he'd been told of the plan to kill him and did nothing to stop it. But if he wasn't guilty of that, he had human trafficking charges waiting for him.

He shoved his keys into his pocket and slammed the truck door, then trudged toward the marina entrance. He wore all black clothing, including a black baseball cap, his hand resting on top, likely due to the increasing wind.

With a key card, he opened the main gate and pulled it closed behind him. He paused. Turned. Looked around. Stood unmoving.

Apparently satisfied he was alone, he strode down the dock, his quick pace sending the structure bouncing. He climbed aboard his boat, his movements sure and swift.

He quickly scaled the steps to the top deck where he scanned the area again and remained in position for a long moment. He shrugged and unlocked the door before ducking into the cabin featuring large windows on the sides.

"He's headed straight for the helm," Gabe said. "He'll probably take off, and we should move now before we lose him."

Hayden glanced at his watch. "It's still early. He already

wanted to bail on the night. If we act too soon we'll spook him, and that won't do us any good. But now that he's here, those of us who are going to tail him on the water should move to Sawyer's boat."

"Oh yeah!" Gabe grabbed the door handle and nearly threw himself out of the vehicle.

Hayden leaned forward. "Top Dog, this is Maverick. Are you prepared to rendezvous? Over."

Hayden tilted his head, obviously listening to Nolan's response.

"Roger, that, Top Dog. Over." He repeated the question to Riddler and once again listened.

Hayden swiveled to look back at Cady. "The others will meet us here. Reece, Abby, and Jude will join Gabe and me in the boat. You'll stay back with Nolan."

"Wait, what?" She stared at him. "I thought I was going with you."

"No."

Just one word, but it had a finality to it, and she knew she couldn't possibly change his mind. She should appreciate having a man so concerned for her safety. She'd never had that in the past. Sure, her father probably worried about her when she lived in the big city and at times handled controversial subjects for her reporting, but he'd never expressed concern.

She didn't think she would actually like it, but knowing a fine man like Hayden cared that much about her warmed her heart in ways she never expected.

Ah, yes. She was falling in love with him, wasn't she? She had a lot of soul-searching to do to figure out what she wanted in her future. But first, she would have to ask what he wanted because he'd told her he didn't want a relationship.

The other team members pulled into parking spaces near the team SUV and got out. Now, she needed to put all her effort into praying for the safety of these fine men and women while they headed toward a potential showdown with dangerous criminals.

20

As Hayden strode down the beach toward the nearby marina, he periodically glanced at his phone to see if Collins moved his boat. Hayden had hoped for a clear night —something that offered visibility and spared them the hassle of rain. So far, the skies held back, despite thick clouds drifting across the moon, dimming the light. The wind showed no such restraint. It came in hard off the ocean, whipping sand at them and stinging their skin. His instinct was to duck against the blast, but they all needed to stay sharp, scanning for any sign of danger.

Reece, Abby, and Gabe had their rifles slung over their shoulders, gripping them tightly each time a gust of wind rolled through.

Jude fell into step next to Hayden. "Nice night for a stroll on the beach, right?"

Hayden shook his head, but his mind was on Collins and the lack of movement on his tracking app. "You sure you hid that tracker on Collins's boat well enough."

"Don't worry about it." Jude squinted against the wind-driven sand. "Collins will never find it, and it's secure enough that it can't easily be dislodged."

"Let's hope that's true." Hayden checked the tracker again, but Collins still hadn't moved.

"Hey, man, I've probably placed more trackers with the FBI than you all have put together, so I know what I'm talking about. Our only potential downfall is battery failure. I put fresh ones in when I placed the device, and there's nothing I can do if they fail abruptly. So barring that, we have months to go with the extended battery models we use."

"Thanks, man," Hayden said, even though the information about the batteries wasn't new to him.

They still had a five-minute walk to the other marina, and he hadn't had a chance to talk to Reece, so he hung back until she came alongside him.

"You gonna be okay with this?" he asked.

She shifted the rifle on her shoulder. "Why wouldn't I be?"

"I'm not talking about today's mission or your skills, but seeing Sawyer Ellis again."

Reece planted a hand on her hip. "No need to worry about me. I can do my job no matter who I have to work with."

She was sidestepping his obvious point. "I don't know what you have against Sawyer. He seems to be a great guy. Maybe he's a little pushy—wanting to be in charge all the time—but otherwise an all-around good guy."

"I've only seen him in action on that one mission, so I wouldn't know about that." The team had partnered with him to travel to a secluded island where a young girl's kidnappers were keeping her prisoner.

For Hayden, it only took one mission to determine Sawyer's qualities, but obviously not for Reece. "I don't think he would've reached the rank of commander if he weren't a decent guy."

A sharp wind whipped off the water, and Reece steadied her rifle. "He also wouldn't have made commander if he weren't pretty straightlaced and decisive. So focused, he can't see life unfolding around him."

"Where you're more a free spirit and like to take things as they come."

She nodded. "Literally two ships that should just pass in the night."

"Except neither one of you want to pass," Hayden said, catching sight of Sawyer's twenty-five-foot sport boat.

Reece frowned. "I don't know about that, but I'm done talking about it. Time to psyche myself up for the mission."

She stepped ahead of Hayden, ending their discussion.

He double-timed it past her to reach the boat first. Sawyer waited in a wide-legged stance at the stern, overhead lights outlining his body. He wore black tactical pants and a black T-shirt, clearly showing off his time spent in the gym. He still had the same neatly trimmed, dishwater-blond hair, fitting for an officer in the Coast Guard.

"Ahoy," he called out in his deep voice.

Hayden stepped up to the boat that had to set the guy back a couple hundred grand. "Sawyer. Thanks for offering your boat again."

"Are you kidding?" He grinned. "Another opportunity to run this baby at top speed and see what she can do? I'd never pass that up."

"Life isn't all about speed," Reece muttered, but it came out loudly enough for Sawyer to flash her an annoyed look.

"Our suspect's in his boat but hasn't left the dock," Hayden said, keeping them on task. "Permission for us to come aboard."

"My boat's your boat." Sawyer stood back but picked up a handful of lifejackets.

"Well, good to hear," Jude said, hopping over the back

barrier. "Just remember that when I want to take someone sightseeing."

"Hey," Sawyer said. "I didn't say this was the Love Boat."

They all laughed, something they needed to break the tension before potentially engaging with human traffickers.

"Everyone wears a life jacket. No discussion." Sawyer handed one to Jude, who took it but stared at it as if it were a creature trying to bite him.

"We'll all cooperate." Hayden gave Jude a pointed look. "I want Reece and Gabe up front. Abby, you have the rear."

Reece planted her feet wide on the boat. "No offense to Abby, but I might do better covering the entire rear of the boat."

Hayden assumed she was trying to get away from Sawyer, but that wasn't an operationally sound decision, and he couldn't allow it. "I need our best marksman in the front of the boat. Any other choice puts everyone in danger."

"You got it," she said, not arguing any further. She would never knowingly endanger other people. Even Sawyer. She snatched a lifejacket from his hand and marched past the captain's seat toward a lower seating area in the bow. Kneeling on a cushion, she took her position on the side of the boat opposite Sawyer. Not a problem for Hayden or the mission as she was right on the front line where she needed to be. And as a bonus, being in front of Sawyer, he wouldn't visually distract her.

Unusually quiet, Gabe trailed after her.

"Abby, behind us," Hayden said.

She took a life preserver and then her respective position without any disagreement.

"And me?" Jude asked.

"Up front, too, with binoculars. Keep your eyes peeled."

"Roger that." He strode to the front, tossing the life

preserver around his neck as he moved. "Make room for your daily dose of funny."

Gabe groaned.

"Crack all the jokes you want now, but you better be serious once this boat is moving," Reece said.

"Hey," Jude said. "You know you can count on me when needed."

"I know," Reece said. "But we've never taken on a foreign human trafficking group before, and this feels different."

"Better to laugh now," Jude said. "So if we have to engage, you're not already in meltdown mode."

"Noted," Reece said, but it didn't sound like she was planning to relax.

Hayden wasn't sure he wanted her to relax, even now. She was their front line of defense, and she had to bring her A-game, however she got there.

He put on the life jacket and took the seat across from Sawyer. "I have a tracker on the suspect's boat, and his location is pulled up on my phone. I'll get an alert when he takes off, and we can follow from a safe distance."

"We'll need to stay back to avoid being spotted—unless we encounter heavy fog or pouring rain." Sawyer looked up at the sky. "They're calling for a storm, but we'll have to wait and see if it actually hits and how bad it gets."

"You're not worried about going out in a potential storm?"

"Yeah, man." Jude glanced back at them. "Might be a little embarrassing to need a Coast Guard rescue."

Sawyer snorted. "Trust me, I know my limits, and I'll turn back long before that would be necessary."

Hayden's phone chimed, and his heart jolted.

"It's go time." He woke up the screen and ran his gaze over the team. Landing his focus on Sawyer, he held out his phone. "Your first coordinates. Do your thing."

"We'll need to wait until he's about four miles out so our lights don't give us away."

"Any way we can run without lights?" Jude asked.

"No way." Sawyer grimaced. "I've come across way too many boaters in my line of work who think like that and end up stranded, hurt, or worse. I'm not ignoring safety rules for any reason."

"Good to know for when I take the Love Boat out." Jude chuckled.

Usually his humor brought down any tension, but not now. The others remained focused.

"We're good to proceed." Sawyer tapped his navigation screen to add the GPS location, then glanced at Hayden. "Can you untie us so we can get underway?"

"Aye, aye, Captain." Hayden chuckled, though his heart hammered against his ribs. He leapt onto the dock, untangled the mooring ropes, and tossed them into the boat as Sawyer revved up the engine, its roar cutting through the stillness of the night.

Hayden jumped into the boat, careful not to face-plant from the momentum, and took his seat.

"Here we go." Sawyer grinned and gently moved the throttle forward.

The boat responded with controlled power, and they slowly eased away from the dock. As soon as Sawyer hit open water, he pressed the throttle harder and the boat lurched ahead. They quickly gained speed until the front end was airborne, and they were nearly flying through the water.

Angry waves rolled beneath them, but Sawyer kept the boat on track. Water spray and forceful wind slapped them in the face. Hayden had to grab onto a handle to stay in his seat, adrenaline coursing through him.

He put his free hand over his eyes to glance across the

boat at the navigation screen. They were tracking Collins's boat, mirroring his path. Dots marking the distance between them soon narrowed, and Sawyer let off on the throttle. They slowed, and the front of the boat dropped down.

He looked at Hayden. "We'll cruise at this speed for a while so we don't catch up to the suspect's boat. Let me know when you want me to close in on him."

Hayden nodded and cupped his hand around his mouth. "Anything up front?"

"Nada," Jude called out.

"Same," Reece yelled.

"Nothing for me either," Gabe shouted.

The answers he'd expected. They were too far away to see Collins. They would have to wait until he stopped to move in closer.

Hayden pressed the microphone on his communications unit, cupping it with his other hand to block out any interference. "Top dog, this is Maverick. Suspect's boat is heading in the direction expected. We're underway, remaining a few miles behind to camouflage the running lights. Over."

"Roger that," Nolan said. "All quiet here. Bandit reports the same with ship in sight. Over."

Hayden still found it funny that the team decided on Bandit for Mina's nickname. No one hearing their transmission would ever suspect she was in law enforcement, which was the very reason they had chosen it. "Copy that, Top Dog. Let me know the moment anything changes. Over."

"Everything okay?" Sawyer asked while keeping his eyes pinned forward.

"Fine. No action."

"Then sit back. At this speed, we have at least a thirty-minute ride to our target."

"Sit back, but don't relax," Hayden called out to the team to be heard above the motor. "Keep your eyes open."

They left the town's light pollution behind and visibility dropped, so Hayden put on night vision goggles he'd brought along. He scanned the area, but found nothing of interest to their mission. Absolutely nothing but dark skies and angry water in all directions.

Time dragged on, the rhythmic, rising and falling of the boat hypnotic, but Hayden kept scanning the area.

"Suspect's boat has slowed and is stopping near target." Sawyer's excited voice carried above the engine.

"Let me check if we're approved to intercept suspect." Hayden lifted his NVGs to his forehead and covered his mouth and microphone again. "Top Dog this is Maverick. Suspect's boat has reached target. Are we cleared to proceed? Over."

"Negative, Maverick," Nolan replied without hesitation. "Hold position. And wait for—hold on. Bandit reporting in now."

The comms went silent, and all Hayden could do was wait. And wait. The adrenaline that had beat within him the last thirty minutes pulsed through him in an exhilarating rush. He tapped his foot to keep from jumping up and pacing.

"Maverick, this is Top Dog." Nolan's earlier calmness gave way to a sharp sense of urgency. "Proceed to target. Urgently. Details to follow. Over."

Hayden fired a look at Sawyer. "Urgent request to proceed to target."

"Roger that!" Sawyer grabbed the throttle. "Hold on." He pressed the lever, and the boat jumped under his touch, leaping ahead and cutting through heavy waves, skimming the top.

Racing.

Hayden glanced at his sharpshooters in the bow of the boat. They repeatedly shifted to maintain their firing position with rifles outstretched, but both of them exhibited superhuman strength and remained in position.

"Maverick this is Top Dog," Nolan's voice came through Hayden's earpiece. "Suspect boat captain spooked by Bandit's attempt to intercede. He's shoving passengers overboard as he flees. Rescue help needed."

Tossing vulnerable people overboard! Disgusting.

Hayden's gut clenched. He wanted to hurl. Scream. Yell.

No. He wouldn't transmit his emotions to the group. He was in charge of this mission and had to remain calm and give concise directions.

He gulped in a breath of salty ocean air and peered at the navigation screen. Not nearly as close as he wanted to be to help, but they'd get there soon. "Roger that, Top Dog. Closing in on target and will assist in any way we can. Over."

He swiveled to face Sawyer. "Can this baby move faster?"

"I'm pushing it now, but let's see if I can open her up more." Sawyer eased the throttle ahead, no doubt with a gleam in his eyes.

Time to update the team. Hayden didn't want to yell across the boat so he stayed low, fought gravity, and moved to the bow. "Heard from Nolan. Mina closed in on Collins. He got spooked and started dumping his passengers overboard as he fled."

Reece grimaced. "In open waters? How awful!"

Gabe slammed a fist into the side of the boat, then rubbed it. "We have to help."

"We'll help with the rescue the moment we get there," Hayden assured them. "Wait for further instructions, but for now keep your eyes open as we approach the target."

Jude shook his head. "This guy is the lowest of the low,

and we *will* save those people. Hopefully Mina's free to stop him."

Hayden nodded and started scooting back through the rapidly moving boat to share the same information with Abby and Sawyer.

"Closing in, " Sawyer said as Hayden reached him. "Should be on target within three minutes."

"Perfect." Hayden waved for Abby to join him so he could update her and Sawyer at the same time. The moment she reached him, he shared the information.

"That dirtbag." Abby growled low in her throat.

"Agreed," Sawyer said. "A real lowlife. We'll have to change our approach. We can't go racing in there with people in the water. We'll have to advance slowly."

Hayden nodded. "Our safest path is to come in behind Mina's boat."

"Roger that." Sawyer gripped the wheel. "Once we reach our coordinates, I'll request a Coast Guard cutter with a ScanEagle System. This new technology will allow us to monitor the subject ship from the ocean and air."

Hayden nodded, thankful Gabe arranged to have Sawyer on their team tonight. "Head to the back, Abby. I'll transmit this information to Nolan so he can share it with Mina."

Abby held out a fist. Hayden bumped it, then they split up. He immediately informed Nolan, then ended their conversation to pass the info on to Mina.

Hayden could now see the lights from multiple watercrafts. The ship sat near to them along with a stationary boat, both riding the rolling waves. The third boat moved slowly away, probably Collins as he dumped people.

Unbelievable to disregard life that way. Abby was right. He was a real dirtbag and not a smart one either.

If he'd let Mina arrest him, he would've been charged with trafficking. But by throwing people overboard to avoid getting caught with them on his boat, he now likely faced attempted murder charges instead. At least Hayden hoped that would be the outcome. Hoped they would rescue everyone and no one would die, turning the attempted murder charge into murder.

What a mess! Hayden prayed everyone would be rescued. Because this operation was now totally out of the team's and law enforcement's control and fully in God's hands.

~

Cady had been on pins and needles since Hayden left, and she wished Nolan would let her out of the vehicle to pace. Anything to relieve her racing heart. She couldn't quit thinking about what Hayden and the rest of the team, along with Mina and her team were facing—in danger out on rough, choppy waters as they tried to rescue innocent people tossed overboard by that loser Wade Collins.

Why, God? Why would You allow this?

Nolan turned to peer at her. "You doing okay?"

"No. No, I'm not." Her tone was testy, and she hated taking out her frustration on him, and yet she couldn't seem to stop herself. "It's bad enough that human trafficking exists, but when men and women who are committed to stopping it must put themselves in such danger to stop it, it hardly seems fair or right."

"Ah," he said, a sad quality to his tone. "You're experiencing the same emotions we face on the job. Something most law enforcement officers do too. But there's no point in wondering why such terrible things happen, or it'll drive you crazy. The only thing you can do is focus on what you can do to help, then let it go."

"But what if someone gets hurt today? Someone you care about."

He curled his fingers tightly around the steering wheel and peered straight ahead. "Then we deal with what happens and make a plan to ensure it never occurs again."

She gaped at him. "You sound so cool and calm about it."

"I might sound that way, but trust me, that's not how I feel. Not by a long shot." He faced her. "The woman I love is out there on the cold, rough sea with ruthless criminals and cold water. Rough seas. Gunmen. All the while trying to rescue innocent people. So no. No! I'm not cool or calm."

She'd never seen him so rattled, but she completely understood his emotions. For his sake, she wished she hadn't forced him to verbalize them.

His phone rang, and he grabbed it. "Mina."

He listened intently. "Good. Glad they're almost there. I know you're surrounded by chaos, but thanks for taking time to update me."

He ended the call. "My team arrived to help, and Sawyer called in the Coast Guard. They're responding, but it could take thirty minutes or so to get the right equipment on site."

Thirty minutes, her brain screamed. Thirty minutes until help could arrive to subdue the evil men on the ship and Wade Collins. Collins had gotten what he wanted—for Mina and the others to concentrate on rescuing the people in the water so he could escape.

But where could he go that the Coast Guard wouldn't eventually catch him? He would have to ditch his boat and disappear by land or air. Was the marina here the best place to ditch his boat?

She and Nolan weren't prepared for that. "If Collins gets away, do you think he'll come back here?"

"Could be," Nolan said. "But there's likely a closer marina where he could put in and not risk returning to a known location where law enforcement could be waiting for him."

That made sense, but... "Don't most marinas prohibit strange boats from docking?"

"They do, but at this hour, there's no one around to enforce it. And now that the Coast Guard's involved, Collins would need to ditch his boat, so he wouldn't care what anyone at the marina thought anyway." Nolan locked eyes with her. "But even if it's only a slight possibility, we need to prepare in case this dangerous man returns."

Cady didn't like the sound of that, but she wasn't a chicken. She would follow Nolan's direction and stand her ground. No matter what occurred.

21

Sawyer's boat raced into place behind Mina's official county patrol boat, and Hayden braced his feet for a quick stop. Sawyer clicked into autopilot, and the boat slowed. The ocean was too deep to use an anchor, but the automated GPS would use bow and stern thrusters to keep their position so they didn't drift off course.

Hayden turned on his searchlight and rolled it over the area to illuminate the scene.

He swallowed and took a step back.

Chaos. Pure chaos.

Flailing victims and their luggage dotted the water. The people screamed for help. Some treaded water. Others dipped up and down like fishing bobbers in the rough waters, seeming as if they might go down for the count soon. They wouldn't make it until the Coast Guard arrived.

The threatening skies opened up and heavy rain pelted down on them. Conditions were bad enough, now this. *Off the Hook* and Collins were long gone, and the large ship that had carried the people was moving at a snail's pace. It ran parallel to the passengers in the water, not threatening them, thank goodness. But at this angle, Hayden couldn't make out any identifying information on the side.

Thankfully, Mina's deputies were in the water, swimming to flailing victims who either didn't know how to swim or were too cold to do so. Reaching them, the victims nearly took the deputies underwater in their attempt to get to safety. But the deputies wore life preservers, likely the only way they remained afloat.

How could one man cause such turmoil?

Heart creasing, Hayden looked at his team to shout out instructions, but Gabe had shot to his feet, ripped off his Kevlar vest, and was kicking off his boots.

"I've got the woman to the right." He dove over the side of the boat without waiting for anyone to comment.

Jude stood on the bow. He'd also discarded his vest and shoes. "There's someone close ahead. I think it's a kid. Going in."

Reece looked back at Hayden, swiped wet hair out of her face. "I'm going in too unless you stop me."

He shook his head. "I need you on overwatch."

She muttered something, but returned to her stand.

Hayden understood. He wanted to go in to help, too, but his entire team counted on him to keep them alive and that meant directing the rescue. Still, it was nearly impossible to stand by while others could die when he could step in to help.

Reece was doing her part too. Neutralizing the threat from the gunmen on the ship, protecting both her teammates and the vulnerable people crying out for help.

Already drenched, Abby made her way to them. "But I can go, right?"

He nodded.

She rushed to the bow of the boat, discarding her vest as well and untying her boots before kicking them off.

"I've got plenty of emergency blankets and a first aid kit under the seats up front," Sawyer said, standing behind the wheel, fisting his hands as if he wanted in on the rescue too. "If you want to grab them, they're starboard side."

Hayden scrambled up to the side opposite Reece, flung off the cushion, and opened the bench seat. He found an entire bag of silver emergency blankets. Thank goodness they'd chosen to use the boat of a Coast Guard commander who planned for emergencies.

"See anyone on the ship?" Hayden asked Reece.

She kept her eye on her viewfinder. "The rain is causing problems with visibility, but I can make out a couple of people. No one pointing weapons at us or others."

"Can you identify anyone?"

"No, but they're all of Asian descent, and before you ask, I don't see Kai."

Hayden had hoped she would've located him. "Keep them in your sight until they move out of range."

"I could use some help here." Gabe's strained, slightly breathless voice came from the side of the boat.

Hayden set down the blankets and leaned over the edge. Gabe raised a shivering woman up toward him, and he grabbed her arms to pull her up to safety. He settled her on a bench seat and immediately shook out an emergency blanket to wrap around her.

"You're safe now." He glanced back at Gabe. "You need a hand?"

"I'm going back." He swam away in a powerful crawl.

Hayden probably should've insisted Gabe get back in the boat to warm up before trying to save someone else, but his teammate wouldn't have listened. If someone was depending on Hayden to help, he wouldn't listen either.

Jude returned with a young boy and lifted him up to

Hayden. Before he could question the strength Jude had left to return for someone else, he'd turned and swam away.

Hayden grabbed another emergency blanket and placed the boy beside the woman. She exclaimed something Hayden couldn't understand and quickly wrapped an arm around the child. Hayden had hoped she was the boy's mother, but even though she was clearly relieved to see him, he could tell he wasn't her son.

Please, Father, please let his mother or father be rescued too. Don't leave him as an orphan.

He kept watching over the area, seeing deputies pulling people into their boat as well. He had no idea how many victims had been rescued, but five people were still in the water. Had the number dwindled because they'd been rescued, or had some succumbed to the choppy waves and cold?

"No! Leave me!" A woman screamed at Gabe as she flapped her hands at the water. "My baby. I just lost him. Find him."

"I'll move the searchlight to them." Sawyer grabbed the handle of the mounted light, and the beam skated over the water, highlighting Gabe and the area around him.

Something bobbed on the far edges of the light. Sawyer aimed it more carefully, revealing an infant floating on the water. Gabe left the woman and swam arm over arm toward the baby.

"Get this boat in closer to him," Hayden demanded.

Sawyer reacted immediately, revving the idling motor. He couldn't risk moving too fast and churning up the water, so they inched toward the woman, Gabe, and her baby. Felt like an eternity passed before they got close enough to help. Sawyer reversed thrust on the motor, piloting them to a stop nearby.

Gabe was two arm's lengths away from the child, when

the child disappeared in the water. He roared in anguish and surged ahead faster, arm over arm, pummeling the water.

He dove into the wave.

Hayden held his breath and started counting in his brain. One one-hundred. Two one-hundred. Three one-hundred. Four one-hundred. Five one-hundred. He reached fifteen when Gabe surfaced with the baby in his arms.

The woman screamed and reached for the boy.

"No!" Gabe shouted. It probably tore him apart, but he knew the baby's best chance was in the boat. He passed the child to Hayden, who lifted him gently, laid him on a cushion, and quickly assessed him.

He wasn't breathing.

Panic surged through Hayden, but his first-aid training kicked in. He gently turned the baby's head to the side and began chest compressions. He'd never performed CPR on an infant before and feared he might hurt him, but he knew he had to press firmly enough to restart the tiny heart.

Reece set down her weapon and came to his side. "I'll take over when you get tired."

Maybe he would tire of CPR on an adult, but only using his fingers, he could continue for a long time. He wanted to continue. He couldn't go in the water himself and wanted to be the one to bring this child back to life.

"Some help here," Gabe called out from the side of the boat.

"I got him," Reece said.

Offering no more than a nod, Hayden kept pressing the child's chest. The baby suddenly coughed, water spewing from his lungs. He coughed again. More water. Hayden's heart soared as he turned the baby over in his hands so he could more easily expel the water.

The coughing subsided, and the baby started screaming.

The most glorious sound Hayden had heard in his life. He grabbed a blanket and wrapped up the red-faced infant.

"My baby." The rescued woman charged him, her eyes frantically going to the child. "*Míngzé. Míngzé.*"

Tears streaming down her cheeks, she took her baby from Hayden's hands and collapsed onto the bench. She held the child close, rocking and cooing in the language all mothers knew.

Hayden retrieved another blanket and circled it around her shoulders, then the other woman moved to them and put her arm around the mother. She looked up at Hayden. "Thank you. Thank Jesus."

Gabe sank to the floor beside them and shivered in the cold. "Good. He made it."

Reece encased Gabe in a blanket, too, and enveloped him in her arms. She gave him a big kiss on the cheek. "I've never been so proud of you in my life."

Gabe didn't respond but continued to look at the woman and her child.

"You good man," the woman said. "My baby alive because of you."

"It's nothing any one of us wouldn't have done."

He might be right, but Hayden still basked in the joyful moment of a positive outcome.

"Besides," Gabe said. "My team got him breathing again. They're the real heroes."

"We need help!" Abby called from the water.

Hayden bolted to the side of the boat to find her holding a young girl, maybe six or seven years old, above the water. He leaned down to pull the little girl out of the icy cold. Jude was right behind her with another woman, so Hayden handed the child to Reece. "Get her bundled up."

Reece gave a nod as Abby hefted herself into the boat and trudged over to Reece and the child. Abby was in good hands with Reece, leaving Hayden free to extend his arms to the next woman who was crying and muttering under her breath in a language he didn't understand.

She reached out to him and grabbed tightly to his arms as if her life depended on it, and it did. She was heavy and soaking wet, and Hayden struggled to ease her over the edge of the boat.

Jude dragged himself into the boat, but collapsed just inside. Hayden tossed a blanket to him. Jude fumbled the packaging with icy cold fingers, so Hayden took it back, ripped the cellophane, and draped the blanket over him.

"Hey, thanks, man." Jude shuddered. "We rescue everyone?"

"Not sure."

Sawyer swung the light around, the beam skating across rough waters. "Looks like it's clear between us and the sheriff. No one needing rescue."

"Are you certain?" Jude asked.

Hayden gave his buddy a piercing stare. "Don't even think about going back in the water right now."

"I can if you need me to." Jude's whole body shivered under the blanket.

"We have to find out if our help is still needed and get everyone warm and dry as soon as possible." Hayden turned to Sawyer. "Does it look clear to pull up next to the sheriff's boat? We need to determine if everyone is accounted for."

"Roger that." Sawyer turned off the spotlight and shifted out of autopilot to start them moving forward.

It felt like they were just inching ahead again, when Hayden wanted to roar up to the boat, jump aboard, and find out from Mina if everyone had been rescued.

He moved over to the woman who spoke English. "Can you please tell the others we'll be hooking up with the sheriff's boat to find out who else was rescued?"

"Yes." She turned to the others.

The young boy jumped up and ran over to Hayden, clutching onto his arm, speaking frantically. "Mama. Mama."

"His mother was on the ship with him," the woman said. "They were separated in the water. Her name is Fen."

Hayden peered down at the boy and smoothed his hand over his blanketed head. "Tell him I'll check the minute I'm on board the other boat."

The woman took the boy's hand and drew him close to her. The young girl escaped from the arms of one of the women and ran forward too.

"She also is looking for her mother, Ming."

"I'll ask about her too." Hayden's voice cracked. His heart had climbed into his throat, and he had to fight to find the strength to leave the terrified children behind and move to the starboard side of the boat.

He sucked in big gulps of air to release his tension as they neared Mina's boat. Once a sightseeing vessel, it had been refitted for law enforcement use. The pilothouse was enclosed with a covered section extending behind it and an open deck at the rear. The rescued victims huddled in the covered area, all wrapped in blankets like the ones Sawyer had brought aboard. They were seated close together, so he couldn't tell how many people had been saved.

Once they reached a deputy who was within shouting range, Hayden leaned over the edge of the boat. "Ahoy! Permission to come alongside."

Mina jetted out from under the covered area and skidded on the slippery deck to the back of the boat. Rainwater had plastered her hair and clothing to her body, and a pair of binoculars hung around her neck. "Come on. Hurry. Give me a report."

Hayden threw her a rope, and she pulled Sawyer's boat

next to hers, then passed the rope to the deputy to tie off. She held out a hand to Hayden.

He grabbed hold of her ice-cold fingers and cleared the distance across the open water to her boat. "Did someone rescue a woman called Fen and one called Ming? We have their children."

"We have a few younger women who have been crying uncontrollably, but no one speaks English, so we don't understand what they're asking for."

Hayden turned back to Sawyer's boat. "Help me get the boy and girl aboard."

Jude tossed off his blanket and went to take the boy's hand to lead him to Hayden. Gabe was right behind him, holding the young girl in his arms, his face stony and angry. The exact feeling building in Hayden for the terror these children had been put through. On the plus side, if their parents were on the other boat, at least they would be spared the terror of being separated from them when their mothers were put into slavery.

But the big unknown right now was if the parents were here.

Jude moved closer to the edge of the boat. The boy clutched him tighter and started crying.

"Don't be afraid." Jude stroked the boy's head and smiled at him. The poor child couldn't understand him, but he surely understood the calming tone and touch.

Jude braced his legs to pick up the child, then passed him over to Hayden. He took the little hand in his and signaled for him to wait.

Gabe hovered protectively with the little girl, his eyes full of reluctance, as if he couldn't bear to let her go until she was back in a parent's arms. With a soft kiss to the top of her head, he gently passed her to Hayden, his hand lingering for a moment before letting her go.

Hayden took each child's hand and led them to the rescued people huddling together in the cold.

"Fen," Hayden called out. "Ming."

Before anyone could respond, the boy broke free and sprinted across the boat, shouting "Mama" over and over. He threw himself into a woman's arms. She clutched him tightly, sobbing as she held him.

Hayden had to swallow hard to keep his own emotions in check. Tears threatened, not from sorrow, but from the overwhelming relief of a life saved.

But then he looked at the girl. No one stepped forward. Her face crumpled, and she began to sob, repeating "Mama," her voice trembling with hope and fear.

Hayden continued walking into the group. They neared the back where a woman sat with her eyes closed, her hands folded on her drawn up knees.

The girl ripped free. "Mama!" she screeched.

The woman's eyes flew open. She lifted her hands to the sky, then pulled the little girl into her arms. They clung to each other, sobbing in pure relief. Another happy ending. Praise God!

They'd managed to reunite children with their parents —but Hayden still couldn't shake his uncertainty. He didn't know if everyone had made it out of the churning water. He turned back to Mina.

"How many rescued people on your boat?" Her urgent tone fought through the wind.

"Three women, a baby, and the girl and boy." Hayden's pride for his team threatened to take over when he shouldn't be thinking about that at all. "So a total of six. How many were aboard the boat?"

"We counted fifteen when they boarded. My deputies pulled in nine survivors."

"Everyone, then."

Mina grimaced. "We didn't see a baby so he wasn't in our count of fifteen. The true count is sixteen."

"Which means there's one person unaccounted for."

"Looks like it, but we don't have anyone who speaks English in our group to help us clarify."

"We do." Hayden went back to the side of the boat to call out. "Someone ask the baby's mother how many people were on the boat including her baby."

"On it!" Abby hurried to the woman cradling her baby to kneel in front of her.

Abby soon returned. "Sixteen. Her baby. The two children we pulled in and thirteen women about her age."

Hayden's heart sank. They'd failed. One woman was missing.

22

_____

"There!" Cady pointed at the docks ahead of her. "It's Collins's boat pulling into the marina. He was dumb enough to come back here."

Nolan raised his binoculars and scanned the area. "It's his boat, all right. Let me try to get Mina on the horn and see what she wants me to do."

He grabbed his phone and dialed.

Cady could hear the ringtone from across the SUV. She continued to watch Collins through her binoculars as he aimed his boat into the slip.

One ring. Two. Three. Nolan's call went to voicemail.

He slammed his fist into the steering wheel. "She's not answering."

"She must be getting a signal because it didn't go straight to voicemail."

"She's probably caught up in something that's keeping her from her phone."

Cady agreed, but terrible visions of what could be occupying Mina's time raced through Cady's brain.

Ugly visions, like criminals on a ship, pinning them down with gunfire.

Rifle reports blasting through the air. Bullets flying. Lives being risked. Lives lost. Hayden may be injured and clinging to life.

Oh, please, please, please. Keep them all safe.

Collins's boat coasted fully into the slip, and he killed the motor.

"I can't let Collins get away—I'm going after him." Eyes fierce with determination, Nolan pressed the keys into her hand. "Call 911 and get backup. If I'm not back in thirty minutes, take the SUV and get somewhere safe."

What? He was leaving her? How did she respond to that? Fear kicked up her pulse.

She searched for something to say, but he'd hung a binocular strap around his neck and bailed out of the driver's seat. By the time she could come up with a single-word reply, he'd silently closed the door and started toward the marina.

A rifle slung over his shoulder, he took slow, even steps toward the marina's main gate, moving in and out of hiding spots. He paused behind trees. Behind structures. Behind shrubs.

Good. At least he was being careful. Gave her confidence in his abilities. But on the other hand, his furtive movements scared her half to death. Being less careful only meant one thing. He believed if Collins saw him, he would come for him, and Nolan's life was on the line.

She prayed for his safety, her heart thumping wildly. Should she just sit here as he told her to do or should she call Hayden? Tell him what was going on?

What good would that do? If he wasn't tied up in whatever preoccupied Mina, hearing about his fellow teammate in danger would make him worry. Right now he was responsible for an entire team, and his mind would be too occupied to be worrying about her or Nolan.

That settled it. She wouldn't call anyone other than 911 as Nolan directed.

Facing facts, she got out her phone and dialed.

She would be alone. On her own. Forced to rely only on herself. Not something she expected to happen today, but it did. At least until she talked to the 911 dispatcher and backup arrived.

She could do this. She had to. She'd gather enough bravery to face whatever might come her way, or as Nolan said, flee the area to safety.

~

Hayden ignored the heaviness in his heart and faced Mina. "We're missing one woman. We have to look again."

"Agreed," she said. "But it's unlikely someone survived this long in such frigid water."

"Still, let's get lights on the water." Hayden leaned out to Sawyer's boat. "There's one woman unaccounted for. Get the spotlight on the open area. Everyone else, binoculars up and search."

His team threw off their silvery blankets and sprang into action. Hayden couldn't stand still either. He took off after Mina, who'd already raced to the front of her boat and climbed onto the bow. He rushed around the covered pilot-house to reach her, working hard to keep his footing on the slippery deck.

The wind had picked up sharply, and the rain came down in bursts—not in soft drops, but in fierce, angled sheets that slashed sideways under the force of the gale.

He planted his feet wide apart to maintain his balance and looked down. Angry, rough waves crashed at the front of the boat, rocking the debris left behind in the water, submerging some of the pieces before they bobbed back up.

Mina ran her handheld searchlight between her boat and the ship. He caught his first look at the ship's name. The *Red Dragon Voyager*. No surprise there.

Her light danced over the water, the rolling waves swallowing it up, like a greedy shark hunting its prey. She continued moving in a grid pattern.

"Wait!" he yelled to be heard above the wind and tumultuous ocean. "Bring your light back. I think there's someone clutching to the luggage you just passed over."

She shifted the light back toward the ship, highlighting a big suitcase. "Yes! Yes! There's someone there."

Hayden didn't waste a second but ripped off his vest and kicked out of his shoes. He plunged into frigid water. The icy waves slapped over him, threatening to swallow him up too. He fought to remain on the surface, where the wind propelled him back with each inch he gained. Heavy rain pelted his face, and he struggled to gain a breath.

Help this woman hold on. Help me rescue her.

Could he do this?

He had to. Her life was in his hands.

Pretend Cady was clinging to life. Ignore the waves whipped into foam by the unrelenting wind.

He dug deep. Found additional strength. Crawled, arm over arm. Pulling hard. Muscles screaming. Tearing. But winning. Advancing. Moving closer.

Rain vanished into the frothing waves as if the ocean was devouring the storm drop by drop, rage meeting rage in an unrelenting clash.

A sound caught his attention.

Could it be the woman's hoarse cry for help or was it the water hitting the ship?

He preferred to believe it was the woman, but if so, she couldn't have much left before she disappeared into the murky depths.

Do better! Move faster! Pump harder!

His motivation doubled. He surged ahead. A large wave collided with the suitcase, ripping her free. Her arms flailed, splashing, and trying to find something to clutch onto. The suitcase. Likely. The icy water consumed her. She popped back up. Coughing, struggling, but with less energy.

He buried his face in the water and sliced through the water one stroke at a time. Kicked until his thigh muscles burned with exhaustion.

He wanted to give up more than he'd ever wanted to give up in his life.

Keep going. Trust God. He put you here for this moment. With His help, you can save this woman's life.

Literal waves of trouble surging around him, he plunged ahead. He didn't have a life preserver or a suitcase to cling to, but he could cling to God. He was Hayden's protection through this storm.

His hand struck the suitcase. Yes! He was there, and the woman had surfaced again. He braced his muscles, preparing for her to throw her body on him and take him under like many drowning victims did.

But she didn't move. Probably didn't have the strength or was too cold.

He raked in a few deep breaths and circled his way around the suitcase to her. She blinked at him. Her eyes were vacant. Looking exhausted. As if she were giving up.

"Hold on. Don't give up on me now." He doubted she understood him, but he infused his tone with hope and encouragement.

He took her arms from the suitcase, and her hands remained curled as if she were still clutching something. He turned her on her back without any fight or argument. Clasping her around the chest, he started to stroke back toward the boat.

Her silent sobs jerked her body amidst the shivering. At these cold temperatures and having been in the water for so long, he doubted she would make it for much longer.

A motor sounded above the storm, nearing him. He glanced back.

Yes! Thank you, God.

Sawyer was moving his boat into position nearby.

Success in sight, Hayden stroked harder.

Pull. Pull. Pull.

Rain lashed at his face, but he cut through the churning waves.

The boat came alongside him. Keeping the woman under his arm, he turned over and made the final few strokes.

At the boat, he tried to lift her up, but had nothing left.

"I got you, buddy." Gabe plunged into the water beside him.

Together they raised the woman high enough for Jude and Abby to pull her aboard.

Gabe looked at him and held up a hand for a high-five.

He managed it, but just barely.

Gabe frowned. "Let's get you out of the water."

Hayden lifted his arms, weakness nearly had him dropping them. Gabe shoved under Hayden's arms, and Jude clutched on. One big surge, and he pushed out of the water. He shimmied over the side, Gabe right behind him.

Reece waited with blankets for both of them. "You had us all worried."

"Hey." He tried to keep his tone light. "I couldn't be the only one on the team who didn't get wet."

They chuckled, but it was forced. "I lost my phone. Anyone have Mina's phone number?"

"I do," Abby said.

"Call her," Hayden said. "Tell her the woman is alive but

in rough shape, and we're heading straight to the nearest boat ramp to get medical attention."

He looked up to see if Sawyer heard. He saluted, tapped his navigation screen, then called out that they would return to the same public boat ramp they'd launched from. "Tell everyone to hold on. If we book it, we can get there in ten minutes."

"Give Mina our destination and have her request ambulances. She can get a faster response than we can. The rest of you attend to the woman. Warm her up with whatever it takes."

They scrambled to get moving. He only hoped they possessed whatever it took, and she, along with the others, survived.

All he could do now was pray. Only time would tell.

Hayden lost his comm's unit in the water too, so he got a phone from Sawyer to call Nolan and update him—plus check on Cady. The call went straight to voicemail.

Hayden snapped to attention and sat forward.

What was going on? Why was his buddy's phone going right to voicemail? That had to be deliberate and not due to a bad signal. If he was still in the SUV where Hayden had left him, he'd have full signal.

So what was wrong? Had something happened to Cady?

He could call her, but he lost his phone with her number and didn't know it.

"Anyone have Cady's phone number?" he yelled.

One by one, the others gave negative replies. His gut clenched, and he turned to Abby, his nearest teammate. "You're in charge when we dock. I'm going to check on Cady."

"Did something happen to her?" Abby asked.

"I don't know, but Nolan isn't answering, so I'll be double-timing it until I lay eyes on her again."

23

Where had Collins and Nolan gone?

Cady swept the marina area with her binoculars. Only movement she found were the waves slapping at the shore and large storm clouds threatening rain crawling across dark skies.

She'd seen Collins descend the steps from the upper level, but then lost sight of him. Nolan had disappeared on the dock about twenty-five minutes ago, and she hadn't seen him since.

Had they encountered each other? She saw zero evidence of the pair struggling on the dock or on the boat. There was simply no sign of anyone.

Twenty-five minutes. Twenty-five long minutes. Alone with only her imagination filled with terrible outcomes. And as a reporter, she could conjure up far more horrible situations than the average person.

She'd remained in the place with no help in sight. The operator had warned it could take some time before help arrived because so many deputies had been dispatched to an emergency. Of course! They had to be helping rescue the people Collins had thrown overboard and were stationed onshore to arrest the gunmen. Or maybe it was a serious car accident.

Either way, it didn't matter. Not really. No one was coming anytime soon.

She checked her watch. Time to bail. She lowered her binoculars for just a second to scoot behind the steering wheel but quickly rested her arms on it again to watch the marina.

Was Nolan really in trouble?

She scanned wide. Still no sign of either man, and she didn't even know if Nolan needed help. He surely was smarter than Collins and could take care of himself.

So why was her gut so tied up in a knot? It wasn't like she'd personally experienced any danger or Nolan had come under fire or anything like that. Seriously, if she was so freaked out here, how would she ever take an assignment in a war zone, where real conflict unfolded around her? Maybe she couldn't do it. She'd never given the danger aspect any real thought.

She'd glossed over the nitty-gritty to think of the stories she would turn in. Perhaps to the recognition she would get for stellar writing. Maybe a Pulitzer Prize. All the wrong reasons to go to a war zone. Her emphasis should be on reporting people's terrible struggles. To show the human cost of war. She certainly would need to have a long think about her motives.

A knock sounded on her window. She jumped. Nolan?

She spun. Gasped.

Stared at the gun pressed against the window. A big black gun.

Collins' gun.

He'd slicked back his dripping wet hair, and his drenched clothing stuck to his stout frame. He hadn't come down the dock. He'd jumped into the water to swim ashore.

Not something she was expecting. Nolan hadn't likely expected it either as he'd gone down the dock.

"Unlock the door," Collins shouted.

She shook her head in defiance.

"Open or don't open. No skin off my nose." He dropped his finger to the trigger. "I'm taking this vehicle with or without your help."

She jerked away from him. The terror in his eyes as he pinned his gaze to her, and his antsy movements said he meant business.

She didn't want to die, but if she opened the door, would he kill her anyway?

She had no choice. Sitting here doing nothing would surely end in her death.

Please don't let me die today.

She held the binoculars in her right hand in case she could use them as a weapon and clicked the door lock with her free hand.

He stepped to the side and jerked the door open, the barrel of his handgun continuously aimed at her.

"Get out," he said.

Fear froze her muscles, and she couldn't move.

"Fine. We'll do it my way." He reached in with his free hand, as if he were going to grab her and pull her out.

"Lay a finger on her and it's the last thing you'll do!" Hayden's beautiful, wonderful voice came from nearby.

Collins glanced back, and she shifted to look in Hayden's direction. His rifle was aimed at Collins. Neither she nor Collins had heard Hayden sneak up on them.

Collins' expression waffled, and his gun arm lowered a fraction.

Now was the time for her to act. She lifted the binoculars and slammed them into the barrel of his gun. His arm went up. The gun went flying.

In the blink of an eye, Hayden was on him. His hand on the back of his neck, jerking him from the truck and tossing him to the ground.

Hayden got Collins on his stomach, his hands behind his back. "Cady, get the handcuffs in the glove compartment."

His words barely registered. Adrenaline swept through her body, making her weak, and her head pounded from the handgun's report. She was safe! Alive!

"Cady?" Hayden asked.

"Sorry." She tried to shake off her stupor as she reached for the glove compartment.

She located a pair of heavy-duty zip-tie handcuffs. She slid out of the vehicle, her legs rubbery and threatening to let her collapse. She held on to the door with one hand and bent forward to give the cuffs to Hayden with the other.

He expertly tightened them on Collins's wrists.

"Ouch!" Collins glared at her. "Not so rough."

"I'll bet that's what the women and children said to you when begging you not to throw them in the water." Hayden jerked up on the cuffs and got Collins into a sitting position.

A crunching noise sounded in the distance, and Cady spun. She let out a long breath.

"Dude," Hayden said, his tone tense. "Where have you been? Collins could've killed her."

"I owe you both an apology." Nolan glanced between them. "I expected him to use the dock or hide out in one of the other slips. It took time to clear all of them. By the time I finished, thirty minutes had passed, and I'd told Cady to leave if I wasn't back by then. But when I got back to the gate, I saw the vehicle was still here and got up here as soon as I could."

"Yeah, well." Hayden scrubbed a hand across his face

and let out a few long breaths. "You didn't do anything wrong. I would probably have handled it the same way."

"I don't think you did anything wrong either," she said. "And I certainly don't blame you for this creep getting to me."

"For what it's worth," Collins said, "I was only gonna drag her out and take off in the vehicle. I wouldn't have shot her."

"So you say now, when charges will soon be brought against you and you're trying to lessen the severity." Hayden stared down on the man as a siren sounded in the distance.

"Finally," she said and explained why law enforcement was so delayed.

"Yeah," Hayden said. "There were several patrol vehicles and ambulances at the boat ramp when we docked."

"How did the rescue attempt go?" Cady asked.

"We rescued everyone," Hayden said, but didn't sound joyous. "They all seem to be doing well, but the last woman is suffering from hypothermia. So we'll see how she does."

"Praise God you found all of them," Cady said, as she offered a silent prayer to God.

Hayden nodded, but glared at Collins. "You'll be lucky to get out of this without any murder charges pinned on you, but you better believe I'll make sure you're charged with sixteen counts of attempted murder. No, make that seventeen, including Cady."

"Now come on." Collins glared right back at him. "I didn't try to kill them. Just didn't want them on my boat."

"Seriously." Cady blinked at him. "Throwing people overboard into frigid water when you don't know if they can swim doesn't in your mind equate to attempted murder?"

"Well, when you put it that way..." He shrugged.

"That's exactly the way we'll put it," Nolan said. "But you can do yourself a favor—maybe reduce the charges. Tell us who's in charge of the trafficking operation and where Kai Nakoa is located."

Collins drew his knees up to his chest. "I don't know anything about that guy, and even if I did, I'm no snitch."

"Fine," Hayden said. "Take all of the responsibility for Kai's kidnapping and the trafficking charges too. Pile on even more prison time. You'll never see the light of day."

"But I-I-I'm not in charge." He lurched forward, his feet sliding down. "They only wanted me for my boat, and I just took the passengers ashore."

"So who gave the directive to meet the ship?" Hayden used a cool tone that belied the anger she knew had to be burning in his gut.

Collins gnawed on his lower lip. "Palmer, okay? Guy's name is Cody Palmer. Is that what you wanted to know?"

"Not exactly," Nolan said. "We already knew Palmer was the middleman, but who's the top dog?"

"No idea," Collins said. "And I mean it. I have no idea who Palmer reports to, if anyone."

Hayden gaped at him. "Palmer tells you when to pick people up, and you've never asked who or if he reports to someone else?"

"I mean, yeah, I was curious, but what difference did it make to me? I did what Palmer asked, and I got paid. That's all I cared about."

Grr. "Exactly. That's all you cared about." Cady had to fight hard not to cross over and kick the man. "Not about the fear these women faced when separated from their children or their husbands or their family. The lives you destroyed. Totally and completely destroyed."

Collins shrugged. "Hey, I didn't know what happened to them."

"But you had a good idea, didn't you?" Nolan glared at Collins.

"As far as I'm concerned, they were people who wanted to be smuggled from another country to start a new life in the United States. That's all I knew."

"Except for the fact that we've been talking about human trafficking here, and you never once disputed it and said they were just being smuggled." Hayden slammed a fist into his palm. "You better be glad deputies are arriving, because I'm this close to telling you what I think about that lie."

Collins sneered. "You won't touch me. Not if you don't want me to bring charges."

Hayden gave Collins a withering look. "Get him out of here, Nolan, before I do something I regret."

The depth of Hayden's anguish swept over Cady. Sure, she'd known the trafficking troubled him, but his time rescuing them from near death clearly impacted him deeper.

How in the world did someone recover from the fear of not getting to these people in time? The pain from one of them dying, if that happened.

Please, help me help him through having experienced such a horrific situation.

Nolan hauled Collins to his feet and dragged him toward a deputy stepping from his patrol vehicle.

Hayden let out a shuddering breath and picked up his rifle to set it against a tree. He looked up at her, his jaw set. "I'm sorry. Can you forgive me?"

She moved closer to him. "What in the world do you need forgiveness for?"

"For leaving you. I should've known something might happen and bring you with me." He rubbed a hand over his head and clamped it on his neck.

She took the last few steps between them and reached for his hand to hold it. "You left me in Nolan's capable hands. None of us could've predicted Collins would come back here. Besides, if I'd been with you, you would've worried about me instead of successfully rescuing women and children who needed you."

"Still. I should've... just should've known better."

"Stop second-guessing yourself. I'm okay."

"But he could've killed you." Looking deeply into her eyes, he let out a harsh, unsteady breath. "I couldn't live with that."

His worst nightmare. Failing to protect someone he cared about.

She took on his pain as if it were her own. "You can't control everything, you know. You can plan and organize as much as you want, but in the blink of an eye your plan can change. God is the only one in control, and we have to learn to trust His choices for us."

"Trust!" His eyes flew wide open. "You know that's my hot button, and I've been struggling with it."

"Oh, mine too. I haven't managed it at all. Especially when it comes to a relationship. I didn't tell you about my mother, did I?" She pulled her hand free.

He took it back and held her gaze. "Tell me."

How they'd veered so far off-topic, she didn't know, but he deserved to understand why nothing could happen between them. "When I was eight, my mom had a late-term miscarriage. Seeing me made her think about the lost baby. She couldn't handle it, and she bailed on me and Dad. I never saw her again. I don't even know if she's still alive. Dad lived in the same house until he moved here, and if she's still alive, she could've easily found us."

A tremor passed through his hands. "I'm so sorry, honey. It was rough losing my parents, but I can only imagine the pain you went through knowing she could've been with you but chose not to be."

If he only *could* imagine it, because she couldn't adequately describe the emotional anguish an eight-year-old goes through when her mother rejects her. No point in dwelling on that. Not when it couldn't be changed. "So you see, it proves marriage doesn't always last. Doesn't survive trials and hardships. If I ever let myself fall in love and get married, why would mine be any different?"

"Not all marriages fall apart."

"I know, but theirs was really strong. They were so happy and good together, and then boom. A bomb was dropped on them, and Mom couldn't come back from it."

"I hear you, especially since I was just in the water and waves threatened to take me down. I know we each have to figure out a way to deal with challenges." He stood motionless, eyes distant, but she kept quiet and waited him out. "Consider this. I couldn't rescue that woman on my own. Too many things were going against me. The cold. The waves. The rain. The wind. Fatigue and on and on. I wanted to give up."

Her heart swelled with a desire to ease his suffering. "I'm sorry you had to go through that. If I can do anything to help, just ask."

"Thank you—but here's the thing. That moment gave me a kind of clarity I'd never had before. I saw the woman holding tightly to her suitcase—her lifeline. And I realized I had to cling to God in the same way, or we both would've gone under."

"I'm glad God was there for you," she said sincerely.

"Me, too, but the big thing was, on the ride back to the dock, I couldn't stop thinking about the storms we face in life. The waves of trouble that hit us, sometimes so hard we feel like giving up. But if we hold on to God, He becomes our anchor—our shelter in the storm—and He'll guide us through. I want to be done with my lack of trust and want to live eyes forward, trusting God, and refusing to look back."

She blinked at him for a few moments. What he said, made complete sense, but as time passed, would he remember this new revelation when one of life's big challenges hit him, would he forget all about it? Not having had the experience, could she even believe it was true in her own life?

She wanted to. How she wanted to. Especially if it meant she and this fine man could be together.

24

As the team and Cady assembled for an update in the conference room, Hayden tried to focus on the rescue. On Collins's admission that he worked with Palmer to traffic women—something they could use to prosecute both of them in a court of law. But his mind kept going back to his discussion with Cady. His revelation. He claimed if he would cling to God, He'd be his protection and show him how to get through storms.

Sure, he believed that in the moment his life was threatened. Even when Collins threatened Cady's life. But now that things had settled down, did he believe it for everyday life? For things like locating Kai. Like bringing these men to justice. Like him figuring out what his future should be with Cady, if anything? Not just him, but for Cady to figure it out as well.

He glanced at her. She claimed she was all right after Collins pointed a gun at her, but there was a shadow of pain in her eyes. Was it from the gun attack or from knowing who actually killed her father? He wished he could've spared her from watching the doorbell video. She would've had to see it at some point, but he felt responsible for not being careful enough to hide it from her until they figured out a good way to present it to her.

Maybe there wouldn't have been a good way. Just like when his parents died. There was no good way for him to hear that news. There was no way to help prevent the shock, the anger, the intense, deep anguish and pain. He just had to hear the devastating news and come back from it, which, if he looked at his life for any amount of time, he would realize that hadn't happened until his discovery today.

Please don't let my recent revelation on clinging to You through storms go to waste. Let me believe it. Embrace it. Live it.

He kept the thought in his head for a few moments, then opened his eyes to see his teammates looking at him. Everyone had changed into dry clothing, and despite it being summer, they'd fired up a small heater in the conference room near Abby, who continued to shiver. The team's expressions were defeated and watchful. Although they'd been successful in figuring out who'd killed Percy and rescuing the women, they still hadn't found Kai, which was their mission.

He got it. Totally got it. But he was the leader of this investigation, and he had to bring everyone back to task and get to work again.

He moved to the head of the table. "I get how you're feeling. Mixed emotions. We were there to save many lives, and that was a win for sure."

"A big win!" Abby's forceful tone surprised him. "Even if our mission was to take someone into custody tonight in addition to Collins, you can't put a price on saving one life, let alone the numbers we did save."

"Collins is a start though," Reece said.

Hayden smiled his appreciation to her for her positive take on what could be deemed an operational failure. "But we still have a job to do, and we need to think positively about finding Kai alive."

"What if Kai hasn't been abducted?" Abby asked. "What if he knew Ivers was after him, and he went into hiding?"

"Makes sense to me," Gabe said. "Especially since the usual leads we see in abduction cases aren't present. No sign of forced entry anywhere. No indication of a struggle. No ransom demand. And on and on."

"What you're saying might be true," Hayden said, "but I think we should proceed under the assumption that Ivers played a role in Kai's disappearance."

"Why can't we work both avenues?" Cady asked.

"Good question," Hayden said. "If he went into hiding, he's not in danger, and he'll come out when he thinks he's safe, so no point in dividing our resources. But if Ivers had something to do with his disappearance, then his life could still be in danger, and he needs us immediately."

Abby fisted her hands and rested them on the table. "So we first get eyes on Ivers. Palmer, too, if Mina doesn't haul him in after interviewing Collins."

"That won't take all of us," Nolan said. "So, at the same time, we can continue pursuing the leads we had before tailing Collins."

"Agreed." Hayden went to the board, picked up the marker and tapped the first item. "We should start with registration for the vehicle used to assault us. Guy's name, Gabe?"

"Alec Mercado."

"And in case we forgot," Jude said, "Gabe got the name in the five minutes or less he promised."

"You know it." Gabe radiated confidence.

"Figured I'd mention it before you did." Jude chuckled. "It's not like you'd let us forget."

Usually the team laughed with him, but this time, all he got were a few strained smiles.

Hayden moved on. "What do we know about Mercado?"

"He has priors and has done time for several crimes." Gabe glanced at his notes. "B & E, armed robbery, assault with a deadly weapon, and domestic violence, to name a few."

Hayden was glad he didn't know the guy's background when they were fleeing from him, or the incident might've hooked him harder than he'd like to admit. "Sounds like the kind of guy who wouldn't hesitate to shoot at us. I'm assuming by now Mina has identified and questioned him. If she found his vehicle, she's likely impounded it and placed him under arrest."

"She said she'd come by after her interview with Collins," Nolan said. "We can ask her about Mercado then."

Hayden drew a big red circle around the guy's name on the board to bring up with Mina. "What about Palmer's Wi-Fi? Have we gone through all the files?"

Abby shook her head. "We still have a few to review, but looks like we've already found the big lead. Now we need to find a legit way for Mina to get the information."

"We sure can't taint the evidence by coming right out and telling her to get a warrant for the video files," Gabe said.

"Shouldn't be a problem now." Nolan gave a weak smile. "Not if Collins rolled over on Palmer, and she knows they're in this together. She'll request a warrant for Palmer's house, and I feel certain she'll include the security cameras. Still, I can casually mention we noticed a doorbell camera when we were surveilling his house. She's sharp enough to read between the lines and know she needs to pull those videos."

Hayden let his gaze travel around the group. "I get that everyone is tired, but watch what you say around her. We don't like withholding information from her, but by sharing anything we know about Ivers, he could walk free."

Cady shook her head. "I don't know how law enforcement officers remember all of that to keep from ruining a solid prosecution."

"Sometimes they don't, and it really stings to see someone walk." Hayden didn't want to bring his team down more, so he pointed at the next item, which was the review of the documents found in the locker.

Reece tapped the stack of papers in front of her. "We confirmed Kai's financial commitment to the Emerald Scorpion Group. It's been going on for months. Plus, there's a signature on the final page that could be Odin Ivers's name. I don't think it's clear enough to prove his involvement, but maybe it can be enhanced by forensics."

"I'll ask Sierra if they can do anything," Hayden said. "If they can, I'm sure she'll need the original signature."

"Let me talk to Mina about getting that to Sierra," Nolan said.

Hayden jotted the information on the board then tapped the next item. "Nick and I have algorithms running to see if we can scrape the dark web for information about the group and if the code names Fletcher gave us are tied to it." Hayden did his best to keep an upbeat tone. "As of now, our efforts haven't returned anything for either of us."

"Speaking of Nick," Abby said, "has he had any success with cracking the flash drive from Kai's bungalow?"

"Not yet, but he'll contact me the minute he succeeds."

"Hearing the conversation between Ivers and Collins," Abby said, "sounds like whatever is on that drive will compromise Ivers's trafficking operation."

"I'm sure you're right," Hayden said. "But there's nothing I can do to speed Nick along. He's working as fast as he can."

Hayden's phone rang. "It's my ICE buddy." He answered. "Adam. Mind if I put you on speaker in front of my team?"

"They're all involved, so they might as well hear this too."

Hayden tapped the speaker icon. "Go ahead, Adam."

"Dude! You've been busy tonight."

"You heard about our rescue of trafficking victims."

"Heard about it? It's all the talk right now. The Coast Guard crew you requested stopped the *Red Dragon Voyager* and boarded the vessel."

Cady had come to her feet and was eyeing the phone as if it were a rattlesnake ready to bite her. "What did they find?"

"Legit cargo for the most part, but four containers held humans smuggled from Beijing."

"Four containers?" Hayden gaped at his phone. "How many people in all?"

"Fifteen people per container, so sixty total."

Reece gasped, and the others bristled with barely contained anger.

"Were they captured in Beijing and forced to come to the United States?" Abby asked.

"No. The worst part is they actually paid to be smuggled into the country. But we all know how this ends. Preliminary reports show the ship makes multiple stops along the Oregon coast, dropping off about fifteen people at a time."

Hayden slammed his fist into the wall, relishing the pain in his hand. "Did you learn anything about the organization?"

"Nada," Adam said. "But give us time and we will, starting with the local contacts who've been farming these people out for quite some time."

Locals. People like Collins, Palmer, and Ivers.

"You didn't happen to find Kai Nakoa on board, did you?" Hayden asked.

"Sorry, no, but his name is on my list of questions for the Chinese nationals we apprehended."

"When will you be questioning them?" Jude asked.

"Soon as I can make my way out there, and we can get a solid interpreter on scene."

"Keep me updated," Hayden said.

"You know I will."

The call ended, and Hayden took a measure of his team-mates' reactions. "Not the information we were hoping for, but it's good to know the ship's occupants were arrested."

Gabe growled. "It's unlikely it's the top men in the Chinese organization."

A murmur of agreement traveled around the table.

The door opened, and Mina marched into the room, likely saving all of them from a pity fest. She looked exhausted. Nolan must've thought so, too, as he hurried to the door to wrap his arms around her. Not something he'd ever done in front of the team when they were in business mode, but everyone who'd participated in tonight's rescue deserved unlimited hugs.

She allowed it for a short period of time before pushing away. "Mind if I grab a cup of Reece's excellent coffee I'm smelling?"

Reece got to her feet. "Sit. I'll grab you a cup."

"Thank you," Mina said, and Nolan led her to a chair next to his.

Reece poured a cup of coffee and cut a huge piece of a cinnamon swirl coffee cake she'd thawed from the freezer and took them to Mina. "Eat this too. The sugar will help."

Mina raised her head and smiled. Reece squeezed her shoulder, then went back to her chair.

Mina took a sip of the hot coffee, then another before

setting the mug down and looking around the group. "I haven't had a chance to thank you all for your work in rescuing the women and children tonight. I never imagined Collins would do such a thing. I probably should've considered he'd do anything to escape prosecution, but it never came to mind."

"Don't be hard on yourself," Hayden said. "None of us could've anticipated he would do something so heartless."

She took another pull on the coffee mug. "You'll be happy to know ICE was involved when the Coast Guard stopped the ship. You may have noticed it's the *Red Dragon Voyager* Olive and Percy told us about."

They nodded their understanding, but no one asked any questions. Mina's eyebrow went up. "You already knew about ICE's involvement."

"My buddy at ICE just called," Hayden said.

"It's helpful to have people you can call on, and with such a large team, your contact list must run deep." Mina forced a tired smile. "I interviewed Collins. Just as he told you, he readily gave up Cody Palmer as the person who hires him to ferry the women from the ship to shore."

"Did he mention any other names in the organization?" Abby asked.

She broke off a piece of the coffee cake. "He thinks there might be someone above Palmer, but he didn't know who. We've brought Palmer in for questioning, and I've obtained a warrant to search his home and business."

"He talking?" Abby asked.

"Spilling his guts. Says he's not going to take the fall for this, and he instantly ratted out our county commissioner, Odin Ivers." She paused and looked at the others. "Your lack of shock over a high ranking official being involved tells me you knew about this too."

Nolan rested his hand on hers. "We couldn't say anything without jeopardizing his prosecution."

"Got it," she said, not at all seeming angry. "Palmer hid the key on the boat after Ivers beached it. Palmer said Ivers has gotten out of control, so he put the key there for us to find the documents to implicate him."

"But if he did leave that evidence, he risked Ivers snitching on him too," Gabe said.

"He said Ivers reported to a Chinese organization and figured Ivers would be too afraid of them to say a word." She popped the coffee cake into her mouth and chewed quickly. "There's really nothing else I can tell you about tonight that you don't already know, other than the last woman rescued is still in the hospital. Thanks to Hayden's quick thinking, her prognosis is good."

Hayden felt his face color at being singled out. "I was in the right place at the right time to see her and didn't do anything everyone else didn't do."

"Still, she owes you her life if she makes it." Mina smiled at him.

Hopefully, her smile meant he'd regained her trust back. "I have a thing about being shot at so do you mind if I ask you if you've learned anything about Mercado?"

"Ah," she said. "So you got someone to run the plates for you."

Hayden nodded, but wouldn't throw Gabe's friend under the bus.

"Then I'm sure you know about his rap sheet. Unfortunately, I don't know anything more about him at this point." She took a sip of the coffee. "He's in the wind, but we've issued an alert for him. Hopefully he'll talk when we bring him in."

"So no connection to Collins, Palmer, or Ivers," Hayden clarified.

She shook her head. "But we've only just started digging into him."

"We were hoping for more information," Abby said.

"You know how it goes with a small department. You have to choose your priorities, and right now it's the trafficked women." She took a chest-raising breath and let it out. "I *can* tell you we recovered a handgun at Mercado's home, which has been sent off to ballistics for comparison to slugs recovered at the scene. The weapon's a 9mm, as were the slugs, so we're hoping we have the right firearm. So far the only other important forensics from the scene is paint transferred from his vehicle to yours, which also is being tested for a match. We've impounded his vehicle, and forensics is doing a thorough search."

Jude bent forward. "I don't suppose you have anything on the other guy in his vehicle."

"Nothing."

Cady blinked rapidly. "But when you find Mercado, you'll keep him locked up, right?"

"Yes. We have enough to hold him."

Gabe gritted his teeth. "Maybe bringing him in will spook whoever he's reporting to, and they'll do something stupid while we're watching."

Mina crossed her arms and looked at each person in turn. "I know I can't stop you from watching potential suspects, but I need to caution you not to spook them, preventing us from making a solid arrest."

Nothing she said would stop them, but they'd embrace the warning to be more cautious. With Collins and Palmer detained, they needed to get eyes only on Mercado and Ivers.

25

Morning came and Cady tried to remain encouraged as she ate a breakfast of fluffy pancakes and tangy sausages in the kitchen with Hayden. Nolan had gone to meet Mina at the cave to get Sierra and her team started on the forensics. Everyone else wanted to get Ivers's surveillance going, but Gabe checked the commissioner's house, and he wasn't home. He moved on to Ivers's office. Another strikeout. It wasn't open yet so they wouldn't be able to locate him via phone for a few hours.

Gabe agreed to remain in place, keeping the commissioner's office under surveillance. But not until after he warned the team members to save him some of his favorite breakfast. Reece had just laughed and promised to make more if there wasn't anything left.

Cady loved how each group member had their own quirks. She'd been totally submerged in their lives for days, and it was like she'd known them for years, and they'd be friends forever.

Man, oh, man. She already knew how hard leaving Hayden would be after this was all over. But not just him. Saying goodbye to his teammates would sting too.

Hayden dropped his fork onto the plate and pushed back. "Reece, you've got to stop feeding us this way when we're so involved in a job and have no time to work off the calories."

She rested a hand on his shoulder. "I promise to tell you when you start getting that middle-aged spread, and I'll personally drag you to the gym to work it off."

Hayden chuckled.

"He has a point," Cady said. "I'm sure I've gained five pounds since I've stayed here."

"If so," Hayden ran his gaze over her, "it's looking good on you."

Reece mocked gagging. "That's my sign to leave the two of you alone."

Hayden glanced at his watch. "That's a good thing because it's time for Betty Lou to call Ivers's office."

Reece's laughter disappeared. "I'm on it. There're pancakes and sausage warming in the oven and fresh squeezed juice and a fruit bowl in the refrigerator if you want more."

He groaned and shook his head. "Didn't I just say I need to stop eating?"

"Yes, but that doesn't mean it's what you'll do." She winked at him and left them.

"I love your teammates, and I'm going to miss them when I go," Cady said before considering how her statement would bring the discussion into the personal realm, an area she wanted to avoid today.

He frowned. "I assume you inherited your father's cottage. So have you decided what you'll do with it yet?"

"I haven't really thought about it." She picked up her silverware and arranged it neatly on her empty plate, careful to miss the syrup so they didn't get sticky. "I have to look into the cost of maintaining it before I can decide, but I don't think I want to sell it. It would be nice for vacations, or maybe I could rent it out."

"Or you could move here full-time and live at the beach."

His hope-filled expression nearly was her undoing, but she dug deep to hide her angst. "I can't work from here."

"Yeah, I know, but I had to try." He scooted his chair closer to her and took her hands. "I meant what I said last night. I'll do my best to trust God and only look forward. I can't promise how successful I'll be, but I'd hoped you might consider dating."

Oh, man, his touch made her want to let go and give in. "I'm sure my feelings for you have been obvious, but long distance dating isn't a great way to begin a relationship. Most of them fail."

"You're probably right, but can you at least consider it?"

She opened her mouth to say yes, but his phone rang, taking his attention. "It's Nick."

His unease melted away, replaced by a burst of enthusiasm the moment he picked up. "Putting you on speaker with Cady."

"I cracked the drive." Nick sounded excited, sure—but the exhaustion in his voice was impossible to miss. "Sorry it took so long. It was worse than some of the military drives I've worked on."

Hayden shot to his feet. "I'm just glad you could do it."

"Oh, there was no question about that. Just about the time it would take to succeed." He laughed. "I know you want the info it contains ASAP, so after I cloned the drive for legal purposes, I also put a clone on our network for you. As soon as we finish here, I'll send you a link and login to access it."

"Perfect."

"That's the good news, but now the bad." His fatigue

seemed to overwhelm his tone now. "I've struck out on the code names on the dark web, but don't wig out. I have a few other tricks up my sleeve, and now that the drive is done, I can put my full attention to the search."

"Hey, thanks," Hayden said. "I owe you big time."

"I might just call you on that. You never know." He chuckled. "Let me know if you have a problem accessing the files. Later, man." Nick ended the call.

"This data could blow things wide open." Hayden shifted as if he couldn't wait to get moving. "Mind if we finish this discussion later so I can get to my computer?"

"Let's go." She stood, too, but he'd taken off before she reached full height. It would take him a few minutes to retrieve the data and make sense of it, so she cleared the table and loaded the dirty dishes in the dishwasher to lighten Reece's load.

In the conference room, she paused at the doorway. Hayden and Jude sat next to each other, each staring at laptops. Phone to her ear, Reece sat directly across from Hayden, and Abby next to her.

Abby closed her computer and slid it away from her. "I'm done with the video files from Palmer's house. I didn't find anything else of value, so hopefully that flash drive will give you the information we need."

"Hope so," Hayden said without looking up.

"Thank you," Reece said in Betty Lou's accent, then lowered her hand to the table. "Betty Lou got the info we need, but it's not good. Ivers is at a statewide county commissioner conference at the Dunes until tomorrow night."

Hayden's head shot up. "The Dunes."

The Oregon Dunes were the largest expanse of coastal sand dunes in America and a huge recreation area and tourist trap not far from Lost Lake. At this time of year, the place would be packed with tourists and off-road vehicles.

"That'll make watching him far more difficult," Hayden said.

"Agreed, but we'll figure it out." Reece stood. "I'll call Gabe and tell him there's no point in surveilling the office. You can find me in the kitchen making his breakfast."

Hayden went back to looking at his computer screen, and Cady crossed the room to stand behind him.

"Whoa!" He sat back. "It's all here. All the incorporation papers for the Emerald Scorpion Group *and* Marine Investment Associates. The Emerald Scorpion Group is listed as a shipping company, and Marine Investment Associates is a consultancy group. Both companies are LLCs, and Ivers is listed as the president and only stockholder for both. They were founded four years ago."

"That would be before he was elected county commissioner." Abby came around the end of the table to join them.

"Big news for sure," Cady said. "But is there anything else?"

"Oh, yeah." He looked back at her, a wide smile on his face. "There are spreadsheets listing the dates, times, and number of women his company trafficked for the past three years. It also lists the amount of money he made per transaction and the money he funneled through Kai's business, starting a few months ago."

Abby shook her head. "So Kai was involved for sure, but it doesn't make sense he had access to this drive."

"However he got the drive, it makes sense Ivers wanted it back." Hayden looked at Abby. "I can't imagine with everyone else saying Kai hated computers that he would be able to transfer this information from Ivers's computer and put it on such a sophisticated drive."

"Yeah," Abby said. "That doesn't make sense. So who owns it?"

"Give me a minute." Hayden clicked on files.

"Ding, ding, ding!" He swiveled and flashed a smile at them. "I don't have an actual name, but the drive is registered to CrimsonX."

A jolt of anticipation hit Cady. "One of the code names Fletcher gave us. Is there any way to search the drive for the other code names?"

"Can do." He typed in *Stub*, and a spreadsheet opened.

"Stub has his own sheet with dates, times, and amounts paid."

Cady pointed at one of the columns in the spreadsheet. "All at three a.m. Could Wade Collins be Stub?"

"Sounds likely," Abby said.

"I'll cross reference the dates to a calendar to see which day of the week these are for." Hayden opened the calendar on his screen. "The transactions occur on Thursdays, so yeah, looks like Collins is Stub."

"And Relay?" Abby asked. "Does he have a page too?"

Hayden's fingers flew over the keyboard, adding *Relay* to the search box. A file popped up, and he opened it to reveal another spreadsheet. "Same column headings as the other spreadsheet, but the dates are different."

Abby got out her phone and tapped the screen. "All the dates listed are Mondays. So if this is Palmer, looks like he got paid before the women arrived. Likely to broker the deal with Collins."

"Then the name 'Relay' makes sense," Cady said.

Hayden sat back. "The most important thing is this conclusively ties Ivers to the Emerald Scorpion Group, and we have the paperwork showing their plan to traffic women."

"So is there any point in tailing him now?" Abby

squinted slightly, lines forming around her eyes. "I mean, we can give this data to Mina, and with everything else we've located, she should be able to arrest him."

"True." Hayden tapped his chin. "But if he has Kai, he might not be willing to tell us how to find him, and Kai could die in captivity."

Abby frowned. "Ivers could have someone watching Kai and he'll release him if Ivers is arrested."

"Or he might not. He might not want to bring someone else into the mix," Hayden said. "And maybe Kai can identify this guy and he won't release him anyway."

"In the video, Ivers indicated he was the only one who could handle getting this drive back from Kai," Cady said.

"Then there's the other option I mentioned in the meeting." Abby looked at them both. "Kai hasn't been abducted at all, and as soon as he hears the news that Collins, Palmer, and Ivers are in custody, he might come home on his own."

Hayden planted his hands on the desktop. "And like I said, we can't count on that. I think our best bet before we turn this data over to Mina is to get eyes on Ivers."

His screen dinged, but he continued to look at Abby.

"I'm not sure I agree about keeping this information from law enforcement," she said. "But say I go along with it. What good does watching him do now?"

Hayden snapped his chair forward. "Now that we have proof of his guilt, we have the ammunition we need to get him to reveal Kai's location."

"I don't know." Abby bit her lower lip. "This plan could go sideways."

"Or it could go in our favor." He glanced at his computer. "Hold on. The algorithm I have running for Ivers just returned a record."

He clicked a few windows, then looked back at Abby. "If you needed a reason to tail him, I have it."

"What?" Cady leaned closer, trying to read his screen.

"Ivers has tickets on a plane scheduled to depart later tonight for Beijing."

"Oh, no," Cady said. "He probably knows about last night, and he's going to disappear."

"Not only that, but China doesn't have an extradition treaty with us."

Abby crossed her arms. "So, there would be no way we could get him back to stand trial."

Hayden jumped up and closed his computer. With or without Abby's agreement, he was clearly going to head to the Dunes, and Cady would be right by his side, finally with a chance to confront the man who had arranged her father's murder.

26

Hayden led the way out of the conference hotel where Odin Ivers was meeting, his head constantly on a swivel, scanning for any sign of danger to keep Cady safe. He raised a hand to shield his eyes from the harsh midday sun beating down on them. Across the road, he spotted the sand dune attraction the enthusiastic program director had said they might find Ivers at.

Hayden pivoted toward Cady. "We'll take the car."

"But the dunes are within walking distance."

"Might only be a short hike across the highway, but I want to have a vehicle nearby in case Ivers tries anything."

"I guess that makes sense." She started across the large parking lot in the direction of the company SUV.

He used the remote to unlock the doors, but slipped ahead of her to open her door. She smiled her thanks and climbed in.

After the emotional reunion from the boat trip, things had remained a bit stilted between them, and he wasn't sure what to do about it. Or if he wanted to do anything about it.

He got the air conditioning going. Even with the short drive across the road, he hoped it would cool off the vehicle.

"I don't get why Ivers would show up here if he was planning to leave town," Cady said.

"Maybe he had some unfinished business with the other commissioners."

"Could be, I suppose."

"We won't know for sure until he tells us. *If* he tells us." At the highway, he waited for traffic to clear, then zoomed across to the dune buggy rental place and backed into the space closest to the front door.

He grasped his door handle, but glanced at her. "I need you to be extra careful here. Follow my lead, and no matter what, let me check things out first and don't get ahead of me."

"I can do that," she said.

They exited the vehicle into blowing sand and strode toward the door where he got his first good view of the dunes. The nearest mound rose beneath the sun. Smooth, silent curves looked as if they were sculpted by unseen hands. Wind raced across the surface, sending tiny grains swirling in a golden shimmer. The world felt still—just sky and sand—but he knew a dangerous criminal lurked in the area.

Cady stared ahead at the dunes. "It's so beautiful and awe-inspiring. Only God could've created something like this."

"Agreed," he said. "Have you ever been in a dune buggy?"

She nodded, but remained locked in place. "I've never rented or driven one by myself, but I've gone on a tour where you have like twenty people in one of those oversized ones."

"Yeah, I've done that too. Not bad. But there's nothing like being in control of your own off-road vehicle to experience more of a thrill."

She looked up at him. "Do you think we'll find him out here? I mean, there are three designated off-road riding areas, and the hotel concierge wasn't sure which one he went to."

"True," he said. "But it makes sense that the group he's with would go to the closest location."

She pointed at a single-story building ahead with a flashing advertising sign on top, looking out of place in the natural landscape. "Guess there's one way to find out if we're in the right place."

He nodded and closed the distance to the door. As he held it open for her, the roar of dune buggy engines on the other side of the building raised his excitement. The scent of freshly brewed coffee drifted out and sent his taste buds watering, but the last thing he needed right now was caffeine coursing through his body when his share of adrenaline would flow once he encountered Ivers.

Cady didn't wait for him but marched right up to the desk, in direct opposition to his directive. He supposed he could take the reporter out of the city, but he couldn't cancel the reporter's curiosity.

"Hi." She smiled at the middle-aged man with a bald patch on the back of his head behind the counter. "Could I please speak to the manager?"

"You're looking at him. Owner and manager, Tyson Pruitt, at your service, ma'am." He planted rough-looking hands on the counter holding boxes of brochures for attractions in the area and cast a suspicious look at her.

His wary demeanor might have put others off, but Cady smiled at him. "I'm looking for Odin Ivers. The sweet program manager at his hotel told me he was here renting dune buggies with his group of commissioners. Could you tell me if he's rented one, and if he's still here?"

"That depends." Pruitt tightened his hands on the edge of the countertop. "What do you want to see him about?"

That adrenaline Hayden had expected to feel jolted through him. They were in the right place for sure. Pruitt wouldn't ask that question if Ivers wasn't here.

Hayden stepped up beside Cady, ready to take over if she crashed and burned.

"Oh, right." Cady slapped her forehead. "I probably should've led with that, shouldn't I?" She laughed, sounding very lighthearted as she looped her hand in Hayden's elbow. "My fiancé and I are in the area to consider it for our honeymoon. Odin is working on a time-sensitive matter. Since we're both in the same place, we're meeting up to kill two birds with one stone."

Hayden admired the way she'd handled Pruitt's question. She didn't say why she needed Ivers, so she couldn't be caught in a lie other than calling Hayden her fiancé.

But Pruitt wasn't buying her story. He smoothed long strands of hair over his balding patch and eyed them, his distrust remaining in his expression.

Hayden needed to do something before that happened.

He wrapped an arm around Cady and gave her a glance filled with the kind of love and certainty he imagined a groom would have for his bride. She sucked in a breath, her gaze remained locked on him.

As much as he wanted to stay locked in those gorgeous eyes, they had a mission to focus on. An important one. He freed himself to face Pruitt. "This is an irregular request, I'm sure, but I really want to get this over with so we can get back to planning our honeymoon."

"You both look like you're eager to get married." Pruitt relaxed and rested his hands on his waist. "Ivers is here. Been here for about thirty minutes with a small group. They're taking turns with a trio of rented buggies. I'll let you through the door so you can talk to him. His group is in the area we call 'the pit.'"

Cady smiled at him. "We're sure to remember your kindness."

"Thanks." He pressed a buzzer under the counter, and the door to the outside swung open, the revving of engines taking over the room.

"I hope that means you'll book buggy rentals for your wedding party from me!" he called out to be heard over the noise.

"I'll be renting those buggies before we leave town," Hayden said emphatically. "You can count on that."

And he would keep his word if he could. No point in missing out on an adventure if he could help it.

They exited to the smell of gasoline from powerful engines. In the pit, multiple ATVs in various colors were parked next to three larger dune buggies. To the left of the pit was a boarding area, where several men and women in casual clothes stood chatting.

Ivers wasn't in the group, and Hayden fought his disappointment. A skinny male employee with worn jeans, a stained white shirt, and red cap with a dune buggy on the front stood by a rope strung across the entrance to the pit.

A bright blue dune buggy came racing in, faster than it probably should have, and sprayed the bystanders with sand.

"Hey, Ivers," a woman dressed in orange athletic gear and wearing a baseball cap shouted. "Knock it off, or you're not going out again."

"Well." Hayden shook his head. "Guess it won't be hard to find him."

Hayden took Cady's hand and marched through the shifting sand toward the vehicle where Ivers was disembarking. Hayden caught Cady glancing down at their hands, a frown forming on her face.

"The man inside is still watching us," Hayden said. "And I figured we'd look more like a couple if we were holding hands."

"Oh, right. Right." Her frown returned, but it was more of a scowl now.

Was she disappointed he didn't really want to hold her hand? He did want to and was enjoying it, but they had to keep their full focus on Ivers.

The man lifted the helmet from his head, and Hayden could officially confirm he was indeed their suspect.

"Ivers, for sure," Cady whispered.

"Yeah," was all Hayden said. He didn't want to draw attention to them just yet.

Ivers dropped the helmet on the dune buggy seat and marched over to the woman who'd yelled at him. "Sorry, Pam. I didn't mean to cover you with sand."

"Or so you say." She crossed her arms. "I'm thinking it was payback from our earlier discussion at the meeting."

"Why would I want to pay you back for a simple discussion?" He blinked at her, an innocent look on his face, but Hayden was seeing right through it to the deceptive man.

"I was being polite when I said discussion." She glared at him. "It was a heated argument, and you know it. I just don't understand what you have against discussing shipping routes in the area."

He ground his teeth together. "I gave you all of my reasons at the meeting."

"But none of them made sense." She shook her head. "Just let it go for now. I'd rather enjoy the next few hours in the sun. We have the rest of the day to argue before our conference ends."

Ivers grumbled something under his breath and stepped

over to a guy on the far side of the group. "Women. They have no place in government positions of authority."

"I can hear you," Pam snapped. "Your take on women is most disturbing."

He rolled his eyes and pointed at the dune buggy. "Go take a ride and lose your misguided hostility."

She shot him a withering look. "If only your female constituents could hear you now."

Cady pulled her hand free and fisted it. "The reporter in me is dying to do an exposé on his blatant prejudice, but after he's arrested, and the truth comes out, his career will be over soon enough and won't need my interference."

"He really is a piece of work. Time to make him pay." Hayden held her gaze. "Let go of that anger so it doesn't interfere with keeping an eye out for problems. It might seem like he's alone, but someone involved in such an illegal enterprise probably carries a gun for protection."

She shivered.

"I don't mean to scare you, but I do want to make sure you're safe." He touched her cheek gently. "I don't want anything bad to happen to you."

"Same," she said, but then turned away to start in Ivers's direction, her face contorted in fierce determination.

They walked up to him and the man he was talking with, and not surprisingly, they were still dissing women and talking about their place as housekeepers and mothers.

Cady flinched. She had to be thinking about the fact that she was finally coming face-to-face with the horrible person who'd arranged to have her father killed. Sure, it wasn't like he'd injected her dad himself, but he'd directed Palmer to do it, who'd acted on Ivers's behalf.

Hayden gritted his teeth as he approached. "Odin Ivers?"

The man whipped around and flicked a glance at Hayden before shifting his gaze to Cady and giving her a thorough once-over. His face twisted into something dirty, and Hayden's skin crawled. He itched to grab the man by the neck. Instead, he drew in the ocean air to control himself. Despite his desire to let his fists tell the guy what he thought of him, he had to stay calm. He didn't want anything to get in the way of a successful prosecution after this creep was taken into custody.

Ivers dragged his gaze away and put all of his attention on Hayden. "Who wants to know?"

"Hayden Kraus. Investigator at Lost Lake Locators."

"Yeah, right. Everybody's talking about you guys. I haven't lost anything or anyone." He gave a relaxed chuckle. "So, not sure how I can help you."

Hayden shoved his hands in his pockets to keep from trying to wipe the smug smile from Ivers's face. "It's not what you've lost, it's who you can help us find."

"Is that so?" He tilted his head slightly, eyes narrowing with curiosity. "Who might that be?"

"Kai Nakoa."

Ivers's body tensed, and he took a slight step back before visibly relaxing his shoulders. "Am I supposed to know who that is?"

Cady bared her teeth at him. "You not only know who he is, you abducted him. If you don't give us his location right now, we'll make sure everyone in your group knows you're engaged in human trafficking and you abducted Kai Nakoa because he could prove your involvement after he took your flash drive."

The jaw dropped on the man who'd been standing next to Ivers. "I don't know who these people are, Odin, but tell them they're way off base here."

"He can tell us all he wants," Hayden said. "But he's the owner of the Emerald Scorpion Group, a known criminal organization involved in human trafficking."

Ivers flexed his fingers. "I've dealt with the Emerald Scorpion Group in my capacity as commissioner, but I had no idea they were involved in anything illegal."

"Right, deny your ownership now, but organizational paperwork on the drive proves otherwise." Hayden gave Ivers a smug smile. "You probably thought an encrypted flash drive wasn't crackable, right? Well, it was, and we possess all the data revealing the money you made from trafficking these poor women."

"I don't know what you're talking about," Ivers said, but his face paled.

"Not enough for you?" Hayden sneered at the man. "You also ordered the death of Percy Vaughn, and I'm sure the DA will be only too happy to charge you with conspiracy to commit murder. That along with the trafficking and kidnapping charges, and you'll never see the light of day again."

Ivers took a full step back, his eyes darting about, panic making him jittery.

Was he assessing the damage that would occur if these people heard about his extracurricular activities, or was he thinking of running?

"There's nowhere to go, man," Hayden said. "You don't have much of a choice in exits. You've got the dunes or the highway. Either way, I'll keep up with you."

He gave Hayden a long look. Glanced at Cady. At his friend.

"Say it isn't true, man," the friend said.

A guilty look crossed Ivers's face, then he shifted back to Hayden. Not for long. Only a brief second. And he took off. Dashing past Cady and knocking her over. Heading straight for a dune buggy roaring into the pit area.

Hayden looked at Cady. "Are you okay?"

"Fine," she said. "Go after him."

"Are you sure?"

"Positive." She waved him off with a flick of her hands. "Go. Now. Before he gets away."

The man in the buggy started to climb out. Ivers grabbed his shoulders and tossed him to the ground.

"Not cool, Ivers!" The man scrambled to his knees. "You could wait your turn, you know."

Ivers paid him no attention but climbed behind the wheel and took off in the buggy. The engine roared, and he spun out, leaving a trail of smoke and the caustic scent of gasoline behind.

Hayden glanced around. Spotted ATVs off to the side, keys in the ignition. He raced past the employee, grabbed a helmet and jumped into the nearest vehicle painted a vibrant red.

"Hey!" the pit employee shouted. "You can't take off on that. It's stealing."

Putting on his helmet, he ignored him and pressed the gas to follow Ivers. Ivers led them down a path lined with trees and scrub and various grasses. Hayden's vehicle was smaller and more nimble, so he rode over the sand with ease until they came upon a wide open area with the beach to the left.

The ocean rushed in and out on the shore, crashing and churning, but Hayden couldn't look at what must be a beautiful sight. He had to be careful not to capsize or crash into the big mounds of sand spilled out in front of them. He soon caught up with Ivers. Hayden beeped the horn on the ATV, warning Ivers he was closing in.

Ivers flashed a look over his shoulder, then one-handed his dune buggy while fumbling under his shirt with the other hand. He pulled out a gun. He lifted it over his shoulder.

Hayden ducked, getting as low as he could.

Ivers fired.

The bullet whizzed past Hayden, just clipping the far side of the vehicle frame. He stayed down, and hopefully out of the line of fire, but he didn't back off. He kept racing forward, praying he wouldn't hit a dune the wrong way and roll the ATV.

That wouldn't be good. Not good at all. He wasn't strapped in, but at least he was wearing a helmet.

Ivers continued to look over his shoulder and fired again. Missed.

Mistake. Big mistake!

"Watch out!" Hayden yelled, warning Ivers of a large dune directly in front of him.

Ivers should've slowed down to ride the crest of the dune. Instead, he'd sped up and hit it head on. Sand dune or brick wall, the difference didn't matter. His vehicle hit the wall of sand, suddenly stopping, and he went flying.

He landed in the dune and didn't move.

Hayden safely stopped beyond the accident scene, ripped off his helmet, and went back to Ivers. His head was buried in the sand, and Hayden dropped to the beach to dig his face free so he could breathe. Hayden wanted to whip Ivers onto his back and force him to confess to everything he'd done and demand he reveal Kai's location.

Instead, he sat back on his haunches. Ivers hadn't worn a helmet and could have a serious head injury. Moving him could exacerbate that and/or kill him.

If he was even still alive.

And if he wasn't?

Then Hayden had screwed up in following the guy, and they might not locate Kai before it was too late.

27

Gunshots finally quieted in the distance, but Cady continued to pace the pit area, her heart beating erratically. What had happened? Was Ivers armed? Had he shot, maybe killed Hayden? She could hardly think straight, so when others in Ivers's group started peppering her with questions, she stepped away and ignored anyone who dared join her. She could explain what was happening with Ivers, but honestly, she didn't think anyone would believe her.

After all, who would think a commissioner could be involved in human trafficking? As a reporter, she had a skeptical outlook on life, and even she wouldn't have believed it at first.

But more of a priority was to know what was going on with Hayden.

Was he okay?

She would've called the police to help him, but Pruitt already reported Hayden had stolen a vehicle. Not the reason she wanted law enforcement involved, but it would bring them to the scene. Her job would be to convince them Hayden wasn't a thief but was following a very dangerous, awful man who needed to be arrested.

Her phone rang. She plunged her hand into her pocket to find it and saw Hayden's name on the screen. Her heart soared. If he was calling, he had to be fine, right?

Her legs trembled with weakness, and it took everything she was made of not to sink to the sand, but answer instead. "Hayden? Are you all right?"

"I'm fine. But I need you to call 911. Get an ambulance for Ivers. He crashed his buggy and went flying without a helmet. He has a pulse, but he's not moving. Tell them to hurry."

No time to revel in her thanks right now. "Where will they find you?"

"If they follow the main trail, they'll see us."

"Okay. I'll call them right now and let you know what they say. Pruitt reported you to the police for stealing an ATV, so they're on the way. I'll make sure they know what's going on."

"Be sure to tell them that Ivers has a gun, and he fired multiple shots at me."

"But he didn't hit you, right?" Her voice rose, giving away her panic.

"Right. I'm fine."

"You're not just saying that so I don't worry, are you?"

"No. He didn't hit me, and I didn't crash my vehicle. All's good. Just get an ambulance here for Ivers."

"Will do." She'd no sooner ended the call and arranged for an ambulance when sirens blared from a distance, and she saw the lights swirling above the building. A single car door slammed.

Had to be the deputy as it was too soon for the ambulance to have arrived. She watched the path to the building, but no one came out. The deputy had to be taking Pruitt's statement. Man, if only she were in on that conversation. No point, though. Pruitt should tell his story first. Then she would refute as much of it as needed to declare Hayden's intent behind taking the ATV.

She tapped her foot and waited. What if the deputy didn't believe her? What if they went after Hayden and arrested him? It would all be figured out in the end, but Pruitt might still press charges.

A young uniformed deputy, one hand on her sidearm, the other on her waist, barreled around the corner.

Pruitt trailed her. He pointed at Cady. "Her. She's the one with the guy who stole my ATV."

"Stay here while I talk to her." The deputy locked eyes on her and approached as if she were a speeding bullet intent on harming her.

Cady took a long breath and let it out. *Please give me the words I need to help Hayden and not harm him.*

The deputy came to stand in front of her, her last name of Booth on her badge. She took out a notepad and fixed an intimidating stare on Cady. "Name, please."

"Cadence Vaughn."

Booth started writing, but before she could finish, Cady said, "And before you ask, the gentleman who took the ATV is Hayden Kraus. We're working on an investigation into human trafficking in coordination with Sheriff Mina Park. Hayden took the ATV to go after Commissioner Odin Ivers, the head of the human trafficking organization, before he fled the area. He has tickets on a plane scheduled to depart later tonight for Beijing. China doesn't have an extradition treaty with the United States, so there's no way we could get him back to stand trial."

Booth held up a hand. "Let's take this a little slower and back up. So you're asking me to believe this commissioner is into human trafficking?"

"Hard to believe, I know, but if you check in with Sheriff

Park or her detective, Elaina Lyons, they'll bring you up to speed."

Another siren sounded, and the deputy spun toward the building.

"That'll be the ambulance I requested for Ivers. He crashed his dune buggy a few miles down the path and flew off it. He's unconscious and needs medical attention."

"You should've led with that." She shoved her notepad and pen into the pocket of her vest. "I don't have time to call for backup, and I can't leave you here, so I have no choice but to take you with me to the accident scene."

She spun and waved Pruitt over. "I need a vehicle for off-roading. Needs to hold two people."

"Follow me." Pruitt gave Cady a scathing look and marched toward the SUVs parked on the far side of the pit.

Two medics charged into the space, and Booth waved them over. "The injured man is on one of the off-road paths a few miles away. The only detail I have is he's unconscious after flying off a dune buggy. He wasn't wearing a helmet. You'll either need to walk or use a vehicle like this one to get to him."

"The vehicle would be faster," the burly medic with a bald head gleaming in the sun said.

"I've got you covered." Pruitt stepped over to the next vehicle. "You can take this one."

"Grab a backboard," the medic said to his partner, and she sprinted away.

"Get in." Deputy Booth pointed at the passenger seat of her vehicle.

Despite his animosity, Pruitt handed her a helmet.

"Thank you," she said. "Once you learn what's going on, you'll understand our behavior."

He just shook his head.

Another helmet was on the seat, and Booth put it on.

Cady slipped into hers, too, and settled into the small vehicle to buckle her seatbelt.

The female medic returned, carrying a backboard, which she and the other medic strapped to the ATV.

Booth gunned the engine, and they shot off with a spurt. Up and down the waves of dunes they rode, Cady's stomach rolling at the swooping movements. She tried to enjoy the beauty unfolding around them but kept her focus pointed ahead until she spotted Hayden sitting by Ivers's body. Ivers lay unmoving, but Hayden bolted to his feet and started waving his arms.

"That's Hayden!" Cady raised her voice to be heard over the throaty engine.

Booth slowed as they approached the body. Hayden remained in place even when they stopped and climbed out.

Cady didn't care if the deputy was with her. She whipped off her helmet and ran over to Hayden to throw her arms around his neck and hug him hard. She leaned back and raised her voice above the sound of the medic's vehicle coming to a stop nearby. "The accident looks bad. Real bad. I'm so glad it's not you."

"I'm fine." He smoothed the hair away from her face. "It's Ivers and his family we need to pray for."

Pray for Ivers? She wasn't sure she was ready for that. Not yet, anyway, but she offered a sincere prayer for his family.

She touched the side of Hayden's face. "When you told me to call an ambulance, I almost hit the ground. Just the thought of you being hurt and losing your life showed me where my priorities should be. Not trying to be some big-time reporter, but being with you if you're ready to start a relationship."

He smiled softly, sweetly. "I'm ready." His expression

turned serious. "I'd kiss you right here to seal the deal, but it seems inappropriate with this man fighting for his life."

She looked at Ivers, surrounded by the paramedics as they put a C collar on his neck before turning him over. "Do you think he'll regain consciousness?"

"I sure hope so. He's our only hope to find Kai."

∽

Guilt ate away at Hayden as he took a seat at the conference table for a late dinner. He'd taken one of Reece's famous, grilled-to-perfection cheeseburgers and put it on his plate, along with her equally famous potato salad. Not that he had any appetite. Not at all. His stomach was still in knots over the accident and Ivers's medical condition. Maybe he shouldn't have charged off half-cocked to question Ivers.

"Man, oh man!" Gabe looked at Reece, hero worship in his eyes. "You've outdone yourself. The best burgers you've ever made. You're giving Submarine Burgers a run for their money."

"Oh, dear, sir." Reece fanned herself with her hand. "I do declare your compliment has given me a case of the vapors."

Gabe threw back his head and roared laughter. "Looks like Betty Lou wants to get in on the compliment too."

Reece and the others chuckled, likely what she was going for to eliminate the subdued mood in the room.

"Save room for dessert. I've got a pan of fudgy caramel brownies just waiting to be cut." She sat down to her own dinner, and the group fell silent.

Hayden glanced at Cady to see how she was handling today's incident. She was looking down at her plate, her fork pushing potato salad around, but she wasn't eating.

"The doctors are optimistic for Ivers's recovery," he said to her, but didn't mention the guy might never walk again.

"I sure hope so, because Kai could depend on him making it."

"And if Kai's safety didn't depend on his recovery? What would you feel if Ivers died?"

She looked up then. "Surprisingly, I don't have any anger toward him at this point. At least not enough to wish him dead."

He took her free hand under the table and squeezed it. "I'm proud of you."

"Thanks, but I don't think it has anything to do with me as much as it has to do with what you talked about earlier. To trust God to work this out and provide justice for my father. It's all in His hands now."

Hayden held her gaze. "We're in God's hands too."

"We are." She gave him a wobbly smile.

He squeezed her hand and let go. His appetite returning a bit, he forked a bite of the tangy potato salad, perfectly made as usual. That bite encouraged him to chomp off a chunk of the burger, and discovered Gabe wasn't just blowing smoke. The burger rivaled any Hayden had eaten in the past.

He swiped a napkin over his mouth and looked down the table at his team. "I don't know about you guys, but I don't want to sit around and wait for Ivers to make it or not. Even if he does, he might not tell us anything about Kai. We need to do something."

"But what?" Reece asked.

"I can print out the information on the drive for everyone to look through," Hayden said. "Then I'll search property records online for Ivers to see if he owns a place where he could stash Kai unnoticed."

"There are plenty of secluded beach houses in the area." Abby held a fork of potato salad midair. "And we're close enough to the mountains. He might have a place there."

"Since properties are recorded by each county, I'll need to get going on that right away." He reached for his computer. "I'll start the printing now so by the time we're done eating, the data will be ready for everyone to review."

"As long as you leave enough time for me to have a second burger, I'm on board." Laughing, Gabe got up with his empty plate and headed for the food table. "Dessert too. Never want to miss one of Reece's desserts."

"Then, if we want to get moving, I better grab the brownies." Reece passed by Gabe and knuckled him on the shoulder.

Hayden might feel more of an appetite now, but he took bites in between sending pages to the printer until all documents and spreadsheets had printed and his food had disappeared.

He set the pages in the middle of the table. "Have at it and divvy up as you see fit."

Hayden moved to the food table and looked back at Cady to see if she'd gotten a brownie while his face was fixed on his computer screen. She didn't have a small dessert plate and much of her meal still sat untouched. Maybe something sweet could tempt her to eat, so he grabbed one for each of them.

"Thanks." She smiled at him. "It was sweet of you to think of me."

"You mean, after I rudely ignored you all through dinner?"

"You had work to do. Work Kai could be depending on."

"Then you don't mind if I ignore you again and scarf this down while searching online property records?"

"Not at all." She pressed her hand over his.

"Aha!" Reece pumped up her fist in passing. "Just like I thought. Hope the handholding in front of us means you're finally ready to announce you're a couple."

"I didn't... I mean..." Cady jerked her hand free, and a flush rose up her neck and over her face.

She was blushing like a teenager, and despite his team butting into something very personal, he found her response sweet.

She shook her head. "What am I doing letting this embarrass me? I'm not some girl who was just caught kissing behind the bleachers. I'm a grown woman who's about to start dating one of your teammates. If you don't like it, I hope over time, you'll change your mind." She lifted her chin and aimed it at everyone giving her their attention. She seemed to want to portray confidence, but he didn't think she felt confident right now.

"Bravo!" Abby smiled broadly. "Way to stand up for the two of you. We've been rooting for you to get together, and we couldn't be happier."

They what? Hayden ran his gaze over his friends' faces. "Since when have you been thinking about us in that way?"

"Since you two first met," Reece said. "And—"

"And you couldn't quit making googly eyes at each other." Jude wiggled his eyebrows and laughed.

The team joined in, and even Cady smiled at Jude's antics, but Hayden didn't crack a smile. He appreciated that his teammates cared enough about him to want him to find a healthy relationship, but everything was too new right now, and he wasn't prepared for this conversation.

He planted his hands on the table. "Why didn't anyone say anything to me?"

"Um, dude," Gabe said. "We have. Plenty of times. And not subtly, either. But you've been too resistant to dating to hear us."

Hayden thought back to times he'd been with Cady and the team when they were investigating the mayor's murder. Vague memories of them teasing him came back. He couldn't remember the details, but as Gabe pointed out, they'd brought it up. When it came to personal matters, there wasn't a single person on the team who would hold back on their opinions. But now wasn't the time to discuss his relationship, even if that meant Cady thought he was embarrassed about them getting together. He would explain later.

"Maybe I do remember some comments in the past." He gave his teammates a deadpan stare. "But now that we've got my personal life resolved, it's time to get to work on finding Kai."

"He's right." Nolan grabbed papers Hayden had printed. "Let's get started on our review."

Hayden sat down and leaned close to Cady. "Please don't think I changed the subject because I'm embarrassed about us. It's just, this is all too new, and I wasn't expecting the team to weigh in on our potential relationship."

She lifted a hand as if she planned to put it over his, but pulled it back. "I totally understand. It caught both of us by surprise, but I'm thankful they support us as a couple."

"Yeah, you're right." Hayden nearly winced at the thought of the tension it would cause among the team if one of them started seeing someone the others didn't care for. "But it's not surprising they're on board with us. You're an amazing woman, and they've already bonded with you."

"And me with them." She beamed at him. "The way I look at it, I'm not only gaining a relationship with a terrific guy, but five other ready-made friends. Six if you count Mina. I'm sure I'll like her too, but I haven't gotten to know her beyond her sheriff persona."

"You'll be fine as long as you don't break the law and she has to arrest you." He grinned.

"All right, like you said—let's get to work, find Kai, and

finally get this relationship started for real." She stood to pick up a few of the printed pages.

He drew his computer closer and started searching for properties in their county. The results only held the home Ivers owned in Seaview Harbor. That was it. Not surprising. Ivers could've hidden ownership of other properties just as he'd concealed the companies, and discovering them wasn't going to be easy.

Hayden moved on to surrounding counties and soon got lost in his work. Over and over he located the county websites and typed Odin Ivers into their search engines. Then Ivers alone. Even Ivers's first and middle initials, which he'd found on the commissioner's bio. But nada. Nothing.

Frustration built, but he wouldn't give up so easily. He expanded to counties farther away. Same result.

He slammed his fist on the table. "Not a single property under Ivers's name other than his main residence."

"Mina's team searched that property while you were chasing him," Nolan said. "So it's a no-go for Kai."

"Which leaves us with nothing at this point." Hayden resisted slamming another fist to the table.

A blanket of silence covered the room.

Abby slapped the documents in front of her. "This guy thinks he's clever. Let's work together like we always do. Show him he's not."

"I'm with you." Cady cast a tight smile at Abby, then looked at Hayden. "This might be a long shot, but what if he bought property under the business names?"

Hayden turned to look at her. "Marine Investment Associates or Emerald Scorpion Group?"

She nodded.

"Hold up." Gabe lifted a finger. "Wouldn't that be unlikely? After all, he's gone to great lengths to hide his affiliation to the companies, and it could be a big risk to have a connection to local properties."

"It's here." Jude waved one of the pages in the air. "The abandoned boat is listed under the asset sheet for Marine Investment Associates."

A lead? Hayden sat forward. "Any properties on your list?"

Jude frowned. "Sorry. No."

Reece tapped a page in front of her. "Before anyone asks, I have the asset sheet for Emerald Scorpion Group and it's blank."

"Zero assets is odd for a shipping enterprise," Nolan said. "And equally as odd for the consultant business to have a boat as an asset."

Abby made strong eye contact with Hayden. "Whatever his reason for choosing that company to record his assets, we should look into it. There could be a property worth pursuing."

"She could be right," Reece said, her gaze brightening. "What if he needed a place to go where law enforcement couldn't easily find him? To do that, he'd have to leave that property off his asset list."

Hayden let the idea sink in. "Yeah, maybe. It's certainly worth checking the county databases again."

He tried not to sound discouraged, but it lingered in his words.

Abby got up and clapped him on the back. "You don't have to carry the full weight of this investigation on your own. Remember, we're here to help."

"Good reminder, and it helps." He smiled up at her.

"We're family first, associates second," she said. "We have your six now and forever."

A swirl of such deep, abiding emotions Hayden hadn't felt since he'd lost his parents hit him. Did he now have everything he'd ever dreamed of? A woman he loved who loved him back and the truest of families who would be with him through thick and thin.

He couldn't look up or risk embarrassing himself by blubbering in front of everyone. He turned back to his computer and entered Marine Investment Associates into their county's database. Abby squeezed his shoulder, then went back to her seat. He fixed his full attention on the churning computer. Hoping this might be the ticket, he tapped his finger on the table as he watched the circle icon rotate on the screen.

No records found.

He let his frustration out on a deep exhale. Okay, fine. This was just the first attempt, and he didn't need to get discouraged. He would try both companies in each county, so he entered Emerald Scorpion Group. No point in holding his breath this time. Not when his expectations had already dropped. And he was right. No records for this company.

"Nothing in our county," he announced to the group. "Moving on to nearby counties."

Using his history to locate the county websites made his search faster this time. He informed the group of the results for each county, so when he hit the last one, they knew he'd struck out.

Gabe tilted back in his chair. "Maybe he doesn't own a place."

Reece narrowed her eyes. "But then, where is Kai?"

Gabe shrugged. "That I don't know, but it's clearly time to consider other options."

"Not so fast." Cady pushed her chair back to look at Gabe. "What if instead of registering under the complete business name, he used an abbreviation?"

Gabe made direct eye contact with Cady. "How would we ever begin to figure out his abbreviation?"

Cady got up and went to the whiteboard where the company names were listed. "He could've used the first letter of each word. So for example." She circled the first letter of each word. "Marine Investment Associates becomes MIA."

"Though I doubt he would expect to have taken a hostage when he formed the business," Abby said. "It's appropriate for our missing person."

"Well, let's check." Hayden went back to their county and entered MIA. "Oh snap! We got a hit under MIA, and the mailing address for the property I just found is Ivers's home address."

"Yes!" Cady pumped up a fist. "This place belongs to Ivers for sure."

Hayden wasn't quite ready to match her enthusiasm. "I'll map out the property, and we can plan a raid to free Kai."

If he was there, Hayden didn't say, because the team needed a win right now.

No bigger win than rescuing Kai from the clutches of the worst kind of criminal.

28

_____

Cady wasn't surprised by Ivers's property. The ramshackle building looked exactly like the photos Hayden had located on the internet. She was still surprised that the team allowed her to come along on what could be a dangerous mission. She had to promise to stay in the SUV just as she'd done when they tailed Collins to the ship. Nolan had suggested she stay at the inn, but Hayden went to bat for her and reminded them all she'd listened the other time.

Of course, Gabe had to point out she'd nearly been killed at the end, but Hayden said they could solve that problem by making sure someone stayed with her, no matter what.

The sun dropped below the horizon as Hayden shifted the car into park. She needed a better view so she leaned close to the window, squinting at the weathered wood cabin ahead. Tucked beneath a canopy of towering evergreens, the front yard was a patchwork of overgrown grass. The windows stared back, lifeless and dark, with no hint of light spilling from the cracks in the door or between the warped boards.

Hayden lifted his night vision binoculars. "Grass is trampled to the front door so someone's been here recently."

Gabe lowered his window and leaned out. "Looks like a truck bumper sticking out from behind the building, so pretty sure there's a vehicle here."

Hayden killed the engine and bent down to his mic. "Sidekick, this is Maverick. Signs point to the building being occupied and a truck parked behind. Over."

At the meeting, the team determined Hayden and Abby would make the initial approach. Hayden because he was heading up this investigation, and Abby because of her experience as a sheriff where she'd approached many buildings with unknown suspects inside.

"Maverick, this is Sidekick. We should proceed with plan. Over."

"Roger that, Sidekick. We're a go in three minutes. Over and out." Hayden looked at Gabe. "You don't leave Cady, got it? If you need help, use your comms and request it."

"I got it, bro. I'm stuck to her like glue."

"Oh, please." Cady rolled her eyes. "I'll never get that visual out of my head."

Gabe laughed, as she intended, but Hayden simply looked back at her. "Abby and I'll move in on the cabin to do some recon and report back. You do whatever Gabe says, even if it means leaving the vehicle with him."

"Of course," she said, but seriously wanted to crack another joke to lighten the tension as her stomach was rolling like ocean waves.

He seemed as if he wanted to say something else, but spun, grabbed up the rifle he'd kept by his side, and swiftly exited the vehicle.

He crept across a patch of weeds and grass to the first tree where Abby waited, but Cady could barely make out Abby's profile. A surge of adrenaline hit her all at once.

She'd vowed to trust God in all things, but at the moment, her trust might be at an all-time low.

"They'll be okay, you know." Gabe glanced at her from between the seats. "They're pros at what they're doing, and nothing bad will happen to them."

She nodded, trying to believe him, believe God, but trust wasn't coming easily, so she sat back and closed her eyes to pray. Not only for Abby's and Hayden's safety, but also for the entire team and anyone inside the cabin.

Please, please, she added. *Let this be the end to Kai's imprisonment and the evildoers brought to justice.*

As Hayden picked his way through knee-high grass, he tried to get rid of thoughts from the last time he'd left Cady behind to go on a mission. But the memory of arriving and finding a gun to her head played in his brain, and he couldn't let it go.

So much for trusting God. He said he would. Not only said it to God, but said it to Cady as well. And he was failing this test placed before him.

Wasn't that just the way things happened? As a Christian, he committed to trying to improve, and something was immediately placed in his life to test his commitment. Sometimes he passed the test, many times he failed. Well, tonight wasn't going to be a failure.

Abby held up a hand, and Hayden stopped behind a tree. A perfect time to pray. So he did, earnestly, until Abby waved him forward. He silently slid through the deep grass under the cover of heavy clouds to join his teammate.

"Movement and flashlight beam behind the window on the right," she whispered.

"Looking at us as if he knows we're here?"

She shrugged. "Let's make sure that doesn't happen so we keep the element of surprise."

Hayden lifted his microphone. "Maverick here. Be advised we have a subject inside the building. Over."

"Roger that," came Jude's voice through the earpiece. He'd taken the role of communicator in the other vehicle. Gabe echoed the sentiment.

"Advancing now. Be ready for instructions." Hayden nodded at Abby, and together, they moved in the shadows toward the building.

Hayden alternated his focus from the windows— looking for a shadow, a beam of light, or any movement inside—to the area where the truck was parked. They approached. An owl hooted from the trees, startling him.

He inhaled deeply and kept going, the grass wanting to sweep around his boots and pull him down. He battled it until they inched up on the corner of the small cabin that was probably no bigger than twenty by twenty. He signaled for Abby to cover him, and he crept toward the window where they'd seen movement.

Inch by painful inch, he advanced until he could dart a look inside without being seen.

Okay, two men inside. One sitting in a chair. The other standing near the door with a rifle propped on the wall a few feet away from him. Hayden took another look at the man in the chair.

His back was to him, and the room's darkness made it impossible to tell whether it was Kai—or if the man was even tied to the chair. He switched his focus to the door. A metal hasp meant to hold a padlock, dangled loose, unsecured.

He held up two fingers to signal the number of occupants to Abby, then moved swiftly back to her. They needed eyes on the truck. With a quick gesture toward the rear of the building, he took off again. They crouched beneath a side window, pushing through a dense tangle of wild blackberries, the thorns clawing at his arms and drawing blood.

Ignoring the pain, he kept moving until he reached the back wall and chanced a look around the corner. A shiny black Ford F150 gleamed in a shaft of moonlight breaking through the clouds, but no one in sight.

Hayden peered into the truck's window. Spotless. Whoever was inside the building cared enough about his vehicle to keep it clean. He checked out the truck bed and waved Abby over. He pointed to the bed and waited for her to spot the rumpled T-shirt with a Ride the Tide logo.

She pivoted and flashed him a smile.

Confident they were out of earshot if they whispered, Hayden bent close to Abby. "Two men inside. One in a chair. T-shirt says it's likely Kai, and he's probably restrained, but I couldn't confirm that. The other one is standing just inside the door, his rifle against the wall a few feet away."

Abby leaned in. "The way I see it, we have two choices. We either spook him from out here and hope he comes out, or we storm the place and take him down before he lays hands on his rifle."

Hayden turned to look over the back of the building. One window, no door. "Let me look for another entrance on the other side."

Hayden got low and scooted under the window to the far corner. He shot a look around the corner, then advanced far enough to determine neither a window nor a door existed on that side of the cabin.

On his way back to Abby, he glanced through the rear window. The view stretched clear to the front, confirming it was a single-room building, and the occupants hadn't moved. He returned to Abby and quietly passed on what he'd seen. "He could have instructions to take Kai out if he feels threatened, so storming the building seems like a better option."

"Agreed." Abby cupped her rifle in her arms, ready for action. "We need to make sure we take that rifle out so it doesn't come into play."

"We bust in. One of us can pin him with the door, leaving room for the other one to go for the rifle. In case the man in the chair isn't Kai, we'll both need to keep an eye on him."

"Good plan, except the door could be locked, and taking time to disable it might give him time to go for the rifle."

"The only lock is a metal hasp and padlock on the outside, and it isn't secured. So we have direct access."

"Good. Good. Since I'm smaller than you, it makes sense for you to breach the door, and I slip behind you for the rifle."

He nodded.

She flashed him an okay sign with her fingers. "First, we request backup, and before we breach, we stop at the window so I can get the lay of the land."

He lifted his microphone. "This is Maverick. Preparing to breach the building. Suspect armed with a rifle. Backup required now."

"Riddler here," Jude said. "We're on our way."

Hayden released his microphone and looked at Abby. " The team will be in place by the time you take a look inside, so let's move."

They crept back around the building to the window. Abby darted up and down, then looked again. She turned and gave a quick thumbs-up.

"Riddler here," Jude's whispered voice came over Hayden's earpiece. "Backup in place. God be with you."

Hayden briefly met Abby's gaze, then eased up to the

door, fearing each step might creak beneath his weight. One step. Two steps. Three steps.

He waited. Listened. No indication their suspect knew they were coming.

Hayden crept into a position where he could break through the door. Abby moved into place behind him. It wasn't hard to imagine her fierce determination.

He raised three fingers.

Lowered the first one. Curled down the second one.

Took a deep breath.

Folded the third one down and charged the door.

Old wood cracked, splintered, and immediately gave away. Swinging the door in, it hit a soft target, not a wall. Perfect. He'd trapped the man. The suspect thrashed, trying to break free, but Hayden planted his feet and held firm, pinning him in place.

Abby plunged past him in a speed he couldn't have managed. She dove for the rifle. Grabbed it up and rolled, bringing it up to point at the suspect.

"Freeze!" she shouted. "Or I'll use your own rifle on you."

The man stopped struggling, and Hayden shot a look at the man sitting in the chair, but he hadn't moved.

"Kai," Hayden called out. "Is that you?"

He received a muffled response as if the man was gagged.

"Okay, stay there and don't move," Hayden said. "And you behind the door. I'm going to slowly release it. You'll come out at a snail's pace with your hands intertwined behind your head." He drew his handgun in case, but eased back to let the man follow directions.

Facing Abby, the man slowly emerged, his hands behind his head.

Abby gasped. "You no-good lowlife."

Hayden wanted to spin the guy around to see who had Abby gasping, but he'd served in law enforcement long enough to know the suspect needed to be cuffed and searched first. Hayden approached him and lowered his right hand to slip it into one half of the zip tie cuff. He followed the procedure with the other one, then patted him down, finding a handgun in his boot and a knife in his pocket.

Whoever the guy was, he'd come prepared to do battle.

"Sit," Hayden said and helped the man lower his body against the wall. Only then did he take out his flashlight and shine the beam of light at the suspect.

Wow! Oh wow! He was gasp-worthy all right, and Hayden had to blink several times to be sure he was seeing straight.

$\approx$

Cady raced from the vehicle toward the cabin. Lights from two police cars strobed through the night, turning the darkness into a circus of colors. She paused to search through the people for Hayden. Talking to Abby, he stood tall on the porch. Relief weakened her knees, and she had to grab onto the rear of a police car to steady herself. He was safe. Really safe. Just as he'd claimed over the comms unit to Gabe. But she hadn't heard his voice and needed to see for herself that he wasn't injured.

But this long-distance view wasn't good enough. She needed to see him up close and talk to him too. She made a beeline for the cabin, but reached the ambulance first where Kai sat on the tailgate. His usual bright smile was nowhere in sight on his rounded face. He looked gaunt with fatigue etched on his features, and his shoulders were slumped.

More than anything she wanted to be with Hayden, but

Kai's dejected demeanor compelled her to stop and talk to him.

She squatted in front of him. "I'm so thankful you're okay, Kai." She glanced up at the medic. "He *is* okay, right?"

The beanpole of a guy nodded. "We'll transport him to the hospital for a full workup, but at this point, he's just dehydrated and sore from being restrained. Seems like he'll make a full recovery."

"He's right, I'm fine. Just a little tired." Kai offered her a weak smile. "I'm sorry to hear about your dad passing. I expected to see him again before his illness took him."

"You haven't heard. It wasn't the illness. It was Ivers. He hired Palmer to inject my dad with fentanyl."

Kai closed his eyes. "If only I'd known what kind of man he was when I got into business with him."

She hadn't stopped to get answers from him, but if he wanted to give them, she would be glad to listen. "How did that happen?"

He sighed. "It started out innocently enough when I gave his son surf lessons. We got to talking one day, and he asked how business was doing. I told him we were struggling a bit. He mentioned he'd been wanting to invest in a local business and asked if I would consider taking on a partner."

Kai tugged at the neck of his T-shirt. "It's not something I would've normally considered, but he caught me at a bad time. That spring had been nothing but rain—no one wanted to be on the beach. With no foot traffic, my retail sales dropped, my rental income dried up, and lesson bookings vanished. Everything tanked."

He glanced past her, eyes distant. "Each month, he gave me money. We called them loans—something I'd pay back once the business was stable again. That cash let me advertise, reach out, bring in people from all over the state. It kept me afloat."

His mouth turned up at the corner. "We're flourishing big time now. It was like finding the granddaddy of all waves except in a business sense."

"But then…" She continued to look at him.

He dropped his gaze to her. "Then he suddenly called in the loans he knew I couldn't pay back."

She felt his pain and anguish not only from his look, but in his tone. "What did you do?"

"Ivers gave me two choices. First was to sign the business over to him." He growled, like an injured animal. "I'd sell the place to someone else before I would *ever* do that."

"And the second choice?" she asked already having an idea what it might be.

"Agree to let him funnel cash through my business." He grimaced. "I knew it would be dirty money. There couldn't be any other reason why he needed it laundered. He didn't tell me how he got the money, and I didn't ask. But then, Ernie Sutton and your dad asked me to take them out in my boat to follow Wade Collins. That's when I learned of the trafficking."

His face paled in the light of the ambulance. "I was sick to my stomach and vowed to find a way to take Ivers down. So I buddied up to him. Pretended I was impressed with what he was doing."

She patted his hand. "That must've been hard."

"You have no idea." He scrubbed a hand over his face. "But I kept it together, and one day I went to visit him at his house. He was in his office working on his laptop with a drive plugged into it. As soon as I came into the room, he ejected the drive and put it in a locked desk drawer. I knew it had to contain something he didn't want anyone to see. Long story short, I broke into his house and stole the drive."

"You were brave to break into the house of someone like Ivers."

"Brave or stupid." He gave a derisive laugh. "I don't know anything about computers—hate them actually—but I showed the drive to a guy I know who does. He said it was seriously encrypted. He couldn't open it, and said not just anyone could. Before I found someone to help me with it, Ivers came after me. With a gun in my face, he warned me to give it back to him, but I wouldn't tell him where it was. So he kidnapped me."

"We found the drive," she said.

He nodded. "That's what Hayden told me, and he also told me it contained all the information needed to put this man away for a long, long time."

"I need to get going, ma'am," the medic said. "You can follow us to the hospital if you'd like to continue your conversation."

She stood and rested her hand on Kai's shoulder. "I'll be staying in Lost Lake, so I'll come by to visit you."

"Thank you." He gave a wobbly smile. "You're as kind as I remember."

She squeezed his shoulder and turned back toward the cabin. She'd nearly reached the porch when Mina came barreling across the property.

"Where is he?" she demanded. "Someone tell me where he is!"

"Inside." Hayden waved her over.

She stormed ahead like a tornado seeking something to destroy, taking the three steps up to the cabin in two smooth leaps. Hayden and Abby followed from the porch, and Cady climbed the steps to bring up the rear.

The man who'd held Kai captive sat on the worn wooden floor, his hands behind his back, his knees lifted.

He was tall and beefy, his blond hair buzzed short like the law enforcement officer he was.

Sergeant Abell, or so she'd been told. Cady had never met him, but from the gossip she'd heard since he was discovered in the cabin, he was a respected member of the sheriff's department, and the deputies were shocked and angry.

Mina stood before him, her feet planted wide, her gaze raking him over. She pulled back her foot as if she intended to kick him, then took a breath and dropped her boot to the floor with a sudden thud. "How could you do this to us, Abe? You've single-handedly ruined the reputation of our department."

He glared up at her. "What choice did I have? You're so stinking popular in the county there's no way I would ever successfully run against you for sheriff. So I was stuck in a dead-end job where I'd make the same salary for the rest of my career."

Mina scowled. "You don't have to be the sheriff to get a pay increase. You could always move up the ranks."

"Could I? Really? Where?" His voice rose with each question. "El's your buddy, and the department needs can only afford one lieutenant. Not to mention, I'm not a woman and can't form the same bond with you as she did. Something I can never change."

Mina shook her head. "Gender has no bearing on my decision-making. Not in the least. Detective Lyons and I are close because she doesn't have an attitude like you do, and she's a team player. Something you never understood and never will."

"Whatever." He rolled his eyes.

"Don't whatever me," she snapped. "Not when I've spent my entire time as a sheriff walking on eggshells around you and trying to make things work for us. Thankfully, I don't need to do that any longer." She huffed out a breath. "But also thanks to you, lawyers for every suspect you ever investigated, every person you ever arrested, will be crawling out of the woodwork demanding their investigations be reviewed."

A snarky grin twisted his mouth. "Guess you're gonna be busy then, and you won't have a competent sergeant to back you up and take the load off."

Mina growled deep in her throat and took a step toward him.

Abby reached out to tug Mina back by the arm. "Don't do anything you'll regret. He's not worth it. Not at all."

"You're right. Time to look at the positive. I'll soon be rid of this thorn in my side for good." Mina scrubbed her hands together as if she were washing something repulsive out of her life. "I promise you one thing. I'll dig as deep as I need to find every one of your roles in this organization and make sure you're charged with them all."

Detective Lyons strode through the door, her expression grim.

Mina faced her lieutenant. "Get him out of here before I say or do something stupid."

"Gladly." El's forceful tone was a verbal assault for the sergeant. "I can't wait to slam the doors behind him."

Hayden helped El get Abell to his feet. Abell pierced Mina with an icy stare. "I look forward to seeing your name dragged through the mud."

El marched him out the door. Surprisingly, he didn't fight her.

Abby stretched shoulder to shoulder with Mina in support of the sheriff. "Don't pay him any attention. He's a bitter man and a sore loser."

"Plus, someone who can't take responsibility for his own actions," Hayden said. "But even if he doesn't, I have no doubt a jury will find him guilty, and he'll go away for a long time."

Abby frowned. "I may not like what he did, and he deserves to serve time, but prison isn't a great place for a police officer."

"He should've thought of that before he got involved with Ivers." Mina straightened her shoulders. "I'll arrange for Sierra and her team to process this scene after they finish their current assignments. Hopefully, Abe's prints and DNA are all over all of them."

"Let us know if you need our help," Hayden said.

"I'll walk to the car with you," Abby said, probably to give Mina a sheriff-to-sheriff pep talk.

Cady grabbed Hayden's hand and led him out to the porch. "When I heard about you and Abby breaching the building the way you did..." She paused and shook her head to tame the acid burning in her gut. "You could've been seriously hurt."

"But I wasn't," he said. "We made a very calculated move —something we've done before and will do again. I hope that doesn't scare you off of being with me."

She bit her lip. "I can't pretend it isn't upsetting, but this is where trust in God comes into play, right?"

"Right."

"Still, I want to hug you right now. I don't suppose that's very professional, and you don't want it to happen in front of everyone here."

"That proves something." He searched her gaze.

"What's that?"

"You still don't fully know me." He smiled at her. "As long as I'm not doing anything wrong, I don't care what other people think. Hugging you is far from wrong and sounds like the best thing that could happen right now."

She lifted her arms gently around his neck, and he

wrapped his around her waist, drawing her in until there was no space left between them. Her gaze held his, steady and full of feeling.

"Along with trusting God," she said softly, "I think this might be the perfect prescription for any worry I have about your safety."

He chuckled, the sound low and affectionate. "Good thing this prescription comes with unlimited refills. I have a feeling I'll need it often. And not just in the difficult moments—"

"But in the moments we create together," she finished for him, then leaned in to press her lips to his—gentle, lingering, and full of promise.

29

Five days later, beneath the golden warmth of the late afternoon sun, Hayden clutched Cady's hand as they walked together toward the public boat launch. In the rush of ocean wind, he escorted her along the path from her father's cottage to the beach, which lay still and nearly empty. The rhythmic lapping of water was the only sound breaking the silence.

Ahead at the launch, Sawyer sat behind the skipper's wheel of his boat, anchored to the dock.

Hayden paused and looked at Cady. "Are you sure you don't want to do this alone?"

She clutched the polished wooden urn holding her father's ashes to her chest. "I'm positive. Having you by my side as I spread Dad's ashes will make it easier for me."

He glanced at the waiting boat. Federal law prohibited scattering ashes on beaches or in tide pools, only allowing dispersal at least three nautical miles from shore. He wished the law hadn't made saying goodbye to her father more complicated and more exhausting, but thankfully, Sawyer had come through for them once again.

Hayden squeezed her hand. "Then let's get aboard and to our destination."

She clutched tightly to his hand, and he led her to the boat.

Sawyer made his way to the stern and gave them a genuine smile. "Nice to see you again, Cady. You too, Hayden."

She returned his smile with an earnest one of her own. "Thank you for sharing your boat again."

"Glad to."

"Ditto that," Hayden said. "Permission to board?"

"Permission granted." Sawyer stepped closer. "What can I do to help?"

"Would you mind holding this while I board?" Cady lifted the urn.

"Not at all." Sawyer reached out to take the precious cargo and moved back.

Hayden helped her aboard, and Sawyer picked up a life-jacket from the bench for her. "You'll probably want to put this on before you take back the urn."

Without a word, she slipped the flotation device over her head, then took the urn from him, holding it with the same tender care Hayden would expect from her.

"Do you have a particular destination in mind?" Sawyer asked.

She shook her head. "Just as long as we obey the three-mile law."

"Then have a seat wherever you want, and we'll get underway."

"I've got the ropes." Hayden jumped to the dock to free the restraints from the cleats.

Back on board, he slipped into a life jacket and moved to the front of the boat where Cady sat near the bow. She smiled up at him and patted the seat next to her. As he dropped onto the hard bench seat, she reached out for his hand, then stared ahead.

Memories of his last trip in the boat with Sawyer came rushing back, and Hayden battled with the emotions until he remembered all of the forensics Sierra had located to cinch the DA's charges against Ivers, Palmer, Collins, and Abe, which pretty much guaranteed them years behind bars. Ivers had pulled through but wasn't talking about his Chinese buddies. He was, however, paralyzed from the waist down, his own personal punishment beyond what a judge would impose on him.

And, on a positive note, they'd worked with Mina to locate Emei's relatives and those of the women and children so callously tossed into the water by Collins, and reunited the families. Such a time of celebration for all of them. Also, it had been bittersweet to learn that Adam had done some digging and found out Mayor Sutton had reported the trafficking to a rookie agent who'd dropped the ball.

The only negatives were that Kai was potentially facing money laundering charges and that ICE had still not gathered sufficient evidence against the Chinese ship owner to charge him.

The motor rumbled, grabbing Hayden's attention. The boat trembled under the power until Sawyer released it to move slowly away from the dock. Once clear of the beach, he pushed the throttle forward, and they picked up speed. Cady freed Hayden's hand to put both of hers on the urn. The wind whipped her hair around, but she continued to clutch the urn.

She'd told Hayden her father had always wished to have his ashes scattered over the ocean, but she'd struggled with releasing him. That changed when Hayden gave her a decorative keepsake bird to hold just enough of his ashes for her to remember him and his love of birdwatching.

Still, today had been hard on her, and he was thinking the surprise he planned for the afternoon should cheer her up. At least he hoped so.

Sawyer slowed the boat and turned on the reverse thruster, bringing down the motor noise to be replaced with the sound of gentle waves lapping against the side of the boat. The waters were unusually calm, and though the wind was sharp, it was warmer than it had been earlier in the day. All in all, a beautiful day to be on a boat in the Pacific Ocean in the middle of summer. Their task of honoring Percy's last wishes was heartbreaking, but beautiful too.

"We've reached our destination," Sawyer called out. "Go ahead whenever you're ready, but please take your time. I'm in no hurry."

Cady looked back at Sawyer and smiled, then stood.

"I can sit with Sawyer to give you privacy if you want," Hayden said.

"No. Stay with me." She clutched his hand. "Unless you'd rather not be here."

He looked deep into her eyes. "I'm in this for the long haul, honey. For better or worse."

He hoped he didn't frighten her by quoting a marriage vow when they would just be starting to date, but her soft smile told him he hadn't stepped wrong with her.

"I'm so thankful God brought you into my life, Hayden Kraus. I'm not thrilled about the circumstances we met under, but it's a perfect example of God turning hardship into something good."

He wanted to hug her. To hold her. But with the urn, that was impossible. The hugging and holding would have to wait until later, after he revealed his surprise.

Cady had thought she would feel such a deep sadness after releasing her father's ashes and would want to go home. But when Hayden invited her to come back to the inn, she eagerly agreed. He had something he wanted to show her. Something he was very cryptic about.

In the lobby, he turned to look at her. "Have I ever shown you the ballroom?"

"Ballroom? How fancy." She watched him for any hint of what was to come.

"It's nothing fancy and definitely not a grand space. Honestly, it's about the size of our conference room—but big enough to host a small wedding reception. The downside? It's still stuck in the sixties, and not the cool mid-century vibe you like—more like your grandma's basement."

Was he thinking about a wedding already? His "for better or worse" comment on the boat and then mentioning the ballroom as a small wedding venue seemed as if he was heading in that direction. Surprisingly, the thought didn't shock her. Sure, she certainly wasn't ready to get married, and he couldn't be either, so her overactive imagination was running away with her.

Time to find out. "Is that what you wanted to show me?"

"It is. Come on." He took her hand, which he'd been doing a lot lately, as if he worried she would get away from him. She could understand that too. Neither of them had wanted a relationship, but this thing between them was inevitable, and they couldn't spend their entire lives running from it.

Well, they could, but it wouldn't be any kind of life.

He started through the lobby in the direction of the conference room and passed the kitchen. She thought she heard voices coming from the door next to the kitchen, but maybe someone was playing a radio.

At the door, he turned to look at her. "If this is too much and you want to leave, just tell me. You don't have to feel obligated to stay. We all understand."

We? She swallowed. So maybe there were people inside. Probably the team, but what was the purpose of this get-together?

He opened the door and led her inside. A small group of people were gathered in a large room, talking to each other. Reece hovered behind a long table with refreshments and a big punch bowl holding cherry-red punch. Cady spotted the rest of the team in various locations, talking to townspeople she'd met, but there were also many people she hadn't met before.

She shot a look at Hayden. "What's going on?"

He turned her to face a large photo display perched on several easels just inside the door. Above it, a banner read, *In Honor of Percy Vaughn.*

"I know you weren't able to arrange a memorial service for your father." Hayden's voice came from behind. "So I wanted to do it for you."

Tears in her eyes, she spun to face him. "You did this for me?"

"I hope it's not too much after the emotional boat ride."

"Too much?" She looked around the space. "All these people knew my father?"

"Yes, and they were glad to have a chance to meet you and say goodbye to their friend."

"Oh, Hayden." She started to cry, and she looked up to try to stop the tears, but she couldn't.

He pulled her into his arms and held her head against his chest, then gently caressed her hair. "I didn't want you to cry, but I wanted you to have a chance to meet all of your dad's friends so they could tell you how wonderful he was."

If she stayed in this room, she was going to completely

lose it, and she didn't want that to happen at what should be an event meant to celebrate her dad's life. She pulled free, grabbed Hayden's hand, and plunged through the door to the hallway.

"You don't like it," he said, a worry line forming on his forehead.

"No. No." She reached into her purse for a tissue and swiped her face. "I love it. It's perfect. I just didn't want to blubber like a baby in front of everyone. I had to come out here to compose myself."

He let out a relieved breath.

"Thank you for thinking of me. For thinking of my father. For being the honorable and kind man you are."

"It's nothing." His face colored. "And I didn't do it alone. Of course, Reece made all of the food. Nolan designed the invitations, and Abby had them printed, then Mina distributed them to the people who knew your father. If you can believe it, Jude handled the decorations with a few tasteful edits by Reece. Gabe was in charge of parking. And I located the pictures for the entryway board, which I hope you can spend some time looking at. After this event is over, Reece is going to have them made into a memory book for you."

Cady smiled at him, and the same happiness was beaming through her body. "How did you keep this from me? Wait, when we pulled up there weren't any cars outside."

"The invitations encouraged guests to walk if they could, and those who had to drive were instructed to park down the hill. If they needed a ride to the door, Gabe was there to transport them."

She shook her head. "You guys thought of everything."

"I hope so, and I hope you'll want to talk with all of the people who loved your father too."

She dabbed her eyes with the tissue. "Is my makeup ruined? Do I look okay?"

"There might be one smudge that needs attention." He moved closer and cupped the back of her head, then swiftly lowered his head to kiss her.

Warm but insistent, much like most of his kisses had been the past few days.

He drew back and chuckled. "Ah, yes. That takes care of the lipstick."

"By removing it, you mean." She raised her finger to swipe away the lipstick transferred to his mouth.

He caught her finger in his. "I have a much better way of giving it back to you."

He looked into her eyes, then slowly lowered his head. His lips touched hers in a tender kiss, not at all like the fierce one that had stolen her lipstick. She liked it, but she needed more. She slid her hand into the back of his hair and pulled his head down. She encouraged him to deepen the kiss, and his arms tightened around her body until she felt as if they were one.

They clung together. Shared kiss after kiss until the door opened.

"Oh, I see." Reece's voice came from behind Hayden.

Cady jerked away to see her poking her head out of the cracked-open door, a knowing look on her face.

She batted innocent eyelashes at them as if interrupting them was no big deal. "Does this mean you have something else to do and won't be coming in?"

"No. I can't wait to talk to everyone." Cady straightened her shirt. "We just got a little distracted."

"I'd say that was more than a little." Reece grinned.

"We'll be in in a minute," Hayden said.

"I'll wait inside, but it seems like you two need a chaperone to make sure you don't get distracted again." Reece turned back to the room, her laughter trailing behind as the door closed.

"I need to repair my lipstick for real, before we do exactly what she said and get distracted again."

"Honestly, now that we've accepted our feelings for each other, that wouldn't be hard to do."

"It's freeing to admit the truth, isn't it?" She reached into her purse for her lipstick.

He swooped his arm in and drew her close before she could locate the tube. "Let's promise right here and right now we'll always tell each other the truth."

She raised her arms around his neck. "Not like my dad. Not like the secret he kept. That truth was almost lost and had to wait for his passing to be revealed."

"Exactly." Hayden gestured between them. "Me and you. The truth. Always."

"Okay then," she said. "Here's my truth at this moment. I'm excited to talk to my dad's friends, but right now, I want to kiss you more than I want to go through the door."

He started to lower his head. "We can do both. And honey, whenever this particular truth comes to you, no worries. I'm more than glad to help you out."

She laughed, but he silenced it with a kiss. A kiss that meant a future together. A kiss that promised a lifetime of love, and a kiss she'd never thought she would find in her lifetime.

Thank you so much for reading *Lost Truth*. If you've enjoyed the book, I would be grateful if you would post a review on the bookseller's site. Just a few words is all it takes or simply leave a rating.

I'd like to invite you to learn more about these books as they release and about my other books by signing up for my **NEWSLETTER** at https://www.susansleeman.com/connect/. You'll also receive a FREE e-book copy of *Cold Silence*, the prequel to my Cold Harbor Series, when you do. If you're already a subscriber, you can sign up again and get the free book and it won't put your name on the list twice, but you will receive welcome to my list messages.

You'll be happy to hear that there will be more books in this series. Read on for details.

LOST LAKE LOCATORS SERIES
When people vanish without a trace and those who go looking for them must put their lives on the line to bring them home alive.

Book 1 – Lost Hours
Book 2 – Lost Truth
Book 3 – Lost Cause – November 3, 2025

Book 4 – Lost Lake - March 2, 2026
Book 5 – Lost Girls - July 6, 2026
Book 6 – Lost Light – November 2, 2026

For More Details Visit -
https://www.susansleeman.com/lost-lake-locators/

LOST CAUSE - BOOK 3

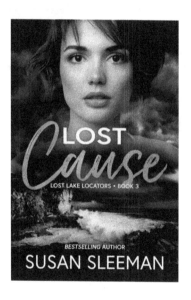

Working together is a challenge...

Detective Burke Ulrich is known for his unyielding dedication to justice and his methodical approach to solving crimes. When a valuable family heirloom is stolen from a recluse's rundown estate on Lost Island, Burke is called in to investigate. Despite the theft appearing straightforward, Burke senses there is more to the case, especially given the homeowner's mysterious history. But when he can't prove

it or find the heirloom, his supervisor tells him to
move on.

But catching a killer is their priority.
Enter former sheriff Abby Day, a sharp and resourceful Lost
Lake Locator hired by the recluse to find the missing heirloom. Abby's involvement immediately irritates Burke, who
is wary of private investigators interfering in police work.
However, as the investigation progresses, Burke and Abby
uncover a complex web of deceit involving long-buried
family secrets, and a string of unsolved crimes connected to
the estate, ultimately uncovering a murder. Burke orders
Abby off the investigation to protect her, but will she listen,
or will she risk her life and a potential relationship with
Burke to catch a killer?

PREORDER LOST CAUSE NOW!

SHADOW LAKE SURVIVAL SERIES

When survival takes a deadly turn, every step forward draws them deeper into danger—where one wrong move could be their last.

Book 1 – Shadow of Deceit

Book 2 – Shadow of Night

Book 3 – Shadow of Truth

Book 4 – Shadow of Hope

Book 5 – Shadow of Doubt

Book 6 – Shadow of Fear

For More Details Visit -

www.susansleeman.com/books/shadow-lake-survival

STEELE GUARDIAN SERIES
Intrigue. Suspense. Family.
A kidnapped baby. A jewelry heist. Amnesia. Abduction.
Smuggled antiquities. And in every book, God's amazing
power and love.

Book 1 – Tough as Steele
Book 2 – Nerves of Steele
Book 3 – Forged in Steele
Book 4 – Made of Steele
Book 5 – Solid as Steele
Book 6 – Edge of Steele

For More Details Visit -
www.susansleeman.com/books/steele-guardians

NIGHTHAWK SECURITY SERIES

When the innocent are in harm's way, these heroes don't hesitate—they put their lives on the line without a second thought.

Book 1 – Night Fall
Book 2 – Night Vision
Book 3 – Night Hawk
Book 4 – Night Moves
Book 5 – Night Watch
Book 6 – Night Prey

For More Details Visit -
www.susansleeman.com/books/nighthawk-security/

THE TRUTH SEEKERS

A team of six forensic specialists bound by one mission: to bring the truth to light. But when chilling mysteries land on their doorsteps, the hunters become the hunted—and the truth they're sworn to protect may be the very thing that shatters their world.

Book 1 - Dead Ringer

Book 2 - Dead Silence

Book 3 - Dead End

Book 4 - Dead Heat

Book 5 - Dead Center

Book 6 - Dead Even

For More Details Visit -

www.susansleeman.com/books/truth-seekers/

The COLD HARBOR SERIES

The cost of protection is high, but for these heroes, no price
is too great—not even their own lives.

Prequel - Cold Silence
Book 1 - Cold Terror
Book 2 - Cold Truth
Book 3 - Cold Fury
Book 4 - Cold Case
Book 5 - Cold Fear
Book 6 - Cold Pursuit
Book 7 - Cold Dawn

For More Details Visit -
www.susansleeman.com/books/cold-harbor/

ABOUT SUSAN

SUSAN SLEEMAN is the bestselling/ award-winning author of over sixty romantic suspense and mystery novels with more than two million books sold. She writes romantic suspense novels that are clean with inspiring messages of faith. Readers love her series for the well-drawn characters and edge-of-your-seat action. She graduated from the FBI and local police citizen academies, so her research is spot-on and her characters are real.

In addition to writing, Susan also hosts TheSuspense Zone.com. She has lived in nine states but now calls Oregon home. Her husband is a retired church music director, and they have two beautiful daughters, two special sons-in-law, and four amazing grandsons

For more information visit:
www.susansleeman.com